Kelli,
    I hope you enjoy
"Charlie" – Imagine
Shelby reading it on your
black sofa!

                Dixie Miller Stewart

Charlie's
MARK

Charlie's
MARK

DIXIE MILLER STEWART

Tate Publishing & Enterprises

Published by Tate Publishing & Enterprises, LLC
127 E. Trade Center Terrace | Mustang, Oklahoma 73064 USA
1.888.361.9473 | www.tatepublishing.com

Tate Publishing is committed to excellence in the publishing industry. The company reflects the philosophy established by the founders, based on Psalm 68:11,
"The Lord gave the word and great was the company of those who published it."

Published in the United States of America

ISBN: 978-1-61777-781-3
1. Fiction: Historical
2. Fiction: Coming of Age
11.05.06

Chapter 1

Mississippi, Early Fall, 1880

The springs creaked as though protesting the weight of him as he placed a dusty boot on the foothold and swung himself up into the buggy. Over the years, the faded leather of the seat had come to match the weathered creases in his face, but he hadn't noticed. His hat brim, its band long ago yielding to the sweat stain, concealed the deep weariness behind his countenance. It went deeper than his sixty-three years and well beyond the long day's stretch past sundown. It was a face Doc didn't show anyone but Jenny.

Jenny didn't need to see his face to know when something was eating at him. Tonight, she whinnied softly, pawing the ground lightly with her good hoof. That impatience suggested the day had been too long for her as well. An hour ahead there would be fresh hay and a stall Doc hoped Johnny had remembered to clean. He settled his bag on the floor, not needing to urge the mare forward. Like him, she had just enough steam left to get home to supper and bed. With practiced deftness, he tamped the last of his snuff behind his lower lip, spilling none, and slumped back, hoping to relax for the first time since before dawn.

He meant to doze and let Jenny take charge of getting them home, but he couldn't close his eyes. Doubts pestered him about having left the young mother alone with her newborn. Her face had been pale, her pulse weak; she'd lost a lot of blood. Even so, though only a girl, she had known what to do to birth her son. *A strong young woman*, he mused, despite how fragile her body seemed, but good stock, courage, and pretty. Too pretty, that had probably been her downfall.

Some no good had gotten her pregnant and then abandoned her. He could tell from the neglect of the place that no man had been around in a long time. It was a white man. Her reticence and the looks of the child told him that much. He was a healthy child but a half-breed. Doc hoped he would have his mother's courage and determination; they would both need it.

There are just two kinds of people in the world: those who leave and those who grieve! Where is this child's father? He'd be willing to bet the father was married. Seemed to him it was the Indian girls, the pretty ones, that the white men could snake charm the most. They'd lie to them and then lie with them until the swell of their bellies made the low-life no-goods run, leaving the young girls to fend for themselves. He'd found their own people didn't always welcome them back. He guessed they felt too ashamed to go home and admit their error to whomever might have advised them against the white man in the first place. "Dadgummit! I'm talkin' like there's an epidemic of abandoned, pregnant Indian girls!" He'd known one other.

Doc thought how it was that one woman wasn't enough for some men and how sometimes one woman was too much for another. That thought led him naturally to Johnny and how Johnny had been the one to find the girl this morning. Doc doubted she would ever have sent for him, even if she knew about him. He didn't think she was from these parts.

Johnny had been riding out this way hunting rabbits, he'd said. But really just wanting to get away from his wife and the houseful of kids and do some thinking…and some drinking, it had turned out. He'd stopped to relieve himself when he heard strange moans coming from an old hut nearby. He'd told Doc he'd been scared to look inside after he'd next heard a sharp yelp. Like a wild animal had its throat cut, he said. He'd paused a second time, turning back to leave and mind his own business, when he'd heard the cry. He thought for a moment that some animal had carried off a human baby.

Then he saw the woman's startled face in the shaft of light that squeezed around the shadow left by his own frame. He said he had never seen a woman look like that: pretty as a picture, even bloodied, sweatin,' and hunched over; like she was scared to death and lookin' at a murder and a miracle all at once. He'd felt fear and a strong urge to get away from something he wanted no part in, thinking only to leave her the rabbit he'd shot earlier and his canteen. He'd been embarrassed to tell Doc the canteen had contained some of Doc's whiskey, but he thought he ought to know. Johnny had ridden hard and fast to fetch Doc.

Doc helped her as much as he could, as if to try and make up for not being there to help her with what must have been a breech birth. Then he split the few logs she had, stoked her fire, skinned and cooked the rabbit, and waited, almost forcing her to take nourishment. Her eyes never once met his, but she hardly took them off her son. Doc kept up a one-sided conversation, delicately returning the baby to her breast, averting his eyes to avoid embarrassing her, explaining it would be a while before her milk came in. He talked about the care she needed for her own healing and for her son. He talked on and on in a stream of words he wasn't sure she understood.

She had a bit of corn and some dried apples. He made her some gruel, adding a last-minute touch of the whiskey to it from Johnny's canteen. Though he hadn't poured enough to do much good, on the other hand, he thought, he hadn't poured enough to do any harm. He gave her some liniment and the bit of lanolin he had and left the uneaten half of the rabbit and the gruel warming on the hearth. He'd come back tomorrow and bring supplies.

It would never have occurred to Doc to grumble about having another patient who wouldn't be paying him. He'd long ago made his peace with the fact that he couldn't serve his conscience and his bank account. Folks here were still struggling from the effects of the war. Many were much worse off now. They were the ones who'd lost their able-bodied men: husbands and brothers and fathers, and some had lost their homes and barns and livestock. Some of their colored folk who'd worked the fields had gone north or to rejoin families from which they'd been separated years earlier. Not all the coloreds had left but enough so that the way of life for their former owners would never be the same; too many fields lay fertile but barren, waiting for a purpose.

Doc ate well because good folks like Johnny paid their bills with rabbit and wild turkey and fruit and vegetables in season. He kept a good garden, telling folks it kept him sane. Sometimes, often enough, he had good venison; he always had butter and eggs, and there were enough widows around to keep him supplied with a cake or a pie. Sometimes they offered more, but he had no interest in another woman since Maddy had passed away. It was her smiles and her arms he still longed for after eleven years.

Jenny had been her horse; she reminded him of Maddy... in a good way. She had Maddy's intuition and way of tossing her head when she disagreed with him. He chuckled to himself. "Maddy was sure enough a sight prettier than you." The mare's steady gait told him she was not offended.

Jenny stopped abruptly in the middle of the road, startling Doc out of his ruminations. He leaned sideways out of the buggy, examining the ground around her feet to see if she'd been spooked by a snake or some kind of rodent. He saw nothing in the gathering darkness; he listened for sounds of escape through the brush. He heard nothing unusual.

He liked the quiet night sounds, sometimes sitting out on the porch until bedtime, letting the moonlight and the fireflies and the occasional falling star provide the visual effects for nature's nighttime symphony. It was in the evenings that he often felt closer to Maddy and to God. But not tonight; tonight he found nothing comforting. He clicked his tongue, making the same sound Jenny heard just about every day of her twelve years. She snorted and whinnied louder than before but didn't budge. Doc was puzzled; this wasn't like her. He clicked again, jostling the reins a little. She snorted and tossed her head. *Like Maddy*, he thought.

"Are you getting stubborn on me after all this time?" Doc growled, finding himself strangely impatient and irritable with his old friend. Jenny looked back but not at him; instead, she looked past him, back down the road. She pawed the ground again but with her damaged hoof this time. Trusting her instinct, Doc released his hold on the reins, letting them drop from his hands across his thighs, as though his own will had scurried off into the night instead of some varmint.

On her own volition, Jenny pulled the buggy back around, swinging wide off the road. Doc had to grip the frame to keep from being bounced out as she drug it over the rough ground and thick undergrowth. Finding the trail again, she headed at a trot back down the short distance they had come, back to the hut. Suddenly, Doc understood what Jenny knew; he just didn't understand how the mare could have known.

She lay there crumpled like a child's doll thrust aside at sup-pertime. The glow from the fire behind her seemed to cast a kind of halo around her head and the shoulder nearest the embers. Her head was tilted at an odd angle against the rocks of the hearth and one leg twisted under her. The young mother had instinctively protected her child as she fell.

The baby lay still cradled in one arm across her bare breast. His eyes were open like those of his mother, but his contained life. He was quiet as though sensing the solemnity of the moment. Doc let out the breath he had been holding since step-ping back inside the hut. "Yes, son," he murmured, "sure looks like you have your mother's courage." He surprised himself with the way his voice broke. "One day old and you already know that a man doesn't get the luxury of crying for his dead."

From some inner reserve, Doc found the strength to bury her. He tried not to make anything of the fact that Jenny stood patiently nearby with her head lowered in what sure looked to him like a bow. He said a fumbling prayer over the grave and marked it with two of the logs he had split earlier, telling himself he'd bring out a decent marker first thing tomorrow. He stroked Jenny's mane, feeling not at all self-conscious about thanking her for adding a dignity and sacredness to this lonesome burial.

The infant fell asleep, sucking on a piece of clean rag Doc had soaked in the gruel. It was the best he could do, and the child seemed to understand that. He slept the seven miles to the Harper homestead. Mrs. Harper had five of her own, counting the young infant she still nursed. A midwife had helped in that delivery, but Doc had driven up to check on her and make sure the mother hadn't gotten ugly with the other kids. He guessed she was mostly a good woman, that there was more goodness than meanness in her, but she could sometimes be meaner than a snake to them, especially when she was nursing a new one. Still, she would never turn away a baby in need of a wet nurse.

"His name is Charlie," Mrs. Harper pronounced, interrupting Doc's explanation of the circumstances. They were seated in the parlor where Beulah brought him coffee, sweetened just the way he liked it. He could detect the lingering supper smells of ham, probably sweet potatoes, biscuits, and turnip greens. Beulah was a good cook. Doc thought about how long it had been since breakfast, and as if to emphasize that, his stomach growled. No one offered him anything else, but he was grateful for the coffee.

Mrs. Harper had agreed to take in the child while they were still standing at her door; she'd reached for him immediately and now cradled him in the crook of her arm with a flicker of tenderness Doc rarely saw in her. The lamplight reflected from her dark hair, and her long lashes cast shadows that made her green eyes look like the sea at sunrise. She would have been beautiful if she smiled and gracious should she ever overcome her resentment of the ravages done to her family and homestead by the Union Army.

Recalling rumors about her, Doc thought she could also have been interesting if her temper wasn't so often misplaced. He knew she was the envy of a lot of women in the area because she got her figure back almost immediately after childbirth… and maybe because she'd married the bachelor every girl hoped would court her. Doc often wondered if those same women still felt that way about Mr. Harper, knowing he opposed the recent changes in requirements for voter registration that so many others supported.

Doc admired Mr. Harper for opposing disfranchisement of the coloreds and the Jim Crow laws. The man had stood up to the belligerence of some of the other men, preparing to defend the rights of his coloreds with his life, if necessary, arguing less about their rights than about rule of constitutional law.

He'd helped an equally courageous and mighty proud Moses and Beulah and the others who remained loyal to his household become fully registered. Doc knew that as a young man, Mr. Harper had advocated for the Thirteenth, Fourteenth, and Fifteenth Amendments and that doing so had probably cost him a position in Mississippi's government.

He wondered now where Mr. Harper was and if he would have any opposition to the fact that a stranger was about to be given his name. The best Doc had hoped for was that Mrs. Harper would take the child in for a few days until another wet nurse could be found.

It was the custom in the community to pass an orphaned child around. Every household who could or would gave each child a place to stay for a few months or a year. The families took turns rearing them until they were old enough to earn their keep or strike out on their own if they had any means to strike with. Consequently, he was surprised that Mrs. Harper was so ready to give the boy her name, yet strangely comforted by it.

He drained his cup and carefully placed it back in the porcelain saucer. Leaning closer to the one lamp in the room that was lit, he wrote down for public registration: "Charles Harper."

"His name is Charlie," Mrs. Harper corrected.

Doc didn't know why this woman intimidated him. She was thirty years younger and half his height, but he felt like a schoolboy who had missed all his spelling words every time they had a conversation, which was as infrequently as he could arrange.

"Uh, yes, ma'am. Uh, Charlie is, uh, short for Charles." *I've addressed crowds of hundreds without this kind of self-conscious stuttering,* he thought.

"Actually," Mrs. Harper immediately interjected, "Charlie is the same length as Charles, same number of letters, so it couldn't be short for the name, could it? He's a half-breed. His name will not be Charles."

DIXIE MILLER STEWART

An hour after daybreak, Doc rode back out to the grave with a stone. Johnny had rummaged through his shed, finding an old grave marker he had kept from the time years back when he'd helped mark graves in Greenwood Cemetery in Jackson. "Chimney town," Johnny called it, because it had been burned down so many times in the war. He'd been too young to fight, but Johnny took pride for his part in honoring the unknown Confederate soldiers who'd been buried there. A hundred of them, there were.

The stone, with its engraving already done, simply read, "Unknown." Doc thought that was somehow fitting. He felt guilty having to admit to Johnny he hadn't asked the mother her name, not that she would likely have answered him. Still, it bothered him that he hadn't even thought to ask. He and Johnny agreed that "Charlie's Mama" was a fine way to honor her and to recognize the hope that came with new life, despite the tragic circumstances of its beginning.

Johnny worked late into the night. He had done a passable, if slightly skewed, job of carving the two additional words on the stone, minus the apostrophe. Doc figured that some future generation would look at that grave stone and be able to put it all together and know that the woman had died unknown in these parts but not without a legacy. There were "unknowns" buried all over the South, leaving it to God to honor their names and their sacrifice and to judge whether their cause had been just.

He'd seen a lot of people die, in the war and in his calling. Some of the deaths were harder to take than others; and for reasons he didn't question this had been one of those harder ones. Not that it hurt him as much as Maddy's—none since had hurt that bad—but all of them since her passing had carried the bittersweet scent of Maddy. She had made him more alive to life; her memory made him more sensitive to death, perhaps more sensitive, he sometimes thought, than a good doctor ought to be.

Chapter 2

Charlie sat tall and proud, hoping Frank would be out on the veranda so he would see him riding by himself beside Oxytak. He felt very grown-up. He hoped Mrs. Harper would see him too, so she'd know how well he could ride and not be mad that he was getting to keep Horse in her barn.

He had been away two months this time visiting Oxytak, as he called his Indian friend. Charlie gave him that name before he learned to pronounce his name correctly, but by the time he could, both had adopted the nickname affectionately. Anyway, Charlie's favorite letters to write were the *O* and the *X*.

Oxytak was his third best friend in the whole world. Doc introduced them when Charlie was maybe just two, after he was speaking well, over half his lifetime ago. Doc thought Charlie should know about his heritage and learn the ways of his mother's people. Cherokee, he learned. He liked the sound of the word.

Charlie loved much about the Cherokee way of life, especially the peace in their homes; he loved their wisdom about nature and hunting and their history and customs. Oxytak wasn't just his friend; he was his hero, like Doc. Oxytak was brave and patient and wise, maybe even more patient than Doc. He taught Charlie many things, just as Doc did, but different kinds of things. Because of Oxytak, Charlie knew what he could eat in the woods and what he must not and what animals were safe to approach and which ones to avoid. He'd eaten his first rattle-snake out alone with Oxytak and had found it to be delicious, as his friend promised.

Oxytak was making a bow for him just his size and would soon be teaching him how to hunt with it and how to set traps so that one day he would be able to help put food on the Harper table. The man had three daughters of his own, but his only son had died. He didn't seem to ever want to talk about that, so Charlie stopped asking when he sensed the man's sorrow.

The boy was still learning how to gain the trust of the deer and other wildlife the way Oxytak had. The Indian seemed to be friends with all animals; at least they didn't bolt and run away from him as they did when Charlie approached. Sometimes he wished he could always stay with Oxytak, but he knew he would miss Frank and Doc too much, and, besides, he liked the choco-late cakes and lemon meringue pies that Beulah made. He would miss her very much too.

He tried hard to like Mrs. Harper; sometimes he did. Some-times she smiled at him or gave him the first biscuit or the big-gest little piece of chicken. But usually she just kept him fetching for her or ignored him. He tried hard to please her too. Doc told him he needed to try to do that. Doc also told him that if he ever did please her, he could know he'd been the first person in Mis-sissippi who ever had.

That's all right, he told himself. *My mama loved me so much she gave her life for me.* He wished he could know what she looked like. Doc and Johnny said she was the prettiest girl they'd ever seen.

Doc said even prettier than Maddy. Johnny said that Charlie must never tell his wife he'd said his mama was prettier than her.

Both men told him he looked just like his mama. They said he had dark hair and eyes like her and her strong jaw. When he asked incredulously if he was pretty, they laughed and said no; he looked like a man. He liked knowing he looked like a man, and he liked it that folks could look at his face and see his mama. It almost seemed to keep her alive.

He never thought much about a daddy. He had Doc and Oxytak, and even Johnny taught him things and let him stay over for supper sometimes when Doc had to go deliver a baby or set a broken leg or something more serious where the yelling could get really loud. Mr. Harper taught him the Bible and manners. He told him how important it was to treat ladies with respect. He'd once asked Doc why Mr. Harper didn't make his wife be nicer, and Doc just said that Mrs. Harper was the one who wore the breeches in that house. It took Charlie a few weeks of thinking about it before he figured out what Doc meant.

Charlie loved life. If he missed anything at all, it was a mama. Johnny's wife had more kids than the Harpers, so he figured she didn't have any more mothering to give to an outsider kid. Mrs. Harper didn't seem to have much either. Doc said maybe losing her daddy and brother in the war had made her be afraid to love anybody more than just a smidgen, even Mr. Harper. He said that Mrs. Harper's mother seemed to lose all her hope and faith when she lost her loved ones. He thought maybe Mrs. Harper decided she just wouldn't love anybody very much so she wouldn't hurt if they died. Knowing that allowed Charlie to feel sympathy for her, even when she was being mean.

Anyway, today was much too glorious to think about anything sad. For the first time, he was riding Horse all the way home alongside Oxytak. Horse had been a present to him from his friend for his fourth birthday. People still thought it was a strange name, and sometimes folks that didn't know him thought Charlie was a little strange for not giving his pony a real name. Being just five years old and so not allowed to argue his point, Charlie just kept the reason to himself.

Horse was the first word the newest Harper member spoke. When Oxytak came riding with it up to the house, thirteen-month-old Lilly looked up from where she was tied to the clothesline playing, pointed, and gleefully announced, "Horse, horse, horse." Charlie had been trying to teach her to speak and was so excited that she said something he just let the name stay so folks would always remember Lilly's first word.

Oxytak and Charlie rounded a bend and came suddenly upon the Harper buggy racing away from the direction of their home place. The boy waved with both arms, excited to see them and wanting to make sure they saw him on Horse; but the Harpers didn't stop. Mr. Harper waved erratically and kept going, turning toward town. Charlie had never seen them racing this fast, ever in his whole life. He and Oxytak followed the buggy, staying far enough behind so as not to breathe in the dusty trail it left. Once in town, they caught up to it in front of Doc's office. It was then that Charlie saw Frank as Mr. Harper lifted him from his mother's lap.

He felt like a wild thing staring first at Frank's bloody face, then at the scarlet smears all over Mrs. Harper's dress, then back at Frank's face and the streak of red dribbling out his mouth. He saw how Frank's blood formed a rivulet, running down Mr. Harper's shirtsleeve, dropping from his elbow, and leaving a dotted trail from the buggy into Doc's office. He took it all in, almost bursting with questions he knew he'd better not ask.

Charlie sat very still outside Doc's operating room, his bare feet dangling from the oversized chair. He was listening carefully for any sounds behind the door, especially for Frank to cry or yell out, but things were quieter in there than they usually were when folks came in all covered with blood. That worried him. Doc often said the folks who yelled the loudest were usually hurt the least. Still, Charlie knew it was serious when they went into the operating room.

That's what Mrs. Harper once called it, and the word had stuck with him. It made the room sound important rather than just a place where he often heard yelling and bad words when Doc was sewing somebody back together.

He thought maybe Frank had been shot in the face. He wished Doc hadn't made him sit outside. Next to Doc, Frank was the most important person to him in the world. Frank was six months older than Charlie, but already Charlie was taller and protective of him. Mrs. Harper said they were so close because she'd nursed them both at the same time.

Every odd-shaped gadget and tool in that room fascinated him. The bottles of strong-smelling liquids, ointments, and salves were things he could do without, but he'd gladly trade his best arrowhead for any one of those shiny tools. He'd once stared into the wooden-framed glass box Doc called a "sterilizer" to see if he could see the germs dying. Doc showed him with a microscope what germs looked like and said he couldn't see them with just his bare eyes.

At one time or another, he had asked Doc the use for every single thing in his office. He thought if he ever really *had* to, he could take out tonsils and maybe even fix an appendix. His eyes glanced over to the precise point where an appendix was diagrammed on the human body chart on Doc's wall. Doc liked to talk as he worked, and Charlie liked to listen; he remembered things.

Charlie even liked the smell of the operating room, although Mrs. Harper always said she hated it. Charlie wondered if she was in there hating the smell now more than she was hating what happened to Frank. And he wondered what instruments

Doc was using in there on his friend. He couldn't imagine how Doc was going to fix the mess Frank was in, blood everywhere and vomit and snot and tears and bloody rags that Mrs. Harper had shoved in his mouth that made him gag.

The door opened, allowing him a peek into the other room, but he could only see Frank's feet and Mrs. Harper's back. Mr. Harper and Oxytak came out the door. Oxytak handed Charlie a peppermint stick and tried to smile reassuringly. But Charlie saw that the smile didn't go all the way up to his eyes, so he knew Frank was not fixed yet. He followed the men out to the front, begging with his eyes to be told what had happened to Frank.

Mr. Harper finally noticed Charlie and said simply, "Son, Frank was running and fell on a pitchfork." Hearing that, Charlie turned his head and poked his peppermint stick to the back of his own throat to see how much the pitchfork might have hurt Frank. He gagged before it hurt very much.

Doc always kept cigars on hand for the men and peppermint sticks for the women and kids. "They help calm the nerves," he always said. Charlie knew Mr. Harper was really nervous because he held a match to a peppermint stick and then asked Oxytak to light his cigar three different times even after it was already lit. He heard Oxytak offer to take Charlie back with him, but Mr. Harper said it might be good for the lad "if Frank made it" for Charlie to be there while he was recuperating.

Mr. Harper's words pierced Charlie's heart. People who didn't "make it" died. The second to the oldest Williams boy caught pneumonia but didn't make it and died. One of the Harpers' horses hadn't made it, and he died.

Sitting and waiting and being afraid that Frank might die is hell, he thought silently to himself then repeated it because it made him feel grown-up. *Hell. It feels like hell to be just sitting and waiting. Hell, he might be dead now. It's awfully darn quiet in there.* He whispered *hell* one last time, knowing he'd get a thrashing if Mrs.

Harper ever heard him say it. Doc told him he needed to stop saying it and even made a pact with him that he, too, would quit.

Charlie was afraid. He'd once heard Doc say, "Charlie isn't afraid of anything." The way Doc said it made it seem like a good thing, and he'd felt proud. But then Doc went on to say that not being afraid wasn't always a good thing, how fear taught a man self-control and wisdom. *Well, Doc will be proud of me now*, Charlie thought. He was very afraid, but he sure didn't feel very wise. He wondered if Frank would have fallen on the pitchfork if he had been there with him.

Close to suppertime, Charlie was finally allowed to come in and sit and stare at Frank's pale forehead, dark circled eyes, and fat lips. His tongue was so swollen his mouth couldn't close, and his cheeks were puffed out like a squirrel's full of nuts. He didn't much look like himself, but Doc had sure done a better job of repairing him than Charlie had feared. There was still a speck of dried blood and a dab of snot just under Frank's left nostril. Charlie wanted to wipe them away but was afraid he might wake Frank and make him bleed more if he disturbed him.

When he'd looked him over and Doc had let him take Frank's pulse, Charlie asked Doc to show him where a "palate" was from the charts on his office walls of all the human parts. Charlie just about had all of them memorized, he thought, but he didn't remember ever hearing about a soft palate and a hard palate, except when he'd slept on them on the floor. Doc said there was no similarity at all. Charlie thought the names of most body parts were interesting and some made sense, but soft and hard palates just didn't.

Doc and the Harpers sat up with Frank all night, turning him from time to time to let blood pour out from his mouth. Doc said he was checking to make sure blood wasn't running down his throat. He said if it did, it would make him vomit and tear loose the wounds where the pitchfork had pierced his tongue and the top of his mouth. But it looked to Charlie like sometimes Doc was almost trying to make Frank vomit. That puzzled him, but he knew Doc was the best doctor in the whole world, and if anybody could fix Frank, Doc could do it, Doc and God. Doc often told him the three of them—Charlie, Doc, and God—made a powerful team. Charlie didn't feel like he was doing his part right now.

Coming in quietly from the toilet, Charlie overheard Doc tell Mr. Harper in a low, worried voice that Frank had lost way too much blood. Between the blood loss and a possible tetanus infection, he said again that Frank might not make it.

Charlie bit his lip so he'd feel pain there instead of in his heart and in that way not cry. He didn't know how that worked, but he did it when he was being spanked by Mrs. Harper. It worked even when he deserved the spanking. If you bit your lip, the other pain didn't hurt as much. He bit harder now, trying to remember if he'd ever hurt this much in his heart.

Doc handed Mr. Harper an article from a medical journal he said was written by two important men who knew just about all there was to know about tetanus infection. He thought they might be close to a cure. After a few moments, Charlie quietly walked over to the stand where Mr. Harper had laid the journal and looked for the names of the two men. He might need to ask someone, maybe Joshua or William, to write to them for help about Frank if Doc couldn't fix him.

They looked like foreign names, Italian or French or something: Carle and Rattone. He'd never seen "Carle" with an "e" on the end, sure that Doc had said "Carl," not "Carly," but he reminded himself that he was only five and that Doc said there was a whole lot more to learn and a much bigger world to see than just Mississippi. Doc had been to New York, Washington D.C., and lots of other important places.

Every once in a while, Doc or Mr. or Mrs. Harper would rouse Frank and carefully put a little bag of ice in his mouth or encourage him to let a small piece of ice melt there. Townsfolk were coming by bringing ice if they had any and fried chicken, cornbread, and cake. Charlie toyed with his food. It just didn't seem fair that he got to eat all this good stuff and all Frank got was ice. He felt better hearing that a prayer meeting for Frank was being held all night in the church and other people said they were praying on their own.

Frank whimpered all night. Charlie lay awake for a long time, wishing he could give him some of his blood. Doc had told him that doctors in London were trying to invent a way folks could give their blood to each other. So far, Doc said all the patients died, but he still believed it would be possible some day.

He asked God to please not let Frank die. He drifted off to sleep, thinking it strange that everyone said how lucky Frank was that the tool hadn't gone through his eyes or all the way to his brain. Charlie thought that wasn't really luck. Luck would have been that Frank hadn't fallen on the pitchfork at all!

Doc let Charlie stay with him the ten days until Frank could be taken home safely. He explained the purpose behind the things he did to help Frank and assured Charlie that he hadn't tried to make Frank vomit but that he was checking his gag reflex. When Doc explained what that was, Charlie was amazed that vomiting was ever a good thing. But, Doc said, the thing that made us vomit, that gag reflex, would be a signal that Frank wasn't getting tetanus. "Lockjaw," he'd said was another name for it. Charlie clamped his teeth together to lock his jaw to see what that would feel like. It felt like he'd never eat another apple or corn on the cob, for sure.

He sat with his friend every day, saying little, letting Frank sleep and mend and gag a little while Doc saw other patients and tended to his other business. He'd finally wiped Frank's nose clean and washed his hands, arms, and chest. There was hardly any sign of an accident now, if he didn't look at Frank's face.

Once back in the Harper home, Charlie read to Frank every day. He hadn't known it was unusual that he could read until Doc told Mr. Harper and the man handed him his Bible, asking him to read something. The book happened to open to pages in Matthew. Charlie looked the two pages over and picked the words beside the big number eighteen to read. He chose those because Doc had told him he thought that was how old his mother was when he was born. Then, like you're supposed to, he started with the little number one first and read: "Who is the greatest in the kingdom of heaven?" He read on, at first thinking maybe it would say his mother. But from the way Mr. Harper and even Doc acted, their eyes turning red and Doc blowing his nose, you'd have thought Charlie was the child Jesus was talking about.

Charlie left Frank's bedside only long enough to tend to his friend's needs. He fetched him his milk with the raw eggs, vanilla, and sugar in it and emptied his chamber pot. He wiped blood from the corners of his mouth when he bled a little in the night. The blood was getting paler and paler. Doc said that was a good sign. He brought him pretty rocks, his best Indian arrowhead, and a tarantula, which entertained them for a day until Mrs. Harper found it tied by a thread to the bedpost and threw it in the chamber pot.

He sat in the window seat looking out the upstairs window and made up stories for Frank of things he saw in the cloud formations about stalking wild bears and fighting in wars. He told Frank all the things about nature that Oxytak taught him.

Every night after their prayers, Charlie would say the same thing, "Good night, Frank. I'm going to lie down on my soft pallet now. Don't be coming after me with a pitchfork." One night Frank chuckled, and Charlie beamed. "Thank you, God, for letting Frank live." Charlie slept soundly that night for the first time in two months.

Spring had seemed to bypass summer and slide directly into fall as life in the Harper household returned to its normal pattern. Frank was not so much the hub of things now that he was getting better. There were crops to be harvested, wagons loaded with cotton lining up at the gin, pumpkin pies being baked, pecans to be gathered, chores and Bible readings and weekly baths— familiar things that gave a sense of order and belongingness to the family. Mrs. Harper was getting back her grouchiness, which always made Mr. Harper attend more meetings in the evenings.

Belle, William, Joshua, and Paul had their lessons. Mr. Harper let Charlie sit in when he wanted now that he knew he could read. Frank wasn't expected to say much or to write but just to listen and play quietly.

They learned about faraway places and about governments and presidents, especially Mr. Lincoln, who had been shot before Charlie was born. He was still Beulah's hero even though he was white.

Along with the older children, Charlie read important things like the Constitution and the Federalist Papers and something called the Emancipation Proclamation. Mr. Harper told them about reconstruction in the south and about what industries helped the southern economy now and what things were built in factories in the north. He didn't understand much of what he read, stumbling over more words than he wanted to, but Mr. Harper was good at explaining things. Sometimes, he remembered to ask Doc about something. Doc knew everything.

There were two things that were different, though. First, the Harpers missed their annual trek to their summer place down

DIXIE MILLER STEWART

south, not wanting to risk the trip so soon after Frank's accident. So there was precious little crawfish or shrimp served that season. Second, Frank talked funny. Doc said his accident left him with a speech impediment. Everyone still said how lucky Frank was that he could talk at all. Charlie thought lucky would have been that Frank didn't sound more like a two-year-old than his old self.

Just before the first frost and shortly after his sixth birthday, Charlie finally got to go see Doc, this time with Beulah. He could stay with Doc overnight. Beulah would purchase the things she needed for Thanksgiving meal preparations, spend the night with her married daughter, and fetch Charlie right after noon dinner the next day.

Charlie was so lost in thought and almost bursting open with sadness that he barely said a word all the way to town. Beulah was a lot quieter too. Charlie supposed she was thinking about her first grandbaby she was about to meet. He'd felt sad for her, too, since he'd found her crying in the woodshed after Mrs. Harper told her no, she couldn't go to town to help her daughter.

Doc had sent word that the baby was born. Ephraim had told Willie, Willie had told Old Andrew, and Old Andrew had told Doc when he delivered the supplies that had been brought up from the rail station. Beulah had asked to go right then, but Mrs. Harper said there was no need for her to waste a trip to town when she had to go anyway in two weeks.

Doc was with a patient when Beulah let Charlie off. She told the boy she was satisfied that Doc was there, seeing his buggy hitched out front, and said Doc had either just gotten back from calling on someone or was on his way to one. Charlie could tell she was mighty glad she'd caught him just in time; she was eager to get to that baby.

Charlie sat on the boardwalk outside Doc's office, poking a lizard with a stick he had once hidden between two planks there.

A boy never knew when he'd need a good stick. Charlie had them stashed in all the places where waiting might be necessary. You could do a lot with them: shooting Union soldiers who might still be hiding in caves and so not know the war was over was one important use, rescuing Confederate soldiers who might still be held captive in caves was another. You could shoot bears, have a sword fight, clean your fingernails if a lady was going to be looking at your hands, and pretend it was a bow or an arrow. There was just no end to the uses for a good stick, not to mention pestering lizards and toads as well as digging them a grave if the pestering went further than you'd intended.

He could hear voices coming from the back office now, so he thought Doc was finishing up. Granting emancipation to the lizard, he hurried in to see Doc shaking hands with the new preacher, and Charlie's heart pumped hard in his chest. He thought about turning around and leaving, but Doc called out to him. Doc introduced Charlie to the new preacher; but before he got all the words out, the man interrupted him and said he'd met him at the Harper place. He nodded briefly to Charlie, thanked Doc, and left.

Charlie settled himself at the table where Doc handed him a man-sized piece of coconut cake Mrs. Thompson had baked. "All right, Charlie," he said, "let's hear it." Doc always knew when Charlie had something important on his mind. Charlie liked that. Oxytak was the same way, but hardly anybody else was.

"Doc," Charlie asked, "what exactly does 'half-breed' mean?"

"Hmm." Doc paused to gather his thoughts. He rummaged around for his pipe tobacco and placed a pinch in the bowl, tamping it down just so. "How is it you're asking that, son?"

He'd hoped Oxytak might be the one to whom the inevitable question would be put. He supposed it was just as well, though, that it had been put to him. Doc knew Oxytak had his own personal battle over mixed-bloods. He had married one, and his father treated her as an outcast for years. That was another reason Doc thought Oxytak would be a good man for Charlie to get to know. The man had suffered a lot, and unlike many men had gained wisdom and forgiveness from it instead of anger and self-pity.

Oxytak hated but understood the bitterness his father felt toward the mixed-bloods and anyone associated with most white men. Doc was always an exception, not only because he was just decent, but also because they had a debt of gratitude toward him and his family. Doc's family had helped their Cherokee friends evade the government's abuse following the Indian Removal Act of 1830. That kindness probably saved their lives. Ultimately, it had prevented Oxytak's grandfather from having to take his family along the *Nunna dual Isunyi*.

Nevertheless, the man, as a young brave, had lost too many of his people along that Trail Where They Cried. They had died of small pox and starvation, and many had simply frozen to death, unable to cross the river in Illinois. Often they had neither the time nor the opportunity to provide a proper funeral for their dead; instead, they sang "Amazing Grace" and trusted in God's grace to provide a resting place for their departed.

Oxytak's parents were children when the soldiers forced their people from their homes. They'd watched the white man murder some of their relatives, plunder and burn their homes, and steal properties that had been in their families for generations. Lotteries dispersed sacred lands of their forefathers to folks who would not even have tipped their hats to an Indian. Oxytak's people still told the tragic stories. Of the many told, one that especially made Charlie cry was that about the white men forcing a Cherokee to kill his own chief and the leader's wife and children.

Doc's father had been a friend of William Thomas, a white man who had been reared by the Cherokee. Because of the friendship, he was able to conceal this small band of Indians from the US soldiers and remain on their vast private land. They had prospered there, frugally managing the small cache of gold they had once mined in Georgia. They established farms on the lands, eventually buying their acreages and raising cattle. They lived simply but not in poverty, growing crops and raising beef both for their own consumption and to sell for profit.

Oxytak had fallen in love with the beautiful half-breed Choctaw girl whose father owned the general store. He had wooed her with her father's and his mother's approval but not that of his own father.

Doc couldn't have hoped for a better match between Oxytak and Charlie. Oxytak was a good papa to his three daughters, but he had long grieved the death of his only son. Charlie won his heart immediately and so charmed Oxytak's father that the man finally welcomed his son's wife and family, if for no other reason than to be able to spend more time with Charlie when he visited.

The older men were eager for Charlie to learn about his Cherokee roots, and that included learning to read from Sequoyah's "syllabary" almost before he could ride a horse. Charlie read and listened to the stories with pride that he had come from such a fine people. The old man told the child about the proud line of Cherokee leaders and their courage, of how his people lived in harmony with nature and had in times past cultivated the "three sisters" of corn, beans, and squash. Already, Charlie admired Sequoyah, who had enabled his people to learn to read English by inventing the Cherokee alphabet.

Charlie's long sigh brought Doc's attention back to the question at hand: "What is a half-breed?" He told Doc about the new preacher calling on the Harpers last month and how he'd said that Charlie didn't seem to look like his brothers. He told him about how Mrs. Harper, who had been right in the middle of a tizzy fit when the preacher rode up, still had the mean look on her face.

"She smoothed her hair and apron and put a big smile on the outside of her face. But when preacher said that, she practically yelled out, 'He's not blood kin. He's a half-breed we took in!'

"Then," Charlie continued, not yet taking a bite of cake, "Preacher dropped his hand, not even shaking mine like he shook William's, who was in the room too. I wouldn't even have been in there when preacher came except William was helping me with my numbers. I'm learning times.

"I asked William what 'half-breed' meant, and he wouldn't answer. I asked Belle, and she said it wasn't nothing bad, and I should just not worry about it. I asked Frank, and Frank laughed and said, 'You are, Chawee.' I said, 'Frank, what is it?' and Frank said, 'I *dote* know. It's what mama said you are and what them *Inyuns* down on the river are, but it's probably not the kind of *Inyun Ostik* is.'"

Charlie reminded Doc that Frank couldn't pronounce words like *Indian* or *Oxytak* anymore and continued. "Then Frank said, 'That's all I know, Chawee. *Dote* ask me anymore!'" Charlie reminded Doc that Frank couldn't say "don't" or "Charlie" either.

So Charlie had waited and waited, his heart heavy, at first happy that Beulah's grandbaby had been born early, thinking he'd finally get to come and ask Doc. He was as frustrated in his way as Beulah was in hers that the baby's early arrival hadn't done either one of them any good.

"But, well, Doc, here I am, and I'm asking you because there's something not very good about it when the preacher won't even shake your hand! I've heard people called half-breed before, but I never was called one, at least not to my face!"

Doc thought to himself that he'd sensed there was something about the new preacher he hadn't much cared for but couldn't put his finger on it until now. The man obviously missed an important point of the faith he professed. He nudged the plate of cake a little closer to Charlie and watched while the boy sliced his fork into the iced end of it.

"Charlie," Doc began, "we've talked about 'prejudice.' You know what that is?"

"Yes, it's like when the man selling Beulah my shoes called her a bad name because she's colored, and it's because of prejudice that Old Andrew has those scars on his neck even though he hadn't hurt any of those white folks."

"That's right," Doc answered. "There's prejudice among all folks, for sure. Always has been. Some folks everywhere have to find others to put down so they can think better of themselves, even though it just makes them look uglier. A lot of folks need to point their fingers at someone a little different from them, sometimes just because of their color. We're talking inside ugly, Charlie, not outside ugly."

"I know," Charlie replied, "but is half-breed a *color*?"

"No," Doc answered, "but you know Indians are called red men and colored folks are sometimes called black because of their skin color, although I have to admit, I've never seen an actual red face or a black face." Doc explained it, and Charlie took it all in without interrupting. "Charlie, do you remember when we read about General Stand Waite?"

"Oh, yes." The boy perked up. "He was a general of the Cherokee. He commanded a whole—was it a regiment?—in the War Between the States. He's one of my heroes and one of Oxytak's too. Oxytak said he once met him. I wish I could have met him. He died before I was born."

"You're right, youngin'." Doc chuckled, always delighted by Charlie's intelligence. "General Waite was a brave, smart Indian man, and rich too, and a Cherokee. He fought for the South, partly because he owned slaves. But he also had a lot of other enemies who tried to kill him, and some of those enemies were among his own people."

Charlie was shocked. "You mean some *Cherokees* didn't like him?"

Doc explained how some Cherokees had been persuaded by the Union to join their side, but General Waite had fought for the South. "And Charlie," he said to emphasize the point, "General Waite was on the side of half-breeds. They call them mixed-bloods, but it's the same thing. A lot of Cherokees were against the mixed-bloods—that is, they were *prejudiced* against them—but General Waite risked his reputation and his life for them."

Doc pretended old age memory loss. "Who is that man you always tell me is your best hero in the War Between the States?"

Charlie smiled for the first time. "You know," he giggled. "It's Stonewall!"

"Oh yes, that's him." Doc laughed.

"Doc, are you going to tell me that General Stonewall Jackson was prejudiced?"

Doc laughed again. "I don't know, I think maybe he had a little prejudice against General Grant and General Sherman and the whole Union Army. What do you think?"

"Yeah, I mean, yes," Charlie mused, the corners of his lips curving into a slow grin as he remembered something. "I bet he was prejudiced against the Confederate soldier who accidentally shot him too!

"Mr. Harper and Beulah both told me about a whole lot of colored folks that are real heroes too," Charlie offered. "Lots of them were heroes in the Reb, Reev...Revolutionary War! And George Washington...not the president, uh, Carver! That's it, and, a funny name... Oh! Booker T. Washington. Don't you like that name, Doc? Booker T. I like it. Anyway, that's two who are still alive. Mr. Harper said they were helping coloreds get educations and learn to do things besides just housework and fieldwork, things to make their lives better. Mr. Harper said they were helping Mississippi's..." He paused, trying to remember the word. "You know…that word that means something like how Mississippi gets its money. I don't understand that part."

"You have quite a mind for facts, son." Doc beamed. "Beulah and Mr. Harper are right. I respect Mr. Harper for not letting bitterness influence his attitude about colored folks. I've read something about this Mr. Booker Washington. He is over in Alabama heading up a school to help coloreds learn. Mr. Carver and Mr. Washington are both helping their fellow men of every color not only get an education or a skill they can use to live in freedom but to add to the dignity and pride of colored people."

"Mr. Carver just may end up making quite an impact on the entire south, not only in Mississippi, son. The word you were searching for is *economy*. He is helping the economy in the South. I don't know that he's ever been in the state, but word of him certainly has. He is teaching all folks to get better uses of their fields by planting crops like sweet potatoes, soybeans, and especially peanuts."

"Moses and Mr. Harper don't know what to plant next spring. Do you think Mr. Carver could come and help them? Mr. Harper needs to make more money. I heard him say the boys were spending him out of his house." Charlie took a long gulp of milk, leaving a white mustache on his upper lip.

Doc used every chance he got to teach Charlie to think for himself, look at all sides of a matter, and to become independent and self-sufficient. Recalling something else he had read about this George Washington Carver, he told the boy, "Mr. Carver also lost his mother as a baby and was very sickly, almost not surviving."

"I'm going to tell Beulah that Mr. Carver is just like me. Now he's my hero too!"

Doc pointed out that each of his favorite heroes was of different color: one was a red man, one was a black man, and one was a white man. "You, Charlie, have both red man blood and white man blood in you. That is what is meant by 'half-breed.'"

In a happier mood now, Charlie nodded his understanding and then teased, "Doc, if part of me is white and part of me is red, does that make me a pink boy?" He fell back in his chair, laughing at his joke. "Pink is Lilly's favorite color. I'm going to tell her I'm a pink man!"

Doc smiled and added, "You can be anything you want. So you see, in a way, being a mixture of both makes you stronger. You've got the best of both kinds of men in your genes. Don't ever let folks tell you that you're not as good as them. You're a whole lot better than anyone I know, Charlie!"

"Yes!" Charlie's regained enthusiasm emboldened him. "I'm a darn sight better than a prejudiced person!"

He recalled something else about Stonewall. "As a matter of fact, Charlie, Stonewall is the man who said, 'You may be whatever you resolve to be!'"

Charlie finished the last of his cake, thinking about what Doc had just said. He laid the fork across the plate and looked steadily into Doc's eyes, man to man. "I'm very glad, Doc, 'cause I resolve to be just like you when I grow up."

It was three days before Christmas, but the Harper household wasn't in much of a festive mood even though the same number of presents was under the tree. William and Moses had cut the same size tree as last year's. Belle and Beulah had decorated the house just the same as they always did. It smelled of pine needles, cloves, and cinnamon like it had in every other year Charlie could remember, but something else hung in the air this Christmas, almost making a mockery of the cedar boughs and mistletoe.

Charlie couldn't *wait* to talk to Doc about this latest and by far worst thing that Mrs. Harper had ever done. He hated being just seven and so not allowed to ride by himself into town. He and Horse knew their way just as well as any adult. Besides, Horse and Jenny were friends, and they hardly ever got to visit.

In late November, Charlie was sent for the week to the neighbors five miles away. He was needed to help with the chores because Mr. Johnston had to go to New Orleans on business. His wife had new twins and six-year-old Benjamin, whom she hoped Charlie would keep occupied by teaching him to read. Consequently, Charlie had to wait twenty-three long days after he got back home before getting a chance to talk to Doc about the very bad thing that had happened to the Harpers while he was away.

It wasn't just that Mrs. Harper had another one of her "tizzy fits," as Belle and Joshua and Paul secretly called them. Even at his age, Charlie knew what the boys now described was much worse than just a regular one where she brought out the razor strap, wildly swinging it wherever it landed on the kids, himself included. This time, she'd outdone herself.

Charlie didn't know if he was glad he'd been at the Johnston's or not. It seemed to him that he was always gone during the most important times. He'd been with Oxytak when the Millers' barn burned down, when Lilly was born, when Belle grew bosoms, and when Frank fell on the pitchfork. This was the biggest.

Doc took one look at the boy's face and knew he'd best make up a story to tell Mrs. Harper that he needed Charlie's help. He had ridden up to the Harper place, bringing a gift as an excuse to see Charlie, expecting him to be bursting with the excitement of the season. Instead, he could see he was about to burst all right, but not with happiness. The boy needed to talk. Though it would mean another trip back tomorrow, Doc gave the weak excuse that he needed him to help shell pecans, saying he intended to give bags to older folks in town whose arthritic hands made shelling too difficult. Charlie climbed in the buggy before Doc had set a foot on it. Jenny whinnied and pawed her good hoof.

The child didn't cry easily; he tended to listen more than he talked, but now he fought tears as he began telling Doc in a rush of words that tumbled over themselves what William, Joshua, and Paul had told him. Jenny folded her ears back as though she, too, wanted to hear.

The brothers told him in front of Frank, who just sat there hugging his knees, not saying anything. Each of Frank's big blue eyes was filled with one enormous tear that Charlie kept watching, waiting for one or the other to spill down his face. In the back of his mind, Charlie was fascinated that the tears could just hang there. But in the front of his mind, he marveled over the balance of perfect awfulness and perfect purity of the story the boys whispered to him.

Charlie told Doc the events that had begun to irritate Mrs. Harper that morning. Things kept going wrong, like Lilly falling into the washtub rinse water and Joshua knocking over the pot full of coffee before anyone had a cup. Doc's own thoughts distracted him for a moment, appreciating again the natural storyteller in Charlie and how he thought more like an adult than a child, so he missed hearing the critical incident that had precipitated the change in Mrs. Harper from irritation to ire.

He heard Charlie continuing, his speech gaining speed and volume. "So when that happened she was so mad, so awful mad, she started screaming and screaming at them and made all the kids go outside and line up against the house. From the tallest to the shortest, that's how she lined them up.

"Then she told them, Doc…she told them she was going to shoot them all! Every last one of them she was going to shoot dead! Doc, they minded her! Except Lilly—Lilly was asleep in the house. So that made Frank the shortest. They stood there, knowing her gun was loaded, and just watched her lift it to her shoulder and aim it right at them! Those kids *still* stood there, Doc! Then Frank...*Frank*...broke rank, I guess you call it, and ran over to Mrs. Harper, crying, saying..." Charlie paused to swallow back tears and continued. "Doc, you know how Frank talks now. Paul told it just like Frank said it. He said, 'No, no, Mama. Dote shoot my bruvers and sisser. Shoot old Frank. Jus' shoot old Frank. Frank cate talk right. Frank not good for nuffin'. Just shoot Frank, but dote shoot my bruvers and Belle!'"

Charlie had lovingly mimicked Frank then swallowed hard and smeared more tears away with his fists before going on. "Then Mrs. Harper just threw her gun on the ground and stomped away, going down into the cellar by herself. She was still there when I got home. Beulah had put Lilly to bed, and Mr. Harper was smoking a cigar and reading his Bible. I went to find Frank and found all the kids dead quiet..." Charlie's voice broke. "I better not use that word. I found them all in William's room, quiet and kinda scared-like, and I asked them what was wrong, and at first no one spoke. I thought somebody had died. Then they told me everything."

Finishing his telling, Charlie slumped across Doc's lap, deep sobs spilling hot tears through the man's trouser leg. He let Doc hold him and comfort him, both arms clinging tightly around Doc's right leg. Doc had never known the lad to cry this way. The sobs seemed too raw and harsh for such a little boy. They rode on in silence, Doc patting and rubbing Charlie's back with a weathered, loving hand. Finally, they arrived at Doc's house, Charlie had cried himself out and grown quiet and still. Doc carried him back to his place behind his office, thinking he had fallen asleep.

"Doc," Charlie said, his voice a hoarse whisper, "Frank saved their lives! Frank is just seven years old, like me. You know he's six months older than me, and he's already saved four lives! What Frank did…what Frank did…made him kinda like Jesus and like my mama. He…he loves his brothers and sister enough to die for them!" The boy was silent for a moment. "I already know two real people…other than Jesus…two *people* who did that, and I'm only seven!

"To tell you the truth, Doc, I'd been thinking that Frank was, well, kinda like a 'fraidy cat. He can't fight, and he's kinda awkward. I love him, anyway, like a brother. I wouldn't care if he's even afraid of a flea. I will always take care of him, but he's afraid of a lot of things." Charlie's voice drifted off for a moment.

"But now I know Frank is the bravest kid I've ever looked in the face. He said he was afraid, but he did it anyway. That's really what being brave means, isn't it, Doc?" Charlie gulped in air with a man-sized yawn and rolled over, pulling his knees up and tucking his hands beneath his chin. "I'm so proud Frank's my friend."

Chapter 3

He rested his forehead against the upstairs windowpane, watching Mr. Harper and William smoking in the back yard. So far, there was nothing to celebrate, but the cigar was to calm their nerves, William told him, as if he knew. Part of him envied William for getting to have his first cigar, and part of him felt proud that Mr. Harper left him in charge of the "sound brigade." Mr. Harper told him that was a very important job for a ten-year-old! His responsibility was to notify Mr. Harper as soon as he heard the baby's first cry or if Beulah called for him.

Frank ran and hid in the cellar, not liking the way his mother was sounding in there. Joshua took Lilly to pick berries. Belle just thought she was really smart getting to help, even though all she did was carry hot water back and forth. Mr. Harper explained that it was not much different than when they had all watched calves or foals being born.

So it was that Charlie was the only one outside the bedroom to hear Jessie's first cry. He felt something that very moment, something like what probably happens when an angel sings in your heart. Even though his orders regarding the sound brigade had been to run downstairs as fast as he could to tell Mr. Harper, Charlie, in fact, walked down them very slowly, pondering the mystery of new life.

Then, he'd felt that magic again when he reached out in awe to touch her little fist and she grabbed his finger; only this time the feeling was even stronger. He thought he might not even be able to explain it to Doc or Oxytak. It was something like he'd seen in Doc's face at times when Charlie caught him looking at him or on Oxytak's face when he looked at his daughters. Come to think about it, he'd even seen it on Oxytak's face for him too.

He lay in bed after the house had grown quiet and the baby was sleeping and thought about the strange and wonderful feelings he had for Jessie now that she was born. It was like he wanted to put his arms around that little person and hug her to him so he could make sure nothing bad ever happened to her, so he could keep her safe and unafraid all her life. More than that, it was like if he had to he could kill bears and bad men all by his self with just his bare hands, to protect her. One minute you couldn't have done that 'cause you'd have been too afraid. But the next minute, the very second the person came into your heart, then suddenly as if by magic, you could. You could fight a bear!

He said his prayers, thanking God for Jessie, and lay back, thinking how he would fight the whole world for her if that were what he ever needed to do. *It must have been what Frank felt when he saved his family!* He thought. *It is what Stonewall felt when he fought those battles. I'll bet it's what miners feel when they go deep into danger to put food on their families' tables.* He had recently read about some miners being killed because their jobs were so dangerous. *It is what men feel for people not as strong as them and why they go to war even though they might die. It's love!* Charlie realized with a jolt.

The summer Charlie turned thirteen, he later dubbed "The Summer of My Contradiction" and wrote a short story about it, sharing it only with Frank and Doc. Years later, Jessie sneaked in and read it, but that was after he'd left home.

In truth, that summer contained many contradictions and contrasts, but he thought it sounded more profound to leave the word in singular form. He'd spent it with Oxytak. He'd gone to Oxytak's speaking as he always did and returned with a voice over which he had almost no control, sometimes sounding like Oxytak's five-year-old grandson and sometimes like Paul, who was twenty-five. He certainly preferred sounding like Paul, but the choice hadn't been his, except to just not speak at all. Also, he'd gone there wearing breeches that were two inches too long and returned with them two inches too short, and they were still shrinking by Christmas.

He'd ridden to Oxytak's in a perfectly happy mood but once there found himself sometimes wanting to cry, sometimes wanting to fight, and other times just bursting out laughing for reasons no one understood.

So while the summer contained some of the best times of his life, it also contained some of the worst. He guessed the worst ones had to happen before the good ones could begin. But whatever his mood at any given moment, he spent a lot of time thinking that summer. He thought most about the changes he was undergoing. He traced the onset of some of them back to the time of Jessie's birth three years earlier. He'd been awakened then to love and to the capacity to hurt, both to feel hurt and, to his shame, to inflict it.

The most important change was brought about by immaturity and a streak of meanness he hadn't recognized until Oxytak called it for what it was. "Son," he'd said with far more kindness than Charlie deserved, "you're at the crossroads of manhood. Becoming a man is inevitable, but the kind of man you become is up to you. What you did today was the act of a prideful bully."

Charlie hung his head, crying in shame.

"Look me in the eye, son. Always look another man in the eye, especially when you're in the wrong."

Charlie lifted his head to meet his mentor's gaze, comforted a bit that he had said "*another* man," and Oxytak continued: "Son, defense of one's life and defense of one's pride are two very different things. A man learns to discern the difference. He'll defend his life and he'll protect the weak, but he'll learn to control his anger and subdue his pride. Otherwise, one or both will control him. You think hard about that."

"Yes, sir, I will."

When he'd covered all the other violations Charlie had committed that day, Oxytak walked away and left Charlie alone in the woods to think for ten days. He'd left his Bible with him and suggested he spend a lot of time in Proverbs.

Being cut off from those he loved and fearing he had lost Oxytak's respect forever was almost more than Charlie could endure. Ultimately, it had brought him closer to God and to a commitment to him, and it had helped him see that it was the loss of his self-respect that presented the strongest challenge.

What he had done still shamed him, and he supposed it would for the rest of his life. He had asked for forgiveness from the boy, his parents, and from God. It had been very hard to do, but forgiving himself was the hardest.

He'd almost killed a boy, and Oxytak was right; no matter how hard he had tried to justify his acts, in the end, they were due to pride. When he reflected back on that day, he was alarmed by his capacity to be so blinded by his own hurt that all he'd wanted was to strike out and hurt another.

It had come about while he was fishing alone at a stream a short distance from Oxytak's town. Charlie approached a group of five or six Indian boys a year or so younger than he and all smaller in stature. Two of them he knew vaguely, but the others were strangers. He casually inquired of their luck that day at fishing.

"What do you care?" one of them sneered. "You ain't nothin' but a nigger-lovin', half-breed, bastard boy that somebody took in 'cause they pitied you! Your daddy never even wanted you!" Emboldened by their greater number, they all started laughing and mimicking the leader, calling Charlie names and making fun of both the circumstances of his birth and the fact that he was neither Indian nor white.

Their words hurt deeply because they mined the secret, buried doubts Charlie had about himself: that in truth he was just what they were calling him: "A half-breed, bastard kid with no heritage, no identity, no roots, unwanted." No matter what he did, he was still on the outside of the Harper family; Mrs. Harper made sure to remind him of that.

Giving no thought to their younger age and smaller size, Charlie charged into the group, employing the defensive skills Oxytak had been teaching him all his life. Martial arts—he knew they were very popular in Japan and China and other places in the Orient. Oxytak had cautioned again and again that his skills were never to be abused and never to be used to inflict harm on another unless his life was in danger. He could use them to prevent a greater harm and to discourage an enemy assailant. He must never, Oxytak had emphasized, use them because he was angry or had his pride hurt.

Forgetting Oxytak's wisdom, Charlie rushed forward, knocking them all down, though some only to their knees. Three of the boys picked themselves up and ran off. One stayed down on the ground, where Charlie's rage had sent him, afraid to rise again. The leader, the main target for Charlie's fury, had tried to run, but Charlie hadn't allowed that. Instead, he slammed him on the ground a second time, where he lay unconscious, a smear of blood trickling from the corner of his mouth. Charlie stared down at him.

The boy came to and seeing Charlie bending over him, began to cry. "Please don't hurt me," he begged.

"I'm done," was all Charlie could think to say. He reached to help the boy up and discovered he'd broken his arm when the kid yelled out in pain. The boy struggled to sit up with his good arm but immediately rolled over, gagging and vomiting.

At the end of his ten days of isolation, a more humbled Charlie was grateful to see Oxytak approaching his lonely campsite. "Son, it is time to come home. We've missed you."

Charlie cried, appreciating and understanding that in Oxytak's quiet manner, he had taught him some needed lessons, forgiven him, and was now welcoming him back into his family.

One of the decisions Charlie made that week was to never again take advantage of someone younger or weaker than him. "I'll just fight with fists like other kids if that ever becomes necessary, sir, and maybe even then only if they're bigger."

The bent of his conversations with Oxytak was different after that week; their talks were better. They were about more important things like growing up and relationships and becoming responsible. Oxytak treated him less like a child too.

Now, he looked forward to talking with Doc about things that he'd been discussing and pondering in his heart. He wasn't really sure he'd be able to explain all his feelings. One reason for that was because Doc told him that every life needed to contain some bad things so that folks would understand and appreciate the good things and not get all high and mighty expectations that God was supposed to make life easy for them.

He said bad things happening made a person real and tested his character. Charlie thought he'd failed his biggest test of character, but Oxytak assured him he had not. Oxytak and Doc both thought wisdom and character and faith in God were probably the most important things a man needed in order to be a man. Both said people grew them mostly from reading God's Word and partly when they learned to look beyond suffering, quit blaming other folks, and be grateful for their blessings.

Doc talked a lot about bad things not always being bad. But Charlie didn't think there could possibly be anything at all good about letting bad things happen to Jessie or Lilly. He wondered if that was what men were for, to have the bad things happen to them so the girls could be spared. Frank already had a really bad thing happen, and he'd be paying for it for the rest of his life, Charlie supposed. He wasn't talking any better, and it didn't look like he ever would. Even grown-ups sometimes made fun of the way he talked. It didn't make Frank cry anymore, but it had always made Charlie want to beat them up.

By summer's end and with the loving patience of Oxytak, Charlie had come to understand something else: he was loved by the people who mattered most to him and respected by those he most respected. That group included white, red, colored, mixed-bloods, and pure bloods. He could identify respect for him in most people's eyes and understood that those good folks were judging him only for his character and how he conducted himself. It had been a difficult and costly lesson to learn.

"Yes, Charlie," Oxytak had agreed, "the most important lessons are usually painful, especially when pride has been the teacher."

But Charlie still got mad when people hurt the people he loved. He had learned to fight with his fists and fight well, making even Mr. Harper twice chuckle over his "skills as a pugilist." He usually got in a fight at school every time kids picked on Frank. He had also fought the boy who made Lilly cry but only when he kept doing it after Charlie twice told him to never pester her again. He didn't always win, but he almost never lost, until today.

Today, his first day back home, was his worst fight ever, no doubt about it; the first one where he'd been badly beaten up. Frank kept telling him it was only because there were three of them and one of him. He knew he was outnumbered, but that hadn't mattered. He loved Oxytak too much not to fight for him, especially for such a terrible thing. It didn't matter that Oxytak would never know; in fact, Charlie didn't want him to ever find out, this wasn't about pride, this was about honor.

The sun had been barely peeking over the eastern hills when Oxytak waked him to make the long ride back in time for the first day of the school year. They waited until Monday to come back so Charlie could attend Oxytak's daughter's wedding on Sunday.

Oxytak's wife had sewn Charlie a new shirt and breeches for the occasion since he had outgrown his clothes in the three months he'd been with them. Oxytak's father gave him his own moccasins, seeming to be delighted that they fit Charlie's feet perfectly. He'd worn his new clothes again today, reminding Oxytak to thank everyone for them again, as he said goodbye and watched him ride away.

Ruffian cowards, as Mr. Harper would later call them, waited until Oxytak had ridden out of earshot on his way back home. Then they mocked him to Charlie, taunting and goading the boy with bits and pieces of the story of how Oxytak's son had been killed. The father of one of the bullies had apparently even boasted to everyone that he had run him down with his horse and wagon and left him lying on the road.

Only later would Charlie get the full story from Beulah, but he'd heard enough there in the school yard to believe he had an obligation to exact long over due justice. Oxytak had grieved the loss of his son for twenty years. Charlie stood agonizing between the lessons so recently learned and the evil that faced him now.

The decision was made for him when one of his tormentors shoved him down onto the rocky yard and another fell on top.

Joshua and Frank helped him home, gingerly bracing him up after almost dropping him, trying first to carry him by his underarms and ankles. The boys were so concerned for him no one thought about sending for Moses and the buggy.

"Boy, Charlie, you were good back there!" Joshua gasped when they'd stopped to catch their breath.

"Yeah," Frank added, "those guys have always been bullies. Stupid bullies is all they are. They've been needing to be taught a lesson for a long time!"

Charlie groaned. "I think I'm probably the one who learned the lesson." He was in too much pain to speak further but quietly hoped he wasn't going to spend his life learning everything the hard way.

"I don't think so, Charlie!" Though struggling to carry his taller friend, Frank was nevertheless quite enthusiastic. "That was the first smile anybody's ever seen on Miss Graham's face in all these years we've been going to that school! That must surely mean that those bullies got what they'd been asking for, for a lot of years!"

Charlie wondered how far the three would have dragged him if the schoolteacher hadn't rushed up, whacking the bigger boys on their backs and shoulders with the cane she kept in the corner for just such occasions. She wrote a note for Mr. and Mrs. Harper, informing them she hadn't seen the start of the fight. However, she thought that since there were three of them and all three older than Charlie by at least two years, it was apparent he'd learned his lesson for whatever responsibility he might share. She added a P.S.: "You will perhaps want to know that all three of the larger boys have nose bleeds, and there appears to be at least one, possibly two, potential black eyes among them." She underlined the word *larger*.

Beulah and Mrs. Harper tended to his wounds while he winced, now not even able to bite his lower lip to diminish the pain. He was determined not to cry. He could hear Paul and Joshua explaining the day to Mr. Harper, William, and Belle. Frank sat on a bench in the kitchen, watching the ladies minister to his friend's wounds, stricken by the injuries he saw. Twice he needed Charlie's reassurance that the fight wasn't because of him. Mr. Harper came in to examine and set his nose, warning Charlie it would hurt but assuring him it would be better for him to have it straightened now.

The entire story about Oxytak's son came out only after Charlie's injuries had been assessed by Mrs. Harper and Beulah and re-examined and announced to all by Mr. Harper: "Both eyes black and almost swollen shut, a broken nose, both lips cut, a loosened tooth, just be careful not to bite on it, that tooth will set again." Then they removed his shirt and found bruises on his ribs from being kicked and lacerations on his back where he'd been dragged over rocks. Beulah clucked and clucked her sympathy. Mrs. Harper kept her lips in a tight line, but she was gentle. Charlie begged Beulah to tell him about Oxytak's son.

"Colored folks," she told him, "come along and found the boy in the road where he'd been run over. They put him in their wagon and carried him to the closest doctor. They'd feared he might die if they took the time to try and find his family." Here Beulah grew quiet for a minute, remembering.

"Even driving him into town to the doctor, the rescuers themselves were attacked and their belongings scattered all over everywhere. That child lingered on a week but never regained consciousness. His parents, who we now know to be Oxytak and his wife, were found and brought in, they never left his side until he died." Beulah shook her head back and forth, as was her way when she remembered sad things. Charlie knew she had a lot of them to remember. He wondered if the child would have lived if Doc had been his doctor.

Charlie hurt everywhere badly, really badly, but he wouldn't have let himself cry from his injuries. His tears finally spilled as Beulah finished telling about the murder of the little Indian boy years ago, filling in the gaps left in the bullies' taunting account. Beulah and Moses knew the family that rescued Oxytak's son, but until today, Beulah had never known whose son that young boy was. "It was murder, just as sure as if they'd shot him." The room grew quiet for a moment as everyone remembered the time Mrs. Harper had threatened to shoot her children.

Beulah shook her head back and forth, back and forth as tears rolled down her round cheeks, grieving again for that little lost life and for the hurt to Charlie, whom she loved as much as her own. Regretful that she had missed so many opportunities to send a cake or a pie home with Oxytak, she made up her mind to remedy that the next time Charlie went to visit. "I would sure have done that already if I'd known it was his boy!"

While Charlie waited for the bath water to heat, Beulah sat beside him, patting the top of his head, the only part of him that didn't ache. She made him a cup of peppermint tea, and Mr. Harper sneaked some of his brandy past Mrs. Harper, assuring Charlie it would help him feel a little better. Charlie thought about asking for a cigar but decided against pushing his luck. However, with every urged sip of the warm beverage, he vowed to never again have another drink of such vile-tasting stuff as brandy.

It took all the Harper males to completely undress him, help him into a tub of warm-but-not-hot water, pull on clean night-clothes, and get him put to bed. He could only lie on his right side and didn't think he would be able to sleep. He didn't wake for seventeen hours.

When he woke, he smelled like Mrs. Harper. Then he remembered she'd insisted he use her good soap because the lye soap would be too harsh for his open wounds. He tried to roll over, and the memory of yesterday's thrashing rushed back. He couldn't lie on his back, and he couldn't lie on his stomach; consequently, he couldn't get over to the left side of the bed. He needed to pee, so he had no choice but to bite his lip and endure the pain.

His pee smelled a little bit like the brandy, and he shuddered remembering how bad it had tasted. Struggling to crawl back under the covers, he mumbled, "This is…this is hell." He managed a stiff grin in memory of the boy he used to be who thought it was grown-up to use that word.

Smelling like Mrs. Harper, remembering that she had tears in her eyes when she saw his bruises and grateful that she had let him use her soaps, Charlie allowed himself to think kindly toward her for a few moments. Then he remembered how she yelled at Jessie all the time as if she had some peculiar resentment reserved just for her youngest daughter. He thought maybe it was because Jessie wasn't a boy.

More than once, he'd rescued Jessie just in time from an unwarranted thrashing or kicks and hair pulling. He had been the one to let her out of the root cellar where Mrs. Harper had banished her for some minor misbehavior, and he untied her from the clothesline when he'd come in from the fields after dark on a cold night. He carried baskets too heavy for her that Mrs. Harper expected her to bear.

Only this year had he been able to cease wrestling with what he thought of as cowardice. Before, he'd struggled between not wanting to risk rejection and what he knew to be the manly thing to do: rescue Jessie from Mrs. Harper's ire. More than once he fetched Jessie from some mishap that Mrs. Harper ignored. If he tried to count the times of her meanness toward Jessie, he thought it would be up to a hundred or more.

Forgetting his sore lip, he tried to smile, recalling how Jessie always waited in the barn to greet him when he came in from chores. The day he'd left for Oxytak's, she'd met him beside Horse, her apron filled with small rocks. "I worked all day yesterday finding these for you. Here." Then she'd wrapped her fingers around two of his and whispered, "Don't tell Mama, Charlie, but I love you most. You're my best, best friend." She had long ago completely captured his heart.

He struggled not to lose respect for Mr. Harper and the boys. They surely must see what he saw in Mrs. Harper's treatment of Jessie, her youngest and fortunately her most spirited. Lilly would not have been able to cope with her mother's anger. Jessie's eyes still twinkled, and when she could, she'd skip away from her mother's grasp, giggling, already too proud to let her mother see tears. Often when she was really hurt, she came looking for Charlie, the only person she'd allow to see her cry.

Over the years, Mrs. Harper had tried to intimidate Charlie by telling him she was going to send him to live with someone else if he didn't toe the mark. When she first threatened that, it scared him even though he didn't exactly know what "toe the mark" meant. He was pretty sure it meant that he'd be banished from their home, though. He couldn't bear the thought of losing Frank. When he was old enough, he knew he could ride Horse to see Frank and they'd always be friends. Now, he felt that same loyalty and protectiveness for Jessie, maybe even more than for Frank.

Mrs. Harper hadn't made that threat to him in almost two years, but he didn't give her an opportunity to do so either, except for his protectiveness toward Jessie. He just stayed occupied and tried not to let her behavior bother him the way it more often did her own sons. Rarely being singled out by her mother, Belle seemed closest to normal and nice enough, but she sometimes threw lesser tizzy fits herself.

DIXIE MILLER STEWART

Lilly was a sweet little goody-goody. Charlie understood that was her way of adapting to a mother whose anger she could rarely predict. Outsiders probably only saw them as a very loving, well-behaved, well-mannered family. They were, but they had secrets and maybe more pain than they showed to others. The closeness of the children acted as a buffer between them and their mother. They seemed closer to each other than to their parents.

Everybody had their own way of coping with their hurt. Jessie's was to stomp off and throw rocks at squirrels. Charlie thought that just made her more lovable; he didn't think she'd ever hit one. Paul was preparing to go to the academy that William attended, and Charlie knew he couldn't wait to leave next fall.

It was Easter, and if the Harpers had any sort of "rite of passage" out of childhood, it was that of taking a horse and wagon into town alone for the first time. This privilege occurred every year on the first Monday after Easter, and it was awarded to that child who had turned thirteen during the past twelve months. The parents, of course, viewed the task in a more practical light. Sending a responsible, middle-age child spared an adult from having to go fetch the supplies the family would need for the months they spent in their summer home "down south," as it was always called. It freed them and the older children to pack and close up the house. Without fail, they left the Tuesday following Easter, even when the weather was least cooperative, even if it poured rain.

The child so honored held the privilege until a younger brother or sister turned thirteen. In that Charlie wasn't born into the Harper family, his arrival on the scene crowded the thirteenth year, as Frank liked to joke. Both boys achieved that status in the same year. Each child took very seriously the honor of this coveted opportunity to exhibit his or her imagined superiority over the younger ones, if only for this one day.

This would be the third such trip for Frank and Charlie. They had the routine down and the long list memorized. It was always the same. It had delighted Frank to lord his superior age over Charlie at first; he was six months older. That had allowed him to handle the reins and make whatever important and unexpected decisions there might be. Now the two were casual in their mutual sharing of the once-prized responsibilities. Today their camaraderie was most important. Although, of course, they went alone wherever they wanted now, there was still the solemnity of the occasion and they understood it would be the last time for them. Next year, Lily would have the honor, and she could hardly wait.

"You know, Charlie, the whole town sets their clocks and calendars according to when the Harpers arrive at Mr. Davis's store every Easter Monday. If you or I took a detour or lost a wheel off the wagon, we could conceivably throw the entire universe out of whack."

"Yep," Charlie answered. "Or if your mama ever got over her mad for Mrs. Cora Lee Folsom and decided to get these supplies from Folsom General Store down south, we'd significantly alter the Davis and the Folsom incomes!"

Frank was on a roll. "And if Papa ever failed to say, 'Julia, we don't need to weigh down these wagons, there's a store right *there*,' then I doubt we'd ever be able to get out of the yard. It could ruin the economy in the south, prevent us from planting our crops, drive Beulah to distraction, and probably so discombobulate Mama she'd miscarry."

"She's going to have another child?" Charlie asked.

"Of course. Otherwise, when Jessie turns thirteen, she'd have to drive it every year from then on, and she'd probably turn into an old maid. Everybody would look at their pocket watches and say, 'Sure 'nuff, here comes ol' lady Harper, Miss Jessie at the helm, just like the last thirty years.'"

They pulled up out front of Mr. Davis's store, and Frank whispered and mimicked what he knew the kind man would say: "Right on time, I see Beulah's list in my dreams every Easter night: seeds, flour, sugar, cornmeal, salt, beans…"

The boys were still laughing when Mr. Davis greeted them with a friendly smile. "Here you are, right on time. I see Beulah's…"

The boys laughed louder; they had known Mr. Davis all their lives and felt affection for him. They chatted with him a moment before beginning to gather the four-month supply of staples, checking off each item from their list. Inevitably, they arrived at the women's things. These they always embarrassedly passed over, leaving the rest of the list for Mr. Davis to finish, pretending every time that they needed to inspect the dry goods at the other end of the store.

In truth, their attention was always more piqued by the men who often gathered there, playing cards around a table Mr. Davis kept for that purpose. To Charlie, it seemed like such a manly thing: drinking sarsaparilla and cream soda, smoking cigars, talking about places and things, most of which he learned about for the first time.

Mr. Davis would not allow alcohol to be consumed there, and he didn't allow cursing, but over the years, Charlie had heard new words. He had learned to first test them out on Doc or William before taking the risk of trying them out with Mrs. Harper.

He'd certainly learned that lesson the hard way. She'd once whacked him on top the head with the silver tray she had been polishing because he'd asked her what "trollops" were. She never answered, so he'd pretty much understood they weren't any kind of fish. The card players talked about trollops being on one of the steamboats that went up and down the Mississippi. To Charlie, they sounded delicious.

Mr. Davis's son, John, was as much a bully as his father was kind. He'd never missed an opportunity to mock Frank's speech problems. He acted nice and polite around his father, but outside the man's earshot, John's true colors came through. He usually colored Frank's face red with humiliation.

Frank and Charlie ran into John coming out of Lois's Eatery, where they went for lunch. Going there was part of the pleasure of their day together. Charlie stiffened to see John, knowing how he treated Frank and remembering a fight he'd had with him once before.

"Well, if it ain't Fwankie Boy."

Charlie stepped forward, his chin raised and his fists clenched, but Frank held him back and took one step to stand in front of John.

"*Weow, weow,* now," John mocked.

Quick as a flash, Frank punched him once in the jaw, knocking him to the boardwalk.

Acting as though he'd just brushed a fly away, Frank casually stepped over John's feet, opened the door of the eatery, and ushered Charlie in. They sat at the counter, still having said nothing. Charlie was stunned but felt admiration.

Frank rubbed his knuckles and wrist for a moment. "Charlie," he spoke slowly and firmly, "you have to let me fight my own fights. I talk funny, but I fight pretty good, when you don't get in my way."

Chapter 4

Charlie steeled himself for the iciness of the water as he deliberately plunged both bare feet into the brook below. After a moment, the shock subsided and the pleasantness of the warm sun on his head and shoulders contrasted nicely with the now-cool numbness of his feet. He removed the two biscuits and honey Beulah made for him from the cloth she'd wrapped them in, leaving the chicken legs for later. He'd finished his chores and done Josh's for him, trading off so he could have the rest of the day free to come here and think. He'd had to beg the Harpers to let him be excused from church on this Easter Sunday. He thought he felt Mrs. Harper's eyes boring into his back as he rode out.

"She's probably thinking I'm a heathen," he told Horse.

Not counting heart-happy places where the people he loved each lived, this was his very favorite place. Here was where he came when he was wrestling with hard decisions or needing to mend from a big disappointment. Here is where he finally found those right answers that were his alone to find and made his most important decisions that were his alone to make. Some things, Doc and Oxytak both told him, a man just had to finally decide on his own.

He sat on the sun-warmed ledge formed by the rocky overhang, looking momentarily at the brook dancing around his ankles. He turned and watched rabbits munching and squirrels racing back and forth in the meadow. Horse was contentedly grazing, not noticing or minding that a bird was perched on his bare back.

Charlie appreciated the harmony and tolerance in nature. Oxytak helped him see the purpose of every living thing and how one kind through its life in turn gave life to another. All were linked in a golden chain that began before birth and continued even after death. The rodent lived on in the eagle that soared. There was a rhythm, balance, and beauty to nature that man sometimes missed when he eyed just one link in that chain too closely.

Behind him was a large clump of trees where through the years he had gathered black walnuts and pecans and picked fruit from the two apple trees that grew there and the three wild plums. Beulah made delicious wild plum preserves, his favorite. He had long understood why his mother chose this place to live alone. It had everything a person needed to survive and for a child to thrive.

Beyond the meadow were denser woods. He'd cut last year's Christmas tree from there, surprising the Harpers. It always amused him that the squirrels in the woods thought the nuts were better in the clump of trees and the squirrels from the clump seemed equally certain the woods held tastier ones. Birds of every color and hue flurried about in both locations, most of them content to serenade from where they were.

On his right was a gentle hill leading up to a small mountain range within which lay a deep valley where he hunted his first deer. He had climbed back up the steep, narrow trail with his buck across his shoulders, at times staggering under its weight but so proud of his success he hadn't minded. The memory of that day brought a smile to his face now.

Oxytak taught him how to hunt just for food and to respect the sacrifice. Here he had learned to field dress the deer and to carve out the coveted tenderloin precisely, although nothing was to be wasted. He'd offered to share his booty with Oxytak, but the man effortlessly felled his own buck. Oxytak's had a handsomer rack, but Charlie didn't mind, he was overjoyed with his.

A bee buzzing around his ear brought Charlie's attention back to this moment in this pleasant place where he sat in the sunshine. Already, though only mid-April, there were wildflowers blooming and grass seeming to almost turn greener as he watched. Bees buzzed everywhere, busy with their sole objective in life, that of providing honey for at least the Harper, Miller, and Johnston households, some of which Charlie now licked off his fingers.

Straight ahead of him was the hut where he was born, the entrance to it facing west at an angle to his right. As he did every time he came here, he imagined Johnny going through the narrow opening and seeing his mama sitting there with him in her arms. He'd formed a picture of her in his mind and thought no one in the world could ever be as pretty as she, although Lilly came close and Jessie was going to be a real beauty. He thought about Doc burying his mama and dignifying her death.

Now Doc was dying. Charlie could no longer avoid the reasons for his coming here today. He had to think through the turmoil his heart was in and sort through all the things dangling from it like sharp razors cutting into him almost every time he moved. It reminded him of when he'd been beaten up and how it had taken him a long time before he could move without pain.

He was feeling a lot like that now, almost unable to move without hurting; but this pain was nothing he could bite his lip to diminish. Doc's pending death was the heaviest burden he'd ever had to bear. This was the first time he had a burden of which Doc hadn't carried the bulk for him. Now, the incidents with Jessie and Frank last night intensified the weight of it.

He had to plan and prepare himself for the loss of this man who was closer to him than a father, and he must find a way to reassure Jessie that he was not abandoning her. He believed if he gave Frank his favorite bow and arrows, then that would make him feel better about spending the summer without Charlie's companionship.

The Harpers were leaving day after tomorrow; he needed to find the right words for his friends today and get over the worst of his grief before he went to Doc's. Otherwise, Doc would have to comfort him instead of the other way around.

Perhaps he could pre-address an envelope and a note to himself that Jessie could carry with her. He would ask Beulah to mail it to him at Doc's if Jessie got in too much trouble. She was still upset with him this morning and hadn't come out to tell him good-bye as she usually did. He missed her running alongside Horse, smiling up at him, saying, "Hurry home, Charlie. I'll be waiting for you!"

He'd told the Harpers at supper last evening about Doc and that he felt he should stay with him instead of accompanying them this summer to their place down south. He halfway expected they would protest, but his argument was prepared. To his relief, they agreed. They understood Doc would need his help and would not admit his health problems to anyone else.

Frank was the first person Charlie told about Doc's health and about his deciding to stay with him this summer. Frank first pleaded with him to come, then reluctantly accepted that Charlie's mind was made up. He hung his head and started to walk out of the room, his disappointment obvious; but he stopped at the door, turned back, smiled and said, "You're doing the right thing, Charlie. I'm sorry about Doc."

Jessie kicked his leg hard under the table when she heard him announce it to the others at supper. As soon as she could be excused, she left the table before anyone else. He couldn't remember a time when Jessie had left the table ahead of him except when she had a surprise for his birthday. Charlie's reason for going with them the last two summers was as much for Jessie's sake as his own or Frank's. Before that, he'd enjoyed alternating the summers between their place and Oxytak's.

He had found Jessie at the edge of the property near the rock pile she spent hours gathering. She kept it for such occasions as these: when she was sad, scared, angry, or very disappointed. "Squirrels don't come out in the evening, Jessie," he teased.

"I don't care!" Jessie retorted, turning her back to him. "I don't need them, and I don't need you! I'm glad I kicked you in the leg! I don't care if you don't come with us! I don't care if Doc dies! I don't care if…if Horse throws you and you break your whole leg and your whole arm, too! I don't even care if Horse breaks his leg!" She fell to the ground in sobs.

Charlie knew she didn't mean anything she said, and he knew she'd never admit it or apologize for it, so he pretended she hadn't said any of it. "I know you're sad that I can't go this year. I'm sad too. I can't think of anyone I'd rather catch crawfish with than you or scratch chiggers with or chase snakes with or have with me when I pull fish hooks out of my nose…"

Despite herself, a laugh escaped Jessie's lips, then another sob, her head still buried in her skirts. Hiccupping now, which made her laugh and cry all at once, she squirmed a short inch farther away from her dearest friend. Charlie knelt beside her. Taking her chin in his hand, he turned her face to him, offering his shirttail. "Here, Jessie-girl, see how much I love you? I'll let you wipe your nose on my shirt."

"Charlie, please, please, please come with us!" The pleading, the tears, the dark curls, the enormous green eyes like her mother's, her hands clutching his arm—Charlie had never found it so hard to disappoint anyone as he was finding it now.

"Jessie, you're the most precious person to me in the whole world. If I could, I would always take care of you. When I grow up and marry someone, I'll—"

"No!" Jessie interrupted. "You have to wait for me. You have to marry me when I grow up!"

They heard Mrs. Harper calling Jessie to bed. Hiccupping and sobbing, she ran from him toward the house, uncharacteristically compliant to her mother's calls. Charlie sat out at the rock pile long after Jessie left, thinking about Doc.

In facing Doc's death, Charlie thought he was also coming to grips with this business of adulthood. He was seeing that it carried with it heavier burdens and many more hurts than it had seemed from the perspective of childhood. Things were more complicated now. At sixteen, he could identify the feeling of love he'd mostly taken for granted all his life. His heart could break in more pieces; his loyalties were no longer as simple as punching in the nose the person who hurt your friend.

Loyalties now pulled him into different circumstances, and none of them could be fixed with a fistfight. Things weren't just black or white or right or wrong anymore. He wondered if Doc and Oxytak had always shielded him from the grays until he was old enough to wade his own way through them.

He thought about how love could still break your heart even when all your loved ones loved you back. It made demands on a man so powerful it could stop him in his tracks or confuse him so that he didn't know what direction to take. Love could make good decisions suddenly seem wrong. Yet, the strangest thing about love, he decided, was that a man was happiest when he was giving up something he wanted a lot so the folks he loved could

DIXIE MILLER STEWART

have something they wanted maybe even a little less. He thought he was ready to do that. He'd seen Doc and Oxytak doing it for him all his life. Even Mrs. Harper sacrificed things she needed so her kids could benefit from her lack. He thought Mr. Harper sacrificed a lot more. He remembered the first time he felt really good about making a sacrifice for someone else.

It happened the summer just before he turned twelve. He recalled how he'd grumbled to himself about having to sacrifice those months to help Oxytak herd and brand his cattle. It was hot and humid riding in the Mississippi summer sun and wrestling with the rebellious animals. He felt a lingering self-pity because he hadn't gotten to go to the summer place with the Harpers and their planned visit on to Biloxi. Bone tired, with rope burns and muscles aching from the day's work, he still had his studying to do by lamplight after Oxytak went to bed. It was something he promised Mr. Harper and Doc; he wanted to keep his word, but he'd even resented that at times.

Yet, riding Horse alongside Oxytak back to the Harpers, Charlie had no regrets at all about the summer. He was pleased that the work was done and done well and eager to discuss with Doc the things he'd read about all summer, like the way people had settled in a place called "the beautiful land," Oklahoma Territory and Indian Territory. Doc believed he should read about it for Oxytak's sake since that's where some of his people lived. Now that he read about it, he wanted to go there someday.

Too, after that summer, Charlie had been able to talk to Doc about the vast and exotic land of China. Some of Doc's relatives, his brother and his family, had gone there by boat as missionaries. They wrote Doc monthly letters telling about their experiences. Charlie thought it was exciting to have people he almost knew doing such important things in such an interesting place.

Doc always said that was one of the longest and most frustrating summers of his life. "I missed you, Charlie—that was bad enough—but on top of your being gone too long, the Democrats and then the railroad unions up north together made a mess of everything else, to boot!"

Charlie recalled he hadn't wanted to offend Doc by laughing at the way he was complaining, so he'd just said he'd heard something about the strike.

"Well, who hasn't?" Doc had asked rhetorically. "But what they don't tell you is how it affects the rest of us! Take my situation: as a result of the Pullman Strike, I've gotten no mail from my family in China. I didn't get the new coat I ordered out of Chicago, nor did I receive the apothecary supplies I ordered back in May, not knowing of course that a dad-blamed strike was starting!"

Doc just hadn't seen anything to feel proud about that summer. The Democrats had passed an income tax bill while the country was still in a panic about the economy. "Who ever heard," he exclaimed, "of imposing taxes during an economic depression?"

Doc believed the country was already in trouble for a lot of reasons. Bank failures and railroads going bankrupt were two major ones, he groused. A bad winter had killed off many heads of cattle out west, a searing summer was killing crops, and along with all the bad economic downturns, there was corruption at every level of politics and even big business. He had no trust in unions, at least not union management, thinking they got in the way of free trade at least as much as monopolies.

Having Federal troops brought out to restore order in the railroad and stop the interference of mail delivery was to Doc a necessary evil but a last straw; it was like taking steps backward in time, he complained.

Charlie didn't know at that time that Doc's bad mood was less about the nation and more because Jenny had died during the summer. His friend was grumbling about everything else, working up to telling Charlie about the loss. "Well, she lived way past her years. Like me," he added, but still it bothered him a lot. He said she was another piece of Maddy that he lost.

Four letters from China finally arrived all at once. Doc read each one aloud to Charlie and then had Charlie read them aloud to him. They were good, long ones; sometimes the family would spend a week writing them, each member adding something to a matter another had mentioned. They often read like books explaining China's politics, society, and gossip, naming people and events in such detail that Charlie felt as if he knew some of them. They wrote thoroughly about their struggles and triumphs, but above all their love for the Chinese people.

Charlie thought he might go there some day, maybe be a missionary if the people weren't all Christian by the time he was old enough. He thought they probably would be, and he hoped they could speak English by then too. He couldn't imagine how anyone had ever learned to read or speak the Chinese language. He couldn't even imagine how the Chinese ever learned it.

Although it was one of Doc's worst summers, it was one of Charlie's best, falling as it did before the summer where he'd had so many hard lessons. Thinking about it brought back the same good feeling in his chest, like he was a better person for what he'd done and accomplished, and not just because of the way Oxytak thanked him for the help. He still held that sense of pride and a greater purpose to those months long after Frank had forgotten about the Biloxi lighthouse and the rows of tinned seafood at the new cannery the family had visited.

On this sun-splashed Easter Sunday, reflecting also on the four years that had passed since that summer, Charlie felt foolish that he had never once given thought to the notion that Doc would someday die. His safe little world had begun to come undone, and it seemed the bad things Doc had warned him about were upon him: Jessie was mistreated, and Doc was dying. He could hardly bear to think about it!

He thought again about sacrifice, gaining a new insight about it also being at the root of Christian love and how, without it, souls would be lost. He thought that when you burrowed down underneath the really important things in life, you always found hurting and sacrifice somewhere in the mix. Important things cost a lot, and the value of a thing was what a man was willing to sacrifice for it, he guessed. Doc had made Charlie the center of his life over the past fifteen years. Charlie had only a summer to give back. He would talk to Frank about paying more attention to Jessie's needs.

The sun was now warm on his back and cast shadows across the water, making it appear black and mysterious in places. Charlie loved this brook and loved the peace that being here always brought him. Sitting here, he sensed his decisions sorting themselves out almost of their own volition. No getting around it, Doc needed him; in a way, it was even a matter of life or death. *Except*, he thought with a stab of pain, *death is part of the equation; this time it will be life and death.*

At the end of this difficult task, there was not going to be a Doc standing there beaming with pride, maybe handing him his second ever glass of brandy or his first cigar. There would never again be a Doc mending his wounds to body, soul, and pride. This time, at the end, there would be Charlie, hoping he'd done all he could to give back to Doc just a little bit of all that Doc had given to him.

The young man reminded himself the words Doc had recently told him: *The test of a man isn't just in how he handles his responsibilities but also in how he determines the relative value of each one.* Then he had added, "Son, a man always has more than one over-sized burden to carry at a time." Charlie didn't know how he was going to carry his without Doc.

Now, he strode barefoot to the hut and bent to enter, surprised that he needed to bend so far down. Again, in one smooth motion, he sat cross-legged on the floor in front of the fireless hearth, as he had done so many times and seasons throughout his life.

"Mama," he said, knowing she could not hear him, "Mama, I want you to know that you don't need to be ashamed anymore. Doc always says that the world is a better place because you were in it. You can look Doc right in the eyes when you see him this time. You'll like him a lot."

Riding back home into the setting sun, Charlie felt a growing peace settling over him.

Chapter 5

May

Forever after, Charlie would look back on those last five months with Doc before he died as the single most significant period in his life. It informed the important decisions he later made and determined the quality of the rest of his years. It largely shaped the man he was to become. Doc crammed into those five months all the lessons of the additional years he had once hoped to invest toward Charlie's manhood. The seeds his mentor planted took root in the good, deep soil that all the previous years had prepared in him. The bearing of the fruit would require more seasons of winters and storms.

At first, Charlie protested the expenditure of effort and energy Doc was making, fearing that the dear, frail man would hasten his own death. Doc wouldn't hear of it. He said he drew energy from Charlie and from what he called his "mission." In truth, Doc's color and vigor seemed to improve so much that

Charlie began to hope that he would have him around longer than the self-pronounced "six months, if that."

In the beginning months, while his strength held up, Doc took Charlie out into the world, in and beyond Mississippi. Later, he brought the entire world into their little space in Jackson. The lesson was not lost on Charlie that a man's world wasn't "out there" nearly so much as it was in his own backyard. More than that, it was in the fertile soil of his mind. Doc was fond of reminding him, "All of life is lived inside our heads, Charlie. If not there, then where?"

Every time Charlie would try to present an argument that life was also in other places, Doc would point out again and again that a person must first run everything he experienced through his mind, that everything "out there" was first seen, heard, tasted, felt, or smelled, and that only in one's brain were these things sorted out and given order and meaning. "Moreover, Charlie, the very meanings the mind assigns to each experience rests less on 'truth' than on the sum total of all the meanings a person has given to previous circumstances in his life."

Doc proved that life was lived wholly in one's mind in the last weeks when he never left his house yet shared his passion for life, politics, medicine, science, business, God, the arts, and nature with Charlie as if they were attending all those events and as if they sometimes sat at the very feet of Jesus.

Many nights were spent discussing the heart and the mind. Charlie, thinking about the almost crippling grief he felt each time he thought about Doc's death, tried to argue that things sometimes happened in a man's heart that bypassed his brain.

"Yes and no," Doc argued, appreciating Charlie's keen mind and willingness to think about important matters instead of living life on a superficial level. "When we talk about matters of the heart, we're talking about feelings. Would you agree with that?"

Knowing that Charlie understood the two were the same, Doc didn't wait for an answer. He pointed out that the heart didn't have any of the five senses; it didn't have perceptions or thought; it didn't have the capacity for intellectual argument or for analyzing truth from fiction or discerning right from wrong or good from bad. He said that the heart decided on a matter pretty much based on whether the thing made a person "feel" good or "feel" bad.

He reminded Charlie that Scripture warns a man that a heart is a deceptive thing.

"Charlie," he said, "that means that a man can't make his decisions just on feelings. Feelings are the shallowest parts of a person. They play games with us, sometimes evil games, where we don't find out the rules until our souls have been bargained or our trust has been betrayed."

"But, Doc," Charlie commented, confused, "I have feelings. You have them. I've seen you cry too. I guess I don't understand. Am I supposed to just not feel anything?"

"No, son, a man has to have feelings. He's a cold thing, like a piece of machinery, if he doesn't, but he's got to filter those feelings through his brain because he's only a wild horse without a bridle and bit if he doesn't.

"There are those," his friend continued, "who argue that God's love and intentions are seen in that wild, unbridled horse. I don't agree. I see that horse as going through life looking out only for himself and his lusts in season, running around, looking proud and magnificent, sometimes, but it's an empty pride. Proud of what? Of having nothing in the end but the glue factory? That kind of wild roaming isn't freedom, though it might be the devil's disguise for it.

"Look at Horse," Doc continued, pressing his point. "Jenny was that way too. They were once wild. They surrendered their wildness for a greater freedom. That's the freedom of knowing your boundaries and limitations and trusting that there is a mind greater than yours that herds you back inside when you stray or fall."

"It is the same way when a man surrenders his life to Jesus, isn't it?" Charlie asked, listening intently.

"That's right, Charlie. To those who don't, God's commandments seem like a bunch of old-fashioned, arbitrary dos and don'ts written by a humorless, capricious old man hidden way up behind the clouds, one who doesn't want anyone to have any fun or happiness. But you and I know our freedom is found within his Word; that it is given to us out of enormous love for his people by a great God who invented fun and pleasure and wants us to live life fully in safety.

"He gave us the rules of the universe and set us free to enjoy the greatest amount of happiness possible if we follow them and trust him when we lose our way."

"Yes, I'm finding that out, Doc, more and more. I sure lost my way summer before last when I broke that kid's arm. That was a hard lesson. I was just acting on pride. I know I struggle a lot with pride, and it sure hurts sometimes."

"When we stray outside his boundaries, it hurts, and we're bothered, and so we return to him and his ways where there is healing and replenishing. He invented love and families, even sex, son. Between a man and his wife, there is no greater pleasure.

"That isn't all there is to a good marriage by a long shot, but it is what folks still have when the bottom has fallen out of their universe. Take those ranchers out west who lost everything or those farmers whose crops burned up. Their houses can burn down, but there is still left the greatest earthly pleasure, and that is love."

"Why do you think people sometimes just quit loving each other, Doc?" Charlie knew some husbands and wives he thought that had happened to.

"Love for and pleasure in each other can't be taken from a couple. They have to voluntarily give them up," Doc answered. "Sometimes they do it one grain of salt at a time—one grain rubbed in a wound and then another and another—but all the while, they're doing it voluntarily. They're choosing salt instead of a balm for the inevitable wounds of life."

Charlie listened intently. He felt proud when Doc talked to him like this; it let him know Doc regarded him as an equal. He interrupted Doc to ask something he'd wondered before. "Did you ever get mad at God because he let Maddy die?"

Doc looked away for a long moment then turned his gaze back to Charlie's. "I did—powerfully mad. I was mad at God for a long time for taking Maddy from me. She had gotten me through the misery of the war. I believed just willing myself to return to her got me through it."

Doc turned inside himself for a moment. Charlie knew from the softening of the lines in Doc's face that he was thinking good thoughts.

"She was so beautiful, so dear to me," he continued. "I fell in love with Maddy when she was thirteen years old, never believing she would some day return that love. She was wiser than her years. She was passionate, fiery, and tender. She could put me in my place when I needed it and turn right around and defend me to others even when she thought I was wrong.

"She was my life, and I thought it was selfish of God to take her from me. That's all I thought I'd ever asked of him for myself that really mattered. Even on the battlefield, I didn't pray for myself. I thanked him every time I was spared. I prayed for my comrades. I even prayed for the Union soldiers. I prayed for Maddy. When she died, I...for a while, it made me doubt he even existed.

"It didn't seem to make sense. My life was in danger day after day in the war. I was barely missed again and again. In fact"—

Doc pulled up his breeches leg to show Charlie where a bullet had pierced his flesh—"I have this as a reminder of how fragile life is. I thought at the time that my life had been spared because God wanted me to come home to Maddy, practice medicine here in Jackson, and take care of her. It seemed like a bargain I'd made with him: I would devote my life to saving as many lives as I could, and he would spare mine. It never occurred to me that Maddy would die before me.

"Here, I've outlived my life expectancy. I've outlived most of my friends, only my sister, twenty years younger, and a brother, twenty-two years younger, are still living out of a family of eleven children. I went for months deciding that a good God didn't take the most important thing in a man's life. I wanted nothing to do with such a God, and since the Bible told me he was good, I no longer believed in the Bible or its God."

His friend grew silent again. Charlie waited, loving the man before him so much his throat ached, seeing no self-pity in this good man at all. He had a message for Charlie, and the lad didn't want to miss it. He didn't want to think about life without him, either. Charlie broke the silence.

"It must have been awful, Doc, to lose both Maddy and God at the same time."

Doc looked up quickly. "You're awfully wise for such a young man."

Doc's voice was tender, and there were tears in his eyes. He had been sitting very still in his favorite chair, but now he cleared his throat and resumed his slow rocking. "Son, you're right. I believed I had lost God and Maddy and that I had nothing to live for. Oh, I wasn't going to take my own life. The thought never entered my mind, but the emptiness was almost unbearable. I had never known life to be so completely devoid of purpose. I would see patients or go about my business during the day, but those acts were just as empty too.

"For the first time in my life, the people who I guess I helped didn't seem to matter. Treating people's sickness or injuries became just a routine I engaged in because it was daylight and a sign out front said I was a doctor. It was my years of discipline as a physician and the experience on the battlefield that defined the motions and techniques I used, not any concern about the suffering the other might be in. I don't think I ever recognized anyone else's suffering during that time.

"I would drink myself into a stupor every night, trying to escape from the sorrow that engulfed me. When I thought about it, I was grateful that during that dark time of my life, I didn't have a nighttime emergency where my help was needed. Sometimes Johnny would come over to put me to bed, and instead we'd both sit and drink until after midnight."

"How did you find God again, Doc? Not that he was lost, but—"

"You're right, son. I was lost, not God. Son, do you know the story in Second Kings four about the Shunammite woman at whose house the prophet Elisha would sometimes stay?"

Charlie nodded his head slowly as the story came to mind. "Yes. Wasn't that the woman who had a baby when she and her husband were very, very old because the prophet Elisha had promised her a child?"

"That's right. What else do you know about her?" Doc asked.

"Didn't her son die, a few years later, but her faith was so strong..." Charlie stopped here, thinking he might offend Doc because the faith of the Shunammite woman had seemed stronger than Doc's. Doc nodded, encouraging Charlie to continue. "That son was all she had. Her husband was much older than she, and the son would be the one to help her in her old age, so when he died, the blessing he had been died too."

"Go on, son," Doc urged.

"Well…" Charlie was reaching far back into the recesses of his mind to remember how it happened, wondering why this was relevant to Doc's finding God again. "She sent for or went for Elisha, and he asked how she was. That's it. She answered: 'It is well.' We readers know it wasn't—her only son was dead—but her faith was stronger than the reality of anything bad that might happen. She had trusted God that far. God had kept his word about the birth of the son in her old age, so I guess it was her faith that God used in working through Elisha to bring the boy back to life."

"Good, good. You know your Bible." He asked Charlie to go to his files under *S* and pull out an envelope marked "Spafford." Charlie did as he was told, enjoying the mystery. He grabbed a peppermint stick before handing the envelope to Doc, who took it without opening it and began to tell Charlie the story it contained.

"Horatio Gates Spafford died about six years ago. I never met him, but we exchanged a few letters. His to me are here in this envelope. Mr. Spafford was a Christian man. His faith was stronger than mine at the time. He was a wealthy man or had been wealthy. His only son died. Shortly after, he lost his wealth in the Chicago fire of 1871. Not long after that, his wife and four daughters were sailing to England when their ship struck another and sank. Anna, his wife, survived, but all four daughters were lost at sea. So in a very short period of time, Mr. Spafford lost just about everything.

"He set sail to join his wife, but for reasons I don't know, that didn't happen immediately. In 1873, he finally sailed out of New York. At the spot where it was said his daughters drowned, Mr. Spafford stood, staring out at sea. In those moments, he wrote a hymn. A friend sent me the newspaper clippings about Mr. Spafford's tragedies and the lyrics to the hymn. My friend thought it would help me regain my faith, and indeed, it did."

Doc began to sing, his baritone voice surprisingly strong and steady. "When peace like a river attendeth my way, when sorrows like sea billows roll. Whatever my lot, Thou has taught me to say, 'It is well. It is well with my soul.'"

Tears rolled down both men's cheeks. Doc's voice wavered a little as he continued the hymn. "'Though Satan should buffet, though trials should come, let this blessed assurance control: that Christ has regarded my helpless estate and hath shed his blood for my soul. It is well. It is well with my soul.'

"There are more verses and, of course, more to the chorus. It repeats the phrase, 'it is well with my soul,'" Doc told him. "You see how the passage from Second Kings inspired the man. Charlie, I broke down and cried about Maddy's death for the first time when I read that man's story and those lyrics. But when I blew my nose and got up off my knees, I knew I had come back to life no less than that young Shunamite man. God had never left me. I had pushed him away in my anger and self-pity. Christ shed his blood for my soul! How could I question his love for me now?

"I felt healed and whole again from that day on. I felt it was well with my soul again. I miss her, but I am assured that I'm going to be with her before long. You remember that, Charlie. You think about that when you're standing at my gravesite. You'll be thinking about your own loss, son… I hate to leave you…" Doc's voice broke again with those words. He didn't hide his tears, but he swallowed hard and took a deep breath to finish his thought. "Son, when my time comes, let me go. Let it be well with your soul."

They sat in silence a few moments. Then Doc added, "Oh, another thing, the Spafford girls drowned on the same day Maddy died."

Neither man paid attention to the tears that continued to run down their cheeks as Doc thumbed through the contents of the envelope. "I wrote a letter to Mr. Spafford, offering him my belated condolences and letting him know that his tragedy had helped restore me. Like the great man I think he was, he answered back that my news had gladdened his heart and made him marvel again at the great and mysterious purposes of our Lord.

"Son, Mr. Spafford was a man of deep emotion and faith, yet deep sensibility. I started out talking about reason and wild horses and ended up talking about the kind of pain that can cause a man to either trust God or to push against everything in life he holds dear. But the analogies don't oppose each other.

"A man has to play the songs in his heart through the chords of his mind. It's the chords that provide the discipline and the order. They keep you on track and honoring your commitments while your heart can be deceiving you, telling you that what's good is bad and what's bad is somehow now good. When you can play the strings of your heart through the chords of your mind, you make a symphony, my son—you make a symphony out of life, yes, indeed!"

"Did you and Maddy make a symphony?"

Doc smiled broadly. He was sensitive to the romanticism in this young man who could tackle a bully and face a mountain lion with the same calmness with which he steadied Horse when he was spooked. Already he was the sort of young man who looked a grown man steadily in the eye when he was offended, not afraid to stand for what was right.

Doc was proud of his protégé and marveled again over the magnificent and strange genetic combination that had produced this fine mind, the product of such a seemingly senseless pregnancy. Pleased that Charlie brought up Maddy's name again, Doc welcomed the opportunity to continue talking about her.

"We did, son. We did indeed make a symphony. It took time, and it took patience on the part of both of us, although more was required of Maddy, especially after the war. Even members of a fine orchestra have to rehearse together. They make mistakes, listen to each other's music, learn the timing, but not even a Stradivarius has ever produced a melody without a master. If the violin plays the music of the heart, it plays it with the mind of the man or woman whose years of discipline guide that bow."

Doc picked up his pipe, having given up snuff some years back. He tamped the tobacco firmly in the bowl, dug for a match out of his shirt pocket, and scratched it across the bottom of his boot. Holding the dancing yellow flame to his pipe, he drew deeply, using the time to form the word picture he wanted to paint for Charlie. The aroma of the tobacco filled the room and was pleasing and civilized. A man needed few things in life, but a good cigar and a good bowl of pipe tobacco were among life's necessities.

Charlie watched, knowing that while Doc's movements seemed slow and casual, the man's keen mind was at work, arranging words in just a way that would make the boy ponder a matter instead of just hear it. Charlie liked the allegory of the Stradivarius; it made sense. He'd seen folks who lived their whole lives with things equivalent to a quality violin but who never disciplined their minds to benefit from it or to help their worlds. Then he'd seen people whose minds were so sharp and disciplined, they'd never permitted any music from their hearts. He wanted to be like Doc. He wished he had gotten to see Doc and Maddy together. He would bet Doc had been a strong, protective, and loving man. Doc said Maddy brought out the best in him most of the time.

For his part, Doc didn't want the young man to think that a good marriage was made entirely in heaven. The lad needed to know that like everything worthwhile in the world, a marriage required work, commitment, and sacrifice. It could be strengthened by the inevitable storms or weakened by them. The only thing certain about a marriage, he had long ago decided, was that it was going to have storms. He thought of marriage as an arena in which God placed two flawed people, not to slug it out, though that might happen, but to work out their own short-comings. It took hardship, disagreements, forgiveness, love, and time to build a marriage. Doc thought each person was a mirror for the other, and if you didn't like what you saw in the other, it probably meant you needed to change yourself.

In the days that followed their conversation that evening, the two were inseparable. There were some things Doc wanted done before he became too infirm. They hitched Horse to Doc's buggy and took medicinal supplies to shut-ins, all of whom had stories to tell Doc either about their infirmities or about those of a loved one. Doc patiently listened to every one, giving each his complete attention.

They fished from the Pearl River, preparing their supper right there on the bank, and examined the night skies for all the con-stellations the two of them together could identify. They visited other Civil War sites, rode out and tended his mother's grave, and many times perused the library. They spent hours and hours in wonderful conversations, sometimes serious and sometimes light-hearted, and sometimes just acting silly and laughing as though they were both almost sixteen years old.

Charlie laughed the hardest when Doc's "etiquette lessons," as he called them, included teaching him to dance. At first, Doc took the role of his dance partner, teaching Charlie the precise moves to as many dances as he could recall. They both kept stumbling because Doc often forgot he was the girl. Char-lie howled with laughter as Doc, pretending to be a pretty girl, would flutter his eyelashes, wave one of Maddy's fans, twist "her" handkerchief, or any of the other signals he said passed unspoken between a gentleman and a proper lady at a dance.

Doc rummaged through Maddy's things until he found her copy of *Asking To Dance*. He had Charlie memorize all the steps and gestures, learning about proper etiquette. Charlie saw that it was similar to reading maps, so he picked up the steps easily in his head. However, dancing them with Doc provided an hour or two of hilarity most evenings as long as Doc's energy held up.

Doc came across Maddy's dance card from a ball they had attended the night he had proposed to her and reminisced. Charlie tried to imagine the romance of dancing with someone you loved and wanted to marry.

When Mrs. Thompson heard about the dance and etiquette lessons, she invited herself that very night to help teach Charlie. He thought she wanted to dance with Doc more than him, but Charlie practiced with her, surprised at how light on her feet she was and how well she danced. Several evenings she brought over her visiting granddaughter. She was pretty, and if Charlie laughed less and took dancing more seriously, it was because he realized the importance of impressing the ladies and not causing them to make a mistake. He had a wonderful time.

Together they often gathered berries with which Doc taught Charlie to make cobblers. Doc had Charlie carry his favorite rocking chair into whatever room that day's project might occur. Charlie retrieved the stick he'd hidden in the boards out front so long ago and presented it to Doc, telling him he needed a baton to better conduct Charlie's activities.

Hours were spent in Doc's office poring over science and medical journals and discussing research findings and inventions. Doc felt everyone ought to have rudimentary and updated medical knowledge. It could save their own or the lives of their loved ones. He impressed upon Charlie the importance of keeping things sterile and now of using the newest medical aid, rubber gloves, when handling open wounds. He told him about the needless deaths up until recent years because otherwise intelligent men and women refused to believe in germs just because they couldn't see them, much less that they could cause infections. He introduced the lad to such giants as Louis Pasteur, Max Planck, Robert Koch, Thomas Edison, and Alexander Graham Bell.

The wise old man taught his bright and eager student everything that came to mind or on which his eyes fell at any given moment. He had him read Mendel's works on genetics and heredity. He showed him how James Simpson's sand filter purification system had improved London's water supply. They discussed the great minds of history and the philosophies that had molded men's thinking over generations. He cautioned the boy more than once that while modern science opened up previously unknown worlds, as God intended it to do, it remained that truth could only be discerned by whether it was in accordance with the Word of God. "God doesn't make mistakes, Charlie. Men do."

Doc had often let Charlie sit in the office when he treated patients under ether; sometimes he needed the extra pair of eyes. He now had him practice on stray cats and dogs, contending that a human life saved was a worthy and noble sacrifice for any animal. However, he assured Charlie, "We're not going to lose our patients. That's the whole point of these exercises." They didn't lose any, and Charlie got the hang of how to neuter or spay an animal and how to measure just enough ether to put a person out if he ever had to. He didn't think he'd ever need to use that information, but, like Doc, he loved knowledge just for its own sake.

Those days when Doc felt stronger were spent re-exploring Jackson. Doc rested as Charlie climbed over the old earthworks that had been constructed by the Union Army during the July 1863 siege of the city.

They picnicked on Mrs. Thompson's fried chicken and lemonade at the location where the Mississippi secession convention had taken place in 1861. Charlie and Doc had engaged in more than one conversation about the terms of the secession declaration that outright stated Mississippi's position to be that of completely endorsing the institution of slavery. Doc confessed to Charlie that as a young man he had been very pro-slavery and had resented the Union's interfering decisions, including the Northwest Territory expansion that he felt weakened the south's influence and power.

"What changed your mind?" Charlie asked.

Doc drained his glass of lemonade and flicked crumbs from the chicken off his vest before answering. "It was a Sunday afternoon, after church. I stayed for a meeting to discuss the unfair treatment of us Southerners by the government in Washington. We complained it was not representing us; that it seemed instead to be trying to ruin us in the south with their legislation, such as favoring the free states. We were all fired up about it, of course. Plans were already in the works then for secession.

"I left the meeting and rode south out of town. I didn't have Jenny then. I needed to think before sitting down to supper with Maddy, knowing she would want to hear about everything that was said. I had been riding maybe fifteen minutes when I heard a commotion a hundred feet or so off my path and rode over to check it out. A group of men had gathered, men who had been in church that morning. They were so riled up with their own lust for blood they didn't notice my presence. Sitting there, I watched three acquaintances of mine finish tying a noose around the neck of a colored man they'd obviously first beaten within an inch of his life.

"The Negro didn't struggle, didn't plead for his life. He remained calm despite their taunts, insults, and obvious intent. That man had no hope of defending himself. But I noticed his faith, and I was struck by the dignity I saw in him the likes of which I had never seen in any of his tormenters. That's what I saw at that moment: dignity in *him*, and I saw meanness and evil in my friends. I saw that colored man looking up and praying with what struck me as peace and calmness. He knew he was going to be the winner in this trial any way he looked at it. For all I know, he might have been praying for his executioners.

"By association, I saw my own evil. I despised myself at that moment for all the times I had sat and watched. I might have gone my way as I'd done in the past, justifying my inaction by saying I had not participated in the hanging. But I knew right then that I was no better than they because I wasn't stopping them, either. It was seeing that colored man's dignity and faith that made me know that whatever inequality there existed between him and me, I had the losing end of it. I wasn't worthy to be his equal! The thought came to me that if I didn't intervene in what they were about to do, I could never again regard myself as a man, much less as a Christian man." Doc stopped speaking.

Charlie waited and waited. Doc sat in silence. "So what happened, Doc?"

"I don't really remember it all. There wasn't a big fuss as you might think. I remember that I had a strong conviction in that moment that what I had to do was more necessary than anything I'd ever done in my life. It wasn't necessary just for that Negro but for myself as well. I remember thinking that if it cost me my life, then so be it because my life wasn't worth living if I could be that callous and cowardly.

"I rode over and grasped the rope above the noose just in time to keep the man from being jerked up. I must have had a fierce look on my face because my friends looked startled. The one immediately untied his end of the rope from his saddle horn, and they all backed off. As I recall, I felt a damn sight calmer than I had felt while I was watching them. I looked every man in the eye. There were more than just the three of them. I knew them all. I looked at them and said, 'I am going to be checking on this man every day that I live. I don't want to ever hear that any one of you has harmed a hair on his head!'"

"That was a very brave thing to do, Doc! I know that white men who defended the Negroes were also sometimes hanged by angry white mobs! You were a hero!"

"No, son, I began to grow up that day. I wasn't a hero. I just stopped being a coward, but I started down the road to being able to think for myself instead of in the customs and traditions of a geographic region. I wish I could say that I stopped justifying slavery under any condition at that moment, but I didn't.

"Right then, I saw *that* colored man as a human being. It took more time for me to see that all of them were equal to all whites in God's eyes. We flawed human beings don't readily accept a different way of thinking. Especially one that is going to cause us to have to face our own flaws or to give up something we regard as our right. We do a much better job of digging in our heels and justifying our view of things while demonizing those who hold opposing perspectives.

"So it took longer for me to see secession as a selfish thing contrived to sustain a way of life that was good only for those who had white skin and only a minority of them. I look back in shame that we whites convinced ourselves the Negro was subhuman. To see him as equal meant we'd have to see ourselves as we really were. It also meant we'd have to pay him, and if we had to pay him, we'd lose our profits and our fine way of life. We lost it anyway, didn't we?

"If any of us harbored a secret guilt about what we were doing, it was certainly twisted in our minds and translated into self-righteous anger against anyone who held up a mirror we didn't want to look into! My personal belief has always been that if the shots hadn't been fired out of Fort Sumter, the war would probably never have occurred. There were negotiations by reasonable men underway trying to work out a sustainable solution. We southerners don't want to admit that we caused the war, any way you look at it. Mr. Harper has a similar story. You should ask him sometime how he changed his attitude about equality. It didn't stop him from keeping slaves, but it changed the way he treated them. I don't think it changed Julia's opinion."

Charlie grinned but said nothing.

Even as an eight-year-old, the age when Doc first brought Frank and him exploring all the indications that a war had been fought here, Charlie had found it patently wrong to justify slavery for any reason. Frank rarely disagreed with Charlie but did so on this one matter. Yet, Frank had no trouble accepting that Beulah and Moses were his equals, even when he'd had to submit to Beulah's switching him on more than one deserved occasion. She would not allow the children to sass her, regardless of anybody's color. "Frank," Charlie had argued, "you just should have been born a half-breed, and then you'd understand human nature a whole lot better than you do!"

"Doc, have you ever had a Coca-Cola?" Charlie asked the question on a lazy afternoon while he and his friend snapped peas and devoured cocoa cookies Mrs. Jamison had sent over. Doc said he had not. "I wonder if you can get a Coca-Cola anywhere in Jackson?" He'd been hearing about the beverage, and now, looking at a newspaper advertisement, his mouth salivated at the words he was reading. "They sure sound delicious."

"I have an idea," Doc suggested. "Why don't we take a trip to Vicksburg, the very place where they were invented a couple years back?" He went on to tell Charlie he'd been communicating with a young physician there who might be interested in moving here and taking over his practice. Jackson had long since needed another doctor. Now it needed at least two more with Doc's retirement.

At dawn two days later, a spirited Horse headed due west pulling their buggy. The plan was to visit the confectionary store where Coca-Colas were first invented and sold. Although it was only forty miles away on the great Mississippi River, Charlie had never been to the city. However, he knew it had been the site of an important battle the Confederacy had lost during the war. "Yes," Doc noted, "a lot of folks knew the war was essentially lost when Vicksburg was captured."

"What did you think when Vicksburg was surrendered that day, Doc?"

The man was silent for a moment, looking out on the beautiful countryside of his beloved state. Fed by the many rivers and streams, there were green meadows; rich, fertile grounds; and tall timber enough to last forever if her people replanted and replenished their lands. He knew this beauty continued all the way into Vicksburg. That city's perch overlooking the larger river gave it charm and vibrancy. It was growing at a more rapid pace than Jackson, but there were also more riffraff of the sort that cities along the Mississippi seemed to invite.

Doc favored Jackson and never ceased to appreciate its beauty and ideal location there on the more constrained Pearl River. He had been deeply saddened by the burnings of his city and the assaults on so much of its structure during the war. He had rebuilt his home right along with the many others who had lost theirs.

He still appreciated the elegance of their Greek revival architectural designs and recalled how their having withstood the sieges symbolized rebirth for the townsfolk and all of war-

DIXIE MILLER STEWART

ravaged Mississippi. His mind flashed back to the day the then new governor's mansion had been dedicated in 1842. He had just hung his shingle not far from it. In fact, his first patient, he now recalled, had been one of the building inspectors who had slipped and fallen on the marble floor.

The rebuilt city of Vicksburg also thrived again, more so with the improvement of the land management along the river. However, to Doc's way of thinking, Vicksburg carried deeper scars than the war battles it had known. Each time he traveled this route, he could almost hear the cries of other sons of the South, cries from beneath dark stains of more innocent blood that had been shed years later.

"Charlie," he finally answered, "sometimes I think maybe Vicksburg's saddest moments came several years after the war." He told Charlie about the many lynchings of three hundred or more black men that had been done there in the middle seventies. He said the coloreds were exercising their rights and freedom and had elected several city officials to represent their interests. "More than a few whites thought the coloreds needed to learn a lesson about keeping their place."

Charlie nodded. "I know," he said sadly. "Mr. Harper told me about it. He said Moses' older brother had been one of the men who had been lynched. Moses said two more of his brothers had earlier fought for the Union farther up on the Mississippi and had both died there on the same day. He said he'd been too young to fight but had lost so many of his family by the time his last brother was killed in Vicksburg that it had taken away any desire he might ever have had to take Beulah and go up north to work. He said Mississippi was his home. His family's blood had been spilled for it on both sides, and he thought the best thing he could do was to continue to work on this land out of respect for its dead."

Doc shook his head, remembering. "Son, you know my attitude about the war and how I feel about slavery. Up until just a very few years leading to the Civil War, the colored were regarded as equals by most folks. Very many of them were American heroes during the Revolutionary War. There were strong, good political leaders among them. They weren't looked at as different by the majority of the white man. I don't believe significant prejudice existed against the black until the South began to fear that slavery would be outlawed.

"The blood that was spilled in Vicksburg in '63 was nevertheless shed with a valor and an honor that those who have never fought for rights and freedom might not understand. I like to think that those boys believed they were resisting the very idea that a representative government could force its will on hundreds of thousands of people, destroying their way of life and essentially eliminating their means of making a living. Our boys fought hard to defend the city against the siege. There were some who were too afraid, but most stood their duty because doing so was a righteous, manly thing to do. They had seen too many of their brothers fall in the previous battle defending Jackson. They knew they might be called to sacrifice their lives as well."

Again, Charlie was struck by the thought of enormous sacrifice, wondering aloud if it had been necessary. "Didn't General Johnston ask General Pemberton to retreat?"

"Perhaps Pemberton continued to believe that Johnston would send in reinforcements even after the general had urged him to not sacrifice any more of his men. As you point out, Johnston wanted him to retreat from the city to avoid further loss of life. Their location was good, but they were vastly outnumbered, and they were nearly starved. Sometimes hunger and thirst are more formidable enemies than cannons and bullets. Some, those who were not there, might remember the general as a little too weak and a little too indecisive. I don't judge him that way, but I am not qualified to judge any man making the kinds of decisions those leaders had to make then.

"Regardless of a man's point of view, for that matter, regardless of which side he fought on, he fought dutifully and honorably. He did, also despite the relentless attacks of fear that very often undermined his courage more than did the other side's gaining the advantage. He believed he was fighting for something more important than his life, even if that cause was simply not wanting his family to be told he'd died a coward."

Again, Doc sat still, seeming lost in thought before speaking. "A man is always most afraid of his own secret weaknesses. You didn't want to die, but there was something bigger than that. Neither did you want to dishonor yourself, your leaders, your land, or your name. You used every strategy available to you to defeat the other side, but both sides fought as equals and with an equal chance of out strategizing even when the sheer numbers were against you.

"I personally believe the Union armies, especially Sherman, acted shamefully in their unnecessary rape of the South. Son, the lesson is that even honorable men are capable of great evil. Great men do evil things when their passion to win becomes more consuming than their passion for righteousness. Perhaps the latter is sacrificed at the altar of the former, or perhaps in war the two are mutually exclusive.

"Pemberton and his men suffered severe dehydration and starvation while fighting against vastly superior ground forces as well as Admiral Porter's barrage from the river. Despite that, they held out for forty days. We will never know whether Pemberton's decisions were made out of hope, faith, or pride. But we can know that his men fought nobly and died honorably."

Doc hadn't talked this much about the war as long as Charlie had known him. Together, the two men had covered a lot of it over their sixteen-year friendship, but not this much at any one time. Charlie had always sensed that Doc didn't like talking about it. He knew his friend had volunteered at the age of forty to both fight and provide medical care. He knew he had done both, as needed, and often both at the same time.

Charlie had always wondered about something he now asked Doc. "Was every man on each side fighting for the same thing? Were some fighting for slavery, others for states' rights and secession, while still others fought for freedom and the union?"

"I seriously doubt they were all fighting for the same thing," Doc mused. "If you look at the secession declarations of the southern states, you see that they were very clear up front that for them it was primarily about the institution of slavery. I'm sure most of the young men thought they were fighting for whatever cause their conscience sparked or leaders assigned. But the important thing, I believe, is less that every man on each side was willing to fight for something. Rather, it was that each man was willing to die for something he valued more than life. Ultimately, that may be the measure of the cause: the valor of the warrior more than whatever worthiness of the fight there may be."

They rode along for a few minutes, neither man saying anything, each caught up in his own thoughts. Charlie knew Doc had seen some horrible things in war that had seared into his soul, yet he had remained a volunteer in a cause he seemed not to value as much as others who had also risked their lives.

He realized for the first time that Doc hadn't joined the war to fight an enemy but to save lives of brothers on both sides, and he had done that. Charlie's admiration for the man grew again. He knew not to even mention his newfound insight, Doc wanted no recognition for what others thought of as heroism, and there it was again: sacrifice. Charlie broke the silence, asking Doc if they ever caught the men who had murdered the three hundred blacks.

"Oh, the whole town knew who they were. It didn't happen all at once, but the violence finally required Federal troops. I had a purpose in bringing up the Vicksburg battle and the men who died there. As I said, to a man, those soldiers fought on under extreme conditions, including starvation and crippling thirst. Grant didn't release the survivors out of any admiration for their courage, though. He released them because he didn't want to have to feed them. He had probably believed they were too demoralized and in shock to ever fight again, but most did. Yes, he met most of Mississippi's sons again back in Jackson and in Tennessee. The South can always hold her head high. Her men are proud warriors.

"Nevertheless, men on both sides there in Vicksburg fought and died for freedom, honor, or unity as each man defined those. I think a small measure of the decency on both sides is that in the middle of heavy battle, each granted a truce, though Pemberton's men were in more desperate straits, to allow the Union men to gather their dead, dying, and wounded out of the Mississippi sun.

"Now to my point, if you'll forgive this old man's mental meandering, the opposite was true in Vicksburg some ten years later. Some of the very men who most complained about the injustice done them and their properties during the war turned around, hid their faces, and apparently saw no injustice in burning the homes and slaughtering innocent men who were unable to defend themselves. Those three hundred men never stood a chance. What was done to them was a vile, cowardly, and evil thing, Charlie.

"Those cowards didn't risk anything. Their cause, whatever they might have contrived it to be, was nothing good or noble. They shattered the lives of hundreds of families with no need of concern that their own were in jeopardy. They weren't fighting to defend anybody! A man who has to force another into submission in order to pump himself up, that is a man without a soul. But a man who then humiliates, tortures, and murders those he has subjugated is the embodiment of evil!"

The two rode on into Vicksburg in silence, each one's thoughts independently thinking over the notion that a man couldn't always choose the evil that came into his life, but he could choose whether or not he would give back evil for evil. Charlie hoped that he would not. He wasn't sure. He wasn't sure that any man could say that he could always do the righteous thing. *We're flawed creatures; and if Doc is right, we each have our own secret fears that we won't measure up when the time comes.*

Charlie tied Horse and caught up with Doc as he strode up the steps to the River Commission building in Vicksburg. Doc wanted Charlie to see the fine building and get an idea of the business conducted there. The commission was responsible, he explained, for a number of important functions along the Mississippi, especially flood control, but also including two of Doc's pet peeves: facilitating commerce and postal service. He promised Charlie they would have their Coca-Colas in due time after they visited with the good doctor and checked into a hotel.

Charlie was so happily preoccupied with the adventures that lay ahead, he failed to notice the gentleman who had stopped in his pathway squinting at Doc. The lad bumped into him, almost knocking him down. Immediately, Charlie grabbed him by his elbow and shoulder to prevent his fall, apologizing profusely.

"No problem. Not a problem, young man." The man hardly glanced at Charlie but held out his hand, "Doc! Doc Whitmore, is that you?"

Doc's grin creased his face from ear to ear. "Joseph Wilson, what brings you to Mississippi? How are you?" The men exchanged greetings and shook hands so hard and so long Charlie worried Doc's arm might drop off.

Doc introduced Mr. Wilson to Charlie, who then shook his hand heartily. "Son, with those shoulders and your height, we can use you in Chicago. I'm trying to put together a winning football team at the University of Chicago!"

"I'm afraid I'm only good at tackling," the lad quickly replied. The men laughed. Charlie instantly liked Mr. Wilson and was curious to know how he fit into Doc's life. Doc seemed to have good friends all over the United States; in fact, all over the world. He received more mail than the governor, Charlie told him more than once.

Doc asked the man again what had brought him to Vicksburg. Mr. Wilson's face frowned as he replied, "I just learned I need to file some papers in Jackson. I thought I could handle it here at the Commission, but I'm told it needs to be done at the capitol. I'm not sure now how I can accomplish that on this trip. I'm here on the steamer the *City of Monroe*. Brought my sons with me before they leave to go abroad for a year. You remember I have twin boys?"

Doc nodded, but before he could speak, Mr. Wilson continued, speaking almost more to himself than to Doc.

"We're leaving out of here shortly after midnight, and I'm told the stopover on the way back doesn't leave me enough time, either. We came by rail out of Chicago to St. Louis and boarded the *Monroe* there. I have to be back in Chicago no later than the eighteenth of May. It was foolish of me to think I could take care of something so important by combining it with a pleasure trip. I should have taken a train directly down to Jackson, but I was certain that the Commission had jurisdiction over the matter. It was the boys who suggested we steam down the Mississippi. They especially wanted to see Vicksburg. That's what they're out doing now. But here I am talking a blue streak, burdening you with my concerns, Doc, and probably not making a lick of sense." He chuckled, adding, "Seems like old times, doesn't it? I'm sorry."

"Charlie and I are heading back to Jackson tomorrow. Is your business anything I can handle for you?"

Mr. Wilson's brows moved together, forming an unbroken line. "Doc, I would be mightily obliged to you if you could. Let me think. I can assign you my power of attorney. We can get that done on board… Doc, would you and Charlie be my guests at supper tonight aboard the *City of Monroe*? We could discuss the particulars of this land deal. I'd like your opinion anyway. I would very much appreciate your opinion, as a matter of fact!"

Say yes! Charlie was thinking, watching Doc hesitate in thought before he spoke.

"Of course we will do whatever it takes to get your business conducted, but Charlie and I have business to attend with a gentleman here in Vicksburg this afternoon, and it may be that I'll need to have dinner with him and his wife."

"It would be my pleasure to host you, Charlie, your friend, his wife, and his ten children if you think you might persuade the man to join you!" Mr. Wilson was quite enthusiastic about spending so much money on total strangers, Charlie thought, deciding the business he wanted help with must be very important indeed.

Dr. Thorpe would not hear of Doc and Charlie spending the night in a hotel. He accepted the invitation Doc extended to dine on the steamer only on the condition that the two men return to his home to spend the night. Charlie couldn't believe their good fortune of having arrived in Vicksburg the very day that Mr. Wilson arrived. He was a little disappointed that he wouldn't get to spend his first night ever in a hotel, but that was before he laid eyes on Mrs. Thorpe.

Red curls made a frame around a face so perfect it seemed more like a painting. Her eyes, a lighter green than Mrs. Harper's, were truly a window into her soul. Charlie looked in and fell in love. Her cheeks were perfectly pink, and her skin was as creamy as Jessie's. Her lips made him think for the first time ever of what it would be like to kiss a woman romantically. He felt stirrings in his heart and body unlike those any other female had ever brought out in him. He realized his mouth was gaping open and that Mrs. Thorpe was speaking to him.

"...stay the night."

Charlie stammered, looking desperately to Doc to rescue him. He saw that Doc was amused by his reaction and trying not to laugh and embarrass the lad but had no intention of rescuing him. Charlie had to speak. "Yes, ma'am. Were you saying that I can—that is, that Doc and I—may spend the night?"

The elegance of the steamer, the *City of Monroe*, would ordinarily have made a stronger impression on Charlie, but touring it required that he leave the company of Mrs. Thorpe. *In truth, the Monroe is more opulent,* he thought, *than even the governor's mansion and Jackson City Hall.* The Wilson twins took him on a tour, starting with the stern, informing him this was one of very few stern wheelers in the Anchor Line fleet, the others being side wheelers.

Charlie carried his own, adding his knowledge about the side wheelers and that they were faster than a stern wheeler, but surmised that when one was on a pleasure trip as the Wilsons now were, one didn't worry about speed.

The Wilson boys showed him their staterooms and the boat's salons, restaurant, and bars. Well-dressed men and women were everywhere, laughing, dining, gambling, talking, and strolling. They pointed out the piano the people from Monroe, Louisiana, had donated to their namesake. Jonathan Wilson sat at the piano and played a few measures of a tune Charlie didn't recognize. David, the twin who was the oldest by two minutes, told him it was from a New York play.

Charlie understood why the boat was called a floating palace. He thought the Wilsons must be very rich to even afford to spend one night, much less the whole cruise to New Orleans and back. Soon, a waiter brought them three glasses filled with a dark, foamy liquid on a gleaming silver tray, offering it first to Charlie.

"Sir." The waiter turned to the lad. "Mr. Wilson has ordered beverages for you young men."

His eyes felt a not-unpleasant sting. His nose was tickled ever so lightly in a way that made him have to smile, and his throat burned just enough to make the Coca-Cola…

"Interesting, don't you think?" one of the Wilson boys asked.

"Yes, that's the word," Charlie agreed. "It is interesting indeed and delicious! No wonder it became such a popular drink. It is my first, you know."

Mr. Wilson seated Charlie between the twins, directly across from Mrs. Thorpe. On one hand, Charlie had hoped to be seated next to her. On the other, he wasn't sure he would be able to carry on a conversation with her without stuttering and stammering. *This way is best*, he decided. He could watch her, take in her beauty, and hear her voice without making a fool of himself. He could tell that the other five men were as captivated by her as he was; it made him feel a little jealous and then a little more self-conscious that he had such feelings for a woman twice his age and married at that!

The talk became lively the minute everyone was seated at the large, round table. Listening, Charlie fingered the snowy white tablecloth and remembered to place his napkin in his lap. He hoped he would be able to know how to use all the glasses and flatware. He decided to watch Mrs. Thorpe to see which ones she used.

Mr. Wilson ordered champagne to celebrate the several important events of the day. "Not the least of which," he noted, "is Charlie having his first Coca-Cola."

And Charlie falling in love, the lad thought and then felt himself blushing. He glanced around, thankful that no one seemed to notice. He watched as the sommelier filled his champagne glass, wondering if Doc would permit him to taste it. Doc made a barely perceptible nod at him, and Charlie smiled.

The conversation seemed to flow naturally from one topic to the next. It had begun with Mr. Wilson's river land purchase and onto Doc's summary of the deal. Doc had pointed out the US Supreme Court "Pollock" decision handed down last year in which it was held that a tax based on receipts from the use of property to be unconstitutional. Therefore, Mr. Wilson's intended use of the properties would net him more income than he had originally calculated.

"Yes," Doc concluded, "the court affirmed that the Constitution didn't deny Congress the power to impose a tax on real or personal property. However, it seemed to find that allotting the taxable income on personal property would pose impossible accounting demands, so for all intents and purposes, the ruling prohibited a federal tax on personal property."

From that, the talk turned to Dr. Thorpe's interest in purchasing land. It lingered a while on Dr. and Mrs. Thorpe's consideration of moving to Jackson, and from there on to the particulars of this steamer and the financial troubles of the entire Anchor

Line, as perhaps reflective of the financial hardships much of Mississippi and indeed the nation were currently experiencing.

Dr. Thorpe noted, "We have the highest unemployment rate in recorded history, and still Washington caters to the bankers." Charlie noticed that Mr. Wilson didn't join in the conversation that ensued. The lad had figured out that he was a part of the "big money" to which Dr. Thorpe referred, although even he had agreed that it was a tough call since both the eastern money and the south and western crops and cattle were essential to the economy.

The friendly group finally agreed that the financial instability throughout the land could not actually be attributed to any one thing. Rather, they said, it was a combination of things such as railroad over building and unstable financing of that, as well as the long drought resulting in lack of cash to farmers and therefore high indebtedness. There had also been the earlier run on the gold supply and a flood on the market of silver.

Mrs. Thorpe turned their talk to the monetary position of "the handsome William Jennings Bryan." Inevitably, the conversation landed on the coming elections.

Charlie loved a spirited election debate, but tonight he was glad to simply sit and bask in the opulence all around him, the wonderful food and service, and the pleasure of the fine company and interesting conversation. He thought the champagne tasted much better than the brandy he had once consumed but not nearly as good as Coca-Cola.

He liked the twins. They were four years older than he but had treated him as an equal all afternoon and evening before dinner, making it a very pleasant time. They made sure he was included in their conversations and were not the least bit arrogant about their ease with money. It turned out that Charlie knew more about Vicksburg's Civil War involvement than they, and he enjoyed having something to contribute instead of asking so many questions. Now, listening to Mrs. Thorpe, he thought perhaps her presence was the single best thing of the day. She was telling them that she had a sister living in St. Louis whom she had not seen in over two years.

In bed that night, Charlie lay with his hands beneath his head, watching a patch of moonlight that seemed to play hide-and-seek with him through the branches of a magnolia tree. He couldn't wipe the grin off his face and relax to go to sleep. *How is it,* he asked himself, *that this summer has been so good when I thought in the spring that I was going to be in grief most of the time and that Doc would need to be tended to constantly?*

He did a mental check of Doc's health. He thought he saw more fatigue in his face and some moments of severe pain, but otherwise Doc actually seemed to be enjoying himself as much as he said he was. Finally, assuring himself that Doc could get along without him for the several days the trip would take, Charlie allowed himself to now dwell on the most excellent turn of events.

Mr. Wilson had made the suggestion that Dr. and Mrs. Thorpe take the *City of Monroe* up to St. Louis to visit her sister on its return trip from New Orleans. Mrs. Thorpe had looked so excited that her husband was clearly finding it difficult to deny her, but he was emphatic that he could not spare the time. See-ing his wife's disappointment, he hastened to offer that she go without him. Mr. Wilson immediately assured them he and the twins would take care of her on the trip up.

"But," Mrs. Thorpe wondered, "who would be my escort back? Please, darling, are you sure you can't take off the time? We would only need to stay a few days."

How had it happened, Charlie asked himself still in disbelief as he lay there, *that it was decided I would be her escort?* He had been distracted by the way her eyes almost sparkled when she was animated and how pretty she looked when her mouth pouted a little in disappointment, so he hadn't heard the flow of conversation until he heard his name mentioned and noticed everyone almost cheering as though in approval of what clearly must be a splendid plan.

"What do you say, Charlie? Do you think you could take care of Charlotte from St. Louis to Vicksburg?" Dr. Thorpe's voice had broken through the cloud Charlie had been floating in for the past several minutes.

Lying in bed now, he retraced the thoughts that had first streaked through his mind when he was invited to escort Mrs. Thorpe home from St Louis. He hadn't wondered about plans or details of how it might come about. Instead, he seemed to experience immediate changes in his own self-regard. Suddenly, he was more mature, more responsible and trustworthy, and somehow even taller.

"Yes, sir," he had responded. "That is, if Mrs. Thorpe will entrust her care to me."

As Dr. and Mrs. Thorpe walked them out to Horse the next morning, Charlie reaffirmed the plan: On May 27, he would arrive in St. Louis, traveling by train from Jackson well in time to meet Mrs. Thorpe in Lafayette Park and thereafter assist her in boarding the *Monroe*. He would have an adjoining stateroom and would be her escort on the return Mississippi River travel. Saying good-bye to her after breakfast was made easier in knowing he would be seeing her again in three weeks. He was filled with anticipation about also taking his longest train ride ever and the first boat trip he'd ever made.

He arrived at noon. With several hours to spare before meeting Mrs. Thorpe, Charlie walked from Union Station to the river wharf. Mrs. Thorpe had told him that May was a perfect time to be in St. Louis. Charlie thought any time was a perfect time to be walking with a beautiful woman by his side, but nevertheless he found the weather more hot and humid than she had seemed to imply.

Locating the *City of Monroe*, he went aboard to make sure their travel plans were in order and was told that Mrs. Thorpe's bags had already arrived. He checked his own and continued his stroll along this busy waterfront. He knew he was gawking at everything. The other floating palaces also had people boarding and strolling on the decks. He read their names: *Henry Stockman*, *Christie*, and *S. C. Club* were three; some of the wharf boats had more romantic names, and it seemed some had none. He headed back to the park, arriving just as Mrs. Thorpe stepped out of a horse-drawn carriage.

He knew his grin telegraphed more to her than he wanted her to know. However, it quickly changed to a frown as he saw for the first time the enormous cumulus clouds that had been gathering behind him as he walked. He had been too lost in thought to notice them, although he was uncomfortably aware of the changing atmosphere. He extended his hand to help her out of the buggy and again felt a jolt of pleasure at her touch.

"I saw that frown, Charlie. Aren't you happy to see me?" she teased as she tiptoed to kiss him on the cheek.

He still felt her lips on his cheek even after she'd pulled away. He hoped his voice wouldn't break as he responded to her. "Oh, very much so, but I'm thinking we should take this carriage on to the landing and board the *Monroe* now. It looks like we're about to have some weather."

"Not at all! I won't have my plans to show you this park spoiled by a few drops of rain! Besides, I have my parasol! Come." She turned and dismissed the cab. "There is much to see. Don't you just love this place?"

Charlie kept one eye on the darkening sky and another on Mrs. Thorpe as she, seemingly oblivious to the oppressive heat, strolled from one point of interest to another, chattering all the while. It was an impressive park, maybe the most beautiful place he had ever seen. He had read about Thomas Hart Benton and so was glad to see the large statue of the man and, of course, the one of George Washington.

"I believe Senator Benton coined the phrase 'manifest destiny,'" Mrs. Thorpe was saying. "I think that was regarding the expansion of the United States, but I'm afraid I'm not a very good historian."

"Yes, ma'am," Charlie replied. "Senator Benton was a very colorful fellow. He fought hard for the expansion and development of all the territories as far west as the Pacific Ocean, believing that unsettled land was a potential threat to the security and the stability of the nation. Doc and I admire him for many things, including his vision for America.

"However, as you know," Charlie continued, "I'm half Cherokee. So, of course I'm more sensitive to the disfranchisement of the natives who dwelled in the lands before the Europeans ever arrived. Benton was a strong supporter of dislocating whole tribes from their ancestral lands so European settlers could take them over. Mrs. Thorpe wrapped her arm in his, sending a thrill all over Charlie and momentarily causing him to forget what he had been saying. "Charlie." He loved the way she pronounced his name, making it seem important. "It must be difficult for you to be half...well, European and half Indian. Don't you sometimes feel pulled in two directions at once?"

"Actually, I do. I have often felt torn between my love for both peoples and for the truly remarkable individuals in both groups. On the other hand, like some other mixed bloods, I've also struggled with bitterness at times.

"I used to get confused and angry either toward the white man or the Indian, depending upon who I was with at the time. Sometimes it felt like I didn't belong to anyone not even the Harpers, and that was difficult. When I listened to prejudiced people I felt shame, regardless of which side they were on. I had a few fights before Doc and Oxytak helped me work through my anger and self-pity and accept that I have been given the gift of life and I should appreciate it instead of resenting the circumstances. Any more, I don't challenge or question other's views in any way to rebel or find fault. Who am I to do that? I'm six... teen." He stumbled on that, hating to remind her that he was not qualified by age to be her suitor even if she had been free to receive him as such.

Charlie looked down at Mrs. Thorpe, pausing to give her a chance to speak. He wanted to kiss her. Where had that thought come from? *Why am I acting like such a dolt? What would it be like to kiss her? I can never kiss her!*

"Too, Doc, Oxytak, and Mr. Harper all taught me that the manner in which men deal with both conflict and with love may very well determine the outcome of every great human endeavor." *I love her.*

""I think you are an insightful young man, Charlie. Please go on. You were talking about things that transcend our day-to-day lives."

"Well, the people I admire most are the ones who have held on to the eternal values and goodness even in the face of strong opposition and risk to their lives. Doc and Oxytak come from two very different societies, yet they have each put their lives on the line for the other, as well as at times opposing their own people on matters they knew to be right. They deeply respect and love each other. In them, I see the greatness not only of two disparate cultures, but of the hope that there is within any culture enough people in every generation who rise above those petty and ordinary things that separate and alienate lesser men from each other."

He watched her struggle with her parasol and offered to close it for her, suggesting again that they hurry on to the wharf. The wind was picking up, too gusty for a parasol. She playfully looped the handle over his arm. "Just a little while longer. Wait right here. Close your eyes. I have a surprise for you."

"Mrs. Thorpe—"

"Charlie," she interrupted, "you may call me Charlotte. I insist you call me Charlotte from now on! As a matter of fact, you should know that my sister called me Charlie and Charlie-girl when I was maybe three and four. Mother made her stop, but I always secretly liked it. What were you going to say?"

She pulled the hair out of her eyes. He watched it blow right back, fascinated by her smallest gestures. Before he could repeat his concern about the weather, she spoke. "Now wait here, Charlie. Close your eyes and count to thirty—no, to sixty. Promise!" She turned, starting to dance away from him.

"Mrs. Thorpe, Charlotte, don't go!" He clasped her arm; the firmness in his voice surprised him, but she seemed not to notice a difference. It felt awkward and inappropriate for him to be correcting an adult, but, he argued with himself, *wasn't this what I was sent to do, look after her?* "I believe we need to find shelter. I don't like the feel of the air. There is at least a bad thunderstorm coming. With the wind picking up, we should either go on to the boat or find a public building for shelter."

"Oh, Charlie, I love the rain. It won't hurt us. Don't spoil my surprise for you. I planned it all day. That's why I sent my bags ahead so that we wouldn't be bothered with them here. To tell you the truth, I got here a few minutes ahead of you to prepare the surprise. The *Monroe* doesn't leave for at least two more hours. Please just give me a moment more, please, please?"

Charlie felt a familiar tug at his heart as he looked down into Mrs. Thorpe's green eyes and saw Jessie's face. Suddenly he missed Jessie terribly and Frank and all the Harpers. Mrs. Thorpe's petulant little-girl charm brought back the memory of Jessie out at the rock pile when she had begged him not to leave her for the summer.

Without waiting for him to answer, Mrs. Thorpe raced away, holding her hair out of her eyes with one hand, pulling up her skirts slightly with the other. She was laughing, calling back over her shoulder, insisting that he close his eyes and give her "no more than two minutes. Count to sixty slowly, and then come ahead!" More from a sense of defeat than willingness, Charlie closed his eyes and began counting.

Even with his eyes tightly closed, he sensed a sudden darkening and became aware of a distant roaring sound. He opened his eyes and looked back. The sky behind him was very dark, and at that moment, a loud clap of thunder sounded, followed immediately by a jagged lightening bolt that streaked across the inky sky to the ground. It seemed to strike only a few feet away. He noticed a lighter outer edge and realized that the darkness was a tornado funnel heading in the direction of the park. He scanned the area in which Mrs. Thorpe had run and saw nothing.

He looked again at the rapidly approaching funnel, squinting as the wind forced his eyelids closed and then immediately blew them open. Tears blinded him, but his eyes instantly dried and stung. Blinking to clear his vision, he searched for a spot of yellow. Air that had been thick with humidity and acrid smells of electricity only seconds ago was now dense and odorless and pelting him with rain and hail. He knew they had only minutes to find shelter before the tornado swept through the park.

Charlie tried to call out to Mrs. Thorpe but the wind seemed to suck the words out of him where they were lost in the roar. He couldn't hear his own voice, yet he seemed to hear Mrs. Thorpe's calling his name. "Charlie! Charlie!" He knew the sound came only from the wind and his conscience for not insisting they seek shelter when he first noticed the weather.

He thought that it had probably been no more than a minute, if that, since Mrs. Thorpe had left his sight, but it seemed like a half hour or more. It appeared likely that she was among the trees that were now bending impossibly to the ground. He glanced about looking for any structure or obstacle down wind he might grasp for stabilization or might otherwise be thrust into and injured. He bit his lower lip and let go of the railing, feeling like one of Jessie's rag dolls.

His body was partially tumbled at breakneck speed seemingly only yards ahead of the awful black wall of churning wrath and unrelenting force. He tried desperately to get a foothold, but that was impossible. His body was traveling faster than his feet could move even when he made his legs extend toward the ground. The wind forced him along as if an unseen winnower was tossing him up one second, dropping him the next. He could only gasp in short breaths, finding that when he opened his mouth to inhale, air was instead sucked out of him.

Wherever he had a chance to look, there were flying objects, some recognizable, most not. There was boarding that now seemed like splinters and huge pieces of objects that defied gravity. The gazebos and statuary that had been in the park just minutes earlier were toppled or, though heavier, were being flung sometimes higher than him. The bandstand was in shambles sailing off in all directions. Again and again, he turned his head to look for her, guessing her direction only because of the path of the wind.

He felt no fear; he felt nothing. His mind raced, clear, calculating, coordinating, his inner calmness belying the outer flailing of his arms and legs that sometimes landed as he had intended and sometimes as the unseen force willed. Tense and focused, he searched for a yellow dress and for a stronghold.

He spotted her off to his left, out of the corner of his eye. She lay on the ground shielded from his earlier view and protected from the force of the wind by a group of boulders. Charlie willed his body to defy this force of nature, rolled into a ball, and somersaulted to Mrs. Thorpe's lifeless form. Hailstones mixed with large raindrops were pelting her face, yet she was not flinching.

In one motion, he flung his body protectively over hers and reached out to grab a large rock that jutted out of a grotto on the lake. This time the wind was with him, enabling him to pull his and Mrs. Thorpe's bodies forward toward the rocky outthrusts. They lay in a slight hollow, sheltered by the rocks. He ducked his head just in time to avoid being hit by a piece of a canoe he had noticed earlier on the far side of the water. He had already seen other boats being tossed in the air like a kaleidoscope of paper kites.

Charlie dug in the toes of his boots and arched his back so as to take his weight off Mrs. Thorpe's lifeless body. He dared not release his hold on the rocks to check her pulse. Something heavy struck hard against his back; he did not so much feel the searing pain as to sense it intellectually. Fighting the impulse to curl up, he held on. The rocks were wet but provided good handholds. Something else small and heavy hit the right side of his head, and he felt a sharp pain and nausea as he struggled to keep from passing out.

As suddenly as it had come upon them, the storm passed on. They were no longer in darkness, and it was getting lighter rapidly. The roar was no longer deafening. Charlie rolled sideways off Mrs. Thorpe and placed his fingers on her carotid artery, as Doc had taught him.

He couldn't tell. His own heart was pounding fiercely, and there was still too much chaos: sirens and foghorns going off all over town, constant crashing sounds, and people whom Charlie thought had probably been yelling and screaming all along could now be heard above the din. Charlie pushed back the rush of feelings that tried again to assault his mind, knowing he could not let them. He needed to think clearly and determine his next move with the goal of getting Mrs. Thorpe to a hospital.

He positioned himself on one knee to lift her, looking around for a nearby house where he could summon help. What he saw stunned him. The only spot in all of Lafayette Park that wasn't several feet deep in rubble was the small area around them. There was nothing left of the beautiful gardens: no blossoms, no structure remained intact. He looked across the street where not thirty minutes earlier he had walked along, admiring beautiful, stately homes that were now in giant heaps of red brick, rock, and wood. He saw stovepipes, chairs, pieces of staircases, large sections of roofs, and horse carriages littering the park and the street beyond. The trees where he had earlier thought Mrs. Thorpe would be hiding had been snapped off like mere reeds in the wake of a boy's imaginary battle. As far as Charlie could see, the entire city was in shambles.

There were signs of life: screaming heard at high pitch; horses running wildly pulling empty buggies, some with missing wheels; and the endless sirens. He saw fires in every direction with black smoke and flames now shooting up against a dark-gray sky. He didn't think anyone in the mansions across the street could have survived. He knew help was probably needed in those homes, but his first act would be to get help here. He called Mrs. Thorpe's name several times, then picked up her slender body, feeling strangely sad to see the soil, rips, and grass stains on her dress but having no idea which direction he should try to walk. She offered no resistance. Her right arm dangled down. "She's hardly bigger than Jessie!"

Charlie staggered not at all from her weight but from the exhaustion of fighting the storm and his fear about Mrs. Thorpe. He paused a moment to center himself, taking a deep breath and stood, resolved to find help for her. He peered above rubble heaps searching for a red cross or perhaps a flag. To himself, knowing she could not answer, he said, "Charlie-girl, where is there a hospital in this city?"

"Charlie-boy, put me down, and I'll show you."

Her words were slurred, but she had a lopsided grin on her face. He might have dropped her in his shock had she not grasped his neck to hold on. She gave him a puzzled smile and then frowned as her eyes regained focus.

"Charlie, you're bleeding. Put me down. We must get you to a doctor!" Only then did she notice the devastation. She clasped her hands to her face in shock and grief with the realization of what must have happened to the city and to them. She seemed to wilt. Charlie drew her into his arms, fearing she would faint again.

"I'm so sorry. I guess I passed out. I was terrified when I saw that enormous funnel behind you. Some help I am!" She drew her hand from his back and noticed blood on it, stepping around him to look behind. "Charlie! There's blood all over your shirt! Why, it's torn. You're badly cut and bruised!" Tearing the hem of her petticoat, she dabbed blood off the side of his face. "You are hurt all over, and I don't seem to have a scratch on me!"

Charlotte knew the city and thought she could find the hospital; however, as she looked around, all the familiar landmarks were now missing, so she was disoriented. She insisted she didn't need medical attention at all, and Charlie refused to go only for himself. Their elation that they had survived intact turned to mounting shock and sorrow as they stumbled in the now-torrential rain, making their way in the general direction of the levee.

Along the way, again and again, they helped remove debris off dazed people or sometimes pulled others out from under huge piles of rubble. Charlie helped Charlotte tear strips of cloth from her dress to use as tourniquets. They scrambled to get inside homes brought to rubble to find drinkable water or blankets for others in shock. They comforted people and offered prayers. Charlie closed the eyelids of people impaled with boards and other objects, both of them swallowing back nausea from the grotesqueness of the deaths. They tried to offer hope to the injured and carried others out of the rain into makeshift shelters, trying to commit everyone's names to memory.

Charlie stopped an ambulance and assisted the driver in lifting an unconscious older woman and a bloodied child into the already crowded wagon. Were there not so many demands upon their sensibilities, they would have crumbled from the grief and growing exhaustion. They learned from a policeman that the hospital had been severely damaged and that the boats at the wharf had been splintered and sunk, drowning almost everyone on board.

Charlie fired questions at the officer like shells from a Gatling gun, incredulity in his voice. "*All* the boats," he asked? "*All* those on board drowned? Were the hospital patients spared? Do we know how many were killed in this? Is the rain extinguishing the fires now? Are the trains running? What about telegraph lines? Telephone lines?"

"Whoa, son, at least I can answer all those questions with one word. *No.*" His mouth closed, and he sat silent, looking through the young man, his eyes matching Charlie's in their sorrow and fatigue. The lad looked at him perplexed; the policeman spoke again after a moment.

"The telephone and telegraph lines are down. There are maybe one or two boats still afloat. The hawsers seemed to have been snapped off, setting them adrift, but those won't be cruising for a while. The east-west track, at least, is down, but I suspect the north-south tracks are just as damaged. There seems to be a lot of damage at the Union station. Let's see, you asked…oh, yes, I believe some patients survived at the hospital… The streetcar lines are down. There are a lot of dead and dying.

"I've got to go. Another thing, though, be very careful. There are electrical wires down all over the city. They're causing most of the fires. Oh, and another thing, the jail was destroyed, looked like the prisoners were too scared to run, but just in case, I'd be careful. Where are you two headed?"

For the first time since the tornado, Charlotte thought of her sister and her family. In stark fear, she inquired of the policeman if her sister's section of town was all right. He thought for a minute. "I believe it is, young lady. I don't believe I've heard a single report of an incident in that part of town."

Charlie left Charlotte in the joyful reunion and care of her sister and made his way to the House of the Good Shepard. The sisters gladly accepted their responsibility of making every effort to get word to Doc and Dr. Thorpe.

The House of the Good Shepard was being used as a makeshift hospital set up to provide medical care for those injured or burned during the storm. It would have been within running distance, except by now, night had fallen and all electricity and gas lamps were out, so he had trouble following Charlotte's directions and making his way through the piles of debris but finally arrived. Charlotte's sister had made him drink a glass of buttermilk and had thrust a slab of ham and bread in his hands as he'd left, so he felt oddly refreshed.

A blood-spattered man looked him up and down, seeing the dried blood from his own injuries and those of others he'd helped earlier. "Sorry, young man. If you can walk in here, you don't need medical attention. We're limiting aid to the more serious injuries."

Charlie's practiced eye took it all in; he told himself that the only difference between this place and Doc's "operating room" was the size and number of patients. "Sir, he hurriedly explained, "I've come to help if you need it. I have a little medical experience. I've done some minor surgery. I can administer chloroform and ether, stitch people up. Do you need my help?"

Before he had finished speaking, the man had taken his shoulders and directed him toward an endless row of crying, bleeding, and sometimes dying patients. He worked all night, doing what he could to assist the doctors, gradually taking on more and more responsibility but not touching those patients who were still impaled by objects or who otherwise appeared to have serious injuries.

He spotted the little girl he had earlier placed on the ambulance. She was pale, with bandages on her head and hand and a makeshift cast on one leg. He asked the doctor about her condition.

"It's not good. I'm not sure she will make it. She hasn't regained consciousness. I can't tell if there are internal injuries. I'm keeping an eye on her."

Shortly after midnight, her eyes fluttered open as Charlie stopped by her bed. She started to cry but tried to stop herself. Charlie held her uninjured hand and crouched beside her. "It's all right if you want to cry. I'm sure you hurt very badly. I know you're scared. You've been very, very brave, but you're safe now; so if you want to cry, go ahead. I'll stay with you a few minutes."

She grew quiet for a minute, letting the tears spill down her cheeks, looking deeply into Charlie's eyes perhaps to see if she could trust him. Charlie wiped her tears away, noticing she didn't pull back.

"Where's my daddy? I want my daddy." She didn't plead; she stated it matter-of-factly.

"What is your name?" Charlie asked, trying to think of an honest answer that wouldn't frighten her.

"Millie."

"Millie, do you know your last name?"

She nodded her head, "My whole name is Millie Marie Morgan. My daddy calls me Three-M because all my names start with M."

"May I also call you Three-M?" She smiled for the first time and nodded her head slightly then frowned from the pain the movement seemed to cause.

"Well, Three-M, your daddy…your daddy…wanted you brought here so we could take good care of you and help your injuries. He knows you are too precious to not have the very best care, and"—Charlie puffed out his chest exaggeratedly—"if I may say so, young lady, you are getting the best care in the world right here!"

She smiled again, giving Charlie courage to go on.

"Do you remember the big storm we had?"

She nodded, new tears filling her eyes.

"Well, lots and lots of people need the kind of help your daddy can give, so while you've been sleeping, he has been out working." Charlie was praying silently that God spare this little girl and her family.

"But I hurt. My daddy always says I have to be brave for him, but I hurt really badly." Her lips were trembling, but she blinked back tears. Charlie wiped away the ones that rolled down her temple.

"I know you hurt. I wish I could make it stop hurting. It will be a few days. You don't have to be brave in here if you don't want to," Charlie tried to soothe her.

She swallowed and pressed her hand against her lips as though to stop them from trembling, tears again welling up. "I want to be brave, but it was really, really scary when the wind blew my wardrobe over on me and the whole house just fell on top. I was really, really afraid!"

"I would have been afraid too. Were you with your mommy?"

"She died when I was two. I'm six now. I don't remember her, but my daddy says she was beautiful and that I look just like her." Charlie told Three-M that her daddy was a good judge of beauty. "I know," she answered with no smugness. He told the child he needed to go help other people but that he would send over a kind lady with soup and water for her. "Thank you," she answered, "and don't forget to send my daddy too. He needs me. I'm his only little girl! We don't have a grandma or a grandpa, either. We just have each other. He really, really needs me."

Charlie kept an eye on the doors; every time a newcomer arrived, he looked up to see if perhaps it would be the child's father. His heart grew heavier as the night wore on and more fearful that the man was dead or too severely injured to come in search of her. Surely he would know that the injured were being diverted here instead of to the damaged hospital.

Just before dawn, a man staggered in through the door, clutching the frame with his left hand to keep from falling. One side of his face and his hands had been badly burned. His clothing was blackened and torn, revealing burns on his chest and one shoulder. His right arm was in a makeshift sling of dirty yellow cloth Charlie recognized to be from Charlotte's dress. Charlie looked into the sunken, tormented eyes of the man. His face bore the agony of a father who had already lost a wife and who was almost crazed by the fear he had now lost his daughter. Charlie hurried to him.

"Are you looking for Three-M?"

It took a moment for the words to sink in. He staggered against Charlie, and both would have fallen had not two other men steadied them. Charlie led Mr. Morgan to his sleeping daughter. It was the most gratifying thing he had done all night.

More and more volunteer doctors arrived from surrounding areas throughout the night. The kindly physician Charlie had first greeted again took him by the shoulders.

"Son, we're both going to rest. We've been spelled. You can't go on like this, or very soon you're going to be one of those serious cases I mentioned!"

Charlie was past exhaustion but hadn't wanted to leave until he knew Three-M would be all right. He gratefully accepted the ride and offer of a bed in the home of the unnamed doctor at whose side he'd worked all night.

A few days later, a rested and bathed Charlie rode back to Vicksburg on the special train Mr. Wilson had arranged. Dr. Thorpe arrived with it, along with other physicians and nurses. He and others in the medical community along the Mississippi had put together vast amounts of medical supplies and other essentials for which the people in St. Louis and East St. Louis were in greatest need.

Tracks had been partially repaired, allowing the train to get near the union station where lines of horse-drawn wagons and buggies waited to cart them into supply centers. Help was arriving in every form and manner as the Associated Press reporters managed to get their stories to their home papers. There was limited telegraph service in East St. Louis, and that newspaper had been able to somehow print a few special editions that were grabbed up before they hit the streets. Charlie read the collections of articles Charlotte had clipped for him.

Before leaving, Charlie had twice gone back to the House of the Good Shepard to visit the people about whom he had the greatest concern or sorrow. Among those were Three-M and her father. He had brought Charlotte, her brother-in-law, and her sister with him, anticipating that having heard the story of the now-homeless child and father, they would also fall in love with her, have compassion for the father, and invite the two into their home while they recuperated. He was right. He grinned now, listening to Charlotte tell Dr. Thorpe again all about Millie Marie, adding that maybe she was ready to have a child after all.

"What if it's a boy?" Dr. Thorpe teased. He'd been holding his wife protectively since arriving in St. Louis.

"Well, then, we'll have to name him Charlie. Wouldn't you agree?"

Chapter 6

Doc met the train in Vicksburg and hugged Charlie tightly for a full minute before allowing himself to speak. Horse greeted him with extra affection, and his gait seemed especially jaunty all the way home. Mrs. Thompson was waiting for them both, sitting in Doc's rocker out front. She had baked a lemon coconut cake for Charlie and made a stew, with biscuits ready to pop in the oven.

The lad welcomed his return to the pleasant routines of life with Doc and their good conversations. The experiences of the tornado, with its seemingly capricious choices of life and death, suffering, and courage had further heightened his sensitivity to the meaning of individual life and purpose. He was more interested now than ever before in probing Doc's mind about every detail of life: nature, science, Scripture, and love, but also industry, technology, and politics. If Doc didn't know about something, he sent the young man to the library for books and newspaper articles on the matters.

Doc also found reasons to send Charlie to Mr. Davis's store. He knew the boy had always been fascinated by general stores and hadn't lost his interest in having one of his own someday. Mr. Davis assured Charlie it provided a good living and a satisfying life if he managed it carefully. He had been taking the time to teach the lad about bookkeeping, purchasing, and inventory management. There was also mutual laughter with townsfolk and shared smiles with pretty girls in which Charlie found a growing interest.

Most mornings were spent picking snap peas, green beans, cucumbers, black berries, and other bounty from the garden, delivering them to the poor, and busying himself with chores in the house. He took Horse for a long, hard ride out to his birthplace. He thought often about Frank and Jessie and wrote them a letter. He mentioned only that he had been in St. Louis during the tornado, knowing it would pique Frank's interest enough to write back and inquire about all the details.

One morning Charlie awoke to find Oxytak smiling down at him. He had brought a mess of just-caught fish, several cuts of beef, and herbs and tonics for Doc, who took some right then, saving the rest for later as Oxytak had instructed. Doc didn't argue; he seemed grateful and offered Oxytak a choice of his pipe or a cigar. Charlie thought back to the time when Oxytak had lit Mr. Harper's cigar over and over because both were so scared that Frank might die that Mr. Harper kept forgetting to pull on the cigar, and Oxytak kept letting the match go out.

The young man made coffee, and the three took chairs out to the boardwalk in front of Doc's office. Passersby tipped their hats, called out greetings, and inquired of Doc's health as they bustled about their business. A pretty girl Charlie assessed to be maybe fifteen smiled shyly at him in a nice way.

Oxytak had to hear every detail of Charlie's adventure news of which he said reached him at home before Doc's letter arrived. Doc had already gathered the news stories of the tornado for Oxytak to read and took charge of the telling of the story, emphasizing Charlie's part in it.

When all the articles had been read and all the questions answered to Oxytak's satisfaction, he nodded his approval one last time to Charlie. Nothing more was said about it, but nothing more was needed. Finally, the talk turned to the presidential campaign. Both men thought they would rather share a supper and a conversation with Mr. Bryan, but they weren't yet convinced he'd be the better president. They agreed that the cash-strapped farmers needed a break from their burdening debts, but was the certain inflation of silver coinage the best thing in the long run for the entire United States?

Neither Doc nor Oxytak cared much for politicians. However, both admired Cleveland, although he was a Democrat, for his courage and convictions as well as his fiscal conservatism. They didn't know enough about Mr. McKinley to make a decision, yet. Nor had they decided if Mr. Bryan was a good man or just a better politician; both men tended to favor the gold standard and oppose income tax.

Bryan was reported to be the best orator around and was also the youngest man to ever run for president. Charlie commented that it would be very interesting to hear Mr. Bryan speak at the Democratic Convention in July. With unusual enthusiasm, considering he thought more like a Republican, Doc said that sounded like a good idea.

Charlie didn't mind hard work, not even occasional kitchen chores because he got immediate results from them: the good smell of a venison stew or cinnamon rolls he'd helped Beulah knead. He'd learned a lot walking the fields with Mr. Harper; he didn't mind the plowing, planting, and harvesting. He enjoyed the end of a day of working cattle with Oxytak. Work gave purpose and structure to daily life and brought its own rewards.

But he hated picking cotton. No doubt about that. It was backbreaking, finger-bleeding, sun-blazing, sun-up-to-sun-down hard work. Yet he loved hearing the singing of spirituals and the good-natured ribbing of the other field workers. He especially loved sitting down to noon dinners where the tables in the fields were piled high with the succulent bounty from the garden and fields and woods. All together, on balance, Charlie still hated picking cotton. So he was glad that the Harpers were more and more switching their crops to other things such as peanuts and potatoes.

"A dependent man is never free. Remember that, Charlie." Doc's voice stirred Charlie out of his reverie. Doc had said that same thing on more than one occasion. "Whether it is the government or your family, even your wife, if you *have* to depend upon them because you refused to learn to do for yourself, you're a bond slave. You're not a free man. That loss of freedom doesn't hit you all at once. It creeps up on you until one day you find yourself complaining a little because something you thought you were entitled to wasn't done quite the way you liked."

Oxytak was measuring his friend's health. Not wanting to tax him, he turned the talk to weather and how the spring rains had benefited the early planting. Charlie left them alone. After a while, Oxytak excused himself, saying he had some errands to run but would be back for supper. Doc sat contentedly in silent thought, his rocking chair gently creaking the repeated sound Charlie remembered from his earliest years.

The lad retrieved the latest book he was devouring, Dostoevsky's, *The Brothers Karamazov*. When he returned to the porch, the rocking had stopped and Doc was asleep, his head resting against the high back, his pipe on the bench beside him.

Charlie read all afternoon until it was time to start supper. Doc picked fresh green onions and baby carrots from the garden and washed them out back. Oxytak returned with a pitcher of lemonade, handing some papers in an envelope to the man and took the chair Doc offered him at the table.

Doc said grace, and Charlie bit into the first hush puppy he had ever made.

"Charlie," Doc announced, "you and I are going to the Democratic Convention in Chicago."

While Charlie hurried to chew and swallow the entire hush puppy he had just popped in his mouth, Doc opened the envelope Oxytak had given him. Reading from the contents, Doc spoke: "It says right here that you and I leave for Chicago on July 7. I imagine we'll still see fireworks along the way. My man, we're going to hear Mr. Bryan speak on July 9, or I don't have a friend in the Democratic Convention! Which I do, so we're going!"

Charlie sputtered cornbread and onion out of his mouth all over Doc as he tried to talk, cough, and swallow all at once. He couldn't believe his ears. Chicago! His face red, his throat scratched, Charlie croaked out, "Doc? Don't you know you're dying?" He hadn't meant to blurt that out.

Charlie's mind was teeming with thoughts about this most incredible news, only one of which was Doc's being too sick to travel. Why had he uttered that one! He was horrified and felt himself turning redder. However, Doc and Oxytak both laughed heartily at the boy's discomfort. Charlie gulped down half his glass of lemonade.

"We're going on one of Mr. Pullman's cars. I can rest there just as well, maybe even better, than I can rest here. You will see some interesting country along the way, and you can read on the train just as easily as you can read here. In fact, I already have some articles picked out that I know you'll enjoy while we travel."

Charlie couldn't believe this was true and told Doc so.

"Oh, it's true all right," Doc assured him, "and that isn't all. We are going on from Chicago to New York City. We are going to see a play, maybe two, and the statue of Liberty, at least."

"New York City?" Charlie stared at Doc, looked at Oxytak for confirmation, then stared back at Doc.

Charlie and Doc boarded train number four at five forty on the evening of July 7 where they had a through sleeper all the way to Chicago. The train was scheduled to make many stops before its arrival the following day at six forty-five p.m., a fact that Doc bemoaned but delighted Charlie all the more. Charlie had taken two short trips on the only north-south bound rail out of Jackson, the Illinois Central Railroad. He chuckled now as he remembered how as a child he had thought it unfair that a train traveling in Mississippi would be named *Illinois*.

Settled in, his heart still racing with excitement, Charlie enjoyed watching the landscape pass faster and faster as the train picked up speed. Until this moment, he had not believed this trip would actually occur. He thought everything was against it, especially Doc's health, but the man had never faltered in his resolve to make the journey. He noticed that Doc took Oxytak's herbs and tonics faithfully.

The lad thought back over the crowded previous month since Doc's surprise announcement, the tornado all but forgotten. There had been so much to attend to, including sending word to the Harpers, making many trips back and forth to the telegraph office, confirming their reservations and other arrangements, and imposing on Mr. Wilson in Chicago to get them entrance into the Coliseum on at least one night of the convention. Mr. Wilson had met Mr. Bryan and promised to try to get Charlie in on a night he would speak although Charlie got the impression that the politician was not Mr. Wilson's choice for president.

Doc insisted that Charlie submit to Mrs. Cameron taking his measurements for a new suit of clothes for the occasion. He

DIXIE MILLER STEWART

wired the measurements, including shoe size, to a haberdashery Mr. Wilson recommended. Then there were the arrangements of travel on from Chicago across the northlands to New York, the hotel reservations in that city, and a list of must-see places. At times, Charlie felt as though he was swept up into a different world were it not for the fact that vegetables needed to be picked, the garden still needed weeding, Horse was to be fed, and meals to be prepared for the two of them. Johnny's sons would take care of those things in their absence.

He fell asleep that night to the pleasant, rhythmic sounds of the train's passing through the countryside, never waking to any of the stops along the way. He found Doc back in the dining car the next morning reading a newspaper.

Mr. Wilson's carriage and driver were waiting for them at the Chicago Union Passenger Depot. The driver had a message for them confirming that they were to be Mr. Wilson's dinner guests and a postscript to Charlie that his new clothes had been delivered by the haberdashery to his hotel room. Charlie was fascinated with the cobbled streets and gaslights as they rode up Michigan Avenue and pulled up to the Congress Hotel.

The men found not one but three suits of clothes and additional shirts and shoes. They were both stunned. There was also Doc's new suit and extra shirts and jacket he had ordered. Charlie grinned, remembering the way Doc had looked almost boyish when he'd announced he was ordering himself some clothes as well, adding, "I can justify that because I'll need a good burial suit." His manner had been so deliberately comical that Charlie could only laugh.

"Doc, should I accept all these things?" Charlie asked, admiring each one. He had never had clothes so fine.

Doc laughed. "I think you'd better. They're made to fit you! Son, this is very generous of Mr. Wilson, but it isn't going to break his bank account. I ordered you just the one, but I see he's paid for everything. He took quite a liking to you, and he's grateful for the money I saved him on the land deal. This trip and these clothes are his way of showing his gratitude. Pick one to wear. We're meeting him in twenty minutes.

"Oh, and he's bringing his seventeen-year-old daughter to dinner. You know the twins are in London with Mrs. Wilson. Joe said his daughter, Rosalie is her name, flat refused to go with them, arguing that she had been to London but she'd never been to a political convention, and not even England could entice her to miss it. She seems to know her own mind, doesn't she?"

"Yes, she does. Sounds a bit like Jessie." Charlie laughed.

The concierge gave them the message that the Wilsons were running late. Doc ordered a glass of champagne and invited Charlie to go explore. They were seated in the Pompeian Room. Charlie thought he was probably embarrassing Doc by gawking at everything and was glad to stroll around. The carpeting was lush and greener than grass; wall murals, lantern chandeliers, and black leather chairs made the room seem exotic. There were perfectly polished brass spittoons, one in front of each green marble column. An enormous, ornate stone fireplace was at the opposite end.

Charlie walked over near the entrance to examine another mural. He heard a female voice, in obvious protest, as she and her companion were entering where he stood partially behind a column.

"I still can*not* believe that you think I would find a mere boy from Jackson, Mississippi, to be a...a...suitable dinner companion! I would so much rather be dining with the Fredericks. At least *their* son is mature and sophisticated. You're telling me this Charlie is, whatever it was you called him. Some sort of a 'heathen."

"*Ah, yes...Jessie.*" Charlie smiled, amused by the girl who clearly lacked her brothers' charm and had seemed to have acquired all the smug arrogance that the others had avoided. In the moment before he faced her, he imagined her to have a nose as sharp as her tongue.

Charlie stepped from around the column as they came parallel to it, bowing low immediately in front of the girl, glancing sideways at her father with a warm smile to assure him he was only amused.

"Princess Rosalie, I presume. Allow me to introduce myself. I am Charlie Harper. I stopped scalping heads several months ago, so I'm perfectly..." Standing tall now, Charlie looked at Rosalie, who except for her dark-red blush was a vision in blue. Her hat and her dress were the same pale blue as her eyes. Her hair was the color of butter, shiny and soft; her lips were fuller and even more inviting than Mrs. Thorpe's. He tried not to stare at them, but he found when he looked in her eyes, he felt oddly vulnerable.

Mr. Wilson shook Charlie's hand, saying, "I would apologize for my daughter, but I think you can handle her better than I. Charlie, it's good to see you. Welcome to Chicago! You have my permission to scalp her if she continues to harass you."

Rosalie found her voice and composure and apologized, adding with good humor, "At least you're not wearing buckskin. Shall we take our seats?"

When the evening was over, Charlie admitted to himself that he had deliberately shown off for Rosalie. She sparked both an excitement and a defensive competitiveness in him that he rarely felt. He didn't mind; in fact, he liked the challenge of showing her that he could hold his own with whomever this Fredericks boy was she thought she preferred. He began by pulling out her chair for her.

The arrival of the waiter gave both young people a chance to collect themselves. The dinner conversation was as lively as had been the last one Charlie had shared with Mr. Wilson aboard the *Monroe*. As if to read his mind, Mr. Wilson brought that up now, commenting that it had been very fortuitous that Charlie had agreed to chaperone Mrs. Thorpe. Charlie changed the subject, noting how helpful to the city Mr. Wilson's supply train had been.

The tables were filled with diners, and the talk from all was about the convention. The topic had been fully explored at the Wilson table by the time dessert arrived. Afterward, Rosalie invited Charlie to accompany her on a tour of the hotel; she especially wanted him to see the underground marble corridor. Charlie was delighted to again be walking with a beautiful girl by his side. He pointed to the gilded gold ceiling, and Rosalie admitted she'd never looked up to notice it. She guided him to the multi-tiered green glass fountain she said had been designed by Tiffany, casually taking his arm, as Charlotte had done, as both admired the remarkable work of art. He smiled inwardly. *I like her after all.*

He fell asleep telling himself he was going to kiss Rosalie Wilson before he died, possibly before he left Chicago. He was up early the next morning, asking Doc's advice on what he should wear for the day's outing. Doc had declined the sightseeing trip, saying he needed to rest up for the convention that evening. Charlie would be spending the afternoon with Mr. Wilson; unfortunately, Rosalie would not be joining them.

Mr. Wilson invited the lad to visit the stockyards and motioned him to the motorcar in front of the hotel instead of a carriage. "I like to drive it from time to time. I still enjoy it. Go ahead and get in. Take a look at it. I'll be right back."

Charlie thought the Duryea was the finest motorcar he'd ever seen, not that he had seen a whole lot. He rubbed his hand over the smooth black leather of the tufted seat, leaning down to look at the engine beneath it. Mr. Wilson had told him there were two three-horsepower motors in it. *No wonder*, he thought to himself, *it won the Chicago Times-Herald Race last year!* He had read about it not long afterward while waiting for Doc to stitch up the cut on the Miller boy's leg.

At first, Charlie hadn't been much impressed with the race when he read that Mr. Duryea had taken nine hours to go the hundred-mile round trip. He knew Horse could do better than that if he was trying to beat other horses. But he read on and learned about the bad weather conditions, snow, and mud and guessed the Duryea might have beat Horse on a good day, on a very long race, not that he would want to ever tire Horse out like that.

The young man decided the best thing about motorcars was that even if the driver got tired, the car kept going—unless, of course, it broke down. Still, when he and Doc had talked about it, Doc had inspired him with the realization that, like everything else, motorcars would get better and better so that maybe the day would come when one could conceivably go all the way from Chicago to Evanston in one hour. *That would be quite something*, Charlie thought. *Fifty whole miles in one hour.* He moved the steering tiller and felt the movement of the wheels underneath the carriage.

Mr. Wilson returned and told the lad more about the car as he drove them along the cobbled streets out of the downtown part of the city. He boasted that the Duryea could actually go twenty miles an hour in really good weather and road conditions if it didn't break down.

As they got closer to the stockyards, the stench was so awful that Charlie couldn't believe people could work here day after day. Mr. Wilson told him there was a long line of people waiting to be hired on in the stockyards. He learned there were more than twenty thousand people working in these vast grounds and buildings, almost all of them foreign immigrants from all over the world. Charlie realized that was almost three times the size of the entire city of Jackson. "Seems to me," Charlie mused, "the Union Stockyards is a city itself."

"You're right," Mr. Wilson agreed, pointing out the miles of railroad tracks that were converging into the area, "and a very productive 'city' it is. I would estimate that at least eighty percent of all the beef and pork eaten by folks in New York, Boston, Philadelphia, and Baltimore is of livestock hauled and processed through here."

Charlie nodded, adding, "I read the stockyards cover more than three hundred acres and that hundreds of thousands of head of livestock are brought here by these railroads. Charlie thought about the conditions these people must live in. He was amazed that they'd all learned to speak English. Mr. Wilson said that most had not; in fact, he observed, very few of the older first-generation immigrants ever learned the language.

"They work hard with most leaving it to their children to assimilate and learn the American way of life. For the most part, the children learn the language and translate for their parents. The various ethnic groups form their own neighborhoods, pretty much keeping to their own kind. That seems to be human nature. We naturally gravitate to what is familiar and safe. They endure a lot of hardships and persecution from locals, however, more so from other ethnic minorities."

"Do you think the immigrants knew when they came to America that life would be this difficult?" Charlie asked, wondering if the folks still felt it had been worth leaving their homeland and the life they had known.

"I think so, son. I'm sure most days they don't have time or energy to think back on what might have been had they stayed. Most of them actually left much worse conditions than they experience here and certainly had less hope for their families. I think they keep their eyes on the future opportunities they're providing their sons and daughters to be citizens of this growing, thriving nation that grants so many more freedoms than any other nation."

They drove around where the cattle were herded. Charlie stared at what seemed like miles and miles of pens containing bawling, stinking animals. As far as the eye could see, there was livestock packed together in thousands of pens. He thought he'd much rather pick cotton than work in the Chicago stockyards. His respect for the immigrants increased.

Rosalie had invited Doc and Charlie to attend the convention with them, not realizing her father had already done so. She thought to ask the driver to take the Harper Street route. "In honor of you, Charlie."

The roar of the crowd inside the coliseum and the press of Rosalie's body against his arm were dizzyingly delightful. He and Rosalie had been caught up in the spellbinding speech given by Mr. Bryan and were happy that he had received the nomination in the fifth ballot. They talked animatedly between themselves how his charisma might very well get him elected even though neither of them necessarily wanted him to be the next president.

The noise was so loud they needed to stand very close to each other to be heard. He was conscious of her body, her scent, and her hair sometimes brushing against his face. He enjoyed the softness of her bosom against his arm. At times, Rosalie's lips just barely touched his ear as she moved closer to tell him something. he bit his lower lip to keep from sighing; his heart was pounding so hard he was grateful for the noise, otherwise certain she'd be able to hear his heartbeat.

She must surely know the effect she was having on him. He was curious to know if all men felt this way, this feeling of being both more powerful and yet more vulnerable by the mere presence of a pretty woman. He was tempted to turn his lips to hers but decided he would wait for a better time to experience his first kiss, wondering if she'd ever kissed a boy—the Fredericks lad, probably.

On their last day in Chicago, Doc and Charlie were joined by Rosalie to explore the city, beginning with a drive along the lake. She took them back to the Coliseum area to where the World's Columbian Exposition had been held. While Doc sipped coffee, Charlie and Rosalie rode the world's first Ferris wheel, which had been inaugurated for the exposition. The panoramic view of the city was spectacular; the girl beside him, beautiful; the chemistry between them, exhilarating.

They learned about the subsequent Wild, Wild West Show that had been produced until recently. Ending the day over a fine dinner in a restaurant overlooking the lake, Doc invited Rosalie and Mr. Wilson to the hotel for dessert and coffee. When they pulled up to the hotel, Rosalie and Charlie spoke up as one, declining dessert, preferring, they said, to sightsee. She suggested Jackson Park "because it's even more attractive at night" and promised they would be back in an hour.

Charlie reminisced about Lafayette Park with Charlotte in St. Louis before it had been destroyed. He found Jackson Park to be just as beautiful and Rosalie just as delightful in a different way. He helped her out of the carriage, and they walked, arms entwined, along a flower-rimmed path lit by gas lamps.

As if reading his mind, Rosalie stopped walking and turned her face up to Charlie. "Would you like to kiss me?" she asked.

"Very, very much," he answered, his voice husky with the thrill of her offer. For months he had been wondering how a man goes about kissing a woman, how he puts his arms around one and touches her lips to his without bumping noses. Should he close his eyes? Should he part his lips; if so, how far? He had thought he would be very awkward until he got it down right. His concerns had been for nothing.

As naturally as he had ever done anything in his life, he gathered Rosalie in his arms, bent his head to her waiting lips, and pressed his softly against hers. All his best imaginings paled to the reality of this moment. Kissing her was unlike any other feeling he had ever known but absolutely the best one. He hadn't wanted to stop and sensed she hadn't either, but he pulled away, hugging her to his chest, neither of them speaking. He was drinking in her femininity, marveling at the feel of her body against his and how fragile she felt yet sturdy, too.

"You are incredible. That was wonderful," he finally murmured against her hair. She responded by reaching up and taking his face between her hands, pulling him down to kiss again.

After a few moments, Rosalie whispered that they needed to get back to the hotel. "My father will never again trust me out with the carriage if we stay any longer, although I assure you I don't want to leave, and I wish you were not leaving my life as suddenly as you entered it, Charlie! You're the first boy I've ever kissed!"

It wasn't until four days later that Charlie told Doc about the kiss. Doc gave the story the full respect it deserved. They were having dinner in Niblo's Garden, a New York nightspot the hotel concierge had recommended. It had been a wonderful day, another one that exceeded Charlie's expectations. Doc had taken Charlie to the Stock Exchange and all the important places he and Maddy had visited on their honeymoon here. Charlie declined climbing all the way to the top of the Statue of Liberty, not wanting to keep Doc waiting. It had been very exciting to take the ferry out to the statue and to actually touch it. It was

New York's newest attraction, a gift from the French in honor of liberty for which Americans were known.

Doc had talked about Maddy more in the past two days since their arrival in New York than he had in a long time. He told Charlie about how much he had loved his wife, how thrilled he had been to be sharing this city with her, and how proud he had felt to have her on his arm. He said if the Statue of Liberty had been here when he'd come with Maddy, they would have climbed to the top and he would have kissed her on every step. It was again seeing this romantic, sentimental side of Doc that had prompted Charlie to tell him about the kiss.

Back in their hotel room, Doc continued the talk he had begun after dinner. "Charlie, we've talked about sexual relations between a man and a woman. I want to talk to you now about making love to a woman."

Charlie was grateful to Doc for the man's willingness to discuss sensitive things while putting him at ease. No one else he knew spoke so openly as Doc did with him. Charlie felt no self-consciousness about the lessons Doc was giving him on every important part of life. Mr. Harper had talked to him about marital sex, but he had seemed perfunctory and awkward. William told Frank and Charlie more about sex than Mr. Harper did.

Doc said he thought Charlie could better understand love-making now that he had known the excitement of desire and how it felt to hold a woman in his arms. He started by confessing he had not been a virgin when he married Maddy and told Charlie that was one of his regrets. "Don't believe the stories you will hear that a man needs to be experienced. It is the experience the two of you have together that makes the sweetest memories. It is the discovering and exploring together that begin the beauty of a couple's intimate life.

"Son, the Song of Solomon is the most romantic book you'll ever read about sexual love between a man and a woman. If a person somehow misses the point made throughout the Bible that God rejoices in the sexual love between a man and his wife, he sure won't miss it there. The good book tells us that in the act of sexual intercourse, a couple becomes one flesh. That also means that there is a joining of each other's spirit. We won't know how that works until we get to heaven. Yet, we do know that there is a purity between a man and woman that is made all the more precious when both know that they are the sole and sacred holder of each other's spirit."

Charlie told Doc about worrying that it would be awkward and embarrassing the first time he kissed a girl. "But, truthfully, Doc, it felt, well, natural, and"—Charlie felt unexpectedly self-conscious—"and very good. So when a man and woman make love for the first time, they won't be self-conscious or uncomfortable. It will be natural like kissing?"

Doc sat for a minute, as if to recall his early experiences. "There's some awkwardness, but it isn't of the sort to embarrass either one. Remember, you're in love and you desire to please your mate. You have to keep in mind that she might not have had the kind of honest discussions about love and sex that you and I have."

Doc lifted his right leg for Charlie to remove his boot, never pausing in his talk. Charlie then reached down for his left leg and pulled off that boot and sock. He noticed the calluses and overgrown toenails and realized with compassion Doc was unable to bend to care for his feet now. He poured a basin of water to begin needed work on them. Charlie nodded for Doc to continue and returned his attention to his feet.

Doc didn't say how touched he was by the boy's love, but he coughed and swallowed before he could resume speaking. "Remember the little flirtations that you and Rosalie exchanged? How your own excitement grew just being near her? That is a very, very small example of the excitement that is a part of lovemaking. There is no comparison between merely wanting to have sex with a woman, no matter how beautiful she is, and the desire for the woman herself with whom you're in love, no matter how plain she might be.

"Your life's partner becomes beautiful to the extent that she feels loved, incidentally. When she knows that your desire is for *her*, not merely for sex, she acquires an inner beauty that is unmistakable. Don't forget that, son. That's a powerful influence a man has over his wife: the ability to make her feel so loved that she also feels beautiful."

"Doc, to tell you the truth, it is all a little scary. It sounds like married people have to invest a lot more in their relationship than I ever thought about, and yet it's all very exciting. I hope I can be the kind of husband you're talking about, the kind you were with Maddy. I've read Song of Solomon in the Bible. Of course, we don't speak like that now, but it taught me that a man and woman are to treasure each other's bodies."

"That's right, son. Sex is the greatest expression of love between a man and woman. When the right time comes, treasure it. Let that excitement always be there between you and your wife. You are to have the patience and the self-control worthy of being called husband! If she is worth spending your life with, she is worth waiting for and she is worth the time you take in preparing her heart, not only her body, to receive you.

"There will be seasons when she will seem like a stranger to you. There will be times when you doubt your wisdom in having married her. But remember, she sometimes feels all that about you, too. Every man has a deep desire to be loved and a secret fear that deep down he is quite unlovable.

"But a woman who says she loves her mate yet doesn't show respect for him ends up canceling out whatever she intends for that so-called love to do. She'll crush his spirit and his pride. A man needs to know that his woman respects him.

"A woman is the more tenderhearted. She needs to be shown love every day. I'm no expert on women, but a physician is often entrusted with the innermost workings of their patients' hearts and minds more than would be, say, their grocer or sometimes even their minister. Evidently, physicians aren't expected to be quite as pious as pastors." Doc laughed at his own humor.

"What kind of man do you think a woman likes…loves most, Doc?"

"Well, now that's hard to say. Depends on the woman, she can fall for a scoundrel or see the depth in a shy, quiet man. It seems to work out that a woman respects and loves the man with whom she feels most secure, safe; one who isn't going to make her doubt herself or her security. The secret is in his willingness to sacrifice his needs, even his life for her. That's a powerful reassurance. Yet, he will do that for her when he knows she trusts and believes in him. You can see that there is always interdependency between the two partners. It is a delicate yet sturdy balance, but it's been my experience that the result over time is genuine love.

"Son," Doc asked, "am I beginning to bore you? I have been bending your ear. I want so much to pass on to you the things I've learned in life. I'm afraid I may be laying a burden on you."

"Heck no!" Charlie exclaimed. " I need to know these things! I admire you for talking to me like this! I want a good marriage, not one that only produces a lot of babies. I need to know how not to have a wife turn out to be like Mrs. Harper, Doc! I want to know how to have genuine love! I just said that, but I don't even know what it means!"

"Genuine love," Doc picked up, "is something mankind has been trying to define since Adam and Eve. I personally found it to be the purified gold that remained when I stopped seeing Maddy so much in terms of what she could do for me. I think it grows to the extent that it embraces the other despite his or her faults; it thrives in an atmosphere of trust and truth. Love craves both. We test our loved one a little bit at a time, finding out if she, or he, still likes us after we've let our temper out or exposed our greed.

"As we mature past the superficial self we wanted them to fall in love with, we develop a hunger to find out if they love the real man we are—the man, for example, who actually hates his neighbor or who struggles against wanting to have sex with another woman because she brings out pure lust. Maybe we're the man who robbed our neighbor or even killed him. Perhaps we ran like a coward and let a friend bear the brunt of a bad fight.

"Every man has his secret shames, so we risk being rejected when we allow our mate to see the nakedness of our exposed, vulnerable, and shameful selves. But when we find that he or she *sees* yet doesn't turn away from us, we know we are genuinely loved. That is grace. Married love is intended to be a reflection of God's grace, and, son, it is a covenant, a sacred one.

Charlie lay awake long after Doc began snoring. He thought over the things Doc had said, committing them to memory. He wanted to grow up and have a happy home of his own; he wanted a wife some day who would respect him. He didn't think he'd have any trouble loving her, but he now understood the importance of making sure his wife would know she was loved. He knew he would never forget tonight's talk; he thought it was probably the best one he and Doc ever had.

The next day they purchased tickets in the orchestra section to "A Trip to Chinatown" in honor of Charlie's interest in the country and Doc's family's presence there. Doc had been disappointed that the setting of the play was in San Francisco instead of China, but both places were almost equally exciting to Charlie, so he hadn't minded at all. The theater was in Madison Square, one of those owned by Marc Klow and A.L. Erlanger, who Doc said now owned the majority of the theaters there.

Charlie's smile widened when "The Bowery" was sung, recognizing it as the song Jonathan Wilson had played at the piano aboard the *Monroe*. He hummed the refrain on their walk back to the hotel, listening to Doc tell him about taking Maddy to see a Shakespeare play in what he thought was the same theater. He laughed and told the lad that Maddy had always teased him that she was jealous of Lillian Russell, Doc's favorite actress at that time.

Doc was growing visibly weaker. Although Charlie pleaded for him to get a wheelchair in New York, he wouldn't hear of it. He did finally admit he was "bone tired" but reassured Charlie that their trip had been every bit as pleasing for him as it had been for his protégé and one he would not have wanted to miss for anything. He said he thanked God every night for this period of remission that allowed him to make the trip. He thought it was most fitting that his first and last trips had been with the two people he loved most in life. Charlie turned away from Doc to keep him from seeing his tears. Doc reminded him, "Charlie, you must set me free when my time comes."

Johnny surprised them at the station in Jackson by bringing Doc's horse and buggy as well as Horse for Charlie to ride. Charlie flung his arms around his old friend, exclaiming he believed Horse would actually climb into his lap if he sat down on the ground. Charlie rode ahead, taking Horse out for a run, as both loved to do, before returning to Doc's house. It seemed like half the town had gathered to welcome Doc home, who sat in his rocker, accepting the well wishes and all the news. He handed Charlie a thick envelope with familiar handwriting. He realized it was his own on the self-addressed envelope he had given Beulah last April for Jessie to write him if she needed him. He tore it open with both delight and apprehension.

It was Frank's and Jessie's answers to his letter sent before he'd left on his trip. Jessie's printing was perfect. She'd drawn three hearts on her sheet of paper with arrows through them, saying, "Jessie loves Charlie." Her message was short, reflecting the labor of a six-year-old:

> Dear Charlie, I can read now but not kursiv, so print your next letter or send more nuz paper notes. I hurd you are a hero; then we read you were going to shakago and NY. I miss you very much. I hope you do not forget me. Hurry home. I'll be waiting for you. I love you. Jessie.

When they had been back home about a week, Doc called Charlie into his office after supper where he had laid out on his large desk unfamiliar papers and boxes. He showed him the deed to his house made out to Charlie and a small investment account also in his name. He had asked the lad several months ago to cosign on his checking account. Doc now showed Charlie the amount of cash he had in the account and explained that there were no outstanding debts. He had made out a list of things Charlie would need to take care of, including where and how he wanted his belongings to be disposed of and what he wanted given to his brother and sister and his nephew and nieces. There were special things he wanted Charlie to have; among them were his pocket watch, his medicine bag and instruments, his leather-bound books, saddle, and guns.

Charlie rubbed his fingers across the fine leather of *The Handbook of Human Physiology*. The contents had always fascinated him; he pretended to read the title again, murmuring aloud the name of the author, Johannes Peter Muller. He kept his eyes downcast to conceal the raw pain he knew they reflected.

Everything Doc had selected for him was further evidence of the man's love for the boy over the years; he remembered all of Charlie's favorite things.

"It isn't much, son, but it will be a stake for you in whatever you want to do in the world. If you want to sell the house, go right ahead. John Davis and I have taught you how to take care of those things. If you want to rent it out, that will be fine, assuming you can find a renter you can trust. I suppose the Harpers will need you to stay there and help with the farm, but you will have this place to escape to if Julia gets bad again after this baby.

"I thought long and hard about whether to spend money on this trip. I saw it as your money and made the decision to do something with it that you would benefit from in a way that you would never have done for yourself. I think you've had a taste of sophistication." Doc chuckled, deliberately choosing that word, remembering Rosalie's comment. "Since that's what the girls want now."

Charlie interrupted his mentor long enough to dish up two bowls of peach cobbler and brought Doc's to him with a glass of milk. He watched Doc take his first spoonful and nod appreciatively.

Between bites, the man continued. "I want to tell you these things! You're a survivor, and you adapt, son. You can go anywhere and be anything you want to be. You're very well read, at least as much so as any college-educated man. You can discuss everything from the social concerns of a Booker T. Washington to the essence of meaning of Plato and Aristotle. You can quote an ancient Confucius or these more modern concepts all of which seek to leave God out of the picture, like Darwin. You have a practical knowledge. You can pick cotton, and you can sell it, stock a store, set a broken arm." He took another bite and a sip of milk. "Um-mmm…and make a mean cobbler!

"Now, I feel better about leaving you. This last, these experiences of some travel and an understanding of these United States as well as a few of the niceties of life are good finishes to most of what I wanted for you up to adulthood. You'll settle on a life's work when the time comes. I don't doubt that. No, son, no one is ever going to look down their nose at you for being a half-breed! I couldn't be more proud of you if you were my son. Why, you are my son. You have always been that in my heart."

For the second time that summer, Charlie awoke to find Oxytak looking down at him; this time there was no smile on his face. Charlie bolted out of bed, pulling on his breeches, asking, "It's Doc, isn't it? It's Doc. How did you know? How do you know these things?"

Charlie stared down at Doc's simple casket. The man had picked it out himself last spring. The minister had spoken fine words, as had the many of the town's leaders. Charlie's words were for Doc's ears only: "You are...you were the finest man I ever knew. Whatever good there is in me is mostly because of you. I want to be like you as best I can be. I choose to honor your memory by striving to have your integrity...and to try to match your character...to keep your kind of faith and to do something good in the world, as you have always done. For all the days of my life, I will thank God for you. Good-bye, Doc. It...it is well with my soul."

Saying good-bye didn't change anything for Charlie. He continued to stare at the casket, desperately wanting to raise the lid and help Doc climb out. Special moments of all the years he had loved this man flashed through his mind. Doc taught him so many important things, but Charlie realized in this moment he hadn't taught him how to let go of what he loved most. He knew his friend was already in a wonderful place. That knowledge gave him some comfort, but he wasn't prepared for this desolate feeling of abandonment.

Most of Jackson surrounded him, paying tribute to her very favorite son; but Charlie had never felt so alone. Every important event of his life had been shared with Doc, and now the most important one could never be. He was paralyzed in his grief, knowing he should turn away or pick up the shovel and cover the casket with the freshly turned earth. He could not move.

A hand crept quietly into his—small, soft, warm, and strangely loving. Charlie looked down at Jessie's upturned face. "Jessie!" He grabbed her and hugged her to his chest. She flung her arms around his neck, squeezing tight.

"Charlie, I missed you so much! I won't die. I am always going to be with you. Don't cry, Charlie, I love you!" She placed her small hand on his cheek, looking into his eyes. "Charlie, I'm sorry for all the things I said. I didn't mean any of them. I didn't want Doc to die! I'm sorry I didn't say good-bye to you. I won't ever do that again! I'll always, always be your best friend!"

Charlie laughed and cried, hugging her tightly before finally setting her down. "Thank you, Jessie. You're the best little sister a boy ever had!" She clung to his hand.

Frank, Lilly, and the rest of the Harpers surrounded him. Mrs. Harper, large with child, had sympathy in her eyes. Frank shook Charlie's hand heartily and then hugged him; the family circled him in support. Oxytak waited until all their condolences had been given then clasped Charlie's shoulders, looking deeply into his eyes, silently reassuring him he would be there when needed.

Frank borrowed a horse from Johnny to ride alongside Charlie. They rode a mile or two in silence, Frank having already told his friend everything there was to tell about his summer. He kept glancing over at him. "You're different, Charlie. It's like…it's like you're older than me now. You're a man, and I'm not!"

"You think its maybe because I kissed a girl?" Charlie teased, racing ahead of Frank, his effort to lighten their moods lasting only for that brief moment. Still riding ahead of his friend, he became aware of the song playing in the back of his mind since leaving Doc's gravesite. It was another he'd learned in New York, "After the Ball." Tears again welling in his eyes, he sang aloud the last line of the refrain: "Many the hopes that have vanished, after the ball."

Chapter 7

Charlie leaned back on the two rear legs of his chair, appreciating the starry, moonless sky. It was after 9:00 p.m., but he wasn't sleepy despite the tiring day that had included chopping the last of the cotton. His attic room was stifling hot for this time of the year; there was not a hint of a breeze through the small window. The children had been sent to their rooms earlier than usual. He wondered if Mrs. Harper had a tizzy fit that day. She had just finished nursing Cornelius, who was born too soon after Ben, he thought.

He had winced when for whatever reason Mr. Harper decided to again plant more cotton instead of another crop. He'd chopped alongside the help all day and then driven the neighboring workers home. Now it was done; that was a good feeling every spring. Despite having to pick the cotton again, he looked forward once more to negotiating the prices come fall. Mr. Harper was pleased with the price he'd gotten for it last year. He'd told Charlie then that he would be sending him to negotiate his crop prices from now on. Mr. Harper had placed more and more responsibilities on the shoulders of Frank and Charlie these past four years since Doc's death. Frank liked the actual fieldwork more than Charlie, while Charlie more enjoyed the business side of farming.

However, there was another reason he was sitting out on the veranda. He needed to think without being distracted by the heat. The veranda after dark was a perfect place for that.

There were two things eating at him this evening. The first, as always, was Jessie. More specifically, her seeming to be more devious with him lately; she seemed evasive whenever he asked how she had spent her day. He had twice asked her about bruises he'd seen on her arms and was pretty sure she hadn't been telling him the truth when she said she'd fallen off the fence. She had also cried out yesterday when he patted her back, as though he had hurt her, and then denied she had cried. He allowed her that little deception, not wanting to further upset her. He resolved to take her aside tomorrow and find out what was bothering her. Whatever it was, he would do all he could to take care of it.

The second matter was less immediate but was a concern that had been gnawing at him for several months. He'd picked up mail today from Doc's box. He still had mail sent there because it made him feel closer to him. Today there was a letter from China with very worrisome news, frustrating because there was little if anything he could do about it.

The Whitmores kept in touch with him, including their daughter, Betsy; he appreciated their continuing contact. A few months back, they had written about the anti-Christian movement re-emerging in opposition to what many Chinese felt was too much western encroachment into their culture, particularly by missionary evangelicals.

Charlie knew the nation had good, decent, hard-working, and enterprising people but seemed always to have corrupt governments. Further, the governments never seemed to be in agreement as to how to protect their people and stabilize their land, although he understood some of that was due to China's vastness. He knew China had been through repeated cycles of wars, plagues, serious droughts followed by devastating floods, and increasing invasions, first by the Mongols centuries back and more recently by European nations.

Charlie's lifelong fascination with China led him to read everything he could get his hands on about its history and politics. He'd read every book on China in Jackson library. He recalled learning in school that her ancient people had invented paper and printing and had been the first to produce silk. One of his treasures from Doc was a finely crafted compass; he knew the Chinese were also credited with inventing the compass.

Those were all very important contributions to the world but said little about the inner workings of the current Qing Dynasty and the court intrigue.

He reflected on their more recent cycle of wars, enforced treaties, losses, and national humiliations. Although it had started before his birth, the country had apparently never recovered. Looking at the situation from China's perspective, Charlie tried to imagine how Americans would react if they were being constantly invaded or assaulted from without and within.

Most Americans had finally pulled together against the British. Charlie recognized it had been due to strong leaders of moral courage and integrity, and even that had been largely due to their willingness to sacrifice everything for the greater good. He wasn't sure how that could ever happen between peoples so different in their foundational beliefs. He marveled again at the elegance and brilliance of the United States Constitution and the wisdom of its designers.

He knew Western influence on China had been increasingly far reaching: investments of money, technology, philosophy, and religion had poured into the country long before he was born. It was on this wave that Doc's brother and sister-in-law had gone there with many other Christian missionaries to evangelize. And it was because of this that they now found themselves embroiled in another internal struggle.

They had fallen in love with the Chinese people and put down roots there, raising their family and now their granddaughter. They seldom could afford to return to the States but less and less often seemed to mind that. Now, things were different. If Charlie read their letters right, they were anticipating a return cycle of the violence in whose heels they had followed so many decades ago.

Today, it had been particularly alarming to Charlie to read that the Whitmores had been among those who had resisted several minor attacks against their town. He learned that Christians lived in growing fear, no longer comfortable going out alone. Noting the tensions and the dangers were increasing, they wrote they were being encouraged to return to the United States. They were proud of their work there—many thousands of Chinese had converted to Christianity—but now the converts, too, were being persecuted and threatened.

Absorbed in his thoughts, Charlie paid no attention to the voices now coming through the open windows from the parlor. He recognized them as Mr. and Mrs. Harper and assumed they would be joining him on the veranda to get out of the heat now that Ben and the baby were finally asleep.

Instead, they lit a lamp and seemed to be arguing. He heard Mr. Harper's more muffled voice, saying, "Julia, I completely trust the lad. He wouldn't lay a hand on Jessie. He loves her like a sister. Besides, I depend on him more than on anyone else. With Moses so infirm, Charlie is the only one in this house who cares whether this farm turns a profit or even survives."

Mrs. Harper's voice was one decibel below the shrilled tone she acquired when she was working into a tizzy. Charlie knew that the only reason it was kept somewhat in check right now was that she did not want to wake the babies.

"He is a half-breed!" She almost spat the words out. "He's half wild! You don't know what that kind is capable of doing! He's not a boy anymore. He's a man. I've seen the way he looks at our girls! Jessie won't leave him alone. Why, she thinks she's in love with him. Does that sound like a sister to you? She climbs all over him! I literally had to give her a beating three times last week for following him around, going up to his room. They're both too old for that now. I will beat her every day if I have to until he leaves here or she finally hates him for the trouble he causes her. Do you hear what I'm saying?"

Charlie didn't wait for Mr. Harper's answer. Now he understood Jessie's behaviors and why even his funniest faces didn't make her laugh anymore.

The sound of his chair legs striking the veranda floor was like a gunshot as he rose and stormed back through the door into the dimly lit parlor. The Harpers were startled. Mrs. Harper recovered first and started to accuse him of eavesdropping. For a second time in Charlie's memory, Mr. Harper shut her up.

Charlie was infuriated by Mrs. Harper's accusations and felt cut to the bone by them, but he was more horrified that Jessie had been her mother's scapegoat because of him.

"Mrs. Harper." His voice contained a steeled fury she had never heard in him. For a moment, she shrank back but then took a step closer, her chin out.

"I don't believe for one minute that you think I'm capable of harming Jessie or Lilly or anyone else in this family. If you truly do entertain such thoughts, then I would question your sanity more than I already do! You are to be pitied more than any other human being: To beat your daughter is vile! To pervert her innocence is contemptible!"

Charlie couldn't remember if he had ever been allowed to speak a sentence to Mrs. Harper on any matter that long. Nor could he remember a time when she had been too shocked to find some demeaning words of insult to return. She was white-faced now; he hadn't seen that in her either. She opened her mouth to speak.

Still fueled by his own fury and indignation from this woman's allegations, Charlie held up the palm of his hand to stop her from speaking. He was not at all surprised that she clamped her mouth shut again. For once with her he felt in righteous control of the situation.

He turned to Mr. Harper. "Sir, I will leave your home, and I thank you for your kindness to me all these years. I've always benefited from your teachings and guidance. You have been very generous.

"You taught me to respect ladies, but, sir, you should have taken this lady over your knees years ago. She has emasculated you, and you've let her. She's made a mockery of your role as head of this home before your sons. They have never witnessed you showing them what a husband ought to be, beyond a breeder of children whom you then ignore until it is too late for them.

"But worse than that, she has emasculated your sons and repeatedly abused all your children—Jessie, most of all—and you've turned your back on it over and over again. I have been taught to believe there is equality in marriage. But, Mr. Harper, there has never been equality between you two! Your wife has been a tyrant for as long as I can remember. And you, sir, with all due respect for the fine Christian man you are, and for admiration for your courage in standing for emancipation in the face of strong opposition, and despite the fact that you've produced nine babies, you, sir, are impotent!"

Mrs. Harper raised her hand to slap Charlie, opening her mouth to protest. But Mr. Harper stayed her with his arm. "Julia, shut up! Charlie is going to leave, but he is going to be allowed to have his say before he goes!"

Charlie nodded a thank you before turning back to Mrs. Harper and continuing, his voice cold and controlled. "You have looked for reasons to vent your hatred onto Jessie all her life. To learn now that you are using me as your excuse to beat her into submission is more than despicable. I do not find pleasure in being rude to you, but you do not recognize truth any other way.

"You have nursed me at your breast, and I am eternally grateful for that. But I have very little respect left for you, and I am embarrassed for you. To think that I have lived in your home all these years and you despised me for my Indian blood is to your shame, not mine. I will never understand why you permitted me to stay, but I am leaving now." Nodding his head again to Mr. Harper, Charlie said, "Good evening, sir."

Charlie strode back out the front door, hurrying around the house to the barn. He saddled Horse and mounted as Lilly, Jessie, Frank, and Beulah all in their nightclothes ran up to him, crying. Jessie thrust an envelope into his hand and turned and ran out of the barn. Lilly hung her head, saying nothing. That she had even joined her siblings in this act of near defiance of her mother showed courage unusual for her. Charlie tilted her chin up and gave her his best big-brother smile.

"Lilly of the valley, you are a fine young woman. Take care of Ben and Cornelius, and be a little more patient with Jessie, okay?" She nodded her head, keeping her eyes downcast.

Frank was crying and apologizing for his mother, begging Charlie not to leave. Charlie looked at him with pity. "Frank, I love you like a brother, but you are just not getting this, are you? Frank, leave! Go to the academy; join the military; go to the Philippians; save yourself; reclaim your dignity. Be a man!"

He had dismounted and had grasped Frank by his shoulders, punctuating each point he was making with a shake to them. Frank looked in his eyes while silent tears rolled down his cheeks. Charlie hugged his lifelong friend for a long moment resisting the gnawing doubt that Frank would ever fully regain the courage he had shown when he offered his life for those of his siblings. Maybe it was his speech impediment that held him in bondage more than his mother's control. Where was the Frank who had punched out John Davis?

He turned and put his arms around Beulah. "Beulah, I will never forget you. I love you, and I thank you for your goodness to me all these years." Tears streamed down Beulah's face as she sobbed her love for him, telling him how much she would miss him, beseeching him to get word to them of his whereabouts.

Crossing diagonally through familiar meadows, Charlie rode Horse less hard than he would have liked out of consideration for his age. They wound their way through trees and down the trails to the hut where he was born. He had long ago created this shorter route. He stopped first at the stream where both he and Horse drank deeply, allowing himself the small respite of appreciating that the stars reflecting from the water sparkled like diamonds.

He stooped to enter the hut, finding matches and a lamp where he had last left them. He sat cross-legged and wept. He wept because of his fury and because of the way his place in the Harper family had been so easily tossed aside by Mrs. Harper. He wept for all of Jessie's pain because of him, for pity of the Harpers whom he loved so much, and for another wrenching good-bye; for aloneness that was becoming all too familiar since Doc had died, and for the hatred that could live in the heart of a mother. When his tears stopped, he bowed his head in prayer, grateful that he still belonged to a loving God. At last, feeling more at peace, he remembered the envelope Jessie had handed him and took it from his pocket.

DIXIE MILLER STEWART

"Charlie, I heard what Mama said. Don't blame you. Must talk. Will be at your place (*not Doc's, yours*)," she emphasized, "tomorrow at eleven. Love forever. I mean it! Jessie."

"Jessie gets it." Charlie spoke to himself. "She always has, but she has paid for her insight. She may be the only one left at home who does understand the insidious poison in that family." Charlie didn't know whether to be alarmed by the risk she was taking or happy that he would have the chance to say good-bye and to talk with her about life things he felt she needed to know. He remembered that Mrs. Harper was going to the neighbor's to help prepare for a viewing. Perhaps Jessie could get here and back without getting caught.

She arrived early bringing a lunch box that Beulah had pre-pared for them both containing enough food for a dozen people. Beulah and Jessie had also gathered the things most important to him and filled saddlebags.

They sat on the rocky overhang, Charlie dangling his feet in the water; Jessie's not yet reaching that far. She had waded across the brook, holding tightly to his hand. Despite the unusu-ally warm day, Jessie had worn her prettiest dress for him—her Christmas dress, she called it, and was careful not to get it wet. He had gathered fruit for them, not thinking she might bring food. He should have known Beulah would see to it that they were fed.

Her eyes were red from crying. His heart was still heavy with everything that had transpired last evening; but most of all, he hurt for Jessie. He knew she had a crush on him in her little girl way. It was completely innocent. She was a sister to him and a very pretty one at that. Already he noticed boys her age showing off for her and knew that before long she'd have a crush on one or two if she followed in her older sisters' footsteps.

She kept feeding him bites of food as he talked, sometimes pushing pieces directly into his mouth. He felt toward her what

Doc must have felt toward him years back in wanting Charlie to learn as much about life as he could cram down him in the short amount of time he had. When he had convinced her he was full, he began to talk in earnest.

He told her about life's demands for courage, sacrifice, wisdom, and faith and made suggestions on how she might better treat her mother without sacrificing her own person. He reminded her she needed to trust God more and to say her prayers, especially when she felt scared or alone. He talked to her about boys and how to be sure she would be allowing only young men with good intentions to court her.

More than once he impressed upon her that she must not only guard her affections but that she must also guard her temperament. "However, your little temper has always been something attractive about you. You've not used it to insult or abuse people but because you've refused to be demeaned and coerced. But don't become like your mother. Jessie, remember that a woman has more power over a man with just her love and respect for him than she ever will with her tongue and tizzy fits! Okay, girl, that's my last… brotherly talk. I hope I've covered everything." The meaning of his words made him want to cry.

She had listened to him, wiping her nose on his shirt and rolling her eyes once when he mentioned other boys. However, anger flashed in her eyes with his last remark.

"Charlie Harper, you are blind and stubborn! I do not love you like a brother. I love you like a girl loves a boy! I always have. Right this minute, I love you more than any boy has ever been loved! I know I'm not yet a woman, but I will mature early. Mama and Beulah and your Dr. Thorpe all say that. I think more like a woman than a child. I always have. You've even told me that before.

"I know you're a wise thinker, and you get things done. You're not afraid of things. You were right in what you said to daddy last night, even about my brothers. And, Charlie, you are very handsome! You are the most handsome man in the whole state. All the girls say that about you. I tell them all to just keep away from you because I'm going to marry you and we're going to have a lot of babies!"

Charlie sat listening to her, amused, saddened, puzzled, yet also strangely uplifted by what he was hearing, even knowing it was from the mouth of a child. Although, he reminded himself, she was eleven, and she was more mature than the other Harper children had been at that age. He wondered somewhere in the back of his mind why he was giving any credibility at all to her professions of love for him.

Her remarks made her all the more endearing but certainly not as mature as she seemed to think she was. Still, he didn't want to insult and hurt her by disagreeing or referring to her young age. He sat struggling with his own pain about leaving her, acknowledging to himself he had stayed on at the Harpers in large part because he felt she needed him. He couldn't even begin to imagine how he would ever see her or Frank again.

Taking advantage of his silence, Jessie continued. "I have always planned to marry you. I wish you would take me with you right now and I'd never see Mama again. I want to go with you more than anything in the world!" She started crying again.

He wiped her tears before he spoke. "Jessie-girl, I can't take you with me!"

"Why not?" she demanded. "I can cook and sew and garden. I can clean house and wash clothes. I can learn to polish your boots, look after Horse... Whatever you need done, I can be a big help to you, Charlie. Please, please!" Again, she fought back tears but seemed determined not to manipulate him with them but only to state her case.

"Jessie, Jessie, listen to me." Taking her chin, he looked into her eyes, oddly stirred by deep feelings he didn't recognize; his heart beat harder. He felt as though he was being drawn into a deep current and somehow unworthy of the innocence and purity shining from her eyes. He saw the darker flecks in their green and thought they were more beautiful than he'd ever seen them. They were steady, unwavering, and courageous, and for the first time, he saw the beautiful young woman she was going to be, not merely the pretty little girl he'd always thought. He pulled his hand back and turned his head away, surprised by his feelings. *Did Mrs. Harper see something in me I don't see?*

"Charlie, I saw love in your eyes!" Jessie's voice was lilting.

"Of course, you did." Charlie tried to sound lighthearted. "You know I've loved you since you grabbed my finger and caught my heart at the same time! You were maybe one day old."

"No, I mean I saw *real* love." She smiled smugly. "It was the kind of look Dr. Thorpe gives Mrs. Thorpe and Andrew gives Belle when she's not looking and he doesn't know I am! Oh, Charlie, say you'll take me with you. I cannot even bear to think about life without you!"

He wished he could. He knew his only chance to resolve the situation was to appeal to her common sense; she seemed to have more than her share for her age. "Jessie, you told me a minute ago that you have always needed to think like an adult. I need you to hear me out and think like one now, all right?"

"All right. But I don't think I'm going to like it," she begrudged.

"No, I don't suppose you will, but here it is, and you will know it is truth. First, I'm too old for you."

"But I'll catch up to you, Charlie!"

"Second, your mother will never permit you to marry me because I'm a half-breed. Your father might not object to that, but he would definitely object to your marrying me without my having a way of supporting you. Wouldn't you agree?"

"Yeeees." She dragged the word out reluctantly, her chin resting on her bent knees.

"Okay, then I must win one of them over, and it isn't going to be your mother because I can't change what I am. But I can change what I do. I must go away. I must leave you for a while until I've, well, made my mark in the world. A man has to make his mark. You wouldn't want a husband that wasn't a provider for all those babies you want to have!"

He knew he was not telling the complete truth. Her father would never agree to their marriage, even if that was something Charlie wanted. Her father expected to marry her off to a wealthy landowner at the very least. Charlie hoped she'd someday marry a man she loved and respected who could make her happy.

He needed some way of appeasing Jessie for now. He was counting on the fact that she would forget him in time, at least forget her infatuation with him, and find a more appropriate match. *This is like me with Charlotte in a way*, he realized, remembering he still had a bit of a crush on her after more than four years.

"Besides, Jessie, you would always regret"—he put a finger to her lips to shush her from interrupting—"leaving home in a fit of angry protest just because you were mad at your mother. You need to make important decisions like that when you are cool headed and using reason."

Jessie said nothing but reached over and took his hand, placing it on top of hers in her lap, bending each of his fingers around it just so. He watched her, overwhelmed with tenderness and swallowing hard, feeling as if he were abandoning her yet oddly feeling he was also being abandoned. But he knew in neither case had the choice been his to make.

She looked at him, her eyes brimming with tears, then back down at their entwined hands. "Who will take care of me now? Who will make me laugh and dry my tears now?" She took his other hand and laid it over their joined two then worked her free right hand beneath his. "Who's going to hold my hand when I'm afraid and tell me things about far away places and be glad to see me every evening? I love you, Charlie!"

She looked up at him again, stating what for her was a simple, obvious conclusion. "God meant us to be together. That's exactly why he put you in our family. We're forever, Charlie."

The trust he saw in her eyes made him want to cry. The first time he'd ever felt strong like a man and protective was when Jessie held his finger, even though he'd been a young boy. He felt that way every time she took his hand; and despite the lump in his throat, he felt that way now.

"Charlie, you just have to come back! I will love you until I die. Wherever you are in this whole big world, I will be there in my heart. I will think of you every day and pray for you every night, and I will wait for you to come back for me when you have made your mark, no matter how long it takes. Come home to me, Charlie. I'll always be waiting."

In ways he could not have explained, he was deeply moved by this moment. Her gestures, her promises, and the sweetness of her made him want to hug her. He did not because he was afraid she would misunderstand his feelings. He still had concern for how she would get along in his absence, but now he wondered how he would get along without her in his life.

"Charlie, how long does it take for a man to make his mark?" She was still looking into his eyes, hers full of trust and complete faith that whatever he said was an absolute truth she could count on.

"Jessie, I don't know. I'd think three or four years—"

"Three or four years! That's forever! That's one-third of the whole time I've been alive! Charlie, that's too long!" Again, tears spilled down her cheeks.

"Jessie-girl, no matter how mature you are, you would still be too young to marry a man before then. Think about it! Besides, I'll be starting from scratch. I don't have a plan or much money.

I will be spending most of my waking hours making a living, so I couldn't even take care of you. He kept their hands together as long as he could, sensing that this would be the last loving touch he would have for a very long time.

She took a deep breath and sighed long. "I knew you wouldn't take me with you. I guess I should be glad you'll come back some day. Last night, when you were saddling Horse, I was afraid I'd never, ever see you again!

"I will spend the time doing things that will make me a better wife to you. I'll read more and get smart like you. I'll learn to cook and to wear a corset. I'll grow bosoms. Frank told me boys like them. So do I, for that matter. I think Mrs. Thorpe has really pretty bosoms, don't you, Charlie?"

His laughter released tension and infected her, and she began laughing and crying as she had done at the rock pile so many years ago. Flashing back to that time, Charlie remembered that her crying and laughing had been under very similar circumstances. She had expressed her intention to marry him, and he was telling her he would be going away for a while.

"Okay, Jessie-girl, you need to get back now." His heart broke to say the words; he was being set adrift from all his moorings; the hurt from that was very raw. Jessie and Frank were as much a part of his life as Horse and as Doc had been. Now even Horse was very old. Oxytak's father was dying. Mrs. Thompson had passed. The China Whitmores were in possible danger. The world was changing into distorted shapes and dark colors, and nothing seemed certain anymore. Tomorrow, perhaps he would look upon his new life with a sense of challenge and freedom; but today, it was only about letting go of the known, the familiar, and, most of all, the people he loved.

"Will you kiss me on my mouth, Charlie?" Her face filled with hope as she turned it up to him and smiled her prettiest.

"No, I will not, young lady!" he scolded. "But I'll kiss you on the cheek and give you a hug." They hugged as if there might not be a tomorrow for them.

Jessie leaned back to again take his face in her hands, searching his eyes. "Charlie, if it's four long years I might lose hope that you'll remember me!"

That's what I'm counting on, Charlie thought. He didn't tell her that he knew when the time came she would find a man more suitable for her. He felt a pang in thinking about Jessie finding a more suitable mate. That was another unexpected feeling, almost like jealousy. He would have to examine that, too, there were so many things to take apart and think through now.

She was still holding his face in her hands. "Charlie, say the words. Say, 'I will come back for you, Jessie, when I have made my mark.'" He made the promise, thinking ahead that having given it, he would keep his word but knowing she would no longer hold him to it by the time his mark was made

Jessie wanted to sit on her horse backward so she could see him for as long as possible. He wouldn't let her but stood watching after her as she stopped again and again to turn back and blow him a kiss. He knew she was crying; so was he.

"Hurry back to me, Charlie, I'll be waiting for you!"

He woke at dawn, took Horse for a ride, and now was pouring his second cup of coffee. He carried Doc's rocker out front; it still felt as though Doc should be joining him. He'd even reached for two cups. He'd thought a lot on his ride about what he wanted to do with his life and future. Doc had helped him develop so many interests, including practicing medicine. He considered politics only because he believed honest people with convictions were needed. But he knew he wanted to be self-employed; he still favored having his own store.

Jessie and all the Harpers had been heavy on his mind the past few days, but he couldn't spend too much time thinking about them. It led him nowhere except further down the trail of loneliness. Still, he admitted that Mrs. Harper had at least done him the one favor of forcing him to establish himself as an independent adult.

He'd picked up three papers and opened the *New York World* now to catch up on news. America had been at war with Spain in defense of Cuba and the Philippines, finally purchasing the latter. However, the Filipinos in turn declared war on America, wearied from hundreds of years of subjugation. They wanted freedom and autonomy.

The explosion of the *USS Maine* this past February was no longer front-page news, but apparently it still had people arguing over whether it had been an accident or a deliberate act by Spain, which of course, that nation denied. Charlie wondered briefly if instead it had been a deliberate act by the freebooters that had been so intent on America going to war with Spain in the first place. He knew both Cleveland and McKinley had opposed going to war. For that matter, most of the more influential nations opposed America on this, having sympathized with Spain instead.

He didn't know what had happened with the *Maine* and doubted truth would ever be determined, but he did believe Spain had been excessively abusive and cruel to the Cubans, and he knew Cuba needed America's help in order to eventually be independent. However, he guessed it was Doc's influence on him that he no longer trusted the motive of any politician in any nation.

Footsteps on the boardwalk interrupted Charlie's thoughts; he was happy to see it was Mr. Davis, who accepted his offer for a cup of coffee. Returning with it, Charlie noticed Mr. Davis reading the open headlines and commented that he, too, had been reading about the Philippine situation.

"Yes," Mr. Davis acknowledged, blowing on his coffee to cool it. "It was certainly a bloody one they fought with Spain for their freedom, so they're not taking it well that America has now, in effect, purchased it for them."

"I don't understand the process of how America or any nation can simply decide to annex another entire population," Charlie responded. "Yet, reading in the *Journal*, I saw that Congress had made Hawaii a territory, after having annexed that island."

Mr. Davis chuckled. "Yes, Hawaii is so far away and now a US Territory. However, I think it has been a clear understanding among the major nations that neither Cuba nor the Philippines are equipped and prepared to suddenly begin self-rule. It may be true of Hawaii as well. I haven't followed that situation."

"I guess we can't blame the Filipinos for not agreeing with the rest of the world. It is their land." Charlie thought to himself that while he might not trust the individual politician, he trusted the intentions of America and its commitment to eventual freedom and self-government for other nations.

Mr. Davis turned down a second cup, needing to get back to the store. "Charlie, Moses dropped by yesterday. He had come by here, but you were out. He said he stopped by the stable and saw Horse was not there either. He was worried that you might have left the area. He told me what happened with the Harpers and wanted me to pass on to you that you were one of the finest young men he'd ever known.

"Son, if I can be of help to you, let me know. I mean that. I'd bring you into the store with me without a second thought if I didn't have two sons who can't wait for me to turn it over to them." The two men shook hands; the sounds of Mr. Davis's footsteps walking down the boardwalk seemed to accentuate Charlie's homesickness.

He sat awhile, feeling an ache in his throat, before turning his attention back to the newspapers. A piece about China caught his eye. It turned out to be a reference to an earlier article printed a year ago quoting Secretary of State John Hay regarding the United States preference for an open-door trade policy in China. There was nothing new in it, the point being made that if the Boxers succeeded in this latest uprising, trade would be closed to all foreigners. Reading between the lines, Charlie understood that to mean America was going to somehow intervene, if only for its own interests. He hoped that was good news; it would perhaps guarantee safety for the Whitmores, but it would also mean another military engagement for America. Perhaps he should volunteer to fight with Mr. Roosevelt.

A week later, he rode Horse to the post office and then over to the telegraph office to see if his query about joining the military had been received there. Lately, every time he saddled Horse he felt a twinge of sadness, knowing there would be another good-bye with Horse, whom he knew would grieve for him as well. It might be years before he returned. Horse would die in his absence. He'd been giving him extra carrots every day from the garden and making sure he had sugar lumps in his pocket at all times.

Old Mr. Campbell looked up, surprised when the lad walked in. "Charlie, you must have a telegraph circuit in your brain. This just now arrived for you. Hope it's what you were looking for!"

Charlie grabbed the message, astonished to see it was from China. It read, "Parents, grandparents killed in uprising. I alone survived. Leaving for Peking Legation Compound for safety. Letter follows. Betsy Whitmore."

"Mr. Campbell." Charlie's urgency startled the old man. "Are you able to send an immediate reply to the office from which this wire just came? Oh, and I want the same message sent to the American Legation in Peking."

He printed out: "Stay at the legation for my arrival. Leaving Jackson this date." Charlie handed Mr. Campbell enough money to cover the cables and more, calling over his shoulder as he ran out of the office. "If I receive an answer, will you send it back that I've departed?" He didn't wait for an answer. He hopped on Horse, both of them forgetting the age of the animal.

Chapter 8

Charlie crammed clothing in the bag Doc had last used for their trip, deciding at the last minute to include his moccasins and buckskins. He liked traveling in them. He wrote a note for Johnny and one to Oxytak.

He pulled out the boxes of letters to retrieve the several maps Betsy had drawn and sent him of points of interest there. She had mentioned in two or three letters her interest in cartography and also sent her fine work to him from time to time, knowing of his interest in China. He remembered her first sketches of the location where they lived near Tianjin, noting the Chinese characters for street names. In subsequent letters, she sent detailed sketches of sequential maps of the eighty-mile railroad they traveled to Peking. He had pored over them, even practicing the Chinese characters for some of the streets and the two cities until he had them memorized. He was very impressed that Betsy could speak, read, and write Chinese.

Doc had introduced them by mail; although once, when Charlie was six or seven, the family visited from China. He was with Oxytak during most of their visit and so missed spending time with the China Whitmores, as he called them. He remembered Betsy as nice and smart and thought of her as vaguely pretty from the photographs her parents sent. They developed a friendship over the years based on his interest in her adopted homeland and her delight in having someone her age in America who shared her interests. Betsy and all the Whitmores knew him mostly through Doc; but because of Doc, they wrote to him with affection.

The map he was particularly interested in now was of the legation compound in Peking. Mr. Whitmore had once described the activities carried out by legations as similar to lesser embassies, so Charlie thought he understood where Betsy was and what protection she should have. Her father's comments were written only four months earlier, and now he was dead, so what of the protection now?

He studied the compound in Peking, committing everything to memory, along with the locations of each representative legation from other nations. Putting his finger on the American Legation, he imagined his cable was being read in that very dot right this minute. Her drawings were precise. *She is a natural cartographer*, he thought. He once sent her the addresses of Rand-McNally in Chicago. He told her about the history of their fairly new partnership and suggested she send her maps to them.

Charlie withdrew his savings from the bank but left untouched the money Doc had given him. He asked for instructions on how to have money transferred to another bank should that ever be necessary, and, just in case, he wrote out a will leaving all his assets to Jessie, including Doc's house. On second thought, he drew a line through that last part and wrote in Betsy's name for the house, giving her first right of refusal of her uncle's home and then Jessie as secondary. Mr. Smith notarized his signature and told him that would suffice.

Mr. Smith listened, nodding his understanding to Charlie's explanation about why he felt it was his personal responsibility to go help Betsy Whitmore. "I don't know who is left alive there in China who would be able to help her or how the missionary system works in that respect. I don't have time to waste to learn they may be unable to help. This is the only small thing I can do for Doc." The banker wished Charlie well and urged him to notify him if he could be of any help.

Horse now in Johnny's barn, munching on every remaining carrot from Doc's garden, Charlie strode to the railroad station. This time, he would not afford the luxury of a sleeper car but was satisfied with the decisions he had made regarding routes and rail lines. The station agent had agreed that his best bet was to travel to San Francisco and, once there, inquire about steamers leaving the port to cross the Pacific.

Here was the adventure in China he had longed for as a young boy. God's working out things in his life always intrigued him. Here was also the distraction he needed in order to be able to leave behind all that he loved. He would soon be twenty-one. *A proper age to apply all Doc's and Oxytak's teachings*, he decided. Waiting for his train at the depot, he yielded to impulse and wrote letters to Frank and Jessie, telling them of his intended journey.

After changing trains in Kansas City, finally headed west, Charlie dozed off, thinking about his trip back east with Doc.

To pass the time on the train, Charlie joined a group of poker players. They nicknamed him "Preacher" because he didn't smoke or drink whiskey, favoring coffee or cream soda instead. He wasn't playing to win big pots but rather for the experience of the game and for understanding the behaviors of men, especially those who were motivated completely by their own gain, regardless of the consequences for another. Henry, a player who seemed to have some wisdom, made a good point: "Preacher," he said, casually blowing cigar smoke in Charlie's face, "any man who intends to make his mark in the world needs to know how to play poker."

More importantly, he learned how to read deceptive men. Their facial expressions only told what they wanted others to know; same way with their fancy words and promises or pretended humbleness. A man's actions told the truth. He was eight dollars ahead when his train pulled into San Francisco.

San Francisco's uniqueness and beauty surprised Charlie. He felt almost as though he had fallen into Alice's wonderland. He found the Spanish architectural influence fascinating and saw evidence of wealthy growth that occurred during the Gold Rush years. He especially enjoyed the contrast of bright sunshine yet soft, cool ocean air. He loved the smell of the sea and the unusual blossoms that gave it a fragrance unlike any other place he'd ever been. Its wharves were a frenzy of activity, even busier than had been the river levees of St. Louis and New York.

There were boats and ships of all sizes, fishing boats teeming with catches, tuna boats just leaving after emptying their catch; there were crab boats arriving from the Aleutians; cruise liners docked, military ships and cargo ships and pleasure sailing vessels in her harbor and in the distance beyond. It was glorious to just watch it all. Strangers didn't mind answering his questions about all he saw. He stopped two sailors to inquire how to go about getting on a ship to China. They suggested he join the navy but good-naturedly directed him to the Pacific Mail Steamship Company a couple of wharves down.

There, he introduced himself to a well-dressed gentleman, explaining the reason he needed to get to China "the fastest way possible." He declined a cruise, explaining he was on a tight budget.

"Ever worked at sea?" the man asked.

Charlie explained he was from upstate Mississippi and had only been on a riverboat, thinking it wiser not to add that the boat hadn't been moving at the time. "I'm able bodied, and I learn fast. Why do you ask?"

"There's a cargo ship sailing for Shanghai as soon as she can get her goods loaded, although ballast is her greatest need for the return trip. She had Filipino hands, but the government ordered them dismissed from American ships. The captain is desperate for reliable hands. He's losing money and off schedule, so he won't be asking many questions if you're running away from something."

Charlie assured him he was not and watched while the man wrote down information about him on some papers.

"You look strong enough. Here you go, son. These will do to get you into China and a return on an English-speaking ship. If you run into any trouble, try to return on one of Pacific Mail's ships. I've included a schedule. This is my card. Use it when you need to. Don't lose it." Charlie looked at the name on the card. *Charles Harper.* The man smiled at Charlie's startled face and wrote the name of the contact person on a second card and directed him to the ship.

Employed, with passage to Shanghai and only in town three hours. Not bad, Charlie. He smiled to himself as he hurried down the wharf. He was put to work immediately loading heavy cargo off wooden pallets and by nets and pulleys into the ship's holds. As he worked, he listened to the sounds of conversations among the dockhands, unable to understand what they were saying except for the occasional English words spoken directly to him. It seemed to be an interesting, multinational crew. He thought he could detect Chinese, Japanese, German, and Russian as well as English being spoken.

There was little time to get to know the men. He hoped he would have a chance to do that once they were at sea. He also hoped the pace would be slower once they were loaded. He was struggling to keep up with these more experienced hands. A

Russian who looked to be about twenty-five and who wanted to practice his English befriended him, readily sensing when Charlie needed help. When the loading was done, the man, Boris, invited him to go for a meal later that evening. Charlie enthusiastically agreed to a cable car ride up Clay Street.

San Francisco was sophisticated and exciting with its hills, cable cars, and rows of colorful Victorian style houses and bays. He liked the interesting landscapes and was fascinated by views of the harbors and the sea beyond. He drank vodka with the good-natured Russian and liked the feeling it gave him, if not the taste. Boris laughed to see Charlie shudder after downing the clear liquid. They walked arm in arm down Market Street, singing, "The Bowery," each happy to learn the other knew the lyrics.

"I learned it in New York where I saw the play about Chinatown," Charlie volunteered.

"I learned it in jail where I saw stars while fighting some Chinamen," the Russian retorted. Both of them seemed to find the remark unusually hilarious. They sang the song all the way back to the ship and boarded to sleep a few hours before leaving port.

Steaming away from San Francisco the next morning was a poignant moment for Charlie. He marveled at the feat of building the magnificent fort on Alcatraz Island and the beautiful Presidio. Still, he was oddly moved by the fact that he was leaving the North American continent and without the slightest notion of what to do when he reached China. Four years ago he had been thrilled to travel the distance from Jackson to Chicago, roughly seven hundred miles. Now he would be traveling over six thousand just to reach Shanghai. He determined it would be at least another thousand more miles north to Peking.

He was eager for news about China and the uprising so was glad to find that many of the Chinese hands spoke English. Some of them, he learned, had families in both China and San Francisco and had a dual loyalty that Charlie well understood.

DIXIE MILLER STEWART

Many had grown up in the Chinatown section of San Francisco. Their late-night discussions helped Charlie get a better grasp of the political and social concerns of their native land. Perhaps it was because they now lived much of the time in the West, but these men felt little if any loyalty to the Empress Dowager Ci'xi or the Manchu Dynasty.

Several of the Chinese crew had parents or grandparents who had been sent over to the United States by China forty and fifty years earlier when their nation had been more open to learning Western ways. They were sent for an education and specifically to learn about the science and other technological ideas that would help modernize China. "That practice stopped," Li said sadly. "China's Empress Dowager no longer approves of it. She is, I think what you say in America, 'wishy-washy,' although she is a shrewd strategist. I will give her that!"

Charlie surprised his Chinese shipboard friends with his interest in and knowledge of their history and politics. He knew the Empress Dowager Ci'xi manipulated and controlled more legitimate contenders for power. He believed she fed the conservative belief that their recent disasters were caused by the foreigners in their midst and thus fueled the Boxer uprising.

He commented on the tragedy that had befallen the young Emperor Guangxu whose short actual rule was called the Hundred Day Reform. Li confirmed that Guangxu had advisors and mentors who influenced his beliefs about reform. "He tried to implement Western innovations and a government more similar to Japan's, like a constitutional monarchy."

"Yes," Charlie noted. "Wasn't he falsely accused of treason by Empress Ci'xi?" The Chinese nodded their heads vigorously, pleased that an ordinary American would know those things.

"True, true! All you say is very true! Our emperor is very young, like you, Chuck!" They had difficulty pronouncing his name and so called him Chuck. "The Empress Dowager has him under house arrest. He lives what we Chinese call a tragic life but you might call a wasted one. He still has interest in a more modernized China but no power to carry it out."

Of equal interest to Charlie were China's actual struggles outside court but of course largely brought on because of the corruption and power struggles within it. He knew the nation had been embattled both from within and without. He mentioned he had read about the Taiping and Opium Wars and heard his new friends complain that largely because of them the French and the British had made inroads into the nation in ways that benefited them at China's expense.

Li believed the Opium Wars had actually occurred so the British could legalize the opium trade out of their own greed with no regard for the harm done to the Chinese. "We gave them tea, and they gave us opium. Tea causes no harm. Opium much harm!" Charlie thought how similar their plight was to that of the Revolutionary and Civil Wars in America. In the former, Americans had been unable to trust the ruling powers in England. More recently, Southerners had come to mistrust the government because it was not ruling in their favor.

He told his friends about the similarities, adding, "Of course, we are a republic in the United States, and you are an empire."

"What is the difference?" Hu asked. "I not so knowing about America."

Charlie thought for a minute. "Perhaps the best explanation is that of America's William Jennings Bryan. He is an American politician who is running for president for a second time. I heard him make a great speech four years ago when he first ran for that office. However, it was on another occasion that he said, 'A republic cannot be an empire, for a republic rests upon the theory that governments derive their just powers from the consent of the governed.' Or words similar to that.

DIXIE MILLER STEWART

"In our republic, the people hold the power and basically grant permission to lead by voting into office those individuals who beforehand establish their intentions for the nation, usually in very vigorous and passionate debate! Mind you, what they say doesn't always coincide with what they do. But if they fail, we will have a chance to replace them by a peaceful voting process.

"In contrast, your dynastic empires have always seemed to rule without the consent of those they ruled. In fact, as we've been discussing, they keep the commoner in subjugation in ways that benefit the rulers, often to the harm of their people. Now, for example, your empress and her court make the decisions under the pretense of benefiting the people. When the people have finally suffered beyond their endurance, they rise up but have no political power, so they rise up in arms."

Li nodded, adding, "Even before the Taiping Rebellion, for the past many centuries of China's existence there have been hundreds of rebellions by the ordinary Chinese at the cost of many, many lives and much suffering. Tragically, most of those rebellions were brought about by starvations and the injustices of a self-serving government."

Charlie asked, "Li, wasn't there a religious aspect in the rebellion you described earlier, the one that ended in 1864 as well as the uprising happening now?"

"In the former, it was felt that Christianity was being forced upon the people who had for centuries followed Confucianism, Buddhism, or any of China's folk religions, as well—"

Charlie hastened to correct Li, hoping he didn't sound disrespectful by interrupting him. "The Whitmores explained to me that the movement was called Christianity but that it was not. Christianity holds that there is one God in three persons: God the Father, God the Son, and God the Holy Spirit. We believe that God the Son voluntarily came to earth as a human being, fully human, yet also fully God..." Charlie saw from the looks on the faces of some that he was losing their interest or otherwise sounding as though he was describing merely another god, this one with three heads.

"Sorry," he said. "I don't mean to try and convert you. I mean to only explain why the form of Christianity that was originated by Hong Xiuquan, of that, uh, cult, was not true Christianity. For one thing, he believed he was Jesus' younger brother. That would not be even remotely possible to a true Christian."

Li spoke up. "I am a Christian, Chuck, a true Christian as you call it. Missionaries from the United States helped my family and me to convert to true Christianity. I was a child at the time. We had practiced Buddhism in my family for generations. "In my heart I have many different feelings about China and the efforts of the missionaries. Yet, I am only grateful to them. I learned that there were false speakers even there, those who only claim to be Christians but teach false doctrines that mislead people. That is true of every great movement. Did you know that Buddhism was the first large-scale missionary movement among the major world religions? They were seeking converts as far back as the third century before Christ."

Li hesitated, looking around to see if he was boring his listeners. But they seemed interested in what he was saying. "Why would I want my people to continue to believe in a religion such as Buddhism? Buddha cannot save anyone. Yet, I honor and respect those who do. I simply think they should hear the gospel spoken and leave it to God the Spirit to woo their hearts. Then the people can choose one or the other.

"That all being said," Li went on, "I have great sympathy for my Chinese heritage. I understand the Boxers and what they are fighting against, even if I do not approve of their brutal manner or, for that matter, believe entirely in their cause."

He turned his face to Charlie, his voice more serious, as though to warn his new friend: "However, they are very well trained, and they are fiercely determined. They believe that the foreigners are all evil barbarians, and of course they are not. But the one point on which I do agree with them is this: they have watched their own people being deprived while the foreigners seem to prosper and receive favors."

Charlie found he could trust most of the men on the crew. Those who seemed less trustworthy didn't congregate with them in the night anyway. He told his friends about his need to get to Peking to rescue Betsy. With the pieced-together knowledge of the others onboard, Charlie developed a plan for rescuing her.

Although Li would be traveling in a northwesterly direction from Shanghai, he volunteered to first help Charlie get rail transportation to Peking. He also provided his Western friend with advice to better assure a safe arrival there. He reminded Charlie that Ci'xi's Manchu forces had joined the Boxers so that his travel would be even more difficult. Li thought it inevitable that railroad lines into Peking would be disrupted and possibly all communications; although the telegraph lines had been intact when he last checked them just prior to leaving San Francisco.

Charlie hoped his cable had reached Betsy. He had been so preoccupied with things onboard, he had not allowed himself to think further about the danger she might also be in. Now that they were preparing to dock and off load their cargo, her situation would become primary.

Li suggested that Betsy should remain secondary until Charlie got to the compound. He warned that Charlie's chances of arriving in Peking without being accosted demanded his complete concentration. Li urged his American friend to be extremely cautious once he left the Yangtze Delta area. He looked over Betsy's sketches of the railroad and the legation area, making some updates and minor corrections on the latter as he recalled from the last time he was there. He spelled out the names of the streets surrounding the compound, asking Charlie to memorize them, and encouraged his belief that Betsy would have gone there along with the other missionaries from the Tientsin area.

Li gave Charlie as much information as he could think of, covering every imaginable possibility, even very remote ones. If the railroads were down, Charlie needed to know the one passable overland route to Peking. There were waterways too, but one needed to know them reasonably well.

"There aren't any street signs there, Chuck, as there are in San Francisco." He grinned to show he was being humorous. Li drew a rough map of the Peking, Tientsin, and Shanghai routes only to orient his friend. He said there were many places where the canals were impassable now.

Also, just to be safe, if he got that far off course, he told him about traveling up the Yellow River and what to expect if he needed to navigate the Yangtze River, commenting that he, Li, would be traveling partway up the Pearl River. Charlie interrupted Li to say that he lived near the Pearl River in Mississippi. Li took that to mean a further bonding between the two. "My ancestors are from the Pearl River area here; yours from the Pearl in America. Perhaps we have a mutual destiny, Chuck."

"Chuck," Li joked with a straight face, "if you were four inches shorter, I'd loan you my clothes. You will be even more noticeable in yours."

Charlie had changed into his buckskins and moccasins. "I know I'll still stand out, but maybe I will confuse them a little."

As a last thought, Li gave Charlie information on how he might be reached and gave him his own schedule of ships that traveled between San Francisco and Shanghai for the next six months. Charlie assured him that he would be back within the month. He saw the look on Li's face as he started to say something but thought better of it. Charlie knew Li had doubts about his friend's success on this mission.

Li spoke, "Just in case, you need to try to get on these ships I've circled for your return trip. You know these are tentative," Li continued. "Governments sometimes commandeer civilian boats or ships into service. There is action in the Philippines and throughout the waters along China. Be careful. Ordinarily, I would be able to assure you that your legation in Peking would provide you with better information, but sadly, Chuck, these are not ordinary times."

Charlie shook hands with those crewmembers with which he had developed a close friendship, especially his Russian friend, Boris.

"We will meet again, my bowery boy friend," the Russian sang in deliberate rhyme and gave Charlie a bear hug. "I envy you, my young American friend. You have an interesting challenge ahead. Godspeed to you!" The big man had tears in his eyes when Charlie finally turned away, hurrying with Li to the railroad station.

He and Li walked around the bustling wharves where the Yangtze emptied into the South China Sea. He found Shanghai to be every bit as exotic but much larger, busier, and vastly more crowded than he had expected. He saw indications of British and American Naval presence. Li told him there were times when many American Naval and commercial boats cruised the river. However, he pointed out there were far fewer Westerners out in the open today than he had ever seen. He was certain it was due to the uprising.

Li had Charlie remain in the shadows around a corner while he inquired if the train was running all the way through to Peking. He was told it was and that it would be leaving in just over two hours. He purchased a ticket for Charlie, wanting him to remain concealed.

"I don't want you to call attention to yourself, Pocahontas!"

Charlie's laughter alarmed Li. "Chinese don't laugh that loud, Chuck," he scolded. "Why are you laughing?"

When Charlie explained that Pocahontas had been an Indian princess, Li smiled. "Yes, big laugh, big joke on me. I was confused. You're no princess!"

Until the minute when Li had to leave for his boat, Charlie had not thought very much about being alone here. Suddenly he was gripped by second doubts. Li noticed. "You have come this far. I will be praying for your safe journey. We have a great God, my fine American friend. I will see you again some day. Just be very cautious. Travel by foot in Peking only at night, and remember, some Chinese speak English."

He would have preferred to board first, but that meant keeping himself exposed by waiting in line. Thinking all would now be on board he walked back to the station just minutes before departure time where, to his amazement, throngs of people were still crowding onto the cars. He tried to act casual as he finally boarded, surprised that a Chinese gestured emphatically that he should take his aisle seat. The man stood while Charlie sat next to another one dressed in traditional Manchu garb with the queue hairstyle. Many passengers carried chickens and buckets of produce or eggs. There were crying babies and distraught parents, but most seemed stoical despite the apparent chaos.

Uncertain about what he should do with his bag, he held it in his lap. He and the man seated to his left exchanged polite smiles, and he smiled at the man and woman in the seats opposite. He noticed that he seemed to be the center of inattention, dozens of Chinese faces pretending not to look at him, with not a single other Westerner in the car.

Well, then, I hope I'm succeeding at confusing them into thinking I'm…Pocahontas. He grinned, remembering Li's remark. But he kept his eyes averted and tried to look relaxed and absorbed in the pamphlet Li had given him on which he had written some translations of essential words.

He wanted to appear to doze, but his mind was alert to every sound and movement. He began to go over his plan, picturing the route he should take from the station to the compound. Li told him to take no chances, reminding him that there would also be allied forces arriving at some point and that he might not be able to tell them from any mercenaries. Li had also suggested that the compound would likely be closed and barricaded for safety. That had not occurred to Charlie; he would deal with it when he got there.

After five or six hours of travel, a man and a woman sitting ahead but on the opposite side of the aisle got off the train, allowing him to move up and take a window seat. The minute he sat down, he realized the change had been a mistake. Now he would be penned in should he need to move in a hurry. However, he decided against drawing further attention to himself by moving again. Another hour passed without incident. Finally, Charlie allowed himself to sleep.

At an early morning stop, he bought some unknown, delicious food in a station. He boarded just ahead of a family with a child who looked to be about eight or nine. The father sat beside Charlie while mother and child sat directly in front. The child kept peeking around his seat to look at Charlie. His father would say something, and the child would sit straight only to soon peek around again. At last, the boy said something to his father, looking at Charlie. The man shook his head, but the child seemed to quietly persist. The mother then spoke, and all looked in Charlie's direction, eyes still downcast.

Charlie placed his hand on his chest. "My name is Chuck." He pointed a finger to his chest and repeated, "Chuck."

"*Chuk*," the child said, looking at his father; again the child and man exchanged words. The father seemed to bow his head to Charlie, got up, and exchanged places with the child who now sat at Charlie's right. Charlie wondered if at least two customs had been broken here: a Chinese child had seemed to assert himself to his father, and the child made eye contact with Charlie. *He's probably seen American Indians and thinks I'm one. Well, I am, more or less*, Charlie thought, amused by the child's rapt attention.

After six or seven hours and several stops, Charlie began to get excited. He would swoop in like Stonewall Jackson, rescue Betsy, take this train back to Shanghai, get to the wharf, get Betsy settled in, and get himself hired on as a now-experienced member of the crew. Or, since he had enough money to purchase passage for both, perhaps he should stay available for Betsy.

He didn't know how long he had been sleeping when he felt the train brake hard, its wheels screaming on the metal tracks. Everyone in the car became alert and reflexively braced themselves for something unknown. Voices could be heard outside the train; they sounded excited, the way the ship's crew sounded when something was about to go wrong on board. Charlie could barely make out dozens of Chinese outside the windows. The train was at a full stop now, and some of the men he'd seen outside were boarding up ahead. He glanced at the child whose eyes were fixed on the seat in front.

He tensed and cleared his mind, alert, ready to respond to what might come next. He heard two men across the aisle whispering to each other. Suddenly, the connecting doors were shoved open from the car ahead. Several Chinese in dark-gray or black uniforms, some with strange head coverings, filled the aisle and looked at the passengers, their gaze falling on Charlie. They looked him over from head to moccasins. Charlie pretended to be mildly interested but unworried. He looked none in the eye as Li had advised.

One of the men spoke to Charlie, who shrugged. "Only speak English." The man looked at the boy beside Charlie and said something that sounded like a question. The boy responded, "*Chuk.*" The men said something else to the boy, who responded with a sentence Charlie didn't understand but which ended again with "*Chuk.*"

The parents remained quiet, but Charlie noticed the veins standing out in the father's neck. After a moment, two of the uniformed men took up the only empty seats, while others went back through the doors from which they had come. There was more shouting and more running back and forth outside the train. After perhaps fifteen minutes, the train began to slowly move again. When it had gained perhaps two thousand feet, an explosion could be heard from behind. The car rocked back and forth but stayed on the track. Charlie realized the tracks had been dynamited.

The uniformed men called out something in unison that might have been a cheer, and the train picked up speed. There was a low-level hum of excited conversation throughout the car. Charlie thought it odd that no woman or child had cried out despite the fear they had to have been experiencing. *Do they know something I don't?*

Wishing to thank the child, he rummaged around inside his bag, searching for some small token to give him. His hand found the packet of maps and Betsy's cable. He remembered he had stuck a photograph of Jessie sitting on Horse and himself standing beside. He hesitated for a moment, reluctant to part with it, but pulled out the photograph, handing it to the boy.

The lad reached out cautiously, looked at his parents then up at Charlie. Charlie showed the parents the picture and gestured his desire to give it to the child. The father nodded his approval; the little boy beamed as if Charlie had given him a real treasure. For the next hour, Charlie looked at the afternoon landscape of this land that was truly as exotic and enchanting to him as it had seemed to be in his childhood fantasies. Everywhere he looked was something interesting and beautiful.

The child sat absorbed in every detail in the picture, clutching it as if it was priceless. Charlie thought back to a time when he had stared the same way at pictures sent to him from China. He felt a slight touch on his arm and turned to the smiling child. Pointing at Charlie in the picture, the boy said, "*Chuk!*"

Charlie nodded and pointed to Jessie. "Jessie." Then to Horse. "Horse." The child repeated the words. *Better than I say anything in his language*, Charlie thought.

Charlie slept again for several hours, awaking as the train slowed to pull into the Peking train station. He looked down at the child and saw that he still held the photo in his hands. *My journey of a thousand miles*," he mused, *ends with a Chinese boy looking at a picture of Jessie and Horse.*

Charlie stood along with the other travelers to get off the train. He was aware that one of the men whom he took to be a militant had maneuvered his way to stand immediately behind him, while the other was up front, the child and his parents between them. He moved slowly forward, finally reaching the steps down to the station.

It was dusk. Li had advised him to wait for nightfall, but that was in order to avoid attention. "That would have been a good idea," Charlie mumbled to himself, "if I were six inches shorter and hadn't already been the center of attention for the past two hundred miles!" Losing himself in the crowd was not going to happen either.

He looked around the crowded platform, double and triple rows of coolies lined up outside the station with rickshaws; more throngs of people swirled to board or to hurry on to their business or families.

Trying to appear casual and unconcerned, Charlie looked the crowd over, spotting ten or twelve of the similarly uniformed men in two groups. He was aware of at least two more of the militants from the train now closing in behind him. Was it only his imagination that he could feel their breath on his neck? When he turned, they turned. He stopped and they stopped. He felt fear. Did they?

If he could escape the station area without incident, he would have about a fifteen-minute walk to the compound. He had hoped to find food and refresh himself until dark. *Now I just hope to get out of here alive.*

A sudden foreboding prompted him to drop his bag, duck, and pivot left; an unsmiling Chinese man was recovering from an obvious kick intended for Charlie's back. The man's transition to a low crouch had been quick and smooth. Charlie also changed direction in a fluid movement, able to strike his assailant with one fast, explosive jab to his jaw, connecting just below his ear.

The man fell backward as three others rushed Charlie with devastating blows to his abdomen and kidneys. The rush from both directions prevented him from anything more than an awkward pivot and a lucky elbow smash to a cheekbone as he felt another excruciating kick from behind. The blow propelled him forward into an assailant's knee, directly into his groin. He experienced intense, hot pain and the simultaneous sharp sensation of a nerve twisting in his neck as he was being taken down to the ground. He felt a kick to the side of his head and then only darkness.

His own moan and the awareness of being carried by his arms and ankles brought him to semi-consciousness. He was vaguely aware of being dumped onto a cart—a rickshaw, perhaps—his face down on rough planking; he felt the cart beginning to roll. He roused momentarily and tried to move before receiving another excruciating blow to the base of his neck and passing out.

Chapter 9

Charlie lay on the ground, conscious of pain all over his body and an intense heat on the left side of his face. He was dimly aware of sporadic gunshots and what seemed to be sounds of light artillery. There were shouts, cries, and eerie chanting—or perhaps only many people speaking at once; he couldn't tell. His head throbbed with pain but cleared sufficiently for him to remember he was in Peking, not Jackson; China, not America.

Flames were rapidly consuming a nearby wall, lapping at the roof directly over his head, he instinctively moved to stand and run, but pain paralyzed him, preventing him from rising to his feet. With a force of will, he rolled away from the flames and tried again to put his weight on his hands and knees but immediately fell forward onto the ground.

A sharper pain signaled his left arm was broken; he became aware of blood running down the side of his face. Struggling to his knees, he gingerly felt around his left eye, confirming it was swollen closed but with an open wound above it that his exertion had reopened. He paused to mentally check for other injuries

DIXIE MILLER STEWART

and to press the heel of his hand on the cut, hoping to stop the bleeding. For all his misery, the most irritating sensation was the blood trickling down his cheek and neck, although the heat from the fire was a close second.

At that moment, a portion of the roof above crashed to the ground, landing near him, igniting nearby rubble. He instinctively rolled over and over on the hard ground, grunting from pain, until his body hit a solid wall. He lay there a minute, gasping, then wiped away the blood that now collected into his good eye. Blinking, looking for an escape route, he saw that he was perhaps fifteen feet from the flames but sensed with relief there was nothing flammable between him and the fire, although the heat was still intense.

Using the wall for support, he climbed clumsily to his feet, stumbling once, recovered, and began to move. He reversed his position and remained crouched both from pain and a need to conceal himself. He pulled his shirt up to protect his face as he moved, unable to get farther away from the fire until he found an opening or a corner.

The fires were ablaze on the buildings to his right, but they looked to be Chinese dwellings in an open area. He hoped that meant they were outside the compound where the missionaries and the others would be holed up. He vaguely remembered moments of consciousness earlier in which he had observed fires being set apparently by the Chinese youths he thought had assaulted him.

Recalling the fight, he knew they were undoubtedly members of the Boxer group. They were too well trained in martial arts to be regular government troops. He felt foolish and naïve now in thinking he'd actually believed he would be able to fight them off. They were not out to win a contest; they were out to kill the hated barbarian. Apparently, his assailants assumed he was dead or that he would remain unconscious and be burned in the fire.

The light from the flames illuminated the darkness, allowing him to make out his surroundings with his one eye. He tried to orient himself, but it was impossible since he had no idea of his location, though he sensed it was far from the train station. His bag was missing, which meant his maps and papers were also gone. He would need to rely on his memory of the compound area; there would certainly be no one from whom he could ask directions. He dare not trust anyone outside the legation area. He wondered how he'd ever find it before someone who wished him ill first found him.

He made himself concentrate and recall the names of streets he had written in Chinese characters and memorized from Betsy's map. However, escaping the flames was the most immediate urgency, that and remaining undetected; he would not be able to defend himself from a Boxer's grandmother right now. He made himself invisible as he moved quietly forward as rapidly as his weakened body would allow, remaining in shadows and once concealing himself behind an overturned rickshaw. Otherwise, he flattened against the wall whenever he saw anyone approaching. He was thankful he'd worn the moccasins.

Charlie saw the ditch a split second before he fell in, gasping from the added pain but thankful he had been able to twist and land on his buttocks. His aching back was braced against a slight if rocky slope. *This almost feels good*, he thought. He took a moment to breathe deeply and rest briefly. He reached for a handhold to climb out, resisting the urge to stay where he was and sleep but quickly pulled back as he heard shouting voices and running footsteps approaching. He ducked down inside the blackness. *I'm dead*, he thought.

He tucked his chin under, with every sense heightened in preparation for the moment he would be discovered. "Father, help me," he silently prayed. The footsteps stopped only feet away from where he huddled. He forced himself to breathe deeply and silently as he cautiously felt about with his uninjured hand for a rock to use as a weapon. He didn't intend to go down without inflicting some injuries. Finding nothing, he accepted that his one hand would have to be his weapon; perhaps he could pull his enemy on top of him as a shield and immobilize him. It would be tricky with two arms, more so with one.

From the sound of the voices, Charlie thought again the people were in some kind of argument. They continued in this manner for perhaps two minutes before seeming to move again in his direction. He shrank as far down inside the ditch as possible. As the militants reached it their footsteps circumvented it and continued on. He heard shouts back and forth now apparently they had separated into two groups going in opposite directions.

Charlie let out his breath in disbelief and tried to relax the knots in his stomach. "Thank you, Father!" Obviously, he was well concealed inside the dark ditch. Of course the Chinese would have known about the ditch and therefore known to go around it themselves to avoid falling in.

He waited a few more minutes to make sure they had all left and then carefully pulled his shirt off over his head. Biting his lip against the pain, he laid his broken arm on the surface and pressed it back into alignment. With his teeth and his right hand, he fashioned a sling from the shirt, managing to tie a crude knot. The pain remained, but the relief provided by the realignment and the sling made it more bearable.

Cautiously raising his head to look about, he noticed something he hadn't seen earlier. He had been moving along what now appeared to be almost solid barricades rather than the wall of a building. He could barely make out a sort of grating about ten feet back to his left; he felt a surge of hope. What he saw appeared to be a water gate. Could it possibly be a gate to the canal he had noticed on the legation map?

Although there were several canals in the city, this was a narrower one, as was the one Betsy indicated. Its size and the fact of the barricades were reasons for his hope. He pulled himself up and half crabbed, half crawled over to look. Peering down into blackness, he couldn't tell what was beneath or behind the grating, but he could now orient himself if indeed this was the canal that led inside the legation quarter. That would explain the barricades he'd been crawling along. He hadn't expected to be approaching it from this direction but didn't have time to second-guess. The sounds of screams and yells all around him were unnerving and the frenzy of their mob anger was obvious even in their strange-sounding language.

Having no vision on his left prompted Charlie to turn back to his right, somewhat more confident that was east—his original direction. He half crouched, half crawled, at times pressing himself low against the sturdy barricades whenever he heard nearby voices. Arriving at a cross street, Charlie searched for the name where Betsy's maps seemed to indicate the signs might be. He was surprised and felt renewed to see the characters for what Li had told him was *Ha-Ta-Men* Street. The compound was on this street!

He turned north, going farther and farther from the fires, keeping in the shadows and moving silently. Grateful for Oxytak's insistence on discipline, Charlie felt some confidence that he was as well trained at evasive maneuvers; he'd also crept up on many deer and other animals in the wild without being heard or smelled. Encountering western guards who might take him down first and ask questions later was a risk, but one he'd choose over encountering more Chinese militants.

He continued for what he guessed to be ten minutes of starting and stopping, crouching, crawling, pausing, and searching for an entrance into the compound. The movements added to his strain and pain, and he was exhausted. Ahead lay another street, much wider and more open than he had expected. He didn't recall there being such a broad street entrance into the legation on the map.

Stepping cautiously into the intersection he squinted in search of a street name, the light from the fire now being only a small help, although the flames were still visible to the south. He barely made out a sign indicating another symbol he recognized. It took him a moment to recall the characters for the street: *Chang an Chich*. His spirits fell; he had gone too far! This was the east-west street he'd seen, located beyond the compound. How had he missed the entrance to Legation Street? Was he somehow disoriented? Was this not the compound, after all?

Listening for approaching sounds and looking about to make sure he was not seen, his eye caught sight of what appeared to be a metal rod lying in the street. He crept over and picked it up. It was a heavy iron bar about fifteen inches long, crudely beveled at one end; holding it gave him a small sense of protection.

As he turned to retrace his steps, Charlie felt an unfamiliar wave of despair. His simple weapon was nothing in the face of thousands of Boxers and the other militants he knew roamed the streets. Exhaustion and disappointment made his pain worse. He hadn't eaten since yesterday noon and had lost a lot of blood. He felt along the cut on his head and his swollen eye, discovering an additional cut to the side of it, but the bleeding there, too, had stopped.

As if to justify his sagging spirits and strength, he reminded himself that since he had left the train shortly before dark, he'd been in strenuous hand-to-hand combat against superior forces, been badly injured and immobilized, rendered unconscious, and almost burned alive. He was running for his life and was now lost in Peking, China, in the middle of a war against that nation's government. If he survived, he thought he'd look back and chuckle over the predicament he'd gotten himself into. For now, he desperately wanted to reach safety and rest.

For a moment, he thought about going back to the ditch to hide and sleep but decided against that. He felt his way back south along the wall, confident again that it was the compound, his movements painfully slower. He took some comfort from the realization he had at least found it and resisted the strong urge to call out for help. He knew he could still attract the attention of the Boxer youths or Imperial troops, some of whom he saw still roaming about. He had no way of guessing the time or how long he had been unconscious, but he sensed it was well past midnight. He knew he had to be concealed somewhere by dawn.

Sliding his hand along the wall, he now felt a rough protrusion he judged to be the more heavily barricaded entrance. This must be Legation Street. He understood why he had missed it, but now how to get behind the barricade without being attacked? He listened for sounds beyond the wall and heard none. He whispered, "Hello. I'm an American." Nothing. He whispered it again a little louder. Again, he heard nothing. He made light knocking sounds, realizing that was stupid; even the Chinese would try that. The only advantage he had over them right now at the compound was that he spoke English and was considerably taller.

Unable to get inside the compound without calling attention to himself, Charlie reluctantly made his way back to the ditch and the water gate beyond. Earlier, he had ruled it out as a possible entrance, but now it seemed his only chance, either that or risk being seen in the ditch come morning. He observed occasional stray silhouettes mostly watching the near-burned out fires, apparently not alert since they would have no reason to suspect anyone from the compound to be on the streets.

He probed and prodded even as he acknowledged that so would the Boxers and the other troops have used every means to get inside the compound; still, there had to be a way. With his good hand, he found a give in the ground against the right side of an upright stone post. He reasoned it might have been there as a result of others trying to break through from this side. Using the rod he'd found, he pried and dug, moving small amounts of stone and earth with each effort. He stopped often to listen for sounds of people approaching. He could still see troops between himself and the dimming firelight, although their numbers seemed to be fewer. He worked for perhaps a half hour, careful to place his diggings to one side so as to replace them from the other side if he succeeded in getting to it.

He lay on his back, headfirst, to test the size of the opening he had made. Grimacing from the pain, he untied the sling and used his right hand to move his left arm down to his side. Doing so allowed him to just squeeze under the water gate, inching his body under and turning his feet sideways until he had completely cleared it. He sat up and replaced his sling, encouraged by this small achievement, and carefully put back the rock and dirt he had removed, pressing it down, hoping it looked natural from the other side.

The most formidable obstacle lay just ahead: the barricade across the canal. It appeared to be twelve or fourteen feet high, at least, and extended well beyond the watercourse on both sides. At each end of the barricade stood a small shelter; given their locations, he guessed they were Chinese guard posts. The thought occurred to him that he might have actually placed himself in greater harm's way if he indeed was trapped between the gate and the barricade in full view of Chinese guards. He whispered a brief prayer, asking for a way into the compound to safety and to rest.

Charlie felt a bit of strength and a great deal of resolve returning. Feeling more secure for now by the total darkness and with the gate between himself and the only troops he could see, he once again explored, prodded, picked at, and jostled everything he could that had any give to it at all. Little by little, using the beveled end of the rod he'd found, he dug a series of small openings in the barricade large enough for a moccasined toe and his fingertips to fit in. Climbing over offered the only opportunity to get inside.

Lifting a foot into the first toehold, he reached for the shallow indentation above it with fingertips so sweaty he lost his hold and fell back down. He leaned his forehead against the wall to rest, his breath coming in shallow gasps, and talked to himself: *No giving up, Chuk, you're out of options.* He rested another moment and then returned to his work, this time making the indentations deeper and slanted downward so as to provide a better hold. He stuck the rod inside the waist of his breeches and again raised a foot, reaching up for the hold above. He maintained his grip with his one good hand, paused, balanced himself by leaning into the wall, and routed out another finger and toehold. Slowly and awkwardly he progressed upward as the night crept inexorably toward morning.

Trembling from the strain and barely able to pull himself over the top; he managed to only straddle the barricade. When he'd caught his breath, he again used his shirt to secure his broken arm tightly against his body. He was able to balance himself to bring his left leg over to the other side of the barricade, paused, taking a deep breath, and dropped down into blackness. He lay there a few minutes until nausea and dizziness subsided.

He willed himself to regain strength, but found he had used up all reserve stamina. His heart was pounding and his clothing was soaked wet with blood and with sweat from tension as he forced himself to again retie the sling and place his arm inside it. Now he had to rest after exerting even slight effort. He had the silly thought that burning dwellings smelled the same in China as they did in America, but grief and terror sounded different. He turned to face the darkness that was the canal, only then grasping that he was inside the compound! Although he was sure he would find further barricades, he had at least reached a modicum of safety, and, if need be, he could find a place to sleep without too much fear for his life.

He felt around, finding a small pebble, and tossed it into the canal. He heard it strike dry rock not far down. He inhaled deeply from relief, breathing in the stench of rotting matter and sewage. *So be it*, he thought and let himself slide into the darkness, landing feet first on an apparent stone bottom. Again, he stopped to rest and to reorient himself relative to where the American Legation would be and realized it should be the first one he came to. If his memory was correct, it would be off to his left on the corner of the canal and Legation Street, probably no more than three hundred feet ahead.

Charlie recalled seeing a bridge across the canal on that street, so there should also be a means of climbing back out and onto the road. He was picturing the map Betsy had drawn; she had indicated that the Russian legation was directly north across the street from the Americans on the far side from where he was.

He trudged on, stumbling, stepping sometimes in shallow water, *but at least not swimming in it*. The thought and his success brought the first grin to his face since he'd said good-bye to the child on the train.

"Hello. I'm an American." Charlie wondered if he needed to continue whispering. He guessed not, but neither did he want to wake the entire compound. He crept along, having no light on this moonless night, feeling the sides of the canal for any sort of brace that might indicate a ladder or steps. He kept straining to see and to hear. The only sounds were those made by occasional youths in the far distance.

The sounds of the terror that had gripped the innocent people who lost their dwellings and livelihood had faded away. He wondered where they had gone, indeed if they had all perished.

He recalled the nightmarish scene in St. Louis when he and Charlotte had survived the tornado. The fires, darkness, chaos, and screams here in Peking had been eerily similar. He hoped the ending this time would turn out as well for him and another lady he had come to rescue.

He extended his right arm so as to slide his hand along the rough, slanted, stone wall of the canal until he became aware that he could now make it out in the darkness. He looked up and saw that dawn was just beginning to break, and against the slightly lighter sky, he saw the bridge over the canal. Relief flooded over him, and he slumped against the rough wall.

"Hello up there. Hello. I'm an American." He stumbled across to the other side. *The American side,* he thought to himself, but he had no strength left to climb out with one arm. From somewhere came the urge to sing. He raised his voice and began singing, "Amazing grace, how sweet the sound…"

Charlie stopped for a moment, swallowing back the lump in his throat made up of a mixture of tears, relief, pain, and fatigue, and from a sudden, poignant thought of Oxytak. He never failed to think of him when he heard or sang those words. His friend had told him about the Cherokees' love for the hymn and how along the terrible Trail of Tears they often had only time to sing it at a gravesite instead of a more proper burial. He sang it, now realizing it was a universal song that every Christian could claim as his own, regardless of the language in which they might sing the lyrics.

"Amazing grace, how sweet the sound that saved a wretch like me. I once was lost, but now I'm found—"

"Mercy me! Where have you come from?"

He awoke to the feel of soft hands shaving his chin. Without opening his eyes, he commented, "Am I about to be decapitated or only have my throat cut?" He chuckled and opened his eyes. "Hello! Are you an angel?"

"I'm Betsy Whitmore. Now lie still, or I will cut your throat!"

"Yes, ma'am. How long have I been sleeping?"

"Shush! Don't move! I'll talk. We have two physicians in the compound. Both have examined you, set your arm, and tended your cuts, bruises, and abrasions. They wondered whether every rickshaw in Peking had raced over you or if the Boxers had thrown you from a train! Your injuries looked rather awful! Anyway, although they are French and German, they were in agreement that you lost a lot of blood and that we should keep you quiet and rested. They impressed upon us that you were otherwise quite healthy and instructed us to keep giving you broth and fluids, let you sleep, and to let nature heal you. That's what we've done now for…hmmm, three days and three hours."

Charlie was incredulous. "I've been sleeping for *three* days?"

"Not entirely. You were unconscious for several hours on two or three occasions, especially when they set your arm. We had nothing with which to sedate you. You talked a lot, but you were feverish and delirious at times. The doctors said your kidneys were badly bruised. We have Chinese Christian friends who are sheltered here who shared some of their medicinal herbs and ointments with you, which they said would also treat whatever infection was causing your fever and bring it down."

She placed her wrist on his forehead, saying, "Your fever broke during the night, and you are still cool. I also have found many of their medicines to promote healing, so you don't need to worry. We've gotten broth and water down you, but you must be famished now. Actually, you've been very polite and grateful. You were quite brave…before you passed out.

"Just so you'll know," she added, her eyes twinkling, "the men bathed you and cut your hair so the doctors could examine your cuts. We've done what we could to clean and mend your buck-skins. You're wearing borrowed clothing right now."

"Thank you for all you've done. I'm very, very sorry about your family, Betsy," Charlie offered, taking her hand. "I grew to love them through their letters and everything Doc told me about them. I also feel a loss, so I can only offer weak condolences to what you must be going through. Then on top of your grief, to have me arrive in this kind of shape is not something you needed at any time, certainly not now. You have been through a lot. I'm sorry to now be adding to your burden. I only meant to help you."

Her smile was genuine with no self-pity. "Thank you. I have shed my tears for my loss, and I will continue to grieve, but my parents and grandparents prepared me for what happened as much as one can ever be prepared. We've known for some time that our lives were at risk. We all chose to continue here, regard-less. My parents arranged for me to leave some months back, but I refused to go. I have no regrets about remaining, but it is time to leave now.

"My parents and grandparents were wonderful Christians with such incredible faith right up to their deaths. They knew they were going to be together in eternity. That gave them a steadfast courage and hope. Their love for the Chinese people never wavered. They were in sympathy with them over the tragic blows to their culture, even with the Boxers. It is this nation that has suffered the most. Not," she hastened to assure him, "at all to diminish what Americans have gone through, but only to say that it has been more severe and relentless and unending in China all my life. You know I was born here."

She resumed her shaving, propping his jaw closed with two fingers so that Charlie didn't have a chance to respond. She continued. "Besides, Charlie, you are not a burden at all. You risked your life to come help me! I felt as though I had family again when I heard of your arrival. You have brought us all renewed hope, seeing your courage and determination. We have needed something different to occupy our minds, and so attending to you has given us that purpose. Why else would I have sent you the cables if I didn't somehow think you might come?"

He tried to speak, but she playfully forced his jaw closed. "Doc told us that you had this tendency to rescue girls in distress." She smiled, releasing his jaw to carefully wipe his face around his cut. Charlie noticed her dimples for the first time.

"I only rescue pretty girls in distress," he flirted. "Especially those who have light brown hair, blue eyes, and dimples."

"Hmm." She pretended to think. "I believe that means I may qualify. Thank goodness I won't need to find my way back to America alone. I assume that I meet your criteria for risking your life on dangerous rescue missions?" She had already pressed his mouth closed again, now working on his right side.

When he could speak, he thanked Betsy. "You haven't cut me once, you know. You could be useful for dressing deer and skinning squirrels. Honestly, I was actually so naïve as to think I was going to storm this compound, grab you, and maybe hire, what, a coolie and a rickshaw? Then we'd race on back to Shanghai and hop on a ship! Talk about being wet behind the ears!"

Hearing that Charlie was up and about, refugees from all over the compound made their way to the camp near the American Legation to meet him and ask questions. All were amazed that he had been able to withstand the assault and somehow get in past their own as well as the Chinese guards and the barricades.

A couple days later, he began exploring, visiting the different legations, speaking sometimes through translators, although he was surprised at how many spoke English. He was shocked to learn they only had one old piece of artillery for their entire defense. He hoped the Chinese didn't know that.

Everyone in each of the legations wanted news of the outside world both afar and as near as what might be happening immediately outside the compound. One man with a strong British accent observed, "Just look at our young chap here, and you bloody well know what's going on outside!"

Their telegraph lines had been cut not long after they had received confirmation of news of their plight and the assurance that help was on its way. It appeared that no nation was going to allow any of its citizens to go without defense any longer than it would take for them to get here. The Americans were apparently arriving from the Philippines. British troops were already on the continent and working their way north. Everyone felt confident that their own nation would be there to rescue them.

The problem was that they had no idea when help could arrive, how many forces there would be, or how difficult it would be to make their way there, given the large number of Boxer and now Imperial forces there were to block the routes. Some within the compound talked of taking their chances by trying to leave secretly. Food and water supplies were already being rationed and would not last indefinitely.

Charlie had several reasons for exploring the area; primarily, he wanted to search out any other weaknesses in their barricades or any other way they might be vulnerable. The barriers were made of wooden beams, bricks, and even rocks from buildings they had hurriedly dismantled in order to use the material for their protection. He examined them as a "white man." Now he switched his perceptions to the heightened awareness of his training by Oxytak. He earlier noticed that some buildings were burned inside the compound from the recent fires. That indicated a high vulnerability. If the Chinese wanted to throw incendiaries, people inside the compound would be trapped.

He learned that the library portion of a nearby school was totally consumed by the fire. Given his love of books and learning, he would have preferred that almost any other building burn down before a library and said so. Betsy agreed. "It was part of the Hanlin Academy. Very elite scholars have studied there who have gone on to be great leaders in China and other parts of the world. They study classics, including translating Confucianism. It is a tragic loss."

Charlie thought for a minute. "If I'm not mistaken, isn't that where Li Hongzhang studied? I'm sorry. I know I just butchered his last name."

"Why, yes! He is a Hanlin graduate. Actually"—Betsy laughed—"you did very well with his name. How do you know of him?"

"Your dad wrote about him in several of his letters. You should know that Doc and I memorized those letters word for word. In fact, I still have every one of them in boxes at Doc's house. Then, Doc and I found some articles on him when we were in New York. He visited the United States and Canada just before we went to New York, so the news of him was quite recent at the time. He's a very intelligent man. I think he's a visionary. Given a choice of meeting him or Ci'xi, I would choose him any time."

"Well, then, I'll invite him to tea," she teased. She agreed that Li was something of a hero to many, even though he was often maligned by Ci'xi. "Probably when she thinks the people look to him instead of to her. However, I've heard he's quite arrogant."

"Perhaps with good reason," Charlie commented. "If truth be known, he's probably the most competent and influential man alive in China today. Li told me he has had to bear the brunt of all the negotiations following wars in which China was defeated. Ci'xi and her court seem to conveniently recede to the background at those times. He has represented China with as much intelligence and dignity, I think, as is humanly possible, given the humiliating circumstances surrounding most of the treaties."

Betsy spoke up. "Yes, I think he very much favors China's adoption of Western ideas and weaponry and Western modernization of industry and political methods. For that reason, he has crossed Ci'xi on many points. She has no trust in Western ways at all, although I believe she once did. Perhaps that is because she feels that China has been betrayed. I personally believe she is a very self-seeking person who has cared little about the people but much about maintaining her own power and lifestyle. My father felt that her fears of losing that power ultimately forced China into war with Japan."

"If I understand it correctly," Charlie added, "I think you're right. It would seem that all Mr. Hongzhang's efforts failed to save China from defeat with Japan. Will they do so now with this rebellion going on? Who will win? Is he bucking Manchu, Boxers, and Ci'xi now? It is unfortunate that so few realize he highly values China's traditions and culture, as he should, given that he is Chinese. But I'm not sure they understand him, or perhaps it is only that I don't understand, quite possible, of course."

"Understand exactly what, Charlie?" Betsy asked.

"Oh, understand that Li Hongzhang's intentions and energies, at least the ones I've read about and those shared with me by some of the men aboard ship, would very much favor China. He seems to hope to preserve the best of China's culture and traditions by employing the best of Western thought, technology, and progress. I can understand that it requires delicate negotiation skills to bring that about. He built the strongest army in China, but rather than preferring force, he seems to rely on diplomacy, intelligence, and, well, practical effectiveness wherever in the world he finds it.

DIXIE MILLER STEWART

"My father felt that Ci'xi more or less forced Li to negotiate at times when the real responsibility was probably hers. "I should have paid more attention, but Li just seemed like one more person in the empress's courts. I do recall my father commenting to someone that Li was pressed by all sides."

"Maybe that's part of the reason I admire him," Charlie commented. "Despite the opposition and the court's betrayal of him from time to time, look at all of his accomplishments in China!"

Charlie was eager to give the man praise where he thought it was well deserved. "He was almost singularly involved in all the important trade and other negotiations with all the foreign powers. That requires a great deal of skill, knowledge, wisdom, poise, and probably self-control!

"Let me start at what I think is the beginning to give you an idea of his vision: he established the China Merchants Steam Navigation Company. I only remember the name because my friend, also named Li, told me about it when we were comparing it with the Pacific Steam Lines.

"With good ships, and so that China would not need to depend on other nations to provide fuel for them, he founded the Kaipin mines. Next, in order to transport that fuel to the docks, he built China's first railroad systems from the mines. Can you see his thinking and planning? Everything he did was to secure China's independence and maintain her ultimate sovereignty! He put to use the most advanced planning and technology that came from other nations, but that also made him seem to some to be sacrificing China's sovereignty, talent, and culture.

"Li also established her first telegraph lines and her first cotton mills. He did all that without borrowing from any foreign country! China financed her own developments.

"So there you have it or as much as I know about it. China, surrounded by grasping foreign powers who want to chip away at her, could engage in trade as it benefited her and otherwise be self-sufficient and as modern or not as she wanted to be, within reason, of course. I recognize that no nation can or should isolate itself."

As he walked about the compound, Charlie listened with some agreement to those individuals who were concerned about supplies and time and who therefore wanted to try to devise a logical plan of escaping the city. They had realistic concerns that all might die inside the compound or certainly that the elderly, injured, and infirm might die of hunger before rescue arrived. The streak of independence he'd inherited from one of his ancestors agreed with that. The memories of being assaulted and the tension of being scrutinized for hours on the train had faded a bit in the three weeks he had been here.

He was disappointed that he was on the continent yet not able to explore China as he had always hoped to do. In particular, he had always dreamed of traveling along the Great Wall and exploring the magnificent architecture, especially those buildings perched impossibly on sides of mountains. How could anyone ever see China's magnificence and still doubt the intellectual and artistic superiority of her people?

Nevertheless, he had seen much of a thousand miles of the incredibly beautiful land and two of its major cities. He had engaged in fine conversations with many of her citizens, eaten some of China's delicious foods, and studied two thousand years of martial arts. Granted, the latter had been packed into a five-minute encounter.

The doctors together had surmised the fracture of his arm would take eight weeks or more to heal. However, Charlie gauged his healing by how rapidly his cuts and bruises were mending. There were only minimal traces of injuries. He felt almost as healthy and hardy as he ever had and reasoned that his bones netted together about as rapidly as his skin and muscle. He resumed daily workouts, which the Chinese in the compound referred to in English as martial arts. He teased them that instead they were American Indian arts.

There had been a steady increase in the firing outside the compound in the last few days. They heard small arms and small artillery but so far, no all-out, organized assault against them. Charlie stood watch one night, which gave him a chance to think more clearly and talk things over with God. He had no other chance of being alone or finding prayer time during the day.

He wished he could strike out on his own. He wasn't contributing anything to anybody's welfare but was instead eating food and drinking water that others might desperately need before the siege was over. He was held back, of course, by concern for Betsy's welfare. He thought he stood a good chance of making it back to Shanghai alone, but not with her; nor would he ever allow her to take the risks involved. Still, he weighed both situations: the risks of staying versus those of trying to leave Peking undetected. An immediate decision was not necessary. His arm needed more time, and he wanted to regain strength in it. He would bide his time and trust that God would guide him.

The compound was abuzz three mornings later. A Chinese Christian sympathetic to the Westerners and who had family inside the compound had made his way there and managed to signal to be let in. The man spoke no English. Betsy knew him and translated for Charlie's ears. He had come to rescue his father from the compound, whom he feared would be killed by the rebels if he remained.

His name is Hong, Betsy explained to Charlie. "His father's name is Tan. Tan, is one of my favorite people in all of China. I grew up speaking Chinese, and although he speaks very little English, he has been my teacher of his culture most of my life; I love him like a grandfather. It was he who, at the risk of his own life and despite his own deep grief, accompanied me the eighty miles to this compound.

"Where is his wife?" Charlie asked.

"She was killed in the same flare up with the rebels as my parents and grandparents. He had intended to return to Tientsin the next day to complete his mourning but has been forced to remain here because the Boxers besieged the compound within hours after our arrival.

"Hong and Tan also have family in San Francisco who have long pleaded with them to come live there. Hong sent his wife and two children ahead some months back when it became apparent that the conflict was not going to diminish on its own. Now that it is not safe for the Chinese Christians, I believe Tan has been almost persuaded to relocate."

"It must be very difficult to give up one's homeland and way of life, especially at that age," Charlie acknowledged, it is almost as if they must take new identities."

"Yes, his wife found it very hard to make that decision."

Hong, it would seem, had made the decision for his father: He had purchased two tickets on a ship departing for San Francisco out of Shanghai in one week. He had waited and waited for his father to return, but now time was running out. He risked his life to come for him rather than sailing on without him.

Betsy approached Charlie where he again stood day watch. "Charlie, please hear what I have to say before you tell me your objections. I want to leave with Hong and Tan tonight. I want you to come with us, of course. I know you have been wishing you could leave here and have only stayed for my benefit. We know that help is on its way, but we do not know when they'll arrive. While I'm sure there are other ships I might take to San Francisco, I have made up my mind to go tonight along with

Tan, Hong…and you. Will you at least listen to their plan of travel to Shanghai tonight when you get off watch?"

Listening to her, Charlie wanted to convince himself it was a reasonable thing to do. "Of course I'll listen. Do you know anything about it to give me something to think about until then?"

"I know very little. Hong has been reluctant to share it in great detail to just everyone, fearing there may be spies inside the compound. That may seem a little overly cautious, but he's wise, like Tan. He is a very respected local leader in his provincial government. As such, it was a difficult decision for him to make when he sent his family to the United States.

"Hong mentioned that he knew there was a very large weapons cache at the *His-Ku* Arsenal. That is along one route. I don't know if he intends to have us arm ourselves. Oh, he said that allied troops are several hundred miles south of here but have run up against heavy resistance. Again, I don't know if he plans to travel by rail. That doesn't seem safe for you and me." She gave him a hopeful smile and turned to go help with chores before he had a chance to reply.

Charlie would listen to Hong's plan before deciding. He was already impressed with Betsy's courage and independence. Along with those qualities, she had the kind of spirit necessary if they were to succeed in this endeavor without her becoming too fearful at any point. Her strength and determination were evident from the moment she told him she had chosen to remain in China last fall despite the danger. If he could be absolutely certain she'd be safer here, there would be no choice to make.

The sun was setting when Hong took Charlie, Betsy, and Tan aside to discuss his plan. Another man, Yaun, whom Charlie thought to be in his mid-twenties, joined them. Through Betsy, Hong explained it in careful, well-thought-out detail. Charlie was relieved to know the plan did not include traveling by rail.

They would be traveling at first by foot and then along several different waterways by vessel. Charlie knew where the Yellow River was, thanks both to his friend Li, and his having examined the area on maps. Hong said the Northern Canal was the only waterway directly out of Peking. However, it was blocked in places that would necessitate their transfer to other tributaries and back again to the Northern Canal, which would eventually lead them into the Grand Canal. Since that canal was also impassable in places, neither would they travel all the way through it. However, he assured them, his route would provide a safer if somewhat circuitous connection on to the Yangtze River and into Shanghai where they would catch their ship to San Francisco.

Charlie was not in a position to challenge Hong's plans. What he knew of the route sounded very similar to what his friend Li had told him as a worst-case situation.

However, Tan knew the route his son described.

Betsy smiled, telling Charlie, "Tan knows every centimeter of ground in his beloved China. He has often helped me with my map-making." She saw Charlie start to laugh, "What's so funny?" "

"I was just remembering how when I was a kid I thought by the time I might get to China they'd all be speaking English."

He wasn't sure that Betsy translated everything, so he wasn't quite as confident as Hong seemed to be. That the other four were confident and eager would have to be good enough as long as he was in China. They would travel the waterways in a sampan that friends were holding for them at a small pier about ten miles from Peking.

Hong led them outside the compound through the north end of the same small canal Charlie had walked from the south when he'd first arrived. There had been little firing from the north position, since the school had burned and there were more buildings for concealment. The man standing guard let them out and wished them Godspeed. The route would be circuitous and somewhat out of the way, but safer, away from the Manchu and rebel forces. They traveled through the night with no incident, although they needed to conceal themselves from time to time as small groups of uniformed men were roaming about. Charlie wondered for whom or what the occasional firing he heard was intended.

Just before dawn, tired and hungry, they arrived at the pier where several sampans and a junk were tied. Hong sang out something, and two smiling friends emerged, who then motioned for all to follow them. Charlie started toward the larger junk, but Betsy took his hand and guided him beyond it to a small, shallow boat. "Hmm, I just sort of naturally assumed we'd be taking the large one there, the junk; considering we've got about a thousand mile cruise ahead."

Betsy relayed his worry to Hong, who smiled and reassured him that his two friends were not accompanying them. The man held out his hand to shake Charlie's, as though that would seal a promise that none would drown.

Charlie wasn't reassured. "I didn't think those two were joining us. I think I can capsize it all by myself!" Betsy smiled, commenting, "Sometimes families live their entire lives aboard such sampans."

They ate something Charlie didn't recognize but found to be delicious and filling, then boarded the sampan with Hong remaining in charge. The young man volunteered to keep first watch and communicated through Betsy that Charlie and the others should try to sleep, suggesting that it would be better if they avoided being seen. He covered them with fishing nets and empty buckets that smelled soured. Hong apparently wanted it to look as though the sampan was only that of local commoners on their way to market. They were cramped, but Charlie was comfortable. Betsy said she was cozy and promptly dozed, leaning against his shoulder.

He put his arm around her to stabilize her; she reached over and took his hand, never opening her eyes. Her hand was soft and warm in his and strangely reassuring. Smiling to himself, Charlie thought no matter the danger or whatever the circumstances, there was often enough the touch of a pretty girl to anchor him to the simple realities of life: love, purpose, character, and faith. At its basic, he thought life was simple; man made it complicated.

He drifted off to sleep, remembering the soft touches of Jessie's little hands in his at Doc's burial, whenever she was afraid, and when he'd said good-bye. It was a lifetime ago. He didn't like being in a world where Jessie and Frank did not also belong, although he would never have wished these dangers on Jessie. He rather wished Frank could have come along; he thought it would have been good for him to find he could survive danger and grow stronger from the experience.

He missed them: Jessie, Frank, and Beulah—all of them. For the first time, he regretted speaking quite so harshly to Mrs. Harper; he'd had no right to. She had made it possible for him to live and to live a good life. He would write her an apology when he got back to America. He fell asleep.

After Hong had also slept and Yaun was taking his turn steering the sampan, Hong, Betsy, and Charlie talked softly about their lives and hopes. Hong spoke first of the wrenching of losing his country and his mother. But his face brightened when he spoke of his wife and two children, how much he missed them, and how overjoyed he was to finally be on his way to them. He spoke of the deep love between him and his wife and of her support for him, regardless of his decisions, whether right or sometimes wrong. Betsy edited his last remark to Charlie, adding she had never known Hong to be wrong about anything, which was why she felt so confident about this plan.

Charlie's respect for Hong grew as he watched the man confidently manage their route while showing deference to his father and consideration for everyone on board. He thought that if Hong had been with him at the Peking train station, the two of them could have given the Boxers a real challenge.

China was losing another fine man, but America was gaining one or two. Tan would be there also; the apple didn't fall far from the tree. Since they trusted Yaun, it was probable that he, too, was another fine gain for America. Charlie hadn't yet had a chance to have a personal conversation with the younger man, but he liked him. He felt sorrow that Tan was starting this new life in the midst of the tragedy of his wife's death, but he found himself envying Hong that he had one to join. He determined to stay in touch with Hong once they were in America and with Betsy.

"We haven't talked about your plans, Betsy. Will you be able to use your experiences in China and your fluency in the language?"

Betsy's face brightened as she shared for the first time, "Yes, but you'll be surprised to learn just what experience I'll be employed to use: Rand-McNally offered me a position in their Chicago office, effective whenever I want. I would never have heard of them if you hadn't sent that information." She sheepishly admitted: "My Christmas present from my parents last year was the thirteen illustrated volumes of the Pacific Railroad Surveys. Just what every girl wants!" She laughed.

"I just loved getting my first rag doll, too!" Charlie teased.

"No, honestly, I was thrilled! But it's just as well that I couldn't bring them, they're already obsolete. There is so much growth and expansion going on in America! I'm thrilled to be having a tiny part in mapping it!"

"Congratulations! In a way, you'll be recording history. Maybe you'll be famous some day; will you be traveling? That seems a little risky for a young woman, not, I assure you, that you aren't probably more qualified than a lot of American men!"

"I don't completely understand the things they wrote about in our mail exchanges, but I'm pretty sure I'll also be working with the US General Land Office. It will be a good way to reorient myself to my own nation after a lifetime in China.

"I am thrilled, honestly, I'd almost do this for free yet I'm going to be paid to travel the United States and be trained on a job I could only dream about before!

"I have a small inheritance coming to me, held in a bank in Indiana where my aunt lives. My plan is to use that to get established in the city, buy clothes, rent a room, and begin a life completely different from anything I've ever known."

They had successfully navigated the transfer from the Northern Canal near Tientsin. Hong explained through Betsy, "Since the railroads have been built between that city and Peking, the canals have been neglected. Silt and other sorts of blockage make it difficult to navigate at all, especially this time of year."

Betsy listened as Hong continued: "He says to tell you the rainy season starts soon, in July, which explains why these offshore slopes are at their lowest right now and the fetch for bigger boats is so limited."

Satisfied they weren't going to sink, Charlie found himself enjoying the pleasant voyage, "There are many more sampans and junks than I guess I expected. All this bustle of enterprise and activity seems so normal, so far away from the hostilities and fears surrounding Peking.

"You're accustomed to it, but I am intrigued by the contrast of antiquity and modernity I see everywhere; the clash between the cultures here; and by the seemingly very different worlds represented." Their sampan was just then passing a modern British Navy steamer headed in the opposite direction. "That is a most comforting sight. Just having an English presence out here feels good." Betsy's nod of her head beneath the net told him she felt the same way. He hoped it carried troops to relieve the refugees.

They would travel along the Yongding River, Charlie thought he remembered…or was it the Hai? Had they crossed that river when he was asleep? He wondered if different individuals gave different names to the same geographical point; if so, it certainly hadn't helped his attempts to memorize things. In any case, they would be traveling on another river before returning to the Grand Canal and on to the Yangtze. After observing the others for many hours, Charlie indicated his wish to take his turn at steering the narrow, flat-bottomed boat.

Betsy translated: "Hong wants to wait until we're away from any military presence."

A half hour later, Hong moved away, motioning for Charlie to take his place.

"Stay clear of the banks," Betsy relayed. "In case you're interested, what you're steering with is called a *Yuloh*." He was pleased that Hong trusted him enough to fall asleep.

As they traveled, Tan and Yaun were in deep conversation but always looking about. They busied themselves with mending and arranging the nets and buckets in ways that allowed them more comfort and concealment but which would seem to any onlookers to be the natural movements of ordinary peasants. They talked softly so as not to disturb Hong. Charlie wondered if life aboard a sampan trained the Chinese to be considerate of others in that way.

Along the shore, he saw people in the villages they passed similarly busy at work, ladies with shoulder-pole baskets filled with crops, he guessed; elsewhere, men and women either filling baskets or stacking empty ones, growing foods, or preparing foods. They were an industrious people, and Charlie fully understood why the Whitmores remained here so long.

Hong awoke and immediately checked to make sure Betsy was all right beneath her net; in taking back the *Yuloh*, he motioned pleasantly for Charlie to now crawl back under. It made Charlie a little apprehensive to learn they still needed to be concealed, and he wondered how he could possibly protect Betsy from an unknown danger.

With Betsy interpreting, Hong distracted him from his apprehension by telling them some of the history of the route they traveled. Charlie was fascinated by the Grand Canal, the longest in the world, he knew. Hong proudly talked about it being one of the best engineering feats in the world, yet it had been built centuries earlier. He described ancient sluice gates, which he explained were still in use to control water levels.

Still ensconced in her comfortable niche, Betsy effortlessly transformed Hong's strange sounds to a factual travelogue: "Hundreds more sluices along the canal ultimately made it possible for Tan's and Hong's ancestors to travel from all over the continent. Rock, stone, and marble were brought from the finest quarries all over China to erect the magnificent palaces and other governmental buildings that you admired."

"I remember reading about the invention of the pound lock, in, what…the tenth-century, I think that's about when it was… and how it had permitted ancient ships to travel upward into extremely high elevations. I'm embarrassed to think how often I have wrongly felt as though life in the United States offers the most modern and advanced of all incredible inventions, industry, creativity, and progress; it has taken this ancient civilization to remind me that men and women have always been brilliant problem-solvers! Some of the earliest solutions to very difficult problems have been much more challenging than many of the modern ones."

Among the more intriguing structures, to Charlie, were the dwellings on stilts. He found it reassuring that people everywhere adapted to environments that outsiders might regard as harsh and made the most of what they had. Beyond the crowded riverbanks and especially where mountains separated, Charlie saw tidy farmlands.

"I guess survival has demanded they crowd around these water sources and find ways to adapt." Charlie commented.

"Yet, through the centuries, many have also been suddenly brought to ruin or even death by flooding and droughts of the very sources on which their lives depended."

Betsy shared their conversation with Hong. He smiled telling through Betsy that his grandparents, Tan's mother and father, had worked three hundred and eighty-seven hectares of crops along here when he was a boy and had been flooded out twice.

Hong's smile fell suddenly, mid-sentence. Charlie turned his head in the direction Hong was looking and heard the first jarring sounds of artillery firing. Their sampan was emerging from behind a mountain range and was just rounding a bend. Ahead were ominous, dark clouds of smoke hanging over a small city sprawled along the river. It had been hidden from view by the mountains.

A line of junks faced the city's wharves back about fifty yards in the river. They were tossing and dipping, apparently from both the recoil of their guns and the force of the returned firing landing in the water just short of their bows. The swells from the churning were furiously spreading out rocking the smaller sampan; at first the effects were merely noticeable.

But the gap between their own craft and the junks was narrowing and the rocking quickly became more fierce. Water splashed inside staining Betsy's borrowed trousers with its filth. Startled, she swiped the mud with one hand, grabbing Charlie's hand with her other. "Do you, do you think we're going to be all right?" She asked, trying not to sound scared.

Tan reassured her in his broken English; Charlie crouched down to hear.

"Manchu...navy...maybe village friendly to Christians" were the only words he could make out from the singsong tones of Tan's best attempts.

A louder volley attracted Charlie's attention back to the scene before them. He watched as a scattering of fires along the waterfront quickly spread, posing an additional threat to a way of life. He saw sampans and other craft around the wharves crush together violently.

Charlie knelt next to Betsy, giving words to the scene before their eyes. "I've seen no place along China's river cities where there aren't throngs of busy people, I wonder where they're hiding or if they escaped into the fields behind. Their sampans and other vessels are destroyed, the only reason they're not submerged is that the water is so low right now."

"So the village is at the mercy of these militants, whoever they are? These hostile forces are people who are surely not unlike the villagers here; people who also belong to this land they're destroying, and maybe us along with it!"

"This ancient land is eternal, Betsy, her people persevere." Charlie knew it sounded lame, but he was struggling too and distracted by worry of how to protect her without alarming her more.

They were no more than two minutes past the bend, if that. Their course would take them directly between the junks and the banks. Charlie's mind raced trying to understand what Hong and Tan might be thinking; and to recall all he'd learned about these apparent combatants using or commandeering what he supposed were formerly commercial vessels. *Why is Hong still heading toward them? Of these "two sides" is at least one friendly to foreigners?*

The exchange of artillery firing increased and was becoming louder and more aggressive, both from the junks and from the shore. The air was pungent with the smoke now drifting into their faces, stinging their eyes.

Between volleys, the popping of small side arms reached Charlie's ears, coming from the direction of the coastline between the sampan and the village. Were the situation less dire, he would have found the contrast of handguns against artillery amusing. His eyes searched the faces of his Chinese friends, trying to detect whatever telltale signs there were of alarm or the lack of it, but their expressions seemed impassive. "Inscrutable," Doc would have said. He tried to keep his own equally inscrutable, but his heart was pounding.

Charlie gave what he intended to be an encouraging smile to Betsy. She was white faced but smiled back at him weakly. "Don't worry about me!" She opened her mouth to say something else but then closed it and looked away, remaining silent. He moved to lay a hand on her shoulder in a way he hoped would offer more reassurance than he felt. She seemed fragile to him clinging to her side of the sampan as it now rocked uncontrollably.

Hong's voice sang out what Charlie thought was at least one long paragraph. But Betsy said simply, "He doesn't think we should proceed."

Hong and Tan exchanged rapid words, their faces finally registering alarm. The expansiveness of Tan's gesturing announced the precariousness of their situation. Hong turned the small craft toward the bank, apparently intending to reverse their route.

Betsy spoke close in Charlie's ear, still needing to shout: "They don't know whether allied or Manchu forces have commandeered the junks; they can't tell which. Tan thinks enemy forces have infiltrated the village, so you can forget what I said a moment ago..."

Before she finished speaking, shots rang out splashing nearer the sampan. As hurriedly as possible, Hong brought the boat alongside the bank about two hundred yards north of the junks.

"Jump!" Betsy hadn't needed to translate. All scrambled out of the sampan into the water.

Hong and Yaun grabbed ropes, secured knots, and tossed one each to Charlie and Tan, their voices in higher pitch, speaking in rapid Chinese. Both men gestured for the others to help pull the craft back around and along the canal's edge. The tepid water struck Charlie at thigh level, but the bottom was sloped and slippery, making it very difficult to maneuver.

Betsy and Tan were on the side of the sampan opposite the shore when it struck a protrusion, her face registered more fear, not understanding the cause of the shudder from the craft. At that moment a violent swell of water engulfed their boat causing it to immediately list to starboard toward the pair. It happened so fast, Charlie could only watch helplessly.

Shouting to each other in Chinese, Tan and Betsy clung to the outside of the vessel but lost their footing and slid under it, their weight adding to the momentum as the sampan continued turning over, swallowing them under its cavity.

Hong reached the two first and pulled Betsy out from under. She sputtered through the mud sliding down her face, "I'm all right, I'm all right. Where's Tan?"

Charlie's glance took in the cut on her forehead, seeing she was otherwise unhurt. He grasped Tan's arm, pulling his head above water, but the man couldn't seem to get a foothold to stand. Charlie braced himself against the sampan, now laying on its side, and helped him up. The man hurriedly swiped the mud out of his eyes, turning his attention toward the threat ahead.

If ever disparate conditions converged at once to create a disaster, this is it! Charlie thought as he looked to Hong for direction out of this one.

An eerie, chilling sound pierced Charlie's consciousness causing his heart to pound harder. He took hold of Betsy's arm and looked around wildly; he'd heard it before while he was sinking into unconsciousness at the Peking rail terminal. He'd heard it again that same night while later running to escape his assailants and more dimly from time to time while safely inside the compound. It was the sound of many human voices raised in a pitched fervor to kill.

"Charlie, some of those are Manchu."

More shots rang out landing in front of them and the eerie shrieks grew louder.

"Betsy!" He shouted to get her attention, pushed her behind the overturned boat, holding her to keep her from falling, and shoved it hard back from the bank. The firing of artillery momentarily drowned out the sounds of the handguns but their waterspouts signaled that the group was still being fired upon.

Charlie pulled Betsy's hand onto the vessel. "Betsy, it isn't going to sink any further. Can you swim?

She nodded and in an attempt at bravado, shouted back, "Like an Olympic champion."

"Good, I want you to move with the sampan back slowly toward the center of the canal. Do you understand?"

She didn't move or answer. "Betsy! Do you hear me?"

She nodded without speaking.

"Good girl; go on." He gave it another shove, and it floated freely.

Charlie knew it would provide only a little protection but hoped it might conceal her. He'd seen two different types of garb, Manchu and Boxers. Knowing that Boxers rarely if ever used guns, he reminded himself grimly of what Betsy's fate could be: Boxers preferred to sever their victims with rusty saws if they couldn't kick them to death.

He estimated a group of fifty or more militants were heading at a run straight for them; not all had guns, but even one was more than his group had.

He shouted to Betsy but deliberately turned his back to her, moving away as rapidly as he could manage, wanting to divert attention from the sampan. "Betsy, no matter what happens, no *matter* what: Stay hidden and take the sampan back north after dark."

She was silent. "Betsy"—he raised his voice louder—"I'm not looking at you so speak so I'll know you heard me."

"Why aren't you and the others coming?"

"We'll be along." He turned, moving away, intending to do what he could to distract the group on shore from the sampan. None had a chance if all attracted attention while trying to scramble toward it. He saw with gratitude that the other men were doing the same. They now turned toward the city instead of away from it, but away from the watercraft where Betsy was concealed.

A single shot rang out from the shore, and Yaun fell, a circle of blood rippling out in the dirty water. More shots splashed the water around them. Tan rose reaching toward Yaun, grief distorting his face.

Hong screamed something to his father. Charlie's voice joined. "Tan! Get down!" He reached to pull him back down just as Tan was hit in the chest once and then again.

The elderly man had slipped down, then stood again, still crouched slightly between Charlie and the shore for mere seconds, and it had cost him his life. Charlie saw the hole in Tan's chest with blood pumping out and the look of surprise on the man's face as he fell back.

"Oh God, please, no, no!" Charlie screamed out. There had been no time to prepare for this, no making of a plan of survival or a proper thank you for his kindness.

Shock numbed him, strangely altering all his senses. Tan's blood had been bright red before, but now it was dark brown. The shrieks and gunfire had been sharp and shrill; now they sounded dull and flat. The tepid water felt icy, the taste of metal was in his mouth, and the stench that had filled his nostrils now smelled of death.

Charlie moved as if in slow motion, but lost his footing in the slippery silt. He staggered back with Tan's body rolling on top of him, sensing more bullets tearing into it. Sickened, with the taste of fear and horror in his mouth, for just a moment he felt tempted to stay down. "Was there peace with Tan at the bottom of this muddy river?"

He gulped air just as water rushed over his head, being forced down by the weight of Tan's body. As suddenly as he had become numb, Charlie came to his senses. Struggling to regain footing, he felt the impact of bullets landing all around him.

"Tan, my friend." Charlie felt his tears and didn't hold them back. "I wish I had known you better. If by some miracle we make it out of here, I vow to see that you are honored for the sacrifice of your life."

Louder artillery fire erupted again from the junks, to his horror it was in their direction. With effort, Charlie managed to kneel and stabilize himself in the sloping water's edge. The three of them—Betsy, Hong and himself—at first seemed caught in crossfire. He bent his head around Tan's vacant face turned now toward him. Charlie closed the man's eyes, his attention for the moment on the immediate danger.

The artillery fire was deafening yet had still not discouraged the militants on shore—the first shells landed short—but they were still firing in the direction where Charlie and Hong stood in the open. "Hong," Charlie shouted, "get underwater, swim underwater!"

Charlie remained crouched behind Tan's body surveying the area. His mind raced to formulate some plan that might improve at least Betsy's chances of surviving. He glanced toward Hong as another volley of artillery firing from all of the junks redirected his attention; shells were landing around them and on shore.

Hope flashed through him as he saw several of the militants go down and watched as the others fled.

"Yoo hoo!" Charlie called out, relief washing over him. He turned, raising a victorious signal to Hong, and saw with horror that the man had been hit. "No!" Charlie's long cry shattered the silence left in the wake of the last volley. He moved, stumbling, sliding, and falling, drinking in the filthy water before righting himself, struggling toward his friend.

Stretching to take hold of his shoulders, Charlie felt revulsion and a sickening in the pit of his stomach as his hand grasped only bloody, jagged bone where Hong's left shoulder had been. He swallowed bile, momentarily so shocked he mindlessly reached out for pieces of Hong's flesh floating nearby, then recoiled from his act, forcing his attention back to Hong's face.

Desperate to comfort the dying man, Charlie tried to think of any word in Hong's language; he knew none of assurance. Yet, he felt compelled to speak to him, if only in English as Hong's eyes began to lose focus.

"Hong! Hong! God bless you. Hong, you are a very noble man!" Searching for something fitting to say as life was leaving Hong's body, he thought to sing the words to "Amazing Grace." His voice cracking with deep grief and shock, Charlie forced himself to sing on: "How sweet the sound…"

A smile curled Hong's lips, his eyes fluttered open one last time before closing on their own. In them, Charlie saw peace.

Further repulsed by the sacrilege to the man's dignity, Charlie nevertheless let go of Hong's body. Sobs escaped him, terrible and haunting even to his own ears, as he watched it sink just beneath the surface of the water. He sensed a numbness spreading over him again, like a blanket on a very cold night that didn't warm the body but made the cold tolerable.

He crab-crawled his way to the sampan. The quiet from it provoking a dulled fear of what he might find. The thought struck him if he could just stand still right where he was, then Betsy would remain alive; as long as he didn't look behind the vessel, she would be as he had left her. His thoughts seemed disturbed, unlike him, *Have I lost control of my mind?* He knew for certain that her death would drive him over the edge beyond sanity.

He found her huddled behind the sampan, shaking all over and sobbing. He held her in his arms, feeling her convulse again and again. He found no words to say to her and no will to utter them if he had. He drew strength from her warmth, her humanness, and the fact that she was alive. They clung to each other until dark. There had been no more shelling and no more hostilities from the shore.

"Betsy, we've got to try and turn the sampan over and go back at least around the bend. Then I'll go ashore to see if it's safe." He waited. His were the first words they had spoken in the hour or so since the… *Slaughter*, Charlie thought. *This wasn't a war skirmish; this was a slaughter.*

He waited for her to speak, but instead she started convulsing again. He held her tightly. At last she spoke. Her teeth chattering, sobs escaping, she continued to tremble. "Char…Char… Charlie, there are b-bullet holes in the b-b-boat."

It was a violation of his sensibilities to merely leave the bodies of his friends in the river, but they had no choice. When he could, if he ever found a friendly Chinese face again, he would tell someone about them so as to give them a proper burial. If he ever made it home again, he would look up their families in San Francisco, if he could find them, and make sure they knew that their men had died heroes. And when he could, he would grieve their deaths and ponder the mystery that had allowed him once again to live while others died around him.

They fell asleep in each other's arms. They had made their way back northeast on foot to where the bend in the river started. Charlie wasn't sure they were entirely safe, but he was positive that neither could go on any farther. He had no idea what to expect. He had no logic about how and who were enemies or why Hong and the others had been so indiscriminately shot. There was nothing about them, was there, that said "Christian" or "enemy"? He was so spent he could barely crawl under a tiny pier, finding space there only because the water level was down.

"*Chuk! Chuk! Chuk!*" Charlie opened his eyes to morning sun and the boy's smiling face where he squatted down, looking into Charlie's. He recognized the child on the train. For a moment, he thought he was back on the train; in that moment, he felt an overpowering sense of dread that all he had gone through over the past month still lay ahead.

Betsy sat up, bumping her head on the pier. She was pale with grief and shock still in her eyes. She managed a weak smile at the boy, speaking to him in a different-sounding Chinese dialect. Charlie listened to them converse for a few minutes. Their conversation demanded nothing of him and so provided a brief respite from the heavy burdens that waking had thrust back on his shoulders. It gave him time to reflect on the past thirty-six hours. He didn't think he would be able to handle another crisis, but he didn't know what a man was supposed to do when the limit to his strength and sanity had been exceeded.

He felt a powerful longing to be home again in Mississippi. He wanted to be sitting on the porch, drinking coffee with Doc or hunting deer with Oxytak or telling Jessie a story and making her laugh again. He wanted to see Jessie smile at him as she had that last day at the brook.

He wanted innocence again; he wished he were not too old to cry. Those things were gone, and so far, the only things that had replaced them were death, shock, pain, loss, and grief. He thought again about his newest friends. Tan had died in his place. All three of them had willingly sacrificed their lives to further Betsy's chances of survival. There it was again: sacrifice and giving so that others may…what?

Betsy turned to him, managing a smile. He saw that color was returning to her cheeks. "Your young man here has quite a hero's crush on you! He met you on the train, said you gave him a horse? No? Well, he tells me that his parents liked you very much, and he's inviting us home with him. He says we can see his house from here."

Charlie laid his arm across the lad's shoulders. "I don't know, Betsy. I've learned some needed lessons here about being more cautious. If my memory serves me, this young man and his parents were, well, maybe at least relaxed with the Boxers who got on the train…I think not far from where they boarded. It may be that they knew each other. I don't have any certainty that we wouldn't be walking back into the hornet's nest."

"He says his father is a servant for the British government. I know they have an outpost near here. It was originally established to keep surveillance on the Russian outpost. I actually believe he is our own God-sent little angel. Besides, think 'baths', Charlie, and food, especially 'food.' I'm famished!"

Given all the enormous difficulties since he had arrived in China, Charlie was still in disbelief that leaving it had fallen into place so easily. Thanks to the British government and underground cable, the details of arranging their transport to Shanghai and passage to San Francisco could not have been smoother. He and Betsy had even been given a wardrobe suitable for the trip. He had young "Michael," as Betsy had renamed him, to thank for it all.

They stood on deck watching the San Francisco skyline grow larger. "Imagine!" Betsy marveled. "If you hadn't been on the same train car as our "Michael," we might still be running for our lives in China!"

She was silent in thought for a moment. "There are no coincidences in life, are there, Charlie?"

"The astonishment," Charlie responded, "is that the British government took responsibility for a proper burial for Hong, Tan, and Yaun."

"Yes, that is amazing, especially in light of the fact that they never admitted they had commandeered those junks or fired on us!"

"I'm very glad that reparations will be made to enable Hong's family to live here in comfort."

The American government kept its word and notified Betsy's aunt, alerting her of her niece's arrival. To Betsy's delight, the family traveled to San Francisco and met the boat as it docked

Shortly after they docked, Charlie wired Oxytak a brief explanation of his absence and promised a letter to follow. Then he went alone to Chinatown to Hong's family to offer his condolences and to tell them their loved ones had died heroes. A neighbor translated for him. It felt strange and disconcerting to be walking these streets; inside Chinatown more resembled the nation he had just left than an American city. He guessed it had provided much-needed comfort of familiarity to the thousands of Chinese railroad workers who had connected this nation's coasts. He was also struck again by the politeness of the culture that required of Hong's family even in their deepest sorrow to seek first to comfort him and put him at ease.

The first thing on his agenda after he returned to Mississippi was a good, long visit with his old friend. Oxytak would appreciate all Charlie's experiences and would provide some needed insight, comforting, and healing.

A distracted, subdued Charlie joined Betsy and her family for a farewell dinner at their hotel where he agreed to a visit with them someday in Indiana. He gave Betsy the address of Rosalie Wilson, promising to also write his friend to expect Betsy to call on her.

They said their good-byes, with Betsy crying, "Charlie, I can never thank you enough. You did indeed rescue me as you came to do."

They embraced for a long moment. No words would have defined the strength of the silent bond between them. "It was a team effort, Betsy, although we lost our leaders. But you made rescue possible by nursing me back to recovery from my injuries."

"But you protected me with your very life!"

"And you translated the languages when I most needed it."

"Well, you're the one who befriended a small boy on the train."

"And it was you who had confidence in him when mine faltered."

They burst into laughter, but each knew their lifelong friendship was forged by the sharing of their most frightening experiences and by the comfort and sanity each had provided to the other. Charlie understood that the deeper relationships were those with whom one had shared vulnerabilities, hardship, and suffering rather than only pleasure and mediocrity.

He had read the front pages of the papers in the hotel lobby while waiting for Betsy and her family. Two stories got his attention: The legation compound in Peking had been reinforced, first by American and later allied troops a few days after Charlie and Betsy had fled; and the Philippines were now engaged in guerilla warfare against America. This story suggested that the Filipinos had not been able to resist the American military but were resorting to a type of warfare that apparently gave them greater advantages. Doc's words came to mind that a man always had more than one oversized burden to carry at a time. Charlie was finding out that was also true of nations.

On impulse, he stopped back by the telegraph office to see if Oxytak might have already received his wire and responded. Oxytak's message warmed his heart: "Son, welcome home. Can you meet me in Guthrie, Oklahoma Territory on your return? Wire me there when you know your schedule."

He caught a train out that very night. He wasn't in the mood for sightseeing; he wanted to go home. He wanted the time to heal and to grieve for Hong, Tan, and Yaun. There had been nothing mediocre about those three unsung heroes. Right now, home was wherever Oxytak would be. He didn't think there were any uprisings or battles of any sort going on in Oklahoma Territory or Indian Territory. He prayed not.

Chapter 10

Charlie was deep in thought as he rode Tan along the verdant bank of the Arkansas River. He was on his way back to Guthrie from the northeast corner of Cherokee Nation. He preferred that name to merely "Indian Nation" or Indian Territory, although he knew the time was approaching when it would all be "Oklahoma." The appeal of the Indians to Washington to have it declared a separate state was falling on deaf ears there. *But then, when had it not?*

He reflected on the terrible circumstances that had spawned the territory. Enactment of the Indian Removal Act of 1830 had wrought unimaginable suffering along the Trail of Tears. Yet, the Cherokee settlers in these parts had risen above the evil done to them and developed and improved this land. Eventually, they had produced a more intelligent and effective Constitution than that produced out of Oklahoma Territory.

There were times when the fighting and struggles here were reminiscent of China's although of course on a much smaller level—land claim disputes, begging the government for rightful considerations, and the long drought that had ended just before his arrival had frayed the nerves of people who had invested everything they had into this land. For some, the "everything" had been little more than hopes and dreams with good intentions of hard work. Those who remained were strong, courageous, dedicated, and yet ever ready to enjoy life. Most of them had a deep faith.

The appointed Governor Ferguson seemed to be effective and honest. Charlie had liked him the one time he'd met him at a meeting between some of the more vocal factions in Guthrie. Oxytak had invited Charlie to attend and when it ended, Charlie remarked to his friend, "I've certainly gained an added appreciation for the immense difficulties in settling any disputes among large groups."

"You're right there, Charlie, "there are always far more demands than can realistically be met, yet no one ever wants to back away from his own claim of righteousness or rights violated."

"I saw that, it seems everyone every where wants the others to do the backing away from theirs."

Acknowledging his bias favoring the Cherokees, Charlie had gained respect for all Indians. His admiration for this half of his heritage had increased greatly now that he was able to interact with so many more of them and do so as an adult. He was impressed by the dignity so many reflected in their negotiations and how they conformed themselves to what was best for the whole tribe, yet individuality was manifested in their achievements and growth. He thought they at least deserved to have their own state.

"Nevertheless," Oxytak suggested, "there are also advantages to the joining of the two territories, east with west under the one name: *Oklahoma*."

Charlie had liked the word the minute it first rolled off Oxytak's tongue years ago. He thought it was fitting that either way the whole area would end up honoring the "red people" with its name.

"You've been telling me about this land since I was old enough to have any comprehension of there being anyplace outside the farm and Jackson. You gave me an appreciation for the history of the Indian people always reminding me that I could be proud of being half Cherokee."

For the first time in many years, he recalled how the new preacher wouldn't shake his hand. It made him smile now as he told Oxytak about it. "The man didn't last long in town, he must have offended a few others too."

Indian Nation had been good to him. In the almost four years he had been here, he had grown to love the beauty of his adopted territory, although he could do with less wind. The deep longing to put down roots had been born that night on the river in China when he wasn't sure he or Betsy would survive. He had felt an intense homesickness, yet his heart had no place to rest itself. The feeling was a bit unsettling. The Harper's place, Jackson, and all of Mississippi seemed to belong to a different person. The boy who had ridden Horse bareback, idolized Doc, and walked arm in arm with Frank was no more.

Whoever he was then had been undermined by Mrs. Harper's denunciations and Mr. Harper's acquiescence to them. Not his character or his faith. They hadn't changed. But for the first many months after leaving their home, he felt as though his identity had been taken from him. He had been building another ever since. Who was he if the childhood that defined and molded the man he'd become turned out to have been a mockery?

"That's not altogether true," he corrected himself. "Doc and Oxytak had at least as much influence on my identity as life with the Harpers." He knew Oxytak respected him and treated him as an equal in every way. He hoped Doc would have been proud of the man he was becoming and how he was putting to use the valuable lessons his mentor had taught him.

Many nights he lay in bed going over talks he'd shared with Doc. The man's mind still astounded Charlie. Doc had stayed abreast of all the latest developments and influences on society and encouraged Charlie to do the same. He taught Charlie to discern truth and to tease out the underlying message of a belief system or movement.

As a result of Doc's urgings, Charlie knew basic philosophies of many of the great thinkers from Socrates, Aristotle, and Plato to Charles Darwin, John Dewey, Oliver Wendell Holmes, and recently, he'd been fascinated by Max Planck's works.

"He could almost hear Doc telling him, "Son, go back to the Bible, always compare truths with Truth then form your own conclusions." Thanks to Doc, his heroes were men like St. Augustine and Martin Luther more than the Greeks and modernists.

Every time he made an important decision now, Charlie was reminded that a wiser man than he had guided him in the direction of prudence and good judgment. Above all, he followed Doc's advice about remaining true to himself and his Creator. His view of the world was largely defined by the truths he found in God's Word; he loved all scientific discoveries and continued to find that they supported Scriptures, not the other way around.

Nevertheless, he knew that his experiences since leaving the Harpers had also shaped the man he was today. They had certainly strengthened his belief that all life has purpose.

He told Oxytak, "If the Bible doesn't make one examine the meaning and purpose of life, surviving something that should have killed you surely will!"

"And what did you conclude from your examination?" Oxytak had asked.

"That a life well lived is one that is on God's terms, not man's, and that success is determined by the degree to which a man has yielded his own will to God's."

"Even when that means he's going to take the bullet for someone else?"

Charlie was quiet for a moment before answering: "I have come to believe that given a choice, knowing then what they now know, neither man would hesitate to agree to that same boat ride!"

"Son, you've not talked much about the night you arrived in Peking, and only very little about the battle that took the lives of your three Chinese friends."

"No, I haven't spoken of it to many, much more to you than anyone. But I waged my own battles with all of it in the first three years."

In truth, Charlie had wrestled with both those terrible events—every moment of them, every move, every image of horror that had burned into his mind. He shared all his fears and doubts with God, acknowledging his presence in everything. He wrestled through them all so that those terrible memories wouldn't lie there in the back of his head and come out to haunt him ever again. He'd been much more at peace this last year.

Examining his life had become an on-going process for Charlie. He didn't take himself too seriously, but he regarded life itself as very sacred, not at all to be taken lightly. He no longer experienced guilt about having survived while others died. He accepted God's decisions on those things having finally believed he'd done all he could.

He named his horse Tan so that every day he would remember to be grateful for the sacrifice of that life. When asked once if giving one's horse the name of a man who had saved your life wasn't a bit sacrilegious, he'd replied, only half kidding, "Not if you respect your horse."

Naming Horse's successor after Tan was the highest honor Charlie thought he could bestow on the man. He sometimes toyed with the idea of naming his first son Hong Tan or Tan Hong. He laughed now. It didn't sound so natural in America… but still, he'd think about that.

He reached a fork in the river and nudged Tan toward the Spring River tributary that flowed more easterly and rode on, turning his mind to the original purpose of his trip, which was to look over a gristmill. The seller seemed like a good man, a German immigrant. He'd come to the territory during the land rush, eventually married an Indian woman, and relocated here to property she had acquired. Four babies later, she convinced him to move farther south to Claremore.

Charlie knew that mineral water had been discovered in Claremore and that it was attracting a lot of people looking to get rich quick. Mr. Mueller seemed more of the sort who would run a better gristmill than a radium bathhouse. As if reading Charlie's mind, the man said his wife was in poor health and believed that having access to the baths would improve it. Charlie examined the accounting records, impressed with the man's meticulous attention to detail.

He next compared the mill's income and expenses over the past five years with those of a lumberyard and mill he was considering. The gristmill was dependent upon things over which God alone had control: drought, storms, late springs, early winters. In contrast, the lumberyard was more attractive because timber was already abundant; prudent management could prosper it. Too, there was an ever-increasing population of people who were using lumber to build businesses and could finally afford to build their own homes. Besides, he was already half owner of a profitable lumberyard; he understood that business. Mr. Mueller looked relieved rather than disappointed when Charlie went back to tell him his decision.

Charlie dismounted and gave Tan a lump of sugar from his vest pocket, running the heel of his hand down the animal's face. Tan nudged his nose into Charlie's palm and kept it there. It had been a pleasant surprise to Charlie to realize he was as attached to Tan as he had been to Horse. Their natures were much alike.

For all its challenges, the territory was a beautiful land. The mountains, if they could be called that, were thickly forested; their plateaus filled with streams and rivers that fed into the watershed that was part of the Mississippi. To have even that remote connection to the river in this small way gladdened his heart as though the two lands were united, his past and his future here together.

He waited for the ferry at Adair to cross back over the Neosho River. He and Oxytak had camped and fished from it when his friend took him all over to acquaint Charlie with the territory. Nearby was where they had talked and planned Charlie's future. Farther down river was the Neosho Fish Hatchery established not long before Charlie arrived. It felt good to be a part of a growing, thriving community where he could contribute and hopefully make a positive difference, as Doc had done in his town.

With Oxytak's considerable help on all requirements for the land grant and Doc's stake, Charlie had managed to do better than he had ever anticipated. He remained in Guthrie, the territorial capital, for the twenty-two months it had taken him to make his business decisions and educate himself on all matters relating to his investments.

That is, he used Guthrie as his hub. He traveled all over the territory, sometimes accompanied by Oxytak, to investigate a business or work one

Although of course on a much smaller scale, he found himself inspired by Li Hongzhang's practices, and they seemed effective. He finally invested in a coal mine and upgraded the railway tracks to it from the main line. He bought acreage with timber, claiming his rightful grant entitlement as half Cherokee, and then invested as a partner in a lumber company, after making certain that it was a well-managed one.

He worked many months in the mine itself, becoming bone weary and blackened along with the others. He was determined to understand the business from the bottom up and, more importantly to him, to know what the miners experienced. He next worked in the lumber mill beginning with cutting timber, hauling logs, and sawing boards. Most of his evenings were spent reading about both businesses until he knew exactly how they should be operated, what problems to look for, and what improvements to make.

In the course of his self-education, he tolerated the snickers behind his back whenever he made mistakes or used the wrong terms. But in short time, he gained respect from the hardworking men when they saw that he put up with the same conditions they did and caught up with them in skill.

In many ways, the men who worked the industries, especially the miners, reminded Charlie of the ship's crew he worked with on his way to China. Here, too, there were mixtures of every language and dialect, hardworking people who had given up their homelands in the hopes of improving lives for the families they either brought with them or expected to establish here. Charlie hoped the conditions were not as bad for them as they had been for their counterparts in the Chicago stockyards.

When he'd been satisfied that he knew enough about the businesses to also leave them in the hands of more experienced operators, he set about looking for a general store, either to purchase or build and start up. He wanted one that looked like Mr. Davis's, with the barrels and shelves and the long counter with room at the back for a card table and chairs. He spent some months looking and paying attention to the direction of the population growth of the territory; he didn't intend to buy a store where there would not be expansion.

He liked the northeast part for its beauty as well as its variety of industries. The many streams provided water and power to communities that were expanding and to farms and mills. Oxytak told him he believed the Grand River area would be a source of hydroelectric power before long. Charlie had read about the hydroelectric progress of Niagara Falls; he intended to go there one day, hopefully with a special someone. At any rate, trusting his friend's judgment was one more reason Charlie leaned toward settling here.

He didn't want a store in Guthrie; the city already boasted many, and there was talk that the capital might not remain in Guthrie once statehood was achieved, whenever that might be. He thought the competition was already stretched and the risk greater than he was willing to take. Besides, it didn't match the dream in his heart. He supposed he was idealizing Mr. Davis's store outside Jackson, at a busy crossroads, but that's what he pictured: a store that would be a central gathering place for locals and travelers. He could keep up with local and federal politics in that way, maybe sponsor occasional concerts and talent contests, and perhaps one day install gasoline pumps if the automobile became more popular out this way.

Guthrie was a fine, fast-growing city. It had none of the old-world charm of Jackson but instead had its own clean, sophisticated, modern look. Building went on all the time—all well-built structures of brick and sand stone the latter mined from around the area. He enjoyed architecture and thought Guthrie's buildings and homes gave it an elegance that somehow reminded him of a small Chicago.

The growth had slowed some. He sometimes thought there were more government offices than anything else, but he'd been able to find everything here he could need. There were all the usual institutions that formed the infrastructure of a thriving city, including several newspapers and more banks. He learned one could run into a lawyer anywhere in town, and never need worry about finding a doctor. There were saloons and dance halls with good musicians making rounds from other cities, so there was a constant stream of news and all the latest trends and newest songs.

The city had just dedicated its brand new Carnegie Library. Charlie became an instant and frequent visitor there. He had books stacked all over his basement level rented room. The books he had been poring over this past month were on architecture and house design. He realized he was jumping the gun somewhat. Before he built, he needed to make a definite decision about where he wanted to live, and that might also depend on what his feelings were for Sarah.

He had spied the pretty woman at a church box supper and outbid every man. The escalating bidding made her blush. He paid eleven dollars and seventy-five cents for her box supper, by far the most ever bid in that town. At least that was what the auctioneer announced and Sarah confirmed.

After that night, he took Sarah to church, square dancing, concerts in the park, and to suppers or on picnics whenever he was in town. She had attended Normal School in Edmond to become a schoolteacher and now taught in one of Guthrie's new schools. He enjoyed her company more than almost anyone else in his life. She was interested in everything, like Charlie, and knew at least as much about United States history, politics, and geography as he did. He hadn't meant their relationship to go beyond a friendship but realized he crossed that line the way he'd kissed her on a moonlit night walking her home from a concert.

The music had been exceptionally good, and they were in fine spirits. The moon was low above the horizon, seemingly so near them Charlie offered to pluck it from the sky for her.

DIXIE MILLER STEWART

The early April night was still chilly, so he took off his jacket to drape it over Sarah's shoulders and left his arm around her. The brush of his hand against the softness of her neck was an unexpected pleasure.

Feeling her respond to him by curving her body into his unleashed a sudden, powerful hunger he'd been denying too long. As one, they moved into each other's arms in a kiss so intense it caught Charlie by surprise. He stepped back to lean against a tree trunk and drew her to him, fitting her slender body between his legs, parted so as to bring himself nearer her height; the effect made him catch his breath. He kissed her mouth and her throat; his hands clasped the small of her back, his fingers pressing her body tighter against his. He was intensely aware of her every curve and everywhere their bodies touched.

Sarah trembled as he slowly moved his hands up her back and shoulders, absorbing her femaleness. A groan escaped from him as she laid her hand against his chest inside his shirt, the other at the small of his back, pressing herself harder against him. He desperately wanted to hold her breasts but made his hands return to her waist. It, too, was curved and inviting. He didn't think he was capable of such self-restraint or that it had ever before been so required of him.

He held her face between his hands and kissed her eyes and mouth again and again. He loved touching her; he had no thoughts, only hunger and a consuming fire. They were both trembling and breathless when finally he held her away from him, releasing a deep sigh; neither spoke for several minutes. He leaned his head back against the tree, running both hands through his hair and clasping them at the base of his neck, taking a gulp of air.

"Sarah, Sarah." He found no further words. He felt a pang of conscience and the thought, *I'm not free to kiss her like this!*

She spoke, her voice a seductive whisper that made him want to reach for her again; he had not known such passion was possible. She stood on tiptoe, her arms around his neck, pulling him down to her. He made himself stop her.

"Sarah." He could barely speak. "You know I'm leaving early in the morning. We...we need to go home."

"Yes." She seemed to wilt against his chest, her disappointment obvious. "You're going to be gone two weeks! I don't think I can stand that!"

"Sarah..." He stopped, realizing with a start that he had been about to say he was not free to court her or to have her hope their relationship might become more serious. But why should he feel that way?

For the first time he was admitting to himself the importance of the promise he made to Jessie almost four years ago. It had never left the back of his mind, but he had kept it there. It wasn't kissing Sarah that thrust it to the forefront of his thoughts; it was Sarah's reaction. She had a right to expect more of him after all these months of seeing her and then kissing her as he had tonight.

She waited for him to finish his sentence. When he did not, she spoke. "I have grown to care very much for you, Charlie. I probably shouldn't be saying this—a wiser woman would wait for you to say it first—but I am in love with you! I want a future with you! If I wasn't sure of that before, I certainly am after tonight!" A splash of moonlight illumined eyes that begged him to tell her he was also in love with her, to somehow take away the vulnerability she felt having made her profession of love.

He kissed her forehead and held her close. "You're a wonderful girl, Sarah." He felt anything he said would be inadequate but nonetheless groped for words that would reflect his sincerity. "You mean very much to me. I have enjoyed being with you more than I can ever remember with another person, except maybe Doc."

"Doc? A man? Oh, I love hearing that maybe you like me almost as much as your best male friend!" Her sarcasm was unbecoming, but Charlie knew she was hurt.

He wanted to lighten the evening so they would not part with this tension; he needed time to think, to decide what he was going to do about Jessie. Not until that was settled would he know what to do about Sarah.

Their conversation was more awkward than it had ever been since the night of the box supper months back. They spoke only of the weather and the moon the rest of the way home. He kissed her lightly on the lips at her door and promised to call on her when he returned.

It had taken him eleven days to make his junket, spending a few days each at the lumberyard, the coalmine, and the gristmill. He was now on his way to look at another possible location for a store and a site to build a home. Reaching the river, he grasped the ropes and pulled firmly, assisting the operator to return the ferry to his side of the Neosho. He nodded to the man and led Tan on to the craft. He'd be heading back to Guthrie tomorrow, yet he had hardly thought about Sarah in any depth. Every time he intended to think about her and sort through his feelings, Jessie came to mind.

Every time he remembered kissing Sarah, Jessie came to mind. He recalled what Doc had warned him about misplacing passion and affections. He didn't know what his affections were for that young Mississippi girl, but he knew he wasn't free to love Sarah until he kept his word to Jessie. Besides, he was longing so very much to see her; he had kept his love for the Harpers buried for too long.

Missing Jessie in particular had been like a small ember that had grown these past ten days into a burning need to see her again. He would not be intrusive; he knew she had a life now that didn't include him. But what loving brother could go this long without seeing his favorite sister? Oxytak had only second-hand news about the Harpers but enough to let Charlie conclude they had all gotten along without him quite well.

He committed right there on the ferry to going back to Mississippi for a visit. The perfect plan formed itself immediately. Next Sunday was Easter! Next Monday, fourteen-year-old Jessie would be taking the wagon to Mr. Davis's store for supplies. That is, if they hadn't switched their business to the larger grocery store that had opened just before Charlie left, and if the Harpers still went down south on the Tuesday after Easter. He could think of no reason why they would not; only Frank's accident had prevented them from going in the seventeen years Charlie had lived with them.

He turned, heading back to Guthrie without checking on the property. He needed to talk to Oxytak, grab a bag, and plot the best railroad route to Jackson. First, though, he needed to be honest with Sarah.

He waited for Sarah outside the school door, noticing with a pang of guilt that her eyes lit up when she saw him. In front of the children, she kept her composure but blew him a secret kiss, obviously thinking his coming back early was because he missed her.

He took her to supper to tell her the whole story about his childhood, his life with the Harpers, the way he had left their home, and his vow to Jessie. Sarah listened intently. *Why does she have to look so beautiful tonight?* He wondered.

She asked perceptive questions from time to time but was mostly quiet, listening, never taking her eyes off his, not even when the waitress came to take their dessert orders. He summarized it all by telling her that he wasn't free to court her romantically until he settled this—indeed until he had closed this last door to his past.

"Am I to understand that you are...that my competition is a *child*, an almost-eleven-year-old girl?"

Charlie was intrigued that her eyes could flash anger, relief, amusement, and sadness all at the same time. Looking into them was making it very difficult for him to hold on to his resolve.

"Sarah, she's almost fifteen now. Granted, that is still a child, but not a little girl. Jessie has been more of a woman...uh, more mature for her age all her life. Girls here in town are married and have babies at fifteen. I'm not going back to marry her. I'm going back because I gave her my word I would. I don't expect her to be waiting for me. That's why I've stayed away this long, so that she would forget her childish crush and by now have at least one young man she thinks she can't live without. But, to repeat myself, I gave Jessie my word." He felt his argument was weak and knew it sounded immature to Sarah; it sounded that way to him.

She continued looking into his eyes for a long time before speaking. "Charlie, there is more to your feelings for Jessie than you're willing to admit, perhaps even to yourself. Your voice softens every time you mention her name. You've said it easily a dozen times since we've been here. It may be as you say, that you regard her as your little sister. For my sake, I hope that is all there is to it. Everything in me wants to discourage you from going back and instead to stay with me and forget a child you've not seen or heard from in four years. But I agree, you need to go to Mississippi and face this, this ghost from the past! Until you do, you'll never be entirely mine."

Her choice of the word *mine* caused him to inwardly wince. He didn't feel as though he was hers in any sense of the word. "Sarah, it may be that I will fall in love with you. You are very lovable. But I don't have those feelings for you now. You are probably my best friend, except for Oxy—" He stopped himself, not wanting to upset her by once again comparing his feelings for her with those of another male friend, but she finished his sentence.

"I know. I know. You like me right after Doc and Oxytak!" Tears came in her eyes. "And now, it seems I'm even behind Jessie. "

"Sarah." He softened his voice, reaching for her hand, which she immediately pulled back. "Jessie is, well, she's in a class all her own. She's pretty special, but as you say, she's a child. It is difficult to express to you our history together. I was her hero. She made some serious vows that she's too young to be held to, but she's also too young to be disillusioned by a big brother figure she trusted to keep his word!

"Look, Sarah, I don't want to leave having you think that when I put this matter to rest about Jessie that I will definitely be coming back with the intention of marrying you. Admittedly, I have thought about our marrying and even thought about the kind of house you might like. I have no other woman in mind. I think you are a wonderful person. I know you will be a wonderful wife, but, well, I'm realizing that I have kept my affections under lock and key."

"The way you kissed me did not suggest they were locked very well, Charlie. That was not the kiss of my big brother!" She wasn't kidding with him. He sensed this normally self-assured, pretty woman fighting for something she was scared she was losing, not even certain she'd ever had. She knew there was no way to win a fight with a memory or an ideal. Like Jessie, he had not been much more than a child when he'd made that promise. He'd only thought he was a man that day.

Sarah's bringing up their kiss stirred him. *What have I become?* He chastised himself for thinking even now how much he would have enjoyed kissing her all the way home. He understood a little better what Doc had meant. He wanted to kiss for the sake of kissing because it was heady and fun and intoxicating. He wasn't altogether sure he wanted to kiss Sarah as much as he just liked kissing.

Charlie placed a telephone call to the Thorpe home. Dr. Thorpe answered, glad to hear from his friend yet surprised by the call instead of a letter or the occasional wire. The connection was surprisingly clear. "Actually, Charlie, it is interesting that you happened to telephone tonight. I saw Jessie in the office just this afternoon. She asked about you, by the way. I like her, always have. She's a bright, spirited, bubbly young woman, but she was understandably down today. She used the excuse of picking up a medical journal of mine, but she wanted to talk to Charlotte. Charlotte then urged me to examine her.

"She had a cut on her temple and deep bruises on her arms and back. She swore me to secrecy, but nevertheless, I intend to talk to her father this week before they leave for their summer place. Julia lost her temper with Jessie and might have killed her. It's happened before, and it has to stop!"

Oxytak drove Charlie to the depot. He knew Charlie's frustration with the inconvenient train route was because he was so worried about Jessie. Charlie grumbled that it seemed to him there weren't as many railroads in the territory as there were in any other state, despite the fact that there were many more now than in the recent past.

"Actually," Oxytak reminded him, appealing to Charlie's love of history so as to distract him from worry, "they're a whole lot more convenient now. Railroads were relatively late in coming here. The reconstruction treaties between the United States government and the Indians stipulated just one north-south and one east-west railroad would be allowed through Indian Territory. When I came out to visit some of my people in 1870, I found out the hard way about the territory's railroad problem at that time. As I think about it, there were more than fifty thousand miles of railroad in the United States then, with thirteen or fourteen hundred of those in Missouri, about the same in Mississippi, and about six hundred or so in Kansas, but none in Oklahoma or Indian Territories!"

He deliberately took the chair facing the door, although his view was somewhat blocked by higher shelving that hadn't been there four years ago. He had no interest in the poker game other than the small satisfaction he felt to be one of the grown-ups now, drinking cream soda and complaining about the president. He recognized Mr. Davis's son at the counter and guessed his dad had finally turned the business over. He trusted that John, too, had matured and had overcome his need to demean others as he used to do to Frank.

Three hours and forty-seven minutes had passed since his arrival in town; no Harper had ever been this late arriving. He was beginning to worry. He wished he had one of Mr. Harper's cigars; he was that nervous.

He looked up from examining the hand just dealt him, and saw her. His heart raced as he watched the beautiful girl she had become stride confidently to the counter and flash the young Davis boy a smile. She was petite and perfect. He laid down his cards, never taking his eyes off her, and made his way to the front of the store until he stood facing her. She was fumbling through her bag and didn't look up at the sound of his footsteps.

"Don't you know everything on that list by now?" Charlie asked, surprised by the lump in his throat. Jessie turned to him, disbelief on her face.

He stood looking down at her. *I love her. I always have. Everything I've done has been for her, for this moment.* He couldn't read what was in her eyes.

"I've come for you, Jessie, like I said I would, if you're still waiting for me."

She blinked back tears, the joy on her face finally apparent. "Have you made your mark, Charlie?"

"I have."

"Have you really come for me?"

"I have."

"Is it forever?"

"It is. It most definitely is."

"When are we leaving?"

"Now. As soon as we take care of that list: flour, sugar, coffee, seeds…" He grinned, and she laughed.

"You remember! Charlie Harper, will you kiss me on my mouth?"

"I will. I definitely will. Just as soon as we take care of that list." He held her to him as he turned to the Davis boy, handing him the list and a stack of bills. "John, here's enough money to cover the Harper supplies and extra for whoever you can find to take them out to their place. Do you think you can gather these things for Jessie? She's going to be occupied. We have some mighty important business to catch up on."

"Yes, sir." John Davis grinned. "But you don't need to pay. The Harpers settle their account when they return for their home supplies at the end of the summer."

"No," Charlie answered. "It is my great pleasure to settle this account. Let me just add a note to it." Not wanting to let go of Jessie, he reached both arms around her to the counter and wrote simply: "I've come for Jessie. I will take good care of her. Charlie."

He picked Jessie up in his arms and carried her out the door and around the corner of the building. Without setting her down, he kissed her on her mouth.

Jessie slept soundly after the hard ride they'd taken across some difficult terrain in order to intercept the train. Charlie had planned this with great care while traveling from the territory. He had checked and rechecked train schedules, rented two horses from a livery in Vicksburg, and remembered to get Jessie a side-saddle. He hadn't counted on her being two hours late. They'd had barely enough time to arrange to have the horses returned before flagging down the train between its scheduled stops.

Charlie tried to think of something to compare with what he was feeling now. He could not imagine heaven being better. He was tired but didn't want to sleep. He wanted to do exactly what he was doing: hold and look at Jessie. He wanted to let his heart rejoice in having found its place again. They hadn't talked of any plans beyond the immediate ones of how to navigate their way to Oklahoma Territory, Jessie's term for her new home-to-be. There had not been much time to talk of anything else, but he had some nagging concern that Jessie so unquestioningly allowed him to simply whisk her away from her family and the life she had always known.

The old anger for Mrs. Harper returned as he looked at the unhealed scar on Jessie's temple and the fading, yellowish defensive bruises on the edges of her hands and wrists. She wore long sleeves, so he had no idea what her arms looked like. He had taken hold of her right hand as they settled into their seats, but she nudged her left under his as well, saying drowsily, "See how perfectly our hands fit together? This is forever, Charlie."

He didn't trust his voice to speak. He held her to him more tightly, certain he could kill a bear with his bare hands if it threatened her. She fit perfectly in the space between his heart and arm as if she belonged there. He felt completely at peace for the first time since Doc's death.

They changed trains in the middle of the night, traveling west across Arkansas. Then changed again in Little Rock. It was there that Charlie thought to ask Jessie to marry him.

"I love you, Jessie. You were right. I've always loved you. Will you be my wife?"

She began to weep. He held her, letting her cry, bothered that he'd been the cause of her tears. He wanted to take them away, not add to them. Finally, she stopped crying, still holding her arms around his waist, her face buried in his shoulder. He tipped her head up to look in her eyes.

"Jessie girl, are you scared? Do you want me to take you back?" He bit his lip, waiting for her reply. She might say she wanted to go home.

"No, Charlie, I don't want to go back! And, no…yes, well, I'm a little scared. I'm scared this is not real. I'm scared Mama will make Papa come after me! I'm scared I'm not the person you remember and that after we get to Oklahoma Territory you'll find you don't want me!" As he used to do to her, she put a finger on his lips to stop him from saying anything so she could empty out her fears and the accumulation of four years of sufferings.

"Charlie, I don't think I'll ever be able to tell you how I have felt all these years waiting for you. There was never a single day when I didn't miss you or a single night when I didn't pray for you. I have imagined you in a thousand different ways from dead to blind with no legs. Each time I'd think something like that, I'd tell myself I wouldn't feel the same about you if you were crippled, but instead, I only felt more love for you, more longing to be with you and to be your eyes or your legs!

"Scared is not knowing all this long, lonely time if you were dead or alive. It's not knowing if you remembered me or would ever return. Scared is imagining you loving another girl! It's feeling my body grow into a woman's and wondering if you will ever make love to me or if I'm just doomed to die an old lady who pined away for the only man she ever loved. It's wondering if I'd ever hear you ask me to marry you!"

"Jessie, I love you. More than anything, I want you to be my wife. I now know I've needed you to complete my life. I want to complete yours. You would be the biggest part of the life I'm building in the territory.

"I'm so sorry for all your pain and despair! I believed all these years that I was doing the best thing for you. You know you weren't yet eleven when you proposed to me." He grinned; she managed a small smile. He continued. "I think I do understand a little bit how you felt because I've had similar thoughts and feelings about you—wondering if you were being courted by someone you were growing to love, wondering if you had forgotten me or shrugged off that day at my birthplace as just a childish crush! All of those thoughts cut into me!

"I guess I've had a thousand different images of you in varying circumstances over these years. I absolutely could not allow myself to ever think of you in another man's arms! But I didn't allow myself the luxury of imagining you in mine either! I had convinced myself that I wasn't even any longer like your older brother but instead just someone you used to know from your childhood."

"Charlie, believe me, I never thought of you as a brother! I thought I made my feelings for you clear that day—"

"You did, sweetheart. Oh, Jessie, the thrill of being able to say that… I want to shout it out." He did, turning to the crowd. "Everybody! Hello, everybody! May I present my wonderful sweetheart, Jessie. I've asked her to marry me, but she hasn't said yes or no!"

Though half asleep and weary, the travelers in the depot all applauded and in unison began chanting, "Say yes, Jess! Say yes, Jess!"

"Yes! Yes! Yes!" He kissed her to more applause from their audience.

"Jessie, I had good reason to believe you no longer cared about me. You…none of you answered my letters!"

"Letters?" she asked in astonishment. "What letters? When did you write me?"

He grew quiet, wondering if he should say the obvious. She spoke. "Charlie, if you wrote us, my parents never told me. I don't mean 'if.' I believe you. I only mean they withheld your letters."

"I wrote you twice, Frank once, and your parents once. I wrote your parents an apology for my rudeness that last night. I first wrote you just before I left for China."

"You left for…have you actually been to China, Charlie?"

"Yes, and that is another story. We've got the rest of our lives to catch up on each other's stories…"

"Oh, you've pretty much caught up on my stories, Charlie! They all begin with missing Charlie and they all end with loving him until I die. That's mine!"

"Your parents must really hate me. I'm thinking now that my kidnapping you like this is going to be particularly grievous. Having you whisked away is bad enough, but whisked by me is going to be really difficult for them, isn't it?"

"Charlie, Papa loves you. He grieved, we all grieved for months and months. Every time we are anywhere without Mama, he brings your name up, pointing out something you did or made, pointing to the crops and saying Charlie this or Charlie that. Frank misses you and still says you're his best friend. Beulah makes your favorite stew and lemon coconut cakes and whispers to us every time, 'This is Charlie's favorite.' William and Frank told me that Dad had a long talk with them about the things you said and even apologized to them. In truth, he has stood up to Mama more, and she backs down to him sometimes. You were right. He should have done that long ago."

"Jessie, I'm glad to hear all that. Thank you. Now, though, we must talk about something more important. With all of those good changes, why is your mother still hurting you?"

She lowered her chin, pressing her fingertips momentarily against her lips. " I don't think I've ever understood why Mama loses her temper and takes it out on me. Papa told me I was more like the Mama he fell in love with than Belle or Lilly. He said Mama's 'spells,' he calls them, didn't start until after Paul's birth.

"Belle once told me that I had taken the brunt of Mama's rage off the others. I guess that's some small comfort, but..." She started to cry again. "It has been really, really hard, Charlie. Somehow it has gotten worse instead of better. I know God sent you back to me in answer to my prayers! If Belle didn't come home from time to time and sit up all night talking with me, I don't know if I would have made it through missing you and putting up with Mama's hatred, trying to protect Ben and Cornelius too. If I didn't have the hope that you would one day come back for me, I couldn't have lasted this long!

"You kept me going, Charlie. You were the reason for everything in my life. I rehearsed in my mind over and over all the things you taught me and said to me that last day at your birthplace. I have tried to become what I thought you would want in a wife. Your integrity has been my guide because I respect you more than anyone I've ever known!

"My friends tease me all the time. They try to get me to let one boy or another court me. I just am not interested in boys my age. They all pale compared to my memories of you at that same age!

"But you know who most helped me keep my faith that you would come back? It was Belle! When I finally told her that I didn't miss a big brother, I missed the man I was in love with, she said she always knew it. And Charlie, she said, 'Jessie, trust me. There is nothing in the world that will keep Charlie from coming for you!'

"But everything is perfect now. You came back, and I won't ever have to put up with Mama again, will I?" Her smile radiated through her tears at the realization that she had been set free from the abuse.

Her words wiped away whatever doubts had still lingered with Charlie about stealing Jessie away. He kissed her tears and held her close.

"Jessie, God kept you going. I don't want you to place me above him. I will fall and fail you many times. You must always hold on to your relationship with Jesus. He won't fail you. I don't even want to try to be more important."

"I love you, Charlie. I love your faith and your wisdom. You're right. I thank Jesus for you. That is acknowledging his sovereignty, isn't it? He and I have had a lot of talks about you these past four years. I know it is his plan that we're finally together."

He hugged her. "Good. Now, I want to try and reassure some of your fears. First, I'm never going to send you back. You are not the same Jessie I knew before. You're a young lady now. I'm not the same Charlie. We will need time to get to know each other. I love you. You mean more to me than anyone or anything in my life. I'm not going to stop after all these years. Trust me?"

She nodded.

"Now," he said, "I think we need to get off the train and get married at the next stop. It is inside Cherokee Nation. Your comment that your mama might send a posse after you—you did say posse, correct?" He grinned. "Seriously, that does concern me. Is getting married today all right with you, or do you want time to plan a grander wedding?"

"Hmm, Charlie, here's my idea of a grand wedding: I say 'I do' to you, and you say 'I do' to me, whichever comes first. Beyond that, I don't have a preference!"

Holding hands, they walked diagonally from the tiny depot across the wide road to the building with a sign out front on which was written only "Hotel." They were both quiet. Charlie had some misgivings about marrying her in this way, but she had urged him again to marry before they got to his home. She had examined a railroad map on the wall in the Fort Smith depot that showed several routes into the territory. She was afraid that her papa might somehow reach there before she and Charlie did. It hadn't helped her worries to know that Charlie had last written her folks from his Guthrie residence.

"I actually think Papa will be happy for me, but I can never know when he is going to stand up to Mama or when he's going to cave in. We had a lot of reliable routines we could always depend on in our house, but Mama's moods and Papa's reactions were never predictable!"

She saw him look around the town and read his thoughts. "What I had in mind was just saying 'I do' to you, Charlie. I meant that. It wouldn't be any better if we were getting married in Paris, France! Yes, let's hurry and get married. That way my parents can't force me to come back, can they?" He didn't think so.

The inside of the hotel was surprisingly attractive. A curved staircase with a polished banister invited travelers upstairs. The walls appeared to be red silk. To the left of the entrance was a saloon with what Charlie took to be a mahogany bar. They could hear laughter from there. Straight ahead was the parlor with chairs nicely upholstered in a gold fabric and a dark-green and gold sofa. Two men sat reading newspapers. Jessie smiled and whispered, "I like it!"

The apparent proprietor and a pleasant-looking, middle-aged woman greeted them warmly as they stopped at the counter. He blurted out, "We're here to get married. Is there a preacher in town?"

There were several.

"Would you mind if we were married here in your hotel this evening?"

The lady's face broke into a broad smile. She immediately introduced herself. "I'm Nora Reynolds. This is my husband, Tom." They shook hands, which seemed to be all Mrs. Reynolds needed in order to seal an unspoken agreement that as of this moment she was in charge of a wedding.

Mrs. Reynolds hurried around the counter and grasped Jessie by her shoulders, holding her at arm's length, looking into her eyes. "You are the prettiest little thing that has ever graced this parlor! And you are the tiniest! Bless your heart. We are going to get you fixed up here. Let's begin by showing you your room." She leaned over and whispered to Jessie, "I'll put you two in the room closest to the water closet!"

She led them up the stairs, chattering away. No one mentioned that there was only Charlie's one small bag. Charlie asked about a general store in town and learned there were two, one at each end, and even a mercantile store "right in the middle between the other two!" She happened to know that Mr. Cox had some fashionable clothes in because he'd just received a shipment from New York that had been on back order and arrived too late for the dedication of the new courthouse building. She smiled warmly again at Jessie, tugging her away a little bit from Charlie's protective arm.

Wrapping an ample arm around Jessie, she hugged the girl to her bosom. "Let me love on this youngin' a bit. I hope Mrs. Cox can fit you. Not many as small or as pretty as you in these parts, honey." She showed them the room and the facilities, brought in extra towels and bedding, and promised to send a bouquet up. "My azaleas and tulips are blooming in profusion this year. Must have known we'd need them!"

Charlie saw Jessie glance at the bed, blush, look up at him, see that he was watching her, blush deeper, and glance away. He grinned. Doc had said it would be worth his time to choose the right moment and the right moves. Jessie was worth waiting for.

Mrs. Reynolds sent help up to fill the tub, first for Jessie's bath, and then later, while the bride examined the hotel's decorations and chatted with Mr. Reynolds, Charlie bathed. He saw Jessie's face light up as he descended the stairs. He could not recall a time when he had been this happy, yet he remembered Doc telling him that in between the bad times, the good times got even better.

Mr. Reynolds had fetched a preacher. He would be there by six o'clock that evening. The missus was already taking care of all the other arrangements; they were not to worry about a thing.

"Not a thing! My, my," Mrs. Reynolds continued, "this is the best thing that has happened in this town since Mrs. Sewell danced the schottische by herself in the middle of the street!

"We had us a real music teacher here for about a year, but he moved on to some big school back east. He taught folks all kinds of music, Russian and German symphonies too, but the schottische is one of our favorites now that Mrs. Sewell christened our new street with her new red shoes!" She made Jessie laugh and relax; Charlie knew it was good for Jessie to be showered with affection from someone so motherly.

They stopped for a catfish meal at a café before continuing on to the Cox store. Happy, playful, and excited, they talked constantly, both becoming aware of how much they had to talk about and how wonderful it was that they had all the time they would need. Charlie told Jessie his hushpuppies were better than these, which prompted her to admit she hadn't done a lot of cooking.

"I know I promised to learn to cook." She looked under the table. "But I will shine your boots, and, in case you hadn't noticed, Charlie Harper"—she stuck out her chest—"I grew bosoms!"

"Oh, I noticed, Jessie. I noticed them right away! They're the reason I'm marrying you!" She threw a hushpuppy at him.

He caught it and continued speaking, taking her hand and lowering his voice. "I noticed how you turn your left toe in when you walk and how you look up to the ceiling first before telling me something difficult for you to say. I noticed that your little finger curves just a bit and how you have a double row of eyelashes. I noticed seven freckles across your nose and how you stand with one hand on your hip when you're thinking. By the way, your eyelashes are the second reason I'm marrying you. I noticed how your hair curls at the base of your neck and how your mouth is the most perfect one I've ever kissed."

"Hmm, perhaps not on my wedding day, but one of these days, when I'm mad at you for something, I'm going to demand to be told about all the lips you've kissed so I can work up a really good tizzy fit! I'll yell at you that you were out kissing beautiful Chinese girls and San Francisco girls and Oklahoma girls while I was pining away for you in Mississippi!" She saw the consternation in Charlie's eyes and laughed. "No, my tizzy fits don't even come close to Mama's. Don't worry. Just don't test me!" she added playfully.

Mr. and Mrs. Cox were as friendly and outgoing as Mrs. Reynolds. They became even more so as Charlie selected several dresses and urged Jessie to pick out whatever she wanted. "Charlie," she whispered, "how much of a mark did you make, anyway?"

"Enough so that you don't have to worry," he whispered back.

They both agreed on the same dress as being the prettiest one in the store. It was two sizes too big, but not to worry. Mrs. Cox had plenty of pins.

It took her thirty-five minutes to pin Jessie into her dress, but when she was finished and Jessie stepped out for Charlie to see, he gasped in wonder, not able to take his eyes off her. He bowed down to her, wearing the new suit of clothes he'd bought. Jessie gave a mock curtsy and took his arm. On their way out the door, they thought to invite the Coxes to their wedding; they agreed to come, insisting that they bring their purchases with them.

There were several more buggies and horses tied up along the street than had been there earlier. Both Harpers were dimly aware of them but so much more aware of each other they gave no thought to them.

Jessie stopped him in the middle of the boardwalk and waited for a gentleman to pass by before whispering, "I want to tell you, Charlie Harper, that I think you are the most beautiful man I've ever laid eyes on. When I saw you in the Davis store, I was stunned. You were always the best-looking boy around, but you've become far handsomer than I ever imagined you being! To see you all dressed up like this now, you almost take my breath away. I am so very proud to be walking down the street with you, so very proud to soon be your wife!"

"Ah, Jessie-girl, you took words out of my mouth."

The crowded parlor broke out in cheers when Charlie kissed his bride, so they hadn't heard him whisper, "Yes, Jessie, my love for you is forever."

The musicians began their wedding song, and Charlie asked his wife to dance, falling more in love with her as they danced to the surprisingly elegant music coming from the fiddlers. "Mrs. Harper, this feels as though we've danced together for years."

"Indeed, my husband, we've been dancing together for at least five years, you don't recall? I'm sure that was you in my bedroom night after night. I mean…" She blushed and looked down away from his eyes. "I meant to say that every night I would imagine you were with me, and I would dance round and round. I would imagine you picking me up and carrying me around an elegant ballroom—"

"Like this?" He asked, picking her up and dancing around and around the floor. The music was powerful and evocative. Charlie felt intoxicated from holding his wife in his arms and the music sounding magically like a symphony. He thought of Doc with gratitude that he had taught him to dance. Jessie laughed joyfully, leaning back on his arm, hers flung wide in happy, trusting abandonment. Her hair spilled down from the up do Mrs. Cox had arranged, cascading down his arm, moving as if in rhythm with the music.

Looking at her beauty, Charlie never wanted to let her out of his arms. He bent to her lips, turning more and more slowly, letting her feet slide to the floor as she clung to him; they forgot everyone else until they heard the applause. As the music ended, they stood, looking in each other's eyes. "Charlie, if tonight is all I will ever have, it is already more than I ever dreamed it would be!"

The guests cheered again, teasing them about waiting until they got to their room; all began introducing themselves to the young couple and wishing them well. A polka was played and then a schottische, which was how they met Mr. and Mrs. Sewell, the latter grabbing Charlie and herself leading him around the floor to the whooping and hollering of everyone.

"Enough of that Russian music. I'm thinkin' it's a good Scottish lad ye'd rather be, Charlie!" He was so happy he even kissed Mrs. Sewell. "Aye, lad, ye'd be Scot all right!"

A dainty, smiling, white-haired lady brought each of them a cup of punch. "I made it myself, special. I call it my wedding punch, but I've never served it at a wedding until tonight. To tell you the truth, I've never even made it until today!" There were cakes and cookies and pies on every surface. Someone had cut tulips and pansies and placed bouquets around and strewn petals on the floor. There was gaiety, well wishes, dancing, laughter, and love.

While the young, unmarried women crowded around Jessie a little later, Charlie slipped away, quietly asking something of Mr. Reynolds. Jessie saw him returning down the stairs and stopped talking midsentence, gazing at him.

As the evening drew to a close and guests began leaving, Charlie noticed Jessie seeming to avoid him somewhat and seeming to try to keep the musicians playing. He walked up behind her, locked his hands around her waist, and whispered, "Jessie-girl, it's time to go upstairs. The party is over." She blushed, and he loved her all the more.

But first, she had a second piece of cake, tried to wipe the counters, and spent five full minutes thanking the Reynolds profusely before finally letting Charlie lead her upstairs. In their room, Charlie handed her the white linen nightgown she purchased that day and pointed to the sheet he'd tacked across the corner.

"Jessie, that's for your privacy. You may undress behind there, but first let me unpin you."

"No! I can do it myself!" She whirled around, turning her back away from him as if to make sure he couldn't reach to unpin her dress.

"Sweetheart." He chuckled. "You're not going to be able to unpin yourself. Let me do it. You'll still have the dress on! I won't see anything. Then you can go behind the sheet."

She took a step backward, protesting again that she could do it herself, and disappeared behind the makeshift curtain. Charlie could hear her struggling and grunting, murmuring to herself. He quietly placed a chair next to the sheet and stepped on it, peeking over the top. Jessie squirmed and wiggled, pricking herself from time to time and making very little progress. She heard his giggle and looked up. "All right, Charlie Harper, help me out of this, but…but keep your eyes closed, you hear me?"

When Jessie came from behind the curtain, Charlie was sitting on the chair with only his shirt removed. The bed was turned back. He had put a tulip on one of the pillows; a pallet was on the floor at the foot of it. She looked it all over, confusion on her face.

Although he wanted to hold her, he didn't want his touch to be misunderstood, so he continued to sit as he spoke. "Jessie, you are sleeping in the bed. I am sleeping on that pallet. We are not going to sleep together tonight. We are not going to have sex tonight or tomorrow night or for quite a while." He was watching her carefully for her reaction, and he saw the scared look go away.

"Aren't we…aren't we married?" she asked.

"Yes, we're married. We're legal. You're protected from Julia. I love you more right now than I did an hour ago. I know you love me. But neither of us knows whether your love is for an idol, someone you only idealized for years and someone to whom you're now grateful for rescuing you, or whether you are in love with the real day-to-day Charlie. I have faults and weaknesses. I'm as flawed as the next man. You've only known me as a big brother. You don't know me as a man. Until you do and know you love this man, all of me, and still choose me, I won't be certain that you love the real me.

"Since yesterday," he continued, "you've been living in a fairy-tale world where Sir Galahad sweeps in and rescues you, complete with waltzes and roses and the excitement of elopement. More importantly, you are too young to have sex. This has all happened too fast for you to have a chance to make rational choices and decisions."

"Do I get a say in this, Charlie Harper?"

He thought her sauciness was a bit of a bluff, but it was the old Jessie, and he loved her for it all the more. He chanced taking her in his arms, nuzzling her hair, cupping her cheek in his hand as he tucked her head under his chin. *You can't imagine how much I want you.*

"Of course, when you've heard my whole plan, but one thing you don't have a choice about is having sex with me. Not anyway soon. That isn't going to happen until you're old enough! And until you have been angry with me a few times and not become disillusioned or regretful that you married this 'old man.'"

"Okay, old man, what's the whole plan?" She had stopped the little nervous gesture of making tiny folds of her nightgown across her lap. She stuck her hand in his, soft, warm, small, and loving. He felt again her trust in him. He did not intend to violate that.

"Jessie, I will tell you all about my, our businesses and properties, maybe tomorrow going home." He paused, smiling. "Home, Jessie. You can't know how much it means to me to think of us sharing a home."

"I know, Charlie. I haven't thought of my parents' house as home since you left. You're what made it home for me. I know that sounds strange. When you left, it became just the place where I stayed and waited for you."

He hugged her and continued. "My plan is this: We will build a house wherever you think you'd most like to live. I can't wait to show you the territory. It is very beautiful. The people are nice and friendly. They're different here, in a good way. People here are carving out new traditions. They don't look backward at what they've left behind or at the destruction of the war. They look forward with excitement, perseverance, and hope to what they can build and do. They have a rugged determination that I respect and a joy and enthusiasm about life that I admire. I know you will too, Jess."

"Oh, Charlie, just hearing you describe them is fun! I'm so excited to be by your side, building a new life in a new territory, a new house, a new me!"

"Jess, I have a preference for where I'd like us to live, but I'm just fifty percent of that decision. My dream, other than kidnapping you and turning you into a runaway child bride, is to own a general store like Mr. Davis's."

"Charlie, I would love that! I remember you told me one time you were going to grow up and have a store. Then you started getting all uppity by going to St. Louis, Chicago, New York, seeing plays, riding the train... Turns out you've been to San Francisco and China! Go on. Tell me your plan. I'm excited!"

"Well, first, it has to be *our* plan. I have done a lot of traveling. Just going to China and back felt like I'd traveled all over the world. I've seen much of the United States, and I want us to see much more together. I've thought about living in a city. I've thought about politics or going to medical school. I've considered many different things. I've been through a lot of dangerous things, so my faith in God has grown stronger, and I know I'm a survivor. When it all settled down and I thought about life, I knew all I had ever wanted was to have a store and to make babies with a loving wife. Naturally, you came to mind."

"Well, ha!" Jessie retorted. "I don't think your plan is going to produce any babies. I believe that still requires sexual intercourse."

He grinned but didn't answer that; he was more intent on having her know his thoughts about how their life would come together. One week ago, he hadn't thought this moment would ever be. He'd almost been tempted to propose to Sarah and believe Jessie had forgotten their vow. It wasn't going to be easy on Sarah for him to return to town a married man; he regretted that much, for her sake.

"Sweetheart, I want you to enroll in school and complete your education. I want you to finish your youth in a healthy, normal way and discover your interests and, well, who you are. Along with an education, that includes making friends your age, some of whom might be married, but most will not be. I want you to enjoy the same activities every other pretty fifteen-year-old girl enjoys. He grinned boyishly, wanting to lighten the tone. Just don't kiss the boys, okay?" He pulled his legs away in time to avoid her playful kick.

"Charlie, I know who I am. I am a mature girl in love with a wise and mature *young* man. My life will be defined by the life we build. Where are we going? What town? I haven't even asked that!"

"Tomorrow we're going to Guthrie, the capital of the territory. I have a room there…a very crowded one because I have been doing a lot of traveling over the state, exploring, working out of town. You and I own half a coal mine and half a lumber yard as well as a couple of other things."

"We do?

"We do. But if you'll agree, I've a mind to buy a store in a smaller area that's growing. We've passed near where I would like to take you and explore. We need to make the decision and then build or buy a house as soon as possible, meet our neighbors, get you in school, and become a part of a community."

She yawned. "Charlie, that sounds like heaven. We'll get to talk like we used to and scratch chiggers together. I want to learn about your businesses, grow a garden. I'd love a picket fence. I love you so much, Charlie! I am going to love being married to you!"

He'd meant to only tuck her in bed, but he lay down beside her on top of the covers, not wanting to be separated by sleep. Her goodnight kiss became unexpectedly passionate and arousing. She obviously felt safe now to tease him and express her desire; he could see it was going to be mostly up to him to keep the boundaries. If he were to keep her trust, he would have to do that.

He leaned back on an elbow to take in the beauty of her, now enhanced by the glow of the lamplight. He tangled his fingers in her long hair and brought it to his lips, the scent of her heightening his desire. He traced her lashes with a finger, noticing how they made her eyes seem to hold mysterious secrets. *The eyes of a woman who knows she's loved*, he thought. He smiled inside. He had loved her all her life, almost all of his.

Charlie watched Jessie's eyes look him over, up and down, lingering on his bare chest. Having her look at him in that way was very arousing. She pulled his head down to her and kissed him with an eager hunger that matched his own as she arched her body toward him, one arm tight around his neck, her other hand on his back. He pulled her close, pressing and pressing, moving together so that there were no spaces between them.

Their tongues ignited fires beyond those either had ever known. He lay her down, his body on hers, his passion overpowering reason, and looked into her upturned, trusting eyes, their pupils wide. Trembling from wanting her and struggling to honor the promise he'd made not ten minutes ago, he buried his face in the curve of her neck until he could quiet his heart and hunger. He made himself roll to her side and tried to smile.

"Charlie, I think I am a woman. I want more and more of you. I want to give myself to you, but I am a little scared." Her voice was a whisper.

"We have a lifetime, Jessie." He caressed her cheek and the softness of her throat and neck, wanting to examine every inch of her. Her beauty and femininity awed him. "Jessie, I've never been given anything in my life so precious. Nothing I have ever cherished even seems of value compared to you! I am so awestruck by you, by this moment, by our love."

"Charlie, that's how I feel about you." Tears welled in her eyes. "I was trying to find words to tell you how completely happy I am to know you are mine, but neither can I find the words to describe what you mean to me." They lay silent in each other's arms for a minute before Jessie spoke again. "Charlie, do you think that's why God invented lovemaking? Because loving someone is so powerful there are no words to describe it, so you *become* love and you join yourself, your spirit and all, with your beloved?"

She pulled the covers down to her waist. He leaned to kiss her again; she reached for his hand and placed it on her breast. He gasped.

"Ah, Jessie, Jessie, do you know what you're doing to me?"

He felt her nipple harden as she pulled her gown aside, inviting him to kiss her there. He gazed at her bared breast—perfect, like everything else about her. He fumbled with trembling fingers to unbutton her gown and pulled it beneath both breasts, caressing them. He felt her tremble and heard her gasp.

Again, mustering the will power to pull away, he tried to prop his head on his elbow but found he was too weak to keep that position, so he laid his head beside hers, his hand on her breast.

"You are so beautiful, Jessie. It seems like a miracle that you are my wife. Your body is exquisite and sacred to me. But, young lady, Mrs. Harper, love of my life, the mere fact that you can deliberately tempt me as you are doing, after what I said, tells me that while you may know something about the art of seduction, you know nothing of what you're doing to me! I am one move away from taking you, and while I want you more than I've ever wanted anything in my life, I meant what I said earlier."

He tried to re-button her gown, but he was trembling too much. He sat up on the edge of the bed. "Sweetheart, I'm thrilled that you are so sexual and passionate, but when you come to me as a woman instead of a fifteen year-old vixen, we'll be doing some serious loving! In the meantime, don't make it harder for me than it already is, all right?"

To her credit, she didn't pout or get defensive. "I didn't know I was being sexual. I...our bodies belong to each other. I love what you do to my body. How will we know when I can come to you as a woman, Charlie?"

"We'll know. Oh we'll know, Jessie girl."

He thought she was sleeping. He lay there wide-awake, his heart still pounding, his aching for her still raw, but he deemed it a good ache and a good raw, no salt in it. Instead, it was a balm—that of knowing Jessie was right there in the room with him, safe, happy, his. His.

From the stillness in the room, Jessie spoke: "It would seem that my groom is rather like a Cinderella man. Only instead of a pumpkin, he turns into my brother at midnight." She laughed happily at her cleverness.

The contrast of his petite, perfect wife against the crowded book- and map-filled room made Charlie wish he had taken her to a hotel instead. Jessie shushed him by kissing him.

"This is so like you, Charlie! You lived in that dreadful attic room, and it was always filled with books and maps, your sketches and poems. I used to go up there when you were away with Doc or Oxytak and sit for hours just to be near you. I read a lot of your books and traced my finger over all the maps. I read your letters from Betsy and Rosalie and was jealous. I saw the poem you wrote about Charlotte Thorpe and was really jealous. I've known your secret life forever, Charlie, and everything I learned about you just made me love you more. I'm glad to be here in this room. It somehow strengthens my reconnection with you, if that makes sense."

He opened his mouth to respond, taking her in his arms. "Have you noticed I have a hard time talking to you without touching or holding you?" he asked instead.

"I had noticed, Mr. Harper. I thought we might need to talk about that. Folks might think we're in love or, worse, that we're married!"

"The problem, Mrs. Harper, is that I start to tell you something important, reach for you, and find that touching you makes me immediately forget whatever it was I knew I needed to say!"

A knock sounded at his door, and Charlie heard Sarah's voice. "Charlie, are you there. I saw your light."

Jessie's face was innocent, trusting, and curious. Since she was closest to the door in the small room, she opened it without concern. Before Charlie could speak, Sarah's face fell. "You... you must be Jessie."

"I am, and you are...?"

"My name is Sarah. I'm sure Charlie has told you about me. I'm his best friend. Well, right after Doc, Oxytak, and you, although I'm not certain that's the correct order."

"No." Jessie smiled. "That would not be the correct order. I'm pretty sure I'm first. Naturally he would not have told me about you."

"Sarah, come in," Charlie invited, feeling unprepared. He had not expected them to meet this way, this soon. He caught Jessie's sarcasm and hated for Sarah to see her this way the first time they met, but the thought flashed. *She's fifteen. Sarah is nineteen. There's a difference in their ability to handle a matter like this.*

Jessie stepped back to let her in. "Three makes it a little overcrowded, doesn't it?" she asked.

"Jessie, this is Sarah. Sarah, this is Jessie, my wife. We were married last night." Charlie watched Sarah struggling to comprehend what she had heard.

Jessie had become quiet and moved away from him a small distance but spoke up now in the silence. "Sarah, we were just going to get a bite to eat. Please join us."

"No. No, thank you. It was nice meeting you. I'll see you again, I'm sure. Charlie, I'm happy for you, Jessie, we'll have supper soon." She turned and raced back up the steps with Jessie looking after her.

Charlie took a deep breath. Jessie's back was to him for a few seconds longer than he would have wanted. He didn't know what was going through her mind, but he was about to speak his when she turned around.

"I'm sorry I was rude to Sarah, Charlie. I tried to make it up to her by inviting her to dinner with us. I'm not so naïve to think that you would not have had relationships with women. You've been an adult longer than I. You're the catch of the century, so I don't doubt that women are attracted to you." Again, she shushed his intention to speak up with a finger on his lips.

"For a minute, I was jealous and angry because she was so, well, so familiar with your room and with you…to just show up at your door. But I saw the devastation on her face when you introduced me as your wife. I loved you for that. I knew you understood that you were hurting your friend, but it was just very Charlie: honest, straightforward. I felt sorry for her. I know what she has lost, and she knows it too. I had that moment to think and realize that you left her—she's very pretty—to come after me. So whatever has gone on between you two was not as important as what exists between you and me. Tell me I'm right, please, please."

He took her in his arms, loving her, loving how the top of her head fit just under his chin. He felt her body curve into his, and for a brief moment he thought of the time he had kissed Sarah. His thoughts weren't about the desire he had felt for her or for the feel of Sarah's body against his. Rather, he thought very briefly about the difference in the way he wanted Jessie and how he had wanted Sarah. He wanted Jessie. Her mind was as important as her passion. Her moods, her jealousies, her tizzy fits if she had any, her thoughts, and heart... He wanted *Jessie;* he had wanted only Sarah's lips and body.

"Jessie, my love, my darling, I am so proud of you! That was an awkward moment for all three of us. Standing there, looking at you and at Sarah, I fully anticipated that you would, well, act fifteen, and for a moment I was so afraid that I would intervene like a big brother. But you were a mature, kind, gracious young woman. You helped all of us through a difficult situation."

"Hmm, does that mean I can sleep with you like a woman, now?

"Nope."

Jessie's enthusiasm for the house that came with the store matched Charlie's for the store that came with the house. The two were situated at a crossroads where there had once been a Wells Fargo outpost. Development was going on all around this area where Oklahoma, Arkansas, and Missouri territories met and where coalmines were thriving. Rivers sprawled in all directions, and timber was plentiful. It was much closer to Charlie's lumberyard and coalmine than was Guthrie. A nearby railroad line was convenient for the mines. Charlie had investigated and found he could join in connecting the rail to a line that fed into Tulsa. The store was doing a thriving business. The seller had married a Choctaw woman whose vast property was in the southernmost part of the territory. She wanted to be back among her people.

Charlie only happened onto the sale because he and Jessie were riding together, exploring the area. He took every opportunity to show her the territory. Jessie fell in love with the house, and they knocked on the door only to ask the name of the builder.

They learned it was called a "Queen Anne" design. Charlie told her it was a perfect name for their new castle.

Their offer was accepted, and the Harpers had a home two and one-half months after they were married. Charlie bought the existing inventory in the store and most of the furniture in the house. Jessie loved it all. "I think I could even learn to cook in this kitchen!"

The sellers were gracious enough to host a welcoming party for them from surrounding communities, bringing in fiddlers and square-dance callers. A country fair soon developed from their idea to give Charlie and Jessie a good start. When Jessie called out to the departing guests at night's end, "See you all next year," a tradition was born.

Charlie surprised Jessie with her own surrey and horse for a wedding present. He'd ordered them from Guthrie, trusting Oxytak to pick out the horse. Charlie had chosen the rig by catalog. Oxytak delivered them on a balmy day in late June, his own horse tied behind. Jessie was away spending the afternoon with a friend when Oxytak walked in the store.

When Charlie had examined and approved of the young mare, he expressed his satisfaction to Oxytak. The man then handed Charlie two letters addressed to "Jessie and Charlie Harper." They were postmarked Jackson, Mississippi.

Charlie tossed a nervous glance to Oxytak, poured them both a cup of coffee and sat down to read. The first letter was from Frank, although he said he was writing on behalf of "everyone else." The second was from Belle.

Charlie's apprehension had been for nothing. Both letters were filled with well wishes, told them they were missed, and beseeched them to write. Belle and Andrew were happy in their marriage, Cornelius and Ben were growing like weeds, Lily wanted to go away to school, Paul was traveling abroad, and Frank was getting help for his speech impediment. Belle's letter had included a bit more about that. "Frank is smitten with his speech trainer about whom he has said, 'She's my age but a whole lot prettier.'" Both writers implied they'd not heard from them except the note Charlie had sent with the store supplies the day they'd left Jackson.

Oxytak noticed Charlie's frown as he laid the letters down. "Bad news?" he asked.

"No, they're good letters, Jessie will be thrilled, but they didn't mention a word about the letters she and I sent them. I've been writing them for years, twice since we've been married. I know Jessie has written at least two times, as well. This is the first word we've had from them, but at least they're not sending out a posse for me." Charlie grinned.

Jessie named the horse Jenny. "I owe a debt to the first Jenny, you know," she said, reminding Charlie that it was the mare, not Doc, who had turned around in the trail and gone back to the hut, thereby saving his life.

She needed the outfit in order to get to school. Four months into their marriage, he was holding to his intentions that she complete her youth and finish her education. The school she chose was a good half-hour away northeast, near Miami. Charlie made a mental note to check and see if starting a school was feasible in their area. He didn't like Jessie having to drive that far every day, especially in bad weather, but she was fearless and headstrong, certain that Charlie's love and prayers kept her from all harm. Nevertheless, his hopes of starting up a school had precipitated their first quarrel.

Charlie complained that Jessie was overreacting to his thought of taking her out of the Miami school. "What would be the alternative?" she demanded. "To go to some one-room school where all ages would attend? I'd be teaching six-year-olds how to read instead of using my mind! I have friends there, Charlie. You're so busy with the store and the mine and the lumberyard and the railroad, I would be alone all of the time without my friends! Besides, what is a half-hour ride? I went farther than that to school in Mississippi!" The clincher had been when she angrily retorted, "Maybe you should have married a school teacher. I know a pretty one in Guthrie!"

"Jessie, that's enough!" She turned away and stomped upstairs to bed early without kissing him at all, much less with the teasing passion they both enjoyed.

Jessie was proving to be a very good student, participating in some way in everything the school sponsored. She joined the debate team and became active in student politics. Soon, the team was competing with other schools, and now it was Jessie who was often gone until after dark. It was the cause of their second quarrel: Charlie was angry that Jessie was staying out later and later more and more evenings a month.

"What do you care, Charlie Harper? You treat me like a sister instead of a wife. You sleep on the floor instead of a perfectly good bed! It was your idea to have me stay a child. I wanted to be your wife. If you don't like what you've created, I'm sorry!"

"If I treat you like a child, try listening to yourself, Jessie. Do you think you sound like a woman? You don't think it's childish for you to throw up in my face that I'm trying to do the right thing by you, the honorable thing? You are too young to be having sex with a man every night and then going to school around a bunch of virgin kids with raging hormones!" Even as he spoke the harsh words to her, he was loving her and wanting nothing more than to pick her up and carry her to bed. He wanted it to be their bed.

If before they married she had imagined a hundred different weddings for them, since their wedding night, he had easily imagined a hundred different ways he would make love to her. He ached for that, comforted only in the thought that they would have a lifetime. He wanted to make love to a woman, not a girl. He had known it would be difficult to live with her in this way; the tension at times became almost unbearable. But, if she found she didn't want to be married to him, she could annul the marriage easier than she could get a divorce.

His resolve sometimes melted into a convulsing, aching longing, especially when he would see her standing in her nightgown with the lamp light behind her, her perfect body outlined. Many times he had stood at their bedroom door, fighting with his own conscience, wondering if he was being a fool not to consummate the marriage. His favorite times were being awakened by her crawling under his pallet on stormy nights, wrapping herself in his arms...or on other nights not stormy at all except for the thunder brought on by their tumultuous desire.

She never practiced restraint; she never made it easier on him. If anything, she made it more difficult; yet he relished those moments, like the one last night before their argument when she had curled in his lap, teasing him with her tongue and her fingers. He had taken to affectionately calling her "evil woman" at those times. Her reply was, "At least you know I'm a woman!"

He left the house without breakfast; he would have prepared it for himself anyway. He hated that they had quarreled, and he hated the words Jessie threw in his face, but he loved her. She was no different than she'd been all her life. *Am I to her?* he wondered.

That evening, he found Jessie at home in her prettiest dress, flowers on the table, and dinner cooked. She sat primly like a woman-child on the edge of the divan, her hands clasped together in her lap.

"I'm so sorry, Charlie. Please forgive me. I am not being a good wife to you. I really do respect you for the discipline you're showing. I know how much you want to sleep with me. I know that you are right in making sure I am mature enough to have sex and risk a pregnancy. I'm certainly not ready for a baby. I feel sometimes like a child when I want only what I want without thinking what is best for us or even sometimes without thinking about your needs and wants."

He loved her for her honesty and the apology and knelt on the floor in front of her, taking her hands in his as she continued, "But I know I love you like a woman, Charlie. I feel like a woman when I look at you, at your body, your shoulders, arms, and belly."

Her voice and words had him spellbound. She spoke the word *belly* in a husky whisper that made him wild with wanting her.

"I love your man's body. I love the hair on your arms. You're like that statue of David in Italy. I am awed by you— your strength, your confidence. You are everything I have ever admired in a man."

Her voice had grown huskier as she spoke. "I think a lot about sleeping with you Charlie, being held by you, making love with you. I want your hands all over my body. I want you to hold my breasts and know they give you pleasure. I grew them for you! I want us to kiss all we want without having to stop so we won't 'go too far.' I want to go too far, Charlie! I am your wife! I want—I want to make love with you so well that you will want to have me every night and every morning because I want you like that!"

Her voice was now a seductive, bare whisper. "I want to be naked with you! I want your maleness inside me. I think about that all the time. I want to feel you inside my…"

She stopped midsentence as a sob escaped from Charlie, and he dropped his head into his hands, shaking it back and forth.

"Don't, Jessie!"

With another sob, he burrowed his head in her lap and wrapped his arms around her hips, the curve of her belly against his head and the triangle below it against his face. He smelled her perfume mixed with her desire for him, and he groaned, trembling from the passion her words had aroused and from the fierceness of the battle going on inside his heart.

Jessie tried to slide her body under his so that she could pull him to her to comfort him; they fell together onto the floor, both crying and clinging to each other.

"Charlie, I planned all afternoon to only tell you I would stop teasing you and making it so hard on you. I really do respect you for waiting for me. But, oh my darling, every time I'm around you I think about making love with… Oh there I go again. I mean to comfort you, and I only make it worse! Darling, should I—I don't want to—but would it be easier on you if I went away, maybe to Normal School in Edmond where Sarah went? If I went away to finish my schooling, would that be better for us?"

His spirits fell even further. "Jessie, if you want to go away, then yes, that would be better for us. I would never want you to stay against your will. But if you don't want to leave for yourself, if you're suggesting it only because of me, then no! I definitely don't want you to leave! I don't like to be away from you even one night. That's one of the worst things about your being in school—that you can't travel with me on my business trips."

She assured him she did not want to leave him, and for a few weeks they were again their happy selves: teasing, playing, going on picnics, exploring, riding horses cross-country, gardening, and reading to each other. Each pulled pranks on the other and fell, laughing in each other's arms. He loved observing her interests widen and enjoyed discussing what they'd read and learned together. They went down to Tulsa to spend the night, shop, and see a play.

Charlie made her his hushpuppies, which she agreed were the best ever. She spent free time helping him in the store, where she charmed all the customers. But home at night, she was careful to not let their passion get out of control or to try and seduce him.

After a few weeks, she became caught up in her own activities again, showing little interest in their home except once to complain that she had wanted a house with a picket fence. She brought home from school girl friends that lived in the surrounding communities and spent more and more time with them. Charlie could hear their laughter from where he was in the store. Then, of course, she needed to take them home during the evenings she and he normally enjoyed together. They went on other short trips together that left Charlie behind.

Jessie was herself—friendly, happy, bubbly—but she no longer responded with any passion to his kisses. She had adopted the new Gibson-girl styles in hair and dress. Charlie thought the look was especially becoming on her and longed for the time when he could loosen her hair from an enchanting girl to the enchantress he glimpsed in her. Now, she often stayed up after their bedtime, saying she needed to study. After church and at gatherings, she spent more time with the young ladies. He hadn't married her so he could sit across the room with the men.

He had never bought her a ring; they rarely spoke of it. She showed no real interest, even when he guided her to the jewelry stores in Tulsa. She hadn't liked any of the choices, but he thought he had at least gotten an idea of what setting she might like. He intended to give her a diamond ring on their six-month anniversary, but it came and went.

Chapter 11

Christmas was pleasant, Jessie was affectionate, but Charlie longed again for the passion they had once shared. He brought it up on two occasions. Jessie had first said, "I can be just as disciplined as you, Charlie!" He hadn't bothered to argue about that.

Several nights later, he watched her step out of her bath and ached for her. When he stepped forward to hold her, she squealed, turned away, and grabbed her robe. "Charlie, you should knock!"

"Jessie! I'm your husband!"

"Well, we have this arrangement, don't we? An arrangement wherein we don't dare do anything that would be…uh, naughty!"

She told him of a planned trip with her girlfriends to the radium baths in Claremore and that she would be gone overnight. Charlie flatly objected. He continued to object despite her insisting she was now committed since it was all her idea. She had the buggy, and she couldn't let her friends down. He argued with her about it being foolish to take those risks, stating emphatically that he did not want her to go. She shut up and stormed to her bedroom. He knew she was mad at him but at least believed she had set aside her trip. She'd dumped his bedding outside the door. He brought his pallet down to the living room for the night.

The next morning, she stopped by the store, saying only, "I'm leaving now." Charlie repeated that it was too dangerous for four girls to be traveling by themselves to Claremore. Incensed by the way she rolled her eyes, he added, "I *forbid* you to go!"

Her eyes flashed fury. "Charlie Harper, you are not my father, you are not my brother, and, frankly, you're not much of a husband!" She ran out of the store, slamming the door, and was gone, riding Jenny bareback instead of the buckboard. She was only a trail of dust by the time Charlie could climb over the crates he'd been unpacking and get out the door.

He instantly regretted saying, "I forbid you." Still, he seethed at her impudent, childish disregard for her safety and his wishes. He was half a mind to close the store and go bring her home. He slammed another crate on the floor, angered all the more that its contents spilled out everywhere.

The bursting open of the door startled him; he looked up, hoping it was Jessie. Two of his miners shouted at him that there had been a cave-in at the mine. There were men trapped inside. They thought there were three still inside, but they hadn't waited around to see. Phillip, the operating partner, sent them for Charlie.

Racing Tan to the mine, Charlie visualized it the way it looked week before last when he was there. Then, he'd walked every cramped foot of the seven or so underground miles of tunnels. He was as much a stickler for safety precautions as Doc had been for hygiene. He always had the colliers go over the precautions every time he visited. He himself checked for methane and other poisonous gas leaks and made sure the ventilation was as adequate as it could be, personally training the fire bosses to apply the Atkinson equation and brattices along every tunnel.

He had insisted on new Davy lamps using the safer gauze adaptations. He purchased the more hygienic-railed cart toilets. His changes had been costly but well worth the expense as far as Charlie and Phillip were concerned. It was proving to be a good mine, producing last year eleven thousand tons of coal and exceeding their expectations. He was proud of their operations. What had gone wrong?

Charlie jumped off Tan before he came to a complete stop, tearing off his jacket as he ran to the entrance to the mine. The scene was worse than he'd prayed for: the main airshaft and what remained of some of the other above-ground structures were barely visible.

An injured man was being taken away. Charlie stopped briefly to shake the man's hand, calling him by name—Josef—thanking him, and telling him he'd keep him in prayers. He rushed on to the mine opening, where perhaps a hundred people were gathered by now. He called every man by name, firing questions at them in staccato fashion: Had the Dragermen been able to get in? How many are left inside? Who? Where was it? Did they know the cause? He was relieved to hear that most had made their way out or been rescued.

"Who's still in there?" he asked, directing a crew to help in clearing the vents. Phillip was standing by the main shaft and motioned for additional picks. Charlie sent three men up with them.

"Ivan Stone and his son are all who are left in there now, Charlie. They were erecting support from the stoping we did this past week. That might have caused the cave-in. Might have been a rock burst, although that shaft is not very deep. Might have been caused by seismic movement, 'cept rest of us didn't feel anything before the accident. We tried to go in after them, but the coal dust was—"

"Where were Ivan and his son?" Charlie fired the question out, interrupting the man. "Draw me a diagram. Here." He handed a stick to a man so covered in coal he couldn't make out his face. Charlie's logic was that the dirtiest man would have been closest to them.

"Yes, sir. I wouldn't have left them. I wouldn't have left them at all. I had come back to get the—"

Charlie interrupted, "Draw the diagram here in the dirt where you think they are!" The man hastily drew the main tunnel and the branch off from it where the roof had caved in. "Beyond that," he said, "is where the Stones had been working."

Determining that Phillip had a crew clearing the airshafts, Charlie grabbed a lamp, dunked his coat in a barrel of water, and wrapped his wet handkerchief around his nose and mouth as he disappeared through the opening. He moved so fast no one realized his intentions until he disappeared inside.

He thought the Stones were about four hundred yards into the east tunnel. It was a new area of what appeared to be good bituminous strata. The digging had just started last month. Charlie's heart was racing as he ran deeper into the semidarkness, his one lamp initially not shedding sufficient light to keep up with his pace. He guided himself by running his hand along the wall of the tunnel, sometimes running alongside the tracks, sometimes trying to straddle one. He passed two loaded haulage engines, grimly reflecting that their payload was not going to be worth the cost in human suffering.

He could see the Stone boy's face clearly in his mind: a handsome lad, intelligence in his eyes. Too young to be doing this dirty work; but at thirteen, he'd been thrilled to be hired, saying his pa had been eleven when he'd first worked the mines in Russia. Charlie knew boys worked in the mines all over the country even younger than thirteen, but he didn't think it was right. He had talked it over with his partner, and both agreed not to hire kids.

The Stone family was determined to earn the money to get their aging grandparents here from the old country; the elderly couple was impoverished, and their lives were in danger there now. Mrs. Stone had waited nine days for Charlie's visit because Phillip told her Charlie was adamant about not hiring youngsters. She pleaded her son's case, describing the dangerous conditions her parents were living in. Charlie took pity on them and reluctantly authorized the hiring.

Why couldn't he remember his name? *Hell! The boy may be lying there dead, and I can't do him the decency of remembering his name?* He thought of Frank and Doc and the time when Frank almost died.

His eyes were burning and tearing, and his breath was coming in gasps; the oxygen was much thinner and the noxious dust thicker. He knew the risks down here, particularly after a cave-in. There was the possibility of an explosion, but more so of additional cave-ins or leaks of poisonous gases. Right now, with no explosion, he wasn't worried about carbon monoxide, but the coal dust seemed trapped. He wondered why it wasn't settling. Was there still activity ahead?

He was moving slower and slower, heaving and coughing, the dust becoming increasingly thicker. He didn't know how far he'd gone; darkness distorted time and distance. He had no intention of stopping, regardless.

He tried to call out, "Ivan! Ivan!" His voice was so hoarse he could barely speak. He heard nothing except occasional small debris and rocks falling; he hoped each time they were sounds made by the Stones. He was beginning to fear he had taken a wrong turn and tried to review his path in his mind. He found it hard to think clearly now and so trusted he was in the correct tunnel and prayed. He prayed silently as he stumbled along, his mind playing tricks on him.

He thought of Jessie as a child and as she had been in his arms on their wedding night. He thought of Li and Hong; he recalled walking through the canal in the compound, and it occurred to him to sing again, but his breathing was too labored; he could barely recite the lines in his mind.

At that moment, Charlie stumbled into a pile of debris, falling before he could determine how to brace himself and keep his lamp steady. *This was where the roof caved in*, he thought and began clawing through rocks, dirt, and some timber. He spotted the end of a pick handle and carefully pulled it from the pile; with it, he made better progress and finally felt air rushing past his ears. He scraped away room to wiggle into the hole that opened up for him easier than he'd expected.

He felt a hand reaching out for him and clasped it, scraped through the opening, and landed hard on his side. He sat up, trying to catch his breath, noticing the air seemed a little better on this side of the cave-in. "Are you both okay?"

"We're a dang sight better now! Pa's got a broken leg and a cut on his head. He was knocked out for a while, but he's come to now. I'm okay. I was knocked out too, but I'm fine; just a lump on my head and a few scratches on my hands. I tried to dig a hole through that solid wall you just came through but had to rest. Our picks and shovels are buried under that pile there. Who are you?"

"I'm Charlie Harper."

"Mr. Harper!" It was Ivan's voice; he sounded weak and hoarse. "The boss is rescuing us! Thank you! Thank you! I've been scared for my son's sake."

Charlie gingerly felt along Ivan's leg, determining the break; he wanted to make sure that moving him wouldn't cause further injury. He felt around for a sturdy board to use as a splint, asking the lad to stay alert to any structural weight shift it might cause. They pulled a two-by-four out that had been part of the framework. Charlie tore his shirt in strips and tied them around the leg and splint.

When Ivan realized what he was doing, he grew silent for a minute then spoke, his voice cracking with emotion. "That's mighty Christian of you, Mr. Harper, coming after us, giving up your shirt and all!"

Charlie remembered the boy's name. "Billy, we are going to need to coordinate our movements here. We'll make that hole more secure, and I'll pass your pa through, all without further disturbing the cave-in."

The boy understood and went to work in the dimming light, mostly by touch, reinforcing the opening Charlie had made and making it possible to pass his father through. Ivan insisted they not worry about him; he could handle it.

"Just get my son out first."

"We're all going out together," Charlie assured. "We're going to make it out, and when we do, we're going to have a celebration."

He had Billy go back through the opening so as to take hold of his father as Charlie passed him through, headfirst.

"All right, Billy, try to brace his head and neck and take hold of his shoulders." Charlie could hear Ivan's breathing coming in raspy gasps. He held the man's legs as steady as he could as they inched him through. "All right, Ivan, you're just about through now. When Billy tells you, turn your good leg down to catch yourself. It's going to be painful and awkward there, as Billy will have most of your weight at that point."

The poor air quality made their efforts much more exhausting for Charlie and Billy. They could only guess the pain Ivan was experiencing; he grunted several times but never protested.

All three were coughing, struggling through the thick, black dust and feeling the effects of inadequate oxygen.

The men heard a rumble and felt a slight tremor as rocks and more debris began falling on them. Charlie crouched slightly to brace Ivan's feet against his thighs and remained still, as did Billy. If another cave-in should occur, Ivan would likely be crushed, if not all three of them. No one spoke.

Billy's reinforcements held. The tremor had been minor, although it kicked up more coal dust. They waited a moment for the worst of it to settle and then resumed the effort to get Ivan through the jagged opening. Charlie heard him grunt and heard Billy offering sympathy and encouragement. Finally, Ivan announced he had his good foot on the ground. Billy slowly backed him out; they heard his broken leg strike the mound and Ivan gasp, but he made no other sound.

Charlie rested, leaning one hand against the tunnel wall, desperately struggling to take a deep breath but seeming to be unable to do so; he had lost his handkerchief somewhere along the way. Finally he passed the lamp through the opening and crawled back through. Each man draped one of Ivan's arms across his shoulders, and they began taking steps toward freedom with Charlie trying to take a larger share of the man's weight.

"Ivan, I can sympathize with you." Charlie's hoarse, raw throat discouraged speaking. "Remind me to tell you about the time I got beaten up and had to be carried like this. I know it isn't pleasant."

"Mr. Harper, this is a whole lot more pleasant than lying on my back side back there before you came down this tunnel! I'm much obliged to you, much obliged."

When they reached the last haulage engine, Charlie and Billy propped Ivan on top and tried pushing him; however, the heavy load and incline, though slight, made it too difficult. They hauled him back down and stumbled on. It was necessary that

Charlie or Billy have the more difficult path walking over the rails, so they switched off from time to time.

Either prompted by worry about Charlie or given the go ahead from the fire boss, several miners met the trio at the entrance to the main tunnel, relieving Charlie and Billy by carrying Ivan the rest of the way out. Charlie thought to ask for a fresh lamp from one of the men, pausing to rest for a minute. He was heartened by seeing them carrying Ivan toward the exit.

Staggering from fatigue, Billy slipped when his boot struck the edge of a rail, and he fell. Charlie stooped to help him, wondering if the lad had actually been more injured during the cave-in than he was letting on. He'd grown quieter, although, of course, their struggle had been laborious. The two could faintly hear the shouts of joy when those outside the mine saw Ivan. It lifted Charlie's spirits, but Billy said nothing.

"Son, are you doing okay?" Charlie asked. "You've been mighty quiet. Are you sure you're not hurt?"

"No, sir. It's nothing."

Under better conditions, Charlie would have laughed at the way Billy looked in the fresh light, as though he was only two enormous disembodied eyes. He was so blackened he faded into the wall of the tunnel. Charlie realized he looked the same.

"Are you sure? Tell me, son," Charlie urged him, clasping him by the shoulder as they knelt there.

"It…it's silly, sir, but I lost my mother's good luck charm back there when we switched sides. Pa's hand got tangled in the string around my neck, and I felt it fall. I just feel bad for my ma. I promised her I would guard it with my life. But she said, 'It's to be the other way around.'"

"What is it, son? Charlie asked. They were both struggling to help each other up off the floor of the tunnel. He appreciated the boy's sentiment; he knew the value of holding on to promises and vows and knew the sense of loss or betrayal when they were broken. He understood treasuring gifts given with hope that they would somehow bring forth a miracle when a precious someone needed it most.

"It's…it's the key to my ma's music box. That box is her greatest treasure. It's the only thing she brought here from Russia." The boy was gasping, but Charlie didn't try to quiet him. "You wind the box with that key, and it plays the song my parents danced to at their wedding. My ma plays it on special occasions, and it is her pride. Pa had it made for her with the first profit he made from his store. He went without so he could save the money for it. She winds it up for very special occasions, and they always dance together. Of course, she'll still have the music box, but I don't know if she'll ever hear it play again. I guess you think that's a pretty unimportant thing for me to be concerned about at a time like this."

"Son, I think it is a very important concern. Next to your life being spared, it's the most important one we have right now. It is a life poorly lived that doesn't contain cherished memories and the mementos that stand for folks and times we love and honor! You go on. I'll go see if I can find it."

He urged Billy to go ahead and share in the deserved applause; after all, the boy had stayed with his injured Pa at the risk of his own death when he could have rescued himself.

Billy hesitated. "No, sir. I can't let you do that."

"I'm your boss, Billy. I'm ordering you to walk out there to your pa. He still needs you! You say you lost the key at the last switch off we made. I remember about where that was. While I still have good light, I'll go back and look for it. You go ahead. Just run your hand along the wall until you see light. Go!"

He groped along the tracks where he believed they had last switched sides. Now crawling, holding the lamp close to the ground, determined. *I am truly a stubborn man*, he thought to himself, knowing that a more rational man would be heading the other way, the direction of fresh air and safety. *No wonder Jessie doesn't enjoy me any more. I'm bossy, stubborn, controlling. I'm rigid, just like she said. What woman wants a husband like me?*

At the thought of her, his heart quickened as it always did. He didn't understand how his love could continue to grow even as they fought and grew apart.

This morning was a disaster. I was stupid to speak to her as I did. She's young. I can't expect her to act older than her age. The thought reminded him of the concern he had for her safety traveling to Claremore. Yet, Ivan and Billy's risk and their subsequent rescue helped him put things in a better perspective. They might have died, but they were now safe. Josef didn't appear to have serious injuries. Regardless of his and Jessie's quarrel, on balance, the day was still a good one.

He spotted the gold key as it reflected his lamplight; it was lying partly underneath a rail. He retrieved it and thrust it deep into his pants pocket, hurriedly rising in the direction of the mine entrance. As he turned, his lantern struck hard against the haulage car, shattering the glass.

In an instant, Charlie grasped the danger of what had happened and was already running when he heard the explosion and felt a shock wave propelling him forward. His last thought had been to wonder what Billy meant when he said his dad bought the music box with his first profit from the store. Hadn't Ivan been mining since he was eleven? Charlie fell, unconscious.

The first things he saw were a blue, cloudless sky and green, tearful eyes, four of them at first. His ears were ringing, and his head and lungs hurt; but even those maladies couldn't prevent him from smiling as he felt Jessie's body across his chest, her hands on his face, and her kisses between sobbing, "Charlie, wake up! Don't leave me. Please don't leave me! Charlie, I love you. Charlie, my darling, wake up!"

He wrapped an arm around her as another roar went up from the crowd. "Jessie...Jessie." He coughed, his voice still hoarse. "I'm so glad you're safe, darling. I'm so sorry for yelling at you this morning, forbidding you—"

She kissed him. "Shush, shush...you are alive. You're out of that hellhole. Nothing else in this whole world matters to me! I'm the fool! I didn't go to Claremore. I knew if I did it would just be proof that I am childish and not deserving to be your wife. That's really why I rode Jenny, to go tell Emily I wouldn't be going so she could tell the others. When I got back to the store, I learned about the accident! Jenny has never been ridden that hard or so fast! I'll make it up to her, and to you, Charlie!"

Jessie looked especially beautiful to him, despite being completely blackened by coal dust, he guessed from hugging him. There were two tear-washed trails under her eyes and a darker ring of black around lips wiped pink again from kissing his. Coal was all over her hair and clothing.

"You could get a job in a minstrel show in New York the way you look right now."

"No pun intended, Charlie Harper, but you are the miner calling the kettle black!" She showered him with more kisses, refusing to let go of his hand while the doctor examined him, pronouncing a moderate concussion and minor lacerations but no broken bones.

Billy knelt beside Charlie, worry on his face. "Sir, if anything had happened to you, I don't think I could have lived with myself. You saved mine and Pa's life and twice risked yours just for something sentimental that doesn't mean anything to you."

Charlie fumbled to remove the key from his pocket and handed it to Billy. "Son, I didn't go back for a brass key. I went back for what it represents, not just to your family but mine and everyone's. I went back because it stands for something much more important than that coal mine. Now you tell your ma I expect to dance to that music box one of these days!"

Billy was speechless for a moment and then pumped Charlie's hand hard, thanking him over and over, staring at the key he had never expected to see again. He rose, turned, and ran, but Charlie had seen his eyes redden. "Pa! Pa! He found it! Mr. Harper found it!"

Two days later, Charlie was back in the store, talking to the stream of local folk and some strangers who poured in to hear all about the accident. It was a close community, so all were eager to either hear more details or add to them or to simply replay that day and to shake Charlie's hand. Many of these good folks had their share of tragedy and death. They didn't always have happy endings when men came that close to death.

Despite a residual headache, his mood could not have been better. Jessie had been showering him with attention and affection, and Ivan was recovering. The doctor hadn't needed to set the man's leg, commenting on the good job Charlie had done.

"I've set a few bones in my day." He chuckled. Of course, Ivan would not be able to work in the mine for some time.

Oxytak surprised him with a visit. "Chief," Charlie often called him now, "I see your sixth sense is a mite slower! You have always shown up when I've been in trouble, although you're five days late this time!" Charlie teased him and poured them both a cup of coffee, and the men sat together at the table at the back of the store. It seemed that Oxytak knew more about the events that went on outside the mine than Charlie did. He filled him in on comments and the efforts to send in Dragermen to rescue him sooner but had been stopped when the mouse died, indicating bad air.

"I deem it a miracle that I survived. For that matter, it is an act of God that we all survived. There's no serious injury, and men have all been raring to go back in. The structures are repaired. They've been working as diligently outside the mine as they ever did inside. The safety check was completed, so they were to start operations again this morning.

"One thing I've never thought to ask," Charlie pondered, "is how I got out of the mine after the explosion. I recall feeling the blast while I was still back in the tunnel. I don't know if I somehow got myself out or if I was rescued. If the latter, and I'm thinking it is, I want to thank those men."

"Jessie hasn't told you?" Oxytak asked, his eyebrows raised in surprise. "Jessie rescued you!"

Charlie set his cup down so close to the table edge it tipped over. He caught it and moved it toward the center, never looking at it but instead staring at Oxytak, disbelief all over his face. "No, that's not possible, Chief. She wasn't there. She's a little thing. She couldn't lift me. She wouldn't have been allowed to enter anyway!"

"Son, I've heard it from three different witnesses now. Jessie is quite the heroine! I'm surprised you don't know."

Charlie finally closed his mouth, only to open it again and manage a weak, "Tell me."

"This is all third party, but I've no reason to doubt it. When that explosion went off, Jessie let out a scream, naturally, but just one, they say; although I think I might have heard it in Guthrie! She wasn't going to stand there and wait to find out you'd been killed. She raced toward the entrance but was caught and held back by three or four women. She tore loose from them. Then a man grabbed hold of her, and another stepped up to help him restrain her. By then, I'm told, the young lad you rescued was already running to Jessie, but he had been on the ambulance farther back with his pa. Jessie wrenched herself from those men, kicking, biting, and scratching."

Oxytak laughed appreciatively. "She must have been a wild cat. As a matter of fact, the word is that the injuries she inflicted on those two men are the worst ones sustained by anybody." He laughed again. "Wish I'd been there to see that little mite of a girl overpowering two men."

"She overpowers me regularly," Charlie managed. "Go on. Are you saying she somehow rescued me?"

"*Somehow* is probably the right word. She tore into that mine, the boy about twenty feet behind her, and five minutes later the two of them were carrying you out and laid you down on the ground. She fell on top of you. Both Jessie and the boy were crying and coughing, the boy telling everyone you'd saved his life and his pa's life, so the least he could do was to protect your wife."

Jessie's excitement about a Sunday picnic made the lingering headache tolerable and the week fly by. He smiled with gladness, watching her busying herself after school with preparations, finding or making little gifts for Ivan's children, selecting candies for them from the barrels in the store, and making a rag doll for their youngest. She, too, had developed affection for Billy and his father since the day at the mine.

They skipped church so as to get an early start and be there before dinnertime. Knowing they were worried about money, Charlie intended to continue Ivan's pay and wanted him to know that right away. Even so, he knew they were hurting financially, especially in light of their saving to bring the grandparents here. Charlie intended to find out more about the parents in Russia also; maybe he and Jessie could help. Their buckboard heaped with enough food to feed the family for a week, and including Jessie's best attempts at blackberry cobblers, they were in fine spirits as they arrived at the Stones'.

"We came from Russia, a small village not far from St. Petersburg in 1887," Ivan explained in response to Charlie's prodding. "There had been pogroms throughout Russia, worsening over the last couple of years. We Jews were under severe persecution. This was by the…government system, mind you, so we had no hope of protection and no recourse when we were attacked or victimized. My store was first vandalized and looted then burned down a few weeks later. Our home was burned down after that, but we had already fled to Maria's parents in the country. I feared for the lives of my wife and daughter and our parents. We all knew we had to make radical decisions or die.

"My parents made the difficult decision to emigrate to Palestine just before we came to America. They would never have left Russia—it was their homeland—had they not understood they would inevitably be killed. They would have no livelihood if by some miracle they survived. It didn't seem to matter that they were elderly. If they were Jewish, they were targets for unimaginable sufferings."

Ivan paused, watching Jessie refill their lemonade glasses and waiting until she sat back down next to Charlie and leaned against him. Crinkles of a smile flashed around his eyes to see their love. "You two are like Maria and me. May you have many fine children!"

Jessie took Charlie's hand. "Oh we intend to, thank you. Please continue, though! How did your parents decide to go to Palestine. Were they Zionists?"

"Perhaps at heart, every Jew is a Zionist, but, no, the Zionist movement had not yet begun. However, the *aliyah* to Palestine—that is, large groups of Jews emigrating there—had been going on in waves. Conditions in Russia were never good for the peasants, the serfs. Of course, we Jews always spoke of a return to Israel, vowing to do so was a part of our religious celebrations, especially Passover and Yom Kippur. But Russia was our homeland, however difficult life was. It was still our home. When my parents had to flee, the Jews in Palestine were the only group of people or place in their hearts where they believed they could also belong. Even had they wanted to come to America, they felt they were too old to start over in a completely new land with strange language and customs.

"My older brother and his family left too. They went over on the same boat. I took them to the dock and watched them sail away. It felt as though my heart was being torn in two. Maria… Ivana was all we had at the time. They were my family, of course, but it is very difficult to say good-bye and know you will probably never see your parents and brother again. They pleaded with us to come with them."

Charlie heard the catch in Ivan's voice and saw the sorrow in his eyes before he glanced away, remembering the parting. Maria reached out and wrapped her arm in Ivan's clasping his hand, tears welling in her eyes as well.

"It must have been heart wrenching for you all," Jessie acknowledged. "What a terrible decision your parents had to make to flee their homeland and all of you!"

"It was not easy for any of us to do, and the government didn't make it any easier even though they were allowing Jews to leave the country at that time. There were hundreds of thousands of us leaving, or so it seemed. We were being looked upon as interlopers, even though we'd been born in Russia. Our families had been born there, and we were as much Russian as you are American, although our Judaism marked us for persecution, military conscription, and higher taxation, for example. We stayed behind a little longer to help Maria's parents.

"But"—his face broke into a broad smile—"we came to Ellis Island and heard about this territory called Oklahoma where people like us were settling from all over the world and where there was opportunity for everyone willing to work hard. Most important have been the freedoms we find here. Freedoms we could not even imagine! We get to keep the money we make and can speak out about matters that seem unfair, although most Americans, we find, have no idea about real unfairness! There has been some rejection because we are Jews, but we do not fear for our lives. We are not afraid to worship. We have become citizens, and we vote!

"We hadn't been able to salvage our belongings. The loss of business from the store made it necessary to use up our savings. I had worked in the mines in Russia when I was a child to help my family out while my father recovered from a serious accident. He had been serving in the Russian military, as was required by all Jewish men from age twelve on. But his injury got him released from that, and I was only eleven, one year too young to be conscripted into the military. Somehow, the authorities forgot about me, so I stayed on in the mines until I had enough money to marry Maria. Best decision I've ever made!"

Maria kissed him on the cheek and spoke up. "By a strange set of circumstances, which I will save for another time, my father had a small market, what you here call a general store. I believe you have one, Charlie. My brothers had both lost their lives, so Ivan helped him out and learned the business. He studied at night to catch up on the education he missed and impressed my father so much that he finally sold us the store so he could fulfill his dream of gardening and taking care of my mother. She lost part of her foot in an accident when I was a small child. He could not have afforded to do that except that we would be paying him back, something every month, although our taxes were being raised and there were threats made over whether the land belonged to us or the government.

"My father also had a small inheritance from his parents who had been respected artisans during the time of the war with Napoleon, so they received a small stipend until recently when the government stopped it. But they had given us most of their money to come here to America. Of course, they stopped receiving much help from us when we lost everything. They are older than Ivan's parents and nearly impoverished. I worry for them all the time."

Ivan spoke. "Maria's parents are the latest victims of pogroms. Living farther away from the city and perhaps still having the artistry of my grandfather honored by the locals, they hadn't gone through what my parents had. At first, they refused to even consider leaving their homeland. Maria is their only living child. It broke their hearts to say good-bye to her.

"I believe that good-bye was harder than the one I had with my parents. However, the pogroms have now left them no choice. They're willing to come here. They were already having a change of heart. They want to be around their grandchildren and their only child, so I believe we have talked them into coming. That is why Billy and I took the job in the mines. It paid best. Now…" His voice faltered.

"Now," Charlie said, speaking up quickly, "you need to let that leg mend, and I am here hoping that you can do me a big favor and solve a problem I'm having."

"Of course, whatever I can do on a busted leg. I can get around pretty good. What do you need, Charlie?"

"Tell me, Ivan, what is the cost of a pound of sugar in these parts?"

"Four cents," Ivan answered without hesitation.

"A dozen eggs and a pound of coffee?" Charlie inquired.

"If you have a guarantee with the local farmers, they'll fetch thirteen or fourteen cents, depending on the agreement. Coffee is fifteen cents a pound. Why are you asking? You already know the answers." Ivan chuckled.

"I wanted to see if you still had the mind of a merchant. I need an experienced man I can trust to go into partnership and manage a second store. Jessie and I have been negotiating to purchase a piece of property on the crossroad down by the Mueller place. That is an ideal spot for a store. There's a new batch of settlers in the area every week, it seems. They're coming to farm, work the timber, and to mine. I figure it will support two families once it gets going. In the meantime, I need someone to oversee the construction, equip it, stock inventory, and, well, manage it without needing to run to me for every decision. You're on the payroll as soon as you agree to this. Thirty-three cents an hour. If the growth in this area continues, I believe you'd eventually be able to buy me out, if you had a desire to do that."

That being settled and Charlie's earning the eternal gratitude of the family for the job and the raise in wages, he turned to Billy. "Son, if it is okay with your pa, I'd like you to come and help me build a picket fence around our home. We could get that finished before your school starts. You'd make about the same as you did in the mine. I'd have to have you do the job of painting it to Jessie's satisfaction. What do you say?"

Three days before the first anniversary of their buying the store and house, and amidst the preparations for their "second annual fair," Charlie received two important packets of mail. In the first was a diamond ring and gold wedding band he had ordered for Jessie. He felt tender and protective toward her just looking at their tiny size four. He would plan a perfect time to surprise her with them, although he was still puzzled why she never seemed very interested.

The second packet of mail contained an answer to the letter he had sent to Charles Harper of the Pacific Mail Steamship Company in San Francisco. He had hoped the man was still there and would remember him. Charlie wrote, asking for advice on ship travel to St. Petersburg, Russia. He explained the situation of Maria's parents and the intention of having them brought to the United States as soon as possible.

Charles Harper did indeed remember him and was delighted to hear, immediately informing him in the first paragraph that both Boris and Li paid him visits whenever they were in port to learn if he had heard from their friend. He included their San Francisco contact information, along with ship schedules sailing in and out of St. Petersburg. He would be happy to help Charlie make whatever arrangements he could from that end, adding a P.S.: "As a suggestion, you might see if Boris is interested in working on the ship's crew to St. Petersburg. He has family there. You mentioned your family is an elderly couple. Perhaps he could be of assistance. He's a good man."

"*I am absolutely not jealous.*" Watching the boys watch Jessie all morning, noticing how they flirted with her constantly, didn't mean he was jealous—at least that's what he argued with himself. He didn't recognize any of them; they were no more than eighteen years old and, he thought, acting considerably younger. *I'm simply concerned for her welfare. Besides, she belongs to me.*

Charlie sponsored the fair, but this year it had acquired a vitality of its own. Beginning with the early spring planning stages, the community came together to develop the event, thus relieving him from most of the responsibility. There were exhibits of crafts, quilting, canning, farm produce, livestock, and contests of every imaginable kind from shows of talent and muscular strength to yodeling, fiddling, races, and horseshoe throwing. Musicians were plentiful.

These good people took obvious pride in their labor, talents, and crafts, and in arranging all other festivities that make a fair successful. Knowing he'd be partial to anything Jessie did, he declined being a judge this year. So it happened that his sole responsibility today was to feed the fair attendees. Ivan and Maria arrived an hour after sunrise to help him set up the food concession. He noticed Jessie leaving the house right after breakfast to pick up her friends. She hadn't stopped by his tent.

All right, I am jealous. She's flirting back and makes no effort to conceal it, either. Although not deliberately flaunting her flirtations in front of him, she seemed to have forgotten he was there entirely. With her everywhere were her three best friends and the same silly boys. He could hear Jessie's laughter above the noise and merrymaking. *She's certainly having a hilarious time without me!*

He tried not to watch the boys flexing muscles and swaggering all over the grounds. They passed Charlie's concession frequently, as their two favorite games were right in front, just across the walkway. In his opinion, they were childish games that required a modicum of brawn but not an ounce of brain.

Charlie kept his feelings in check by attending to his customers, although it was becoming increasingly necessary to remind himself he was more mature than Jessie's new clique. He resisted the temptation to go show off for her and show up the boys, certain that his strength and coordination at twenty-six were still greater than theirs. On at least two occasions he pretended he had not felt an urge to break the arm of the boy who tried to put his around Jessie. To her credit, both times she shrugged him off and stepped away, not that the brazen bruiser got the message.

But Charlie worried that the truth was on display today: *Jessie is not in love with me*, the thought hurt.

It was pretty clear. "She no longer thinks of me as her husband." That would explain, he decided, her disinterest in wearing a wedding ring. As long as the boys didn't know she was married, she could have them all eating out of her ringless hand. He couldn't force her to love him; this was one of the primary reasons he had not claimed her sexually. She needed to be able to freely choose him from the population of available suitors.

Today, he wanted to ring the necks of them all and knew he was capable of doing so, but what would he prove by that? He hated it more than he had ever hated anything in his life, but he had to accept the inevitable: he was more like a beloved older brother to her now. Her affections would soon be settling on one of these swaggering, immature, unintelligent boys or another like them. If he weren't tied down to the food concession, he would take a long, hard ride on Tan to clear his mind.

These were unfamiliar and quite unpleasant feelings; he was angry with himself for wallowing in his self-pity. He had himself to blame and no one else. He would certainly talk with Jessie tonight. It was not his nature to feel sorry for himself, but he knew he would be grieving the loss of Jessie's love for the rest of his life.

It had also been his intention to present his plan to Ivan and Maria today for rescuing her parents and bringing them here. Based on his conservative calculations and projections on what he expected Ivan's store to yield, the man would be able to feed his family, turn a profit, and still make payments on the loan Charlie wanted to offer. He had added up the costs for bringing them out. He wanted Jessie by his side to help convince them to accept his offer of a loan in this way. He knew neither would accept charity.

With all her fun, Jessie hardly glanced in the tent, much less to sit down with him to talk. There had been no time to speak about it to the Stones anyway. The turnout for the fair was so much greater than anticipated; he'd hardly found a moment to chat with them all day. In that respect, he was glad to stay busy and not ruminate about Jessie more than he already was. He noticed her and Maria talking, nodding to each other and hugging. Maria handed Jessie a covered basket, probably the peach pie she'd promised she'd bring; seeing them together cheered him a bit.

Seeing Oxytak poking his head under the food tent was a balm for Charlie's churning emotions. The timing was perfect, too, with a late afternoon lull in the activity. The fair attendees were thinning out.

The men hugged. "Chief, you've done it again. You've shown up at the right moment. I want to… No, I think I need to talk to you about a personal matter, if you don't mind."

"That's why I'm here, son."

Charlie drew him aside to a table at the far end of the tent. Maria and Ivan were in conversation at one nearer the front where noise from the passersby would mask the words between the two men.

Charlie got straight to the point. He confided in Oxytak everything regarding the past year of his marriage. He spared no detail: the fights, the passion, the very difficult struggles to keep his vow to respect her youth, the doubts he had as to whether Jessie married him because of her childhood fantasies or to get away from her mother, and his belief that she was too young to have sex.

"I made a vow to her on our wedding night that I wouldn't touch her until she was more mature and had completed her education."

Oxytak was silent a few moments. "Charlie, I knew there was a magnificent love and a powerful tension between you two, but I couldn't put my finger on what it was. Now, I understand. I see your points, and I admire your restraint. It's another measure of the good man you are. You're a stronger man than I. I could not have lived with my wife for one week much less a year as you and Jessie have done. Few men could. For that matter, few women could who love their men the way Jessie loves you."

"Chief, that's my point. I guess I no longer believe she does love me in the way you're implying, as her lover… Well, I guess I can't expect her to think of me as her lover but as her husband. I don't believe she thinks of me…I guess it would be difficult to think of me as her husband, too, since we don't—"

"Here are my thoughts, Charlie. First, she is a young woman, not a little girl. I've thought of her as a woman since the day I met her again in Guthrie. She's proven herself to be mature in her judgment and wisdom, if not always her temperament. I remember you telling me how considerate she was of Sarah. You say she's accelerated in her studies. I'm told young folks go to her for advice they don't trust their parents with. Every woman I know of every age respects her, and that is saying a lot considering how pretty she is. Another woman might have aroused jealousy, but Jessie is always considerate and genuinely interested in the other person.

"You tell me today that her passion for you has waned. I take that to mean only that she has been trying to live by your terms and within your boundaries while also protecting her own emotions. She was fully ready to give her life for you at the mine accident. If that isn't a powerful testimony of love, I don't know what is."

Charlie sat, weighing everything Oxytak was saying. He nodded his head imperceptibly as his friend's words rang true.

"Son, I'm with Jessie in this matter. You've been denying her something her heart, spirit, and body all tell her she needs and has every right to; but beyond her right to have a sexual relationship with you, her soul needs that oneness with you."

Again, Charlie nodded. "That is what I've needed too."

"A woman needs to be joined with her husband in a sexual union not one bit less than a man needs that, and she needs to experience all the many joys that accompany that union, including the confident assurance that her body gives him great pleasure just as she receives it from him. She's not going to feel completely married until that happens, and you really can't expect her to. In a very real way, she isn't yet married to you.

"Seems to me in denying her that very essential intimacy you have risked pushing her into the arms, certainly the attention, of some other man. Men aren't blind. She's a beautiful woman, but they don't all have your integrity."

Charlie told him what he had been seeing today, all day—Jessie flirting with the boys and one of them acting possessive of her, with her not outright putting him in his place. He said they hadn't quarreled since the mine accident, yet Jessie seemed to be taking him for granted. "Pretty much like she would an older brother!"

"Son, Jessie has better sense then to give her affections and the woman she is to just any boy! You're selling yourself short there. Jessie is a good judge of character. Proof is her waiting for you all those years!

"However, you've been pushing her away from you. Not intentionally, but in a one-sided effort to define what you believe is right for her. In that sense, you've denied her both the right to express her deepest love for you and the respect for her wisdom in knowing who she is and what she wants."

Oxytak's comments recalled to Charlie's mind the beautiful words Jessie had told him on their wedding night when he had no words to tell her how deep were his love and emotions at the time. She had said she thought God gave lovers the pleasure of a sexual relationship so as to become love rather than merely try to describe it. It struck Charlie now that even then she had understood love, maybe better than he!

Oxytak spoke again, "I don't know why you have believed you must not consummate your marriage. Perhaps it is your guilt for the difference in your ages and having married her so young. Son, you did rescue her from an abusive situation. That was a good thing, but it doesn't define the marriage. Whatever her age, Jessie has loved you completely. She is a woman now. That's how she loves you. When I see Jessie looking at you, I see a woman's love."

Everything Oxytak said made perfect sense to Charlie. Why hadn't he been able to see all this before? Jessie made at least as many sacrifices and often the wisest decisions in their marriage. She was struggling in it, denied her very basic right to express her love and identify her own needs. He had discounted her passion, thinking it was his own that showed the greater sacrifice and discipline. How blind he had been! He now felt he hadn't been much better to her than her mother! He was ashamed that he'd been so narrow minded about her needs. He nodded now to Oxytak's wisdom.

"She just might have grown up right under my nose, and I've been too blind to see."

"Think about it," Oxytak urged. "If she has normal, mature desire for you and you have made sexual love and even her passion conditional on your terms, how is she supposed to cope with that?" Both sat in silence for a while, Oxytak in his wisdom letting Charlie contemplate the things he'd heard. Finally, he rose, his hand on Charlie's shoulder. "Son, I'm glad I came. Give Jessie my love."

Charlie watched him walk away. He was so absorbed in the things Oxytak had said he didn't think to say good-bye.

A few straggling customers wandered in for the next hour, allowing Ivan and Maria to enjoy the remainder of the fair. Charlie polished and re-polished tables, lost in thought and remorse. Everything Oxytak said was right. Charlie felt humbled by the truth in it and grateful for the love that seemed always to surround him. Yet he realized how often he took it for granted. Was Oxytak's lesson too late?

His ponderings were abruptly interrupted by the boisterous laughter coming from the young people entering the tent. It was Jessie and her friends. The boys took it upon themselves to move three tables together so they could sit as a group, piling the prizes they won for the girls on a fourth table. Two of them pulled chairs from under a fifth and propped their dirty boots on those.

Jessie smiled at Charlie warmly but didn't speak and made no effort to introduce him. Her girlfriends were clearly so enamored by the boys they all but ignored Charlie, except to make their selections among the remaining pies and cakes as if their waiter didn't exist. *Am I also simply taken for granted by her friends as well?* The insight made him ponder more whether in fact he treated Jessie like a big brother rather than the lover he longed to be.

Charlie brought their orders, no more impressed with or intimidated by the youths than he would have been by a bunch of ten-year-olds, but he was curious to know what attraction they held for Jessie. Nonetheless, he granted respect to the group as he had done to all his customers all day. He smiled at her but didn't single Jessie out, although he wished she were with him instead of with them. He asked the boys to remove their feet and replace the chairs for other customers, pointing out there was no other available table.

"Well excuse me!" One of them exaggerated his pretended apology. "Looks to me folks are staying away from this place in droves, but here you go." He looked around his table to make sure the others appreciated his cleverness.

The group got louder as well as sillier in Charlie's opinion. The boys referred to him as "old man" at one point when telling him to bring another entire pie. Charlie smiled to himself, thinking the banana cream pie would fit perfectly in the middle of the thug's face. None showed any manners or respect. At least he didn't hear Jessie laughing like the other girls. To him they were shallow and immature and not worth his concern, but Jessie was. He heeded Oxytak's words and hoped he would be able to make it up to Jessie. He would see to it that they talked it all out tonight.

When their food had been consumed and their boasting had reached a new level, the boy who had insinuated himself next to Jessie all day spoke up, asking about plans for that night. He reminded them there was a dance in Miami that evening and, looking directly at Jessie, invited the girls collectively to join them there. "Even better…" Charlie bristled at the leer he saw on the boy's face as he spoke to Jessie. "Pretty girl, I could ride with you in the buckboard, and your friends can ride behind my friends here on their horses. What do you say to that?"

Already approaching their table, Charlie waited the eternity for Jessie's answer. Whatever it was, and no matter the cost to him or their relationship, he had no intention of allowing her to go to Miami tonight. They would talk, and if she still wanted this kind of freedom, well, he would deal with that when he got to it. His heart was breaking, but he tried to smile.

Jessie stood as Charlie arrived at their table and turned to him with the teasing look on her face that always made his heart pound from wanting her. She wrapped both arms around his waist, looking up at him, her eyes shining with love.

"No, boys," she said, still looking at Charlie. "I won't be going to the dance. I'll be spending the night with my husband."

Charlie swept up his mite of a woman who he was learning was mightier than he and carried her away before the shocked expressions of her friends.

"Jessie," he whispered, "I am going to make love with you tonight. You can bank on it, woman!" Her kiss let him know that was her plan too.

A while later, he sent Jessie home, finding her presence by his side even more distracting than her being with the boys had been, although it was the kind of distraction he relished. She gathered Maria's basket and her bag, blew him a kiss, and flashed him the special smile that was his only.

His heart pounding with anticipation and rings in hand, Charlie paused briefly outside their bedroom door, momentarily puzzled by the sweet sounds of a familiar melody. He recognized it as the music he and Jessie danced to on their wedding night. The beautiful symphony brought back a rush of memories of the thrill he'd felt having Jessie in his arms. He felt a surge of the same headiness of that night, recalling holding his beautiful bride as they swirled around the floor. There had been only the two of them and the music, and even that seemed more to be coming from the joining of their hearts than from the violins.

The door was slightly ajar; he pushed it open. Jessie stood just inside, wearing that smile and a sheer negligee. The light from the lamp behind her caused the folds of the material to shimmer around her perfect, woman's body. She had fastened the gown only at her waist so that the swell of her breasts was revealed in the opening and a bare thigh showed provocatively below. Her hair was swept up in the winsome Gibson girl style she knew he liked.

Charlie sucked in his breath at the sight and promise of her. He stopped at the door to slowly look her over. "Jessie, you have never been more beautiful!"

He entered the room and held out his arms, barely trusting his voice to speak. "Mrs. Harper, may I have this dance?"

He lifted his wife in his arms as he had done that first evening. That night, they had danced to the provocative, passionate sounds of three country violins magically transformed into the strings of an orchestra. Tonight, the lovers danced to a small symphony encased in Maria's music box sitting on a dresser. And again, Charlie let Jessie's body slide down his so that she stood tiptoed, barefoot on his toes as the music wound down, their lips not parting until it stopped.

"It is Tchaikovsky's." Jessie's voice was low and breathless. She paused to kiss him again then continued. "Waltz from *The Sleeping Beauty*! It is"—he kissed her—"the same music Maria and Ivan danced to on their wedding night in St. Petersburg. That's why he bought her the music box! How perfect for us, Charlie! It is almost symbolic of both our wedding night and tonight."

She took a step back, enjoying the pleasure the sight of her gave him. Her confident, sensual expression thrilled Charlie more than anything she had ever done to tempt him before.

Her voice still husky, she murmured, "You once told me that we would know when I could come to you as a woman. We know, Charlie."

She spoke while making a slow, seductive turn, full circle, knowingly keeping the lamp light always behind her. The effect was as intoxicating as she intended it to be. Her back now to him, she let her gown slide from her shoulders to the floor, finishing her turn facing him, her lips parted, her breath seeming to catch in her throat. He saw her eyes close involuntarily in response to the rush of his breath, herself overcome by the passion she had aroused in him.

One hand encircled her waist as he loosened her hair with the other. His desire surged as he watched its silkiness fall around her shoulders, provocatively parting at her breasts. Lifting her, he bent and kissed them, overcome again with wonder and awe of her. "Jessie, Jessie, my woman, my wife. I love you so very much!" His kiss muffled her reply, but her ardor matched his.

He carried her to their bed, aware again that there were no words adequate to describe his emotions. "Jessie, no man has ever wanted a woman as much as I want you."

She kept her arms around his neck and her face buried in his throat. Feeling her eyelashes brush against his skin, he caught his breath, finding even that simple gesture to be exquisite. She molded her body into his for a moment; they were both trembling as she let him lay her on their bed and unblushingly watched his eyes caress her.

Overwhelmed with tenderness and passion, Charlie fumblingly placed the rings on her finger, whispering their wedding vows. "Tonight, I take thee, Jessie, as my wife, to have and to hold forever."

Her tears of surprised joy thrilled him. "And I take thee, my wonderful husband."

Her movements graceful and sensual, Jessie raised herself to her knees. "I want to see you naked, Charlie! I want to see all of you!" She fumbled to unbutton his shirt, her hands shaking, his hands doing magic things to her body, fueling her desire, their mouths hungrily drinking each other in.

The feel of his wife's breasts against his bare chest was far more wonderful than any of his imaginings over the past year. At last, they were naked together, unable to keep their hands from exploring each other's bodies.

"Charlie Harper," her voice shaking with desire, "thank you for waiting so that I might know this night as a woman."

Epilogue

Charlie died of pneumonia at the age of forty-one. He fell ill after becoming wet and chilled from digging holes to install gasoline pumps outside one of his general stores. Jessie was seven months pregnant with their seventh daughter at the time of his death. She named that child Charldene in honor of her husband. They had no sons. Charlie was as adored by his daughters as he had always been by Jessie.